Jill 9

Jill 9

J.D. Tynan

A Better Be Write Publisher, LLC
North Carolina***New Jersey

Jill 9

A Better Be Write Publisher
For Information:
A Better Be Write Publisher
9001 Ridge Hill Street
Kernersville, NC 27284
www.abetterbewrite.com
ISBN: 0-9767732-9-5
Book Cover Designed By Joe
Printed in the United States of America

~Dedication~

This book is dedicated to all the men and women of law enforcement and all branches of the military—Thanks for keeping us safe.

~Thank You~

A special thank you to my editors, Rick and Nina, for catching my errors and helping to iron out the kinks in my story. I'll never forget you, Rick! Thank you to Mark Bredt for being my hero and *saint.* I owe my undying gratitude to my husband, Jim, and my two young children for giving up a little time with *Mommy* so I could finish this book.

~Prologue~

In the small town of Darien, Connecticut, after a long day of football practice under the hot August sun, Ian Hamlin sauntered up to his best friend since childhood, Elias Webber, and handed him a bottle of lemon-lime Gatorade. He'd seen him through good times and bad, but lately his friend just seemed a little *off.*

"Where's your head today, dude?" Ian asked.

Ian usually told it like it was and today, along with every other day for the past two weeks, Elias's mind had seemed to be anywhere but on the practice field. This season coming up, the Darien Cougars were looking at a chance for a state title if they could just keep up their undefeated status and continue their long-running winning streak from last year. Ian needed that to happen more than anything and counted on his friend to snap out of his funk and get his head into the game.

They were both about to start their junior year at Darien High School, but unlike his friend, Ian desperately needed a college scholarship in order to even consider higher education. It's not that his family was hurting for money in any way, but he hadn't been born with a silver spoon in his mouth like Elias had.

Envy had been an all too familiar part of their friendship for the past seventeen years and sometimes it was painful for Ian to see Elias get everything from autographed basketballs, to ski trips to Vale, to new designer high-tops. Ian had to sit by and watch his best friend reap the rewards of being a rich, spoiled-rotten brat.

Year after year, Ian got sick and tired of being the one who had to work hard to get what he wanted.

1

Everything from algebra to finding a job at the video store had been a challenge for young Ian, who had always had a hard time opening up to people, while Elias's world just seemed all too easy. Elias was one of those tall, blonde, perfectly sculpted boys with deep hazel eyes. His hair looked sun-kissed even in the middle of winter, almost as if he belonged on a beach in California. He was at least a good three inches taller than Ian, and even he had to admit his best friend was the best looking guy in their high school. Getting good grades also came easy to Elias, as did dating, and now he had just been chosen as the starting quarterback. But here he was blowing it and it pained Ian to sit back and watch him taking yet another good thing completely for granted, never feeling remorseful about anything. It was almost as if he lacked the capacity to empathize with the rest of the human population.

"Nothing, dude," Elias shot back viciously. "Get off my back."

Elias turned abruptly to avoid the gaze of his best friend, whom he envied more and more every day. Ian had a wonderful mother who cooked real food and spent time at school. She brought snacks for the team after a hard workout and even gave Elias warms hugs, as if he were her own son. She held a position on the PTA, shouted the loudest at their baseball games and even made the team matching duffle bags to take on road trips. Ian's father was also as doting as they come. He headed the booster club, never missed any football or Little League games and took them fishing whenever they asked. The rage Elias felt inside was teetering closer to the edge, and every day all he could do to keep from strangling his best friend, was to remind himself that he had a brand new BMW convertible.

"Look," Ian said, as he caught up to his friend. "I know having your dad gone is hard and all, but you're the starter. It's all you, man, and you need to get your shit together or we can kiss our season goodbye."

They both climbed into Elias's new, black BMW convertible. All Ian could do to prevent himself from losing control and beating his best friend senseless was to remind himself that he still had his father around daily. Ever since Elias' father up and flew the coop, things had been shaky around the Webber house. Elias seemed even more irritable and it was just a matter of time before the young man snapped.

Three months passed, in which Elias grew angrier with each passing day. Ian tried many times to understand exactly what his best friend was going through, but because his home life was as stable as it got, he just couldn't understand his rage. The worst part was that Elias had to welcome a few new family members into his home. Needless to say, Elias hadn't wanted to go home since Dick and Tanya moved in.

"It's really not that bad."

Ian slunk down on the couch and listened to his friend go on and on about his new stepfather and his stepsister from hell. Three days prior, Elias's stepfather and eight-year-old stepsister, Tanya, had finally moved in, bringing an entirely new reason for Elias to feel angered. His mother hadn't known Dick Swenson for more than a few months before marrying him and inviting him and his brat to take up residence in his house—he *same* house that his father once lived in. It had been a long three days living with Elias camped out on his floor.

Ian raked a hand through his jet-black hair and sharply exhaled. "It could be so much worse, dude," Ian chuckled to keep the mood light. They had just lost the state football championship the day before, but at least enough college scouts were present to keep his college hopes alive. It was a loss for the team, but Ian had made every catch, scored a couple of touchdowns, and even played on special teams to show his versatility.

"How so, *dick-weed?*" Elias shouted and then slammed his beer can against his forehead until it buckled

3

under the pressure and wrinkled against his furled brow.

"You could have *two* evil stepsisters," Ian chided and then did the same with his own empty can of Coors Light. He got up and relieved himself in the bathroom before cruising upstairs to his bedroom to finish up the game of chess they had started the day before. Ian's bedroom looked like every other average teenager's room, with clothes piled on the end of the bed, posters of half-naked women hung on his walls, and left over pizza crust sat atop his dresser.

"Whoa!" Ian passed by his bedroom window and stopped short. "Look at that," he yelled out to his best friend, but his gaze remained on the awesome spectacle of naked breasts. Naked breasts that were attached perfectly to an impressive body that was equally naked; her nipples were dark like her hair that even matched the curly hair between her legs. "Come here, dude."

Elias Webber went willingly, rarely able to say no to his best friend. His life sucked these past four months, but after hearing that his father was making an attempt to get his mother back, he had high hopes that life would once again be good. It would be good again if his dad would just come back. Back to where he belonged, but having Dick in his mother's bed wasn't helping much.

Elias took the stairs two at a time. Every muscle in his body ached from the beating he had taken on the football field the day before. He steadied himself on the windowsill with both hands as he stared through the glass, across the lawn and into the window of his new stepsister's bedroom.

"Dude, who is that?" Ian leaned against the glass and sent his best bud a glare for apparently holding out on him. How did a babe like that end up in Elias's house without Ian knowing all about it? They were best friends after all, and best friends share everything. "Who's the babe?"

"She's Tanya's nanny and she's off limits."

"Dude? What the hell does that mean?" Ian peered harder and wished he had the foresight to keep binoculars in his bedroom since she was by far the most beautiful girl he'd ever seen.

Elias glared hard into his friend's deep blue eyes. "It means— she is off limits."

Ian chuckled and wiped the drool from his lips. "Man, she's hot."

"Someday, she'll be mine," Elias hissed under his breath and narrowed his eyes on the pretty, young nanny. "She will be all mine."

~ Chapter One ~

"Jill, Jill," **Anita** said as she softly shook her best friend curled up under blankets, trying her best to keep warm in their drafty, small apartment. "Wake up!"

"What?" Jill sat straight up, raked her hands through her long, dark hair, and glared at her frantic roommate. Before she could totally focus on Anita's face, she noticed the sun had already begun peeking in through the moth holes in the curtains.

"Oh shit!" She said as she jumped up and rushed for the bathroom after seeing her digital alarm clock blinking midnight, over and over, like a beacon that was reminding her yet again that she was going to be late for her new job.

"What the hell is wrong with this place?" Jill shouted from under the lukewarm spray of the shower. "This is the third time this week." She shivered under the barely-there trickle of yellowish water. The water pressure couldn't hold up to the thickness of her long dark hair, so she usually had to wash it every other day and usually in the sink. She could very well be one of those women who use the excuse; *I have to wash my hair tonight.* Although Jill rarely had the chance to use that line.

Anita peeked her head into the bathroom and plugged in her curling iron. "It's just old. Now that you have a real job, maybe we should think about moving." She raked her hairbrush through her long blonde hair and pulled it up behind her ears. "I mean really, you're the Channel 12 weather babe. What kind of statement are you making by living in this dump? You're about to be famous."

Anita having not yet finished her master's degree in marine biology still waited tables at Ross' Bar and Grill, while dreaming about getting into a place that actually had continuous electricity, curbside parking and didn't reek like General Ming's Chicken. "*Paaa-lease,*" she begged. "I can't take it anymore. Do you know that last week, I actually gagged when Ryan suggested that we get Chinese Food and take it back to his place? I felt so bad for the guy. He thought I was gagging because I didn't want him. We need to get out of here."

"Anita," Jill poked her head through the curtain hiding the mildew covered shower stall. "I've had the job for two days. I think we should wait until I actually make it on the air before *moving on up*...if you know what I mean."

"Fine." She finished applying her mascara and pulled her little black skirt up around her ample hips. "But if I have to wait too much longer I'll be begging Ryan to let me rent his couch and you know how I feel about that."

Jill chuckled lightly and finished the quickest shower she had ever taken.

* * * *

The Channel 12 News station took up the entire corner of 17th Avenue and Broadway in downtown Vancouver, Washington. It was the first of its kind; the first station to broadcast the news from the other side of the Columbia River, as opposed to all the Portland stations that had hogged the Pacific Northwest airwaves for so long. Vancouver was a fast growing metropolis, but of course still relied on Portland for many things.

Jill didn't remember a time in her life when she hadn't wanted to be a meteorologist and after seven long years of school and an internship at a moderately small station in San Francisco, she finally made it to the big time.

"Better late than never," her assistant, Tom Riley, said with disdain, feeling he deserved the position as opposed to Jill the wonder-babe. The term *weathergirl* was so passé and yet here he was working for a woman at a mediocre new station in Vancouver of all places. "It might be nice if perhaps you actually got to work on time everyday. Its only day three and you aren't *that* pretty."

Jill's jaw dropped open. She'd met some petty people in her life, but Tom Riley takes the cake. If it was up to her, and it wasn't, she would dropkick his ass to the mailroom. He never smiled, looked like a mouse, and reeked like day-old cheese.

"My power went out again. It's not my fault."

"Whatever." He went back to his latte and handed her the latest reports from the National Weather Service. Jill flipped through them quickly and bit her lip when he said, "Can you read those without your cheat sheet, or would you like me to translate for you?"

"I can manage," she said haughtily and raced to the production booth to smooth things over with Reed Langley, the head producer. Casually flattening the wrinkles from her beige skirt, she lengthened her spine and smiled. "I'm really sorry. It won't happen again."

He looked up at her over the rim of his bifocals. "What won't happen again?"

His eyes were the deepest shade of charcoal gray that she'd ever seen, matching his silver gray hair perfectly. If he were ten years younger or she were ten years older she'd be hot on his tail and demanding that he talk dirty to her in her earpiece, being as she was just a bit frustrated from lack of sex and more importantly, lack of sleep. Anita was right. They needed to find a new place and quick so she could get some sleep and get her mind out of the gutter.

It dawned on her he probably had better things to

do than stare at the clock and wonder where the new weathergirl was. "Nothing." She felt it best not to confess something so trivial. After all, she still wasn't technically on the air yet and her training was all behind the cameras, so no harm done.

Jill went about her day, followed Reed around with clenched buttocks and sweaty palms. She hung on his every word and treated him like the god he was because, after all, he was the man who had taken the chance and hired her when she lacked even one minute of on-air experience. That fact was most likely why her assistant hated her and treated her with a venomous bite.

The newsroom was set up fairly similar to the station in San Francisco. The studio was moderately sized, the dressing rooms were about the size of a standard walk-in closet—but comfortable, and from every window was a spectacular view of the Columbia River and the fast growing city of Vancouver. Jill familiarized herself with the ins and outs of the station and then of course, it was just a matter of meeting the staff, seeing how the anchors ticked and taking lots of time to schmooze the bagel guy to make certain that she got breakfast daily.

Jill's day ended at seven thirty p.m. and not wanting to return to a lonely, stinky apartment, she stopped by Ross' Bar and Grill on her way home. Ross' was located just a few blocks from the station snuggled in on 12th Street between a Barnes and Noble and a Starbucks. A full service nail salon sat above the famous restaurant and Esther Short Park was directly across the street. Jill fidgeted with her cocktail napkin and waited anxiously, while Anita finished pouring a microbrew for a fairly high-maintenance customer.

"Let me try the porter," the man said, as if he were a microbrew aficionado.

Anita turned and rolled her eyes, then gave Jill a cross-eyed look of boredom.

The customer swirled the glass. He sipped, licked

the foam from his lips, and scowled. "How about the Hefeweizen?"

"Jesus," Jill muttered under her breath. She'd never had to do such menial tasks for the public and she really hadn't a clue as to how Anita has done it all these years.

"Beefeater Martini. Slightly dirty with four olives. . .please." Jill dropped her elbow on the bar and blew her long, dark bangs out of her eyes. "Make it a double," she said to Anita.

"Bad day?" Anita didn't miss a beat and keeping the impression that Jill was just another customer and not her best friend, she could actually give her free drinks and carry on normal conversations without anyone being the wiser. "Want to talk?" She dried her hands on her black apron and gave her friend a warm smile.

"No. I just think Tom hates me. Reed thinks I'm a wet-behind-the-ears bimbo and I think the bagel guy actually thinks I want in his pants. I swear to God, I hate men. I really do and I'm not just saying that this time. This time I really, really mean it."

Anita laughed whole-heartedly and dropped her elbows onto the deep mahogany bar. She gazed deep into her friend's warm brown eyes and smiled with a devilish intent. "You need to get laid."

"Ha," Jill said a bit too loud, and plucking an olive off her tiny pink sword shaped skewer, nibbled on it while her stomach rumbled from lack of food. "Are you not listening? I just said. . .I. *hate men.*"

Just then, a rather attractive, perfectly dressed specimen in a dark suit sat down beside her at the bar and winked. "Don't let the looks fool you. I'm really not a man." He put his hands into the air in mock surrender. "I swear it's true."

Jill laughed and sucked down an entire ounce or two of chilled alcohol. "I'm sorry," she said apologetically and then blew the errant bangs from her eyes once again.

"It's all right. I pretty much hear it from my wife

every other day, so I'm immune." He smiled and Jill was actually relieved that the man was married and she hadn't just offended a perfect stranger who could very well be the man she was supposed to marry.

Her shoulders were tense with the struggles of modern day life, surviving being single, and just because she hadn't had a real orgasm since Seinfeld went off the air.

I do need to get laid, Jill thought and sulked, staring at her martini until another just like it was set down in front of her. She looked around and followed her best friend's finger that was pointing to the man who had bought her another drink.

Sitting on the opposite side of the bar was a blond-haired surfer boy with a smirk on his face and a Corona grasped in his large hand. He nodded, held up his beer and smiled. He was easy on the eyes, but she always had a thing for dark haired, brooding men. Surfer boy just looked too damn happy. Not to mention smug.

"There's your boyfriend." Anita giggled. "Go for it," she said as she bobbed her eyebrow, giving her best friend permission to seek out gainful, uncomplicated sex and if Jill wasn't such a romantic at heart and a sensible woman, she would have fallen for it hook, line, and sinker. But alas, it just wasn't her style. She preferred to be courted, showered with flowers and chocolates while being swept off her feet by a mysterious stranger with eyes as clear as the Caribbean Sea.

Jill shook her head and mouthed a thank you to the kind stranger, and then glared at her friend.

"What? You're never going to find *him,* so just drop your demure act and take a chance with a real flesh and bone man. He's hot, he's single, and I'm positive that he's not bisexual. What more could you ask for these days?" Anita said with a sigh.

"I'm not waiting for *him* anymore, but I do want something better. Something more substantial than hot sex

11

and a great butt." She sulked. "Don't you believe in fate?"

Anita rolled her eyes. They'd had this conversation at least twice a year for the past twelve years. "I do believe in fate somewhat, but this has nothing to do with it. You have got to get over this obsession with some kid you saw a million years ago. You're not going to find him. You don't know his name, and I would bet tonight's tips that you wouldn't recognize him if he bumped right into you. It's over. Get on with life and stop searching for a shadow."

Jill thought about what Anita said the entire way home. She pulled her nearly dead, twelve-year-old Chevy Cavalier into the only spot left on the street, just a block from her apartment and couldn't shake the feeling she was right—again. He *was* just a shadow. She remembered his deep blue eyes, the way his jet-black hair hung over his eyebrows, and his perfect rippled chest—but that was all she remembered. He had never spoken to her. He never touched her. He was just a faint memory; an image that she saw on a hot summer's day twelve years ago.

* * * * *

New Haven, Connecticut is where the team of FBI agents were receiving more information about another death in a long line of horrendous murders on the east coast. Agent Ian T. Hamlin had never seen anything so horrific in his six years with the bureau. He peered down at the last eight-by-ten glossy and held his breath, fearing the vomit he was holding back would somehow emerge in front of his superiors and his entire team of investigators. The fluorescent-lit room seemed to be spinning, so he inhaled sharply to stop the imaginary movement. This had been a long time coming, and he feared it *was* coming. He hoped for the best, but wasn't entirely surprised that yet another young woman had wound up dead.

"This is the fourth Jill Walker in four years. What are we missing here—besides the obvious?" Special Agent

Pete Morrow shook his head as he sipped some hot coffee from behind his desk. "I don't get it. Most serials don't target on name alone. It seems to me that someone out there has a serious grudge against the name Jill Walker and he or she will stop at nothing until they get the right woman."

"Why did we not see this coming?" Agent Will Harrison piped up during the long silence.

"We did." Agent Hamlin let out his breath with a groan as he tipped back in his chair to engage the baffled group of agents. "Two years ago, after the third Jill Walker was murdered, we informed the other six Jill Walkers on the east coast and even had this one under surveillance for months. Nothing ever came of it and our manpower was pulled by the powers that be. We thought it was over."

All eyes shot to the point man on the case, Agent Ian Hamlin. "I guess he's back." Ian said with a hiss. He couldn't believe it. The son-of-a-bitch was back.

Ian got all necessary files and photos together and finished up his meeting with the rest of his team before storming from the room. The door slammed loudly behind him and if it weren't for all the other manly men walking about, he would have dropped to his knees and wept like a child. He'd let her down in the worst way and now he had to make it right.

Ian followed Will Harrison out of the front door, and then taking the elevator down to the parking garage, climbed into his black Chevy Tahoe. "I can't believe this happened." Ian said, shaking his head. "It doesn't make sense."

"Nothing about this killer makes sense. I've read up on every one of the first victims, and nothing but the names and similar ages of these women fit into any kind of plausible scenario." Will Harrison agreed with his partner about the oddities of the Jill murders. "What are you thinking?"

"I think it's time to pay a visit to the other two Jill

Walkers in Connecticut."

"You heard the boss." Will said with a disapproving glare. "He doesn't want to move on this until Monday."

"Yeah--well, the boss is wrong." Ian started his car, pulled around the corner and took out his list of addresses that he swiped from the Jill Walker murder file; a file that two years ago he hoped he'd never have to reopen.

Ten minutes later, they pulled up to the Walker residence in East New Haven. Ian scowled at his partner as he finally got out of the SUV and followed him to the front door. The house was an older style; one of those classic Connecticut homes with a large yard out front with the walkway to the front door lined with azalea bushes, roses and purple pansies and plenty of trees to shade the backyard. Then Ian rapped lightly on the yellow door and removed his identification from his inside jacket pocket.

A woman looking to be in her mid-fifties opened the door as they held up their identification. "Can we have a minute of your time, Mrs. Walker?"

"Sure," Ruth Walker opened the door and called out for her husband, Gordon. "Gordon, this is Agent Hamlin and Agent Harrison of the FBI." She made the introductions once her husband was by her side.

Gordon's face tightened, some color faded from his cheeks, but he kept his cool and sat down next to his wife on the couch. It had been quite a few years since the murder and he prayed that this was just a friendly visit— although his gut said otherwise. "What can we do you for?"

"Actually, if it isn't too much trouble, we'd like to speak to your daughter, Jill."

Mrs. Walker kept a tidy home. Ian noticed that right away, as he surveyed his surroundings. The antique furniture was free of dust and clutter and the room smelled of freshly baked cinnamon rolls.

Gordon and Ruth looked wide-eyed at Agent Hamlin, and then exchanged sullen glances with each other. Ruth recalled, all too well the last time she saw her daughter's smiling face. Her heart ached as she looked back upon that fateful day over thirteen years ago.

It had been overcast and dreary that day outside the Westport Memorial Hospital. Her hand wrapped tightly around Gordon's as she reigned in her emotions and wiped the remaining tears from her eyes. She wanted to remain strong for her girls and show them she had every confidence in what they decided to do. She fully understood that Dr. Singletary was world-renowned for this type of risky surgery and both her daughters were aware of the risks, making it somewhat easier for her to bear. But it was still difficult for Ruth to put her trust in a man who now held her daughter's lives in his hands. Jill and Jane had recently turned seventeen and were about to undergo a lengthy surgery to finally separate them from each other. As Gordon led her down the long, fluorescent-lit hallway on their way to the surgical ward, Ruth reminded herself to breathe.

When they finally entered the room, Dr. Singletary's team was assembled around the oversized hospital bed of the two young girls. Ruth's heart ached as she slowly walked toward the girls. In the past, the doctor's warned against the high-risk operation to separate them, but since Jill was in need of a liver transplant, they decided to try the risky surgery. Ruth knew it had been a difficult life for the two girls—especially for Jill; her organs had been failing for nearly three years, which meant plenty of time spent in the hospital. It was as if her body couldn't survive without the help of her sister's strength, and it was because of that she was ready to attempt it. Ruth knew Jill loved her sister that much and it was her only wish—to give her sister a shot at a normal life, a chance at love, and finally the freedom from being looked upon like a freak. Jill vehemently insisted on the surgery, and they felt obliged to let the girls do as they wished. Sure, they had been given the odds, and had been lectured about the severity of their

15

*actions, but they felt that it was important that the two
siblings who had been joined at the hip since the day they
were born have some sort of shot at a normal life.*

*Ruth held tight to the frailer of the two girls and
gave her a gentle squeeze. "We love you both and we'll be
right here when you come back. We'll be right here."*

*Gordon gave Jane a big hug and a kiss on the cheek
as a tear streamed along the contour of his cheek. "You'll
both be just fine, and when you're all done, we'll go out for
ice cream." As far as fathers go, Gordon had always been
there for his daughters, who most people referred to as
freaks. Jane was the strong one of the girls. In fact, she took
after him in everyway; big bones, strong jaw, and she ended
up with the dominant version of all the organs. She was
strong as an ox with the heart of a stallion, unlike Jill who
was frail and weak and could barely keep any weight on her
fragile frame. It killed him to think that Jill may not make it
out of surgery, but if it meant that Jane might live a more
normal and happy life, then that's the way it had to be. It
was Jill's wish—possibly her last wish, but it was her
decision just the same.*

*The apprehensive parents watched their daughters
being rolled down the long hall toward surgery. Tears
stained their cheeks in high hopes that both girls would
make it to the other side.*

*Those were the longest and hardest sixteen hours
of Ruth's life before Dr. Singletary emerged from behind
the double doors near the dimly lit waiting room. His head
hung low and despite a heroic effort, he had to confront
the parents of Jill and Jane Walker and inform them that
one of their daughters had not survived.*

"I'm sorry, but there must be some sort of
mistake—" Gordon tried to say, but was cut off by Agent
Harrison looking up from his little notebook.

"Her last known address is here. Jill Rene Walker,
age thirty. That is your daughter, is it not?" Will sent Ian a

wondering gaze.

Ruth's eyes welled with tears as her husband lightly patted her trembling hand.

"There must be some kind of mistake, gentlemen," Gordon went on. "Actually, it happens often, but our daughter Jill died thirteen years ago in surgery. The girls were conjoined twins and she never made it off the operating table during the surgery to separate them. Her sister Jane lives with us from time to time, but we still get mail for Jill and those damn Visa companies are always calling to offer her lines of credit."

Ian and Will winced slightly in apology for their mistake. Ian looked around the living room walls and noted the photographs of the two girls. The agents exchanged glances and made their way toward the front door. "I'm so sorry for bothering you and I'm sorry for your loss." Ian extended his hand and Gordon gave it a firm shake, as he rose off the couch.

"What is this about?" Gordon asked curiously. "Does this have anything to do with Jane? Do you know where she might be?"

"No sir. I'm sorry, but I don't know Jane. I was just looking for Jill. That's all I can tell you. Thanks for your time." Ian said as he and Will let themselves out.

When they were finally out of sight, Ruth broke down into hysterical sobs and Gordon took her in his arms.

"Shhh." Gordon rocked his wife. "I'm sure it's nothing, darling. It's nothing. I'm positive that it didn't happen again. Don't worry, we'll find her." He pressed a kiss into the top of his wife's head and said a prayer to God, hoping that it was true. *By god, please let it be true.*

* * * *

Two weeks and three days after she first came to Channel 12 news, Jill was seated in front of the well-lit

17

mirror and getting made-up for her debut as Vancouver's first female meteorologist. Finally, at the age of thirty-two, she was getting her big break.

"This is Jill Walker, coming to you from Vancouver, Washington." She rehearsed the line again without smearing the lipstick across her white teeth that time. Each time she rehearsed it, she got better and better about not smearing the pound of lipstick she had on her lips.

The makeup artist teased her bangs, fluffed up the back of her newly highlighted hair, and brushed a dollop of rouge onto her olive-toned cheeks. "This is Jill Walker, coming at you from the Couv. It's going to be a hot one, so break out the sunscreen and don't forget to drink plenty of water." She giggled and plucked an errant eyebrow that looked out of place. "Jill Walker, signing out and wishing you a peaceful tomorrow." Jill smiled at her reflection. *Not too shabby.*

"You're something else," Tom snickered from behind her. "What's with the Jill Walker shit? I thought your name was Jill Wallokowski."

"It is, but it's a bit much, don't you think? I need a quick, catchy name. Besides, if I ever get famous, I'd be afraid that some psycho would hunt me down and chop me into a million pieces." She laughed at Tom's agape expression. "Hey, it could happen."

"Which part? The part about you becoming famous, or getting hacked into a million pieces?" he snickered with condescension and she knew he was hoping for the second choice. He was a hard man to get to know, but at least by then she was used to his Limburger scent.

"Both." She shivered and became more adamant about the idea of keeping her personal life—personal. She'd read too many true-crime-stories about stalkers and whom they like to target. The threat of being targeted by a creep was all too real, even in smaller cities like Vancouver.

She finished in the makeup chair and after what

seemed like an entire can of hairspray, her newly styled hair was cemented into place just as the production assistant shuffled her to the large blue screen that would be her permanent home five nights a week. Her adrenaline surged, but now was not the time to get a case of the jitters. She had wanted this her entire life and her dream was about to come true.

Leaning in closer to see the teleprompter, she inhaled deeply, said a private prayer to God, and took Vancouver by storm.

The cameras seemed to love her as she lit up the screen with an abundance of energy and vitality. Even Tom Riley had to admire the way she made rain sound like it was a good thing. The room was quiet and tranquil as the staff and executives stared in awe at the capable and beautiful Jill Walker. Reed Langley couldn't have been prouder. In fact, he was already making plans to plaster her pretty face all over the city buses. She was golden, and he had been the brilliant mastermind who had taken the chance and hired her.

* * * *

Three hours north of Vancouver, a very aroused, very winded man, sat upright in bed and knocked the heavily breathing woman off his lap and onto her side of the bed.

She pulled the white, satin sheet up around her naked breasts and glared over at her lover. "Elias," she sputtered and flipped her long blonde hair over her shoulder. "What the hell are you doing?"

"Shhh," he hissed at the naked woman and grappled for the remote control. Turning up the volume, he almost thought he was dreaming. After blinking a couple of times to make sure, he stared deeply at her sculptured chin, her full lips, and her big eyes he had fantasized about for the past thirteen years.

19

It was her. It was Jill. Tanya's nanny was standing in front of him, reciting the weather in Vancouver, Washington, of all places. Shaking his head in disbelief, he stared blankly at her face and was once again mesmerized by her beauty. She had only been a fantasy for all these years and now, now after thirteen years, he would finally have a shot at getting what he wanted all those years ago.

"It's gonna rain. Big deal, honey. We can go to Cancun instead of Orcas. It doesn't matter to me." Sara said in frustration. It's not everyday that a man tosses a perfectly good woman off his dick and demands that she stay quiet so he can hear the news of all things. Sure, she could understand it happening during a hockey match, but never for the weather.

"Shhh," he hissed again and licked his lips in anticipation. His mind was already reeling about how he was going to make her his own.

* * * *

"You were beyond wonderful! I never knew you were so bubbly. How the hell did you do it?" Anita hugged her friend after a long day and even longer night. Anita had waited anxiously for Jill to walk through the front door of their apartment.

"Lots of coffee, I guess. Was I really that good? I didn't look stupid. Did I have a double chin? Did I smile enough, or too much, or hell, did you understand me perfectly or did I mumble—because I tend to mumble when I get nervous, and oh God, Anita, I was so fucking nervous."

"You were great. Now stop being neurotic and tell me all about these." Anita motioned to the giant box of long stem red roses.

"I don't know." Jill bit her lip with uncertainty, but nothing could keep the broad smile from spreading across her glowing face. "They were delivered to the station for me from a secret admirer. Pretty good for one night, huh? I already have an admirer."

"Let's hope it's not a stalker who wants to chop you into a million pieces and keep you in his freezer." Anita shuddered and grabbed the bottle of Belvedere vodka from behind the bag of frozen peas.

"I think it's time we found a more suitable apartment," Jill said with a smile, finally feeling comfortable about moving.

"That's wonderful, because in two weeks, we're going to be homeless. I gave Ling our notice two weeks ago." She giggled and then held her breath, waiting for Jill's response.

Jill laughed and gave her a hug. What more could she do? Anita Long had been her oldest and dearest friend for the past fifteen years since they had graduated from David Douglas High School in Portland, Oregon. Anita had been there for her through thick and thin, good times and bad. They had even both moved to Connecticut together before starting college. Anita had the brilliant idea of becoming nannies and that is just what they had done. Every summer during their years at the University of Oregon, the girls would head east and spend their summers on the southern Connecticut coast along Long Island, South Hampton, and sometimes even Cape Cod.

Jill would do just about anything for her best friend and that meant spending a little extra money a month so they could live comfortably until either Anita graduated and found a real job, or one of them got serious enough about a man. Up until lately, that had never been an issue for Jill and Anita, but since Anita's biological clock started chiming loudly; she'd been on the hunt for the future father of her babies.

"I think something in Vancouver would be nice. The downtown area has really taken off. I bet we could get a great apartment."

"Actually, Jill," Anita said as she bit her lip. "I was thinking more along the lines of a house. You know—with a yard—more room and a garage." Her eyes lit up with a dreamy expression. "Think about it. We wouldn't have to sunbathe in the park anymore and who knows, I may want to plant a garden."

"I guess that would be okay." Jill shrugged and sipped her martini. The idea of having fresh veggies and herbs did have its appeal. "You really do make a mean martini. Why would you want to give up a talent like that just to play doctor to a bunch of helpless fish?" Jill teased and kicked off her high-heels. "So, is this thing with Ryan, the-wonder-schlong, getting serious?"

"As serious as you can get with a twenty-five-year-old I guess." Anita sighed and eased back against the horrible dingy couch she'd inherited when her great aunt Marta passed away. "The sex is great; the conversation is bearable; he says—*like* a little too much, but he has potential to be a good dad to our kids one day. He's fun and energetic."

"Yeah, but he's just a baby himself," Jill scoffed before chewing the large green olive that had been rolling around on her tongue. "Men can't get serious until they hit thirty. It's a well-known fact. I read it in Cosmo and Cosmo never lies," she said with a smirk and then burst into laughter.

It was then the phone rang. "Hello," Anita said into the receiver. "Hello? I can hear you breathing." She rolled her eyes at her friend. "Blow yourself!" She finally snapped into the phone and slammed it down. "Now that we can afford it, perhaps we should check into caller ID."

"We?" Jill chided. "Since when can *we* afford it?"

"I just meant. . ."

Jill's warm embrace cut her off from explaining further. "I was kidding. Let's start house hunting this weekend and yes—caller ID would be a wonderful thing," she said as she gave her friend a quick peck on the nose, went to her room and crawled into bed for the night.

~ Chapter Two ~

Two weeks later, Jill pulled up in front of the older, bright-yellow house that they had rented and stood to stretch a kink from her leg. "I can't believe you talked me into this. It looks like something out of a horror movie." Jill walked toward the large house, carefully stepping over the row of decimated rose bushes lining the front yard.

"It's quaint." Anita smiled from the wrap-around front porch. She let her finger slide down the chain of the porch swing to set it in motion.

"It's spooky," Jill said and cringed. "But I love the backyard."

"You love the kitchen, too," Anita scoffed, as she sat down on the swing and kicked her feet onto the railing. "And the large bathroom with the jetted tub. . .and the walk-in closet, and the fact that it has two fireplaces. Come on. It's homey."

"It makes my uterus ache," Jill finally admitted outright.

Anita's jaw dropped. "You feel it, don't you?" She reached her feet back onto the wooden slats of the deck.

"I do not," Jill said haughtily. "I just meant that this should be a family home. There should be tricycles in the front yard and a wading pool out back."

"You feel it. I knew it!" Anita chuckled lightly, getting up to help her friend move the rest of their

24

belongings into the large house. She felt a bit relieved that her friend was also feeling the incessant pangs of a biological clock.

The large house wasn't dilapidated in any way and it definitely had potential, but the appliances were from the seventies—avocado green in color. The floors were solid hardwood that could use a little refinishing. The foyer was bright and sunny thanks to all the windows designed to let in the morning sun. Curtains of faded blue were mounted from the windows in the kitchen and the kitchen was roomy. The two larger bedrooms were on the lower level, except for one upstairs that the women planned on using for a home office and a place for Anita to study. Screen doors on both the front and back doors creaked and the backyard was the perfect size for a couple of lawn chairs, a small garden, and a volleyball net. It reminded Anita of her grandparent's house, but until she actually finished school and could buy a place of her own, this would just have to be home for the next year or so.

As Jill moved her things in, she liked it more and more, but her uterus was taking an absolute beating. Visions of children pitter-pattering on the hardwood just made her realize how far she was from having a family of her own.

* * * *

New Haven never felt like home, but to Ian Hamlin that is what it had been for the last two years. He could hardly believe it had been only that long since his divorce was finalized. *What was I thinking marrying that tramp anyway?*

Kicking the door open with his heavy boot, he shimmied in past the screen door. He set the bag of groceries onto the beige countertop, pulled a bottle of Corona from the brown bag and popped it's top. He took a long, drawn-out pull from the bottle, feeling he deserved it after the day he had. It was then that the cell phone on his hip chirped, halting his idea of getting shit-faced and forgetting his troubles for the night.

"Hamlin," he muttered in frustration. Listening intently to the details being relayed for his benefit had him clenching his jaw. "Fuck." His eyes closed tightly as he groaned and leaned against the counter top. "I'll catch the next flight out."

So much for Friday night, he thought to himself. He knew his life belonged to the bureau and that for the rest of his working life, he'd be called away at a moment's notice without regard to his relationships, his house, and his big black dog, which he finally let go live with his folks down in Darien. Nothing ever got in the way of his job. He'd spent years in school, worked three jobs to make ends meet, and this was the end result. No personal life to speak of other than a poker game with the guys here and there.

This case weighed heavily on his mind the past two weeks. Actually, it had for the past two years since they never did find the psychopath and now it seemed that it's happened again.

Originally it wasn't even Hamlin's case. When he moved from Seattle shortly after his divorce, it was his first assignment with the New Haven office and one way or another, he felt somewhat responsible for Jill-Four's untimely death.

It took him no longer than ten minutes to pack an overnight bag with necessities: a razor, his toothbrush, a change of underwear and a clean black t-shirt. His hand momentarily paused in front of the box of condoms in his medicine cabinet. He'd bought them two years ago and hadn't even broken the seal on the box yet. Sure, he had thought about it once or twice. Even contemplated carrying one around in his wallet like he did when he was seventeen, but he knew nothing would come of it. He'd been burned and hadn't a clue as to how to get past it.

Shaking his head with furled brows, he bypassed the box one more time and slammed the mirror shut before heading out the door.

* * * *

Memphis, Tennessee is where he ended up after a short flight and a couple of bags of salted peanuts. Agent Will Harrison met him at the gate with a large manila envelope containing a few rather graphic photos along with every detail that led the FBI to believe their serial killer had moved off the east coast. Harrison quickly updated Ian as they walked through the crowded parking lot toward their rental car.

"Nothing about this fits any profile. He's moving out of Connecticut and into Memphis?" Hamlin closed the car door, snapped his seatbelt shut and stared down at the horrific photos.

"And get this," Harrison began, as he pulled out into traffic; he lit up a cigarette before finishing his sentence, a cloud of smoke leaking from his lips. "Her name is Jill Stevens, but she had been Jill Walker up until three months ago. Clearly this son-of-a-bitch had either stalked her, or had done some serious homework. Either way, this is one pre-meditated homicide."

Hamlin exhaled slowly, with a hint of a hiss at the end. "Son-of-a-bitch. How can we catch this motherfucker if he doesn't play by the usual rules? How the fuck are we supposed to get a handle on him?" He slammed his hands onto the dashboard in frustration and pulled out his cell phone. "I want a list of every Jill Walker east of the Mississippi," he muttered to Agent Harrison while waiting on the line for the New Haven office to answer. When a research analyst finally answered he quickly gave her his instructions. "Hey, It's Hamlin. Are there any other Jill Walkers in Memphis?" He waited with bated breath, hoping that another woman would not have to die before he got his hands on this sick fucker. "No?" He shot a glance of relief at Agent Harrison. He continued his conversation with the analyst on the phone. "I want a list in my hands of any and all women and girls who are now, or have ever been, named Jill Walker who are within a radius of six hours from here and I want it *yesterday.*" He clicked his phone shut.

"That's a pretty tall order. What are you thinking?" Harrison asked, the lights of the city streaking by as they raced down the interstate. They continued trying to make sense of the latest murder, while Ian read the preliminary report on the latest victim. The air was humid and causing his black t-shirt to cling to his rippled chest. He read down the page and shook his head at the cold hard facts in front of him. This latest Jill had been returning from her Biology class at the community college, when she was apparently abducted and taken to an empty field behind the science building where she was then killed. It looked just like any other random act of violence to the Memphis Police who had first taken the call, but Ian knew better.

"I'm thinking that eight hours ago he slashed up another young woman and if he's going after another one, I want to be there before him," he snapped.

"Fuck, man. It's not *your* fault. You can't possibly protect every Jill Walker out there. It's fucking impossible," Will said with a slight fatherly tone. He turned left near the community college and pulled up in front of the latest crime scene where the investigators were waiting to brief them.

"I'll be the judge of that. Besides, I'm not talking about *every* Jill Walker, just the ones in the area. I mean really, how many can there be?" Ian asked, hoping there couldn't be *that* many.

* * * *

The following morning in Vancouver, Jill had just awaken with the sunrise, ready to start her day. The weekends weren't her favorite days of the week anymore because she actually loved her job. She loved being on television twice a night, five days a week. Her neighbors in the Wallingford district of south Vancouver were actually starting to recognize her when she took her morning runs.

Wallingford stretched out around the south side of Vancouver Lake and ended up across the railway tracks that led straight downtown. It was a far better trail to run than anywhere she had ever run in Portland because she had never felt safe there. The parks in Portland were filled with overgrown trees and bushes, and sometimes women would go out jogging and never return. Scary things happen even in God's country, but Jill felt safe in Vancouver. Vancouver already felt like home and it was nice to be recognized.

"Morning, Mr. Lange," she shouted out to the nice elderly man who proudly owned the best-looking yard on the street. The pink and yellow roses were pruned, the hedges were perfectly aligned, and even his lawn was free of dandelions and clover. She hadn't broken a sweat yet because the dew hadn't evaporated off the leaves and the temperature wasn't anywhere near reaching its morning high of fifty degrees. It was the beginning of June, and early summer in the Pacific Northwest meant lots of sunshine, but cool mornings and cooler evenings. Jill knew more about the Pacific Northwest weather than anyone she'd ever met, since she had been paying attention since she was six years old.

Her sixth birthday was the day that she decided she wanted to know what kind of cloud that was high in the sky.

"I think that's a cumulus cloud sweetie," her father said from the bow of their little fishing boat. "Cumulus ones fly high and fluffy."

"How do they get up so high?" she asked. He answered the best that he could, but her father was a dentist, not a meteorologist, so his answer had something to do with where God wanted them to be in the sky. Jill asked question after question that day out on the lake and from that point on, she had been somewhat infatuated with anything pertaining to the weather.

With two more miles to go as part of her daily

exercise routine, Jill stopped a moment to catch her breath. She had always been a bit on the thin side. It was in her genes and she was tall; five-foot-ten to be exact, and after her junior year of high school her mother had even suggested modeling, but she declined because she still had her sights on becoming the all-knowing weather goddess.

"Nice day today," Mrs. Miller yelled out from behind the car she was washing, almost as if she were thanking her for the cool brisk morning. "Not a cloud in the sky. Just like you said last night."

Jill smiled and continued down the sidewalk that lined her suburban neighborhood. The trees were already bursting with leaves that swayed slightly when the east winds blew.

Someday she'd be wrong about the weather and those same people would be glaring at her and blaming her for ruining their picnics or trips to the beach. *Oh well*, she thought as she rounded the corner. *I'll cross that bridge when I come to it.*

When she finished her jogging loop and returned home, a bright white delivery van was parked out front of her new home with the tall gangly deliveryman already on the front porch holding a bright colorful bouquet of summer blossoms.

"Jill Wallokowski?" he muttered, as she walked up behind him. He tried not to notice her pointy nipples through the white sports bra she was wearing, but failed miserably and kept his eyes staring down at her heaving chest.

"That's me." Jill smiled despite the fact that the horny teen was nearly drooling.

He handed her the bouquet and then his face lit up with recognition. "Ain't you that babe on the news?"

"Yep!" Jill smiled and shuffled past him and into the house.

"For me? You shouldn't have," Anita joked, beaming in mock surprise, and then got serious. "Another secret admirer?"

"I hope not," Jill shuddered dramatically and set the flowers on the kitchen table. "It's for Jill Wallokowski, not Walker."

"Oh." Anita sat back down at the table to finish her tea. "My bet is on your Papa."

Jill ripped open the tiny envelope and smiled. "Right you are," she gushed. "I do love that man."

"You make me sick," Anita groaned. "Have you ever wondered if maybe you're holding out for a man just like daddy because you think that man is perfect? This really could be detrimental to your ability to successfully scan prospective husbands."

"Oh for Christ's sake," Jill snapped and rolled her eyes. "Psychology 101 again? I thought you already fulfilled those pre-requisites."

"Not psychology," Anita grinned and held up the latest edition of *Cosmopolitan.*

Both women laughed. The phone rang and again had them curbing their hysteria. This time it was Jill who answered, but not before checking the number on the caller ID, only to find it displayed the word 'blocked.'

"Hello," she said cautiously. "Hello," she said again and hearing only the sound of someone breathing on the other end. "I know you're there. Who are you?"

"You're so puuurr-ty," the voice whispered into the phone.

Her face turned pale. Punching the off button, she dropped the phone to her side. "That was spooky."

"Who was it?"

"Someone who said I was *puuurr-ty.*"

"Ah, fuck," Anita growled. "You're unlisted. I don't get it."

"It's probably just some punk kid dialing randomly," Jill said, hoping it was true. But they had received several calls just like that one over the past two weeks. It hadn't mattered one bit that they changed their number and had started fresh. Someone was still finding a way to crawl under her skin and make her shiver.

"You can think whatever you want, but if I were you, I'd read the damn manual for that phone and find out if there is a way to block that number. I know there's a way you can do it," Anita said with a serious tone.

* * * *

Two time zones to the east, Ian Hamlin was getting the news he had been waiting for.

"There's four Jill Walkers in Tennessee. There are also three in Kentucky of which two are minors. Are we just looking at adults or do ten-year-olds count?" Will asked, as he flipped through the report that had just been sent to them at the latest murder scene. He knelt down near the trampled grass and made some notes.

Hamlin was still pacing around the area, taking in every minuscule detail and processing the information to memory, as he sipped coffee, and then raking his hand through his black hair answered, "I don't fucking know, but it would not hurt to see how many are out there, I guess." He looked down at the chalk outline where the latest victim had been, dark blood still evident on the bushes and matted down grass. "The other five victims were between the ages of thirty-two and thirty-four. This latest one was thirty-three. I'm thinking the ten year old is safe for now, but I still think we should notify her parents, just to be on the safe side."

"You really think this is a good idea?" Will asked sternly and stood up from his squatted position. Hamlin was his superior and all, but he had a notion that Hamlin was taking things to the extreme, due to the fact that he felt somehow responsible for Jill-number-four's death. "What if we just keep them under surveillance for a couple of weeks and not tell them. I think this kind of information might scare the fuck out of these poor ladies."

Hamlin glared viciously and took aggressive steps toward agent Harrison. "Scare the fuck out of them? I don't care if I make them all piss their pants. They need to know that there's some psycho freak out there brutally killing women with the same name as them and I don't see it stopping anytime soon. I think the guy's after someone and my gut tells me that this is far from over, so yeah—I'm going to scare the fuck out of these woman and hopefully they will listen to me and move to fucking Siberia."

Harrison actually chuckled. The moment of levity was broken by the sound of a cell phone chirping on agent Hamlin's hip.

"Hamlin." He stood still, drew in a sharp breath, and tilted the phone toward his chin to relay the news to Agent Harrison. "They found another body."

* * * *

Elias Webber's penthouse apartment in downtown Seattle was directly facing Puget Sound. He had no sense of design, so the inside of his penthouse was mostly painted white. Cold and sterile would best describe the kitchen. The living room had a splash of color, but mostly he kept everything the way the previous owner had had it. It didn't feel like home, but then again, no place that he stayed in felt like home to the overindulged man. He stayed there often during the week as his lavish spread in Sequim was just too long a drive after a hard day of making deals, signing papers, and all in all reaping the rewards of being the CEO of his father's billion-dollar company, Webber Software.

Pulling the naked Sara to his chest, he kissed her hard and then not very nicely told her to get out. "Go shopping."

"You're such a bastard," she snapped at him, pulling her long blonde hair into a ponytail. "Someday you're going to wake up and I'm not going to be here."

He rolled over and lit up a cigar. *That'll be the day.* He took a couple of deep drags, exhaled a long stream of gray smoke, and gave her a wink. "Don't let the door hit you in the ass."

He got out of bed, walked into the living area and looked over at the kitchen counter after the irate woman finally left him alone. A manila folder remained sealed on the counter.

He walked slowly toward the kitchen. His chest rippled slightly, as he leaned over and pressed his finger to the button at the top of the coffee maker. His long blonde hair hung down to lightly tickle the tops of his shoulders before he pulled it back and secured it behind his ears.

His father hated his son's long hair, but Elias ignored him since he despised his father so much that he never cared what his father thought. He would have rather chopped it all off when he took the position of CEO, but the fact that his father hated his hair kept his blonde locks intact for the past three years.

Elias had spent a couple of years surfing in Australia, Hawaii, and the Fuji Islands before finally succumbing to his father's wishes and returning to the States. It hadn't been his plan to ever be that involved with the man who had once walked out on him and his mother, but since he never finished college and his mother flat-out refused to send him any more money, he really did not have much choice.

He raised a naked muscular thigh over the barstool, sitting down on the thick-cushioned padding, and then slid his middle finger under the secured tab of the manila folder. He had paid good money for the information he'd requested on Jill and hoped it would be worth the wait.

He'd been waiting for this longer than he wanted. "Jill," he muttered breathlessly and opening the envelope, looked at a photo of her jogging. A photo of her running into the supermarket was next. Then one of her pulling into her driveway, followed by one of her sunbathing topless in her backyard. Once again, he felt himself becoming mesmerized by her beauty.

He'd wanted her from the moment they met when

34

he was just seventeen and first moved in with is family as their live-in nanny. That very first night, he crept into her bedroom and slid under her bed just so he could catch a glimpse of her naked. She was so pretty. So young and tight and since she was nineteen and all, he had fantasies about her knowing all about sex; about what girls liked, and how she would be the one to teach him everything he needed to know. He'd wanted to explore her body, to press his hands against the flat of her stomach and work his way up to her breasts, inch by inch. He'd wanted to smell her pussy and figure out just what a clitoris was. Convinced she was experienced in every way had him tongue-tied and anxious whenever he was around her, not allowing him to utter only a couple of words to her those first few days that she lived with them. Finally after a week of acting like a drooling idiot, he was ready to make his move...but then she left right after the fatal car accident that killed little Tanya and his step-father Dick and he had never gotten his chance.

It was then the sound of the coffee pot chirping brought him out of his daydream.

Pouring a cup, he began to look at the other items in the envelope. Everything and anything that he wanted to know about Jill Wallokowski was sitting in front of his face. He virtually had the woman's life held tightly in his hands. There were phone numbers, address, license plate number; then names of her best friend, her parents, her brother, and even her boss. Everything, including how after two weeks of constant surveillance, there didn't seem to be any indication of a steady man in her life. That would just make things that much easier.

"She's mine," he chortled loudly and let out a chuckle. "All mine."

* * * *

Monday night at Ross's Bar and Grill wasn't particularly busy, especially at one in the morning. The place was nearly closed down for the night, but Anita had a couple of important people at her bar. One more important than the other of course.

"I'll try the pale ale," the less important man on the other side of the bar said politely. Anita did what every other barmaid would do and smiling, pulled a glass from the cooler and tilted the Mirror Pond tap until the amber colored beer began pouring into the icy glass.

"So," Anita glanced over her shoulder to finish her conversation with Jill while she waited for the twenty-four ounce mug to fill up. "Did he say when this was going to happen?" She handed the beer to the thirsty customer, thanked him and propped her elbows on the bar in front of her best friend.

"This week. I have to go to Seattle on Thursday morning."

"Holy shit." Anita giggled loudly. "You're going to meet Willard Scott and Al Roker. You're about to be on national television. Do you realize that? This is huge."

"Shhhh!" Jill blushed slightly. "It's not that big of a deal. It's just a couple minutes of airtime with me standing beside them. I don't even have to say anything. I just have to smile and look pretty." Jill sipped her martini and smiled over Anita's shoulder at the handsomely big overgrown teddy bear of a man, who was also a fire fighter. *How lucky is Anita?* "There's your boyfriend," She whistled quietly and smiled at the tall dark haired man walking toward the bar.

Anita looked back over her shoulder and grimaced. "He's a fucking dead man!"

"What, trouble in paradise? I thought that you said he might possibly be *the one.*"

"I did think that -- last week. Now I need to get tested for STDs."

"Ah hell." Jill bellowed, wishing she already had a few drinks in her, so she'd have enough guts to walk up and kick the guy in the balls. "I'm so sorry. *Fucking men!*"

"He doesn't know I know yet, so be cool." Anita swallowed the lump in her throat and turned on her smile to greet the no-good-two-timing-piece of dog shit. "Hi," Anita growled trying to keep her emotions in check.

"Hey Babe," Ryan said with a devilish smile.

Jill resisted the urge to stick her finger down her throat, finished her martini with a single swig, stood up and excused herself to use the powder room to avoid having to watch what was about to happen. As she did, she lost her balance slightly and was jostled by a large man who grabbed her arm to steady her.

"Are you all right?" His other arm slipped around her waist to keep her balanced. "I'm so sorry. I didn't see you." His hazel eyes twinkled slightly in the dim lighting of the lounge. He released her arm and straightened to his full height, making him about four inches taller than Jill.

She momentarily lost all control of her thought process. Probably just the rush of alcohol to her brain. Either that, or it was just because she hadn't been man-handled in so long that it caught her off guard for a minute. She liked it.

She bit her lip and smiled. "It was my fault. I turned around too quickly. I'm sorry."

"Are you leaving?" He grinned and looked at her empty glass.

"Oh." She flushed slightly. "No, I'm just...I well... I have to powder my nose." That always sounded so much better than, 'I have to pee.'

"Oh, well in that case, I'll let you make it up to me by letting *you* buy *me* a drink." His teeth were so perfect it was almost unnatural.

Jill chuckled lightly. "You're so chivalrous."

"Is that a no?"

She stepped back to take in the whole picture. Tall handsome blonde wearing Armani and demanding that she buy him a drink. The man definitely had potential and so far, she was impressed with his sense of humor. Still, he did look too perfect. Her head cocked slightly to the side. Even his hair was perfect. *The man clearly spends a fair amount of time on that long, thick head of hair.*

"Thanks, but I should really be getting home. Maybe some other time."

"Can't blame a guy for trying." He lightly brushed her hand with his and gave her a wink.

Jill turned around after watching the man leave. Her heartbeat still not yet returned to normal. She mentally slapped herself in the head for turning down a perfectly good male specimen, but he just didn't set her vagina on fire like *he* had. He being -- the young hunk that she had seen on the beach all those years ago. His eyes so hot on hers that she thought she'd died and gone to heaven. That day at Compo Beach in Westport, Connecticut, twelve years ago was the first day and the only day since that her knees had actually buckled because of a boy. Even in junior high school during her first kiss, or the first time a boy touched her boobs didn't cause that *weak-kneed-trembling-stomach* feeling that she had felt that day that he looked into her eyes on the beach. Jill shuddered in recollection and felt a shiver of tingly prickles race up her spine. She'd never forget those heavenly blue eyes for as long as she lives. Nor would she forget how he made her feel with just a glance. She did think the tall blonde was attractive, but unfortunately, she wanted more, much more than just good looks and great hair.

Elias left Ross's Bar and Grill a very confused man. He wasn't used to rejection and had honestly expected Jill to fall at his feet. *Who the hell does she think she is?* The air was cool, yet Elias was a bit hot under the collar. Seeing her again, in the flesh was bringing back so many memories -- some of them painful ones.

His car was parked three blocks down from the bar and it seemed like the longest three blocks of his life as he repeatedly went over the encounter with Jill in his mind. *Was she not amused by my charm?* Clearly, he had to try something different next time for Jill was more guarded and reserved than he anticipated.

Chapter Three

After a long run in the hot sun and a piece of plain rye toast for breakfast, Jill headed for the bathroom and a shower, only to be halted by the phone ringing in the kitchen. In her soft fluffy socks, she slid across the smooth hardwood floor and picked it up on the third ring.

All she heard was deep breathing. "Hello," she said again and waited. "I know who you are. I have caller ID."

"You're so puurrty," the creepy voice said breathlessly.

That was all she could stand. Hanging up, she yanked the phone cord from the wall, and shivered; then headed into the bathroom after double-checking the locks and pulling down the blinds in her bedroom.

When she finally got out from under the cool shower, Jill heard sobs coming from down the hall. After securing her towel around her, she rapped lightly on Anita's door. "You okay, sweetie?" Without waiting for a reply, she walked in and sat down next to her on her friend's oversized pink bed.

"It wasn't supposed to happen like this. Not like this and not with him."

Anita sobbed hard onto her friend's shoulder.

"I know you're upset, but you did the right thing. You dropped kicked his ass and you'll bounce back. I know you will."

"That's not it." Anita sniffled and slowly opening her clenched fist, exposing the early pregnancy test she held. She dropped it onto the bed and sobbed harder.

Jill lifted the long piece of plastic and examined the tiny window with two thin blue lines clearly showing. Sucking in a breath of sheer panic, nausea and extreme jealousy, she bit down on her lip and fumbled with her words. "A baby?" She actually let a tear or two roll out before getting it together to embrace her friend again. "Honey, are you okay? Are you happy about this? Are you going to keep it?"

Anita's face revealed itself as she peeled her cheek off Jill's bare shoulder. "Are you insane? Of course I'm not okay! I'm fucking freaked out of my mind. I just broke up with the jerk and you know what...you and Cosmo were right. He said, and I quote, 'I'm not ready to commit myself to *like* one babe. I got *like* five more years to party before I grow up. I got lots of pussy to *like* chase and places to *like* go, babe, I'm sorry.' He actually said he was sorry that he had lots of pussy to chase. I can't have a baby with a man like that. What the fuck am I going to do?"

"You're going to stop spitting on me..." Jill laughed and dried off her face with the corner of her towel. Anita burst into laughter and then began crying again as Jill continued. "And then you are going to think about this calmly and rationally. How long have you known?"

"Ten minutes." She sniffled.

"Okay," Jill got serious. "Cosmo says that it takes at least fifteen minutes for the reality of pregnancy to actually sink in, so we wait." Her lips quivered with the threat of laughter.

Anita's eyes became as wide as silver dollars.

"I was kidding." Jill pulled her into a big bear hug. "I love you, sweetie. It's going to be okay."

All she could do was embrace her friend and listen to her wail about everything that was suddenly so wrong. Jill tried looking at it from a completely different perspective and started saying about all the things that were right. Like how they live in a wonderful house with a yard just three blocks from a school. Or like the fact that Anita is almost done with school and that neither of them have boyfriends. Perhaps this was supposed to happen. Jill pressed a kiss into Anita's hair and led her out to the kitchen for tea and cookies.

Half an hour and a half a box of tissue later, Anita finally pulled her long blonde hair up into a high, tight ponytail and sipped her herbal tea with a smile.

"Let's make a list," Jill said cheerfully. "Why you should keep it and why you shouldn't. I personally vote for keeping it, but it's your choice. I just think that in today's society it is possible for a woman to have it all. Especially since you live with me. We could do it together."

Anita sent her dear friend a grim smile; admiration for her best friend clear in her misty blue eyes. "I can't do that to you. You're going to find a good man one of these days and you deserve to have your own life. I'll be fine." She sucked back her sobs. "I'll just make it work. Besides, I'll be finished with school by the time it's born." She smiled brightly and patted Jill's hand.

Returning the smile, she had to admit that Anita was a strong, capable woman who really could handle anything.

"I want this baby. I really do."

"That's what I thought," Jill replied. "Are you going to tell *The Jerk*?"

"Yeah -- someday."

Thursday morning Jill stopped by the station on her way out of town. For the following morning she would be airing live from Channel 12's sister station in Seattle, with Al Roker and Willard Scott, and couldn't be more excited if she tried.

Tom Riley was sitting at her desk picking at a bouquet of dead blackened roses.

"What's this?"

"Why, they're for you, pretty lady." He sneered and held out the card.

Jill stepped back, her eyes wide with mortification. "I don't want it. Give it to the police."

Tom rolled his eyes and opened it. "It's blank

except for a number."

"Like a phone number?" Jill asked, trying to get her heartbeat under control.

"No, just the number 9."

Jill still refused to grab the card, but she leaned over his shoulder and took a look. Just as he had said, there was a large number nine scribbled in red ink. She shrugged. "Are you sure they were for me?"

"Positive. They were in a big box with your name on them. Security says they hadn't seen them until this morning, but they just assumed that someone had forgotten they were there. I don't think someone meant to send you dead roses."

Jill shivered. Never in her wildest dreams would she truly expect to receive this kind of negative attention. Sure, she liked to joke around about being famous and having her own stalker, but this was beyond scary. Not to mention the phone calls that she had still been receiving. *Perhaps*, she thought, *now would be a good time to make a phone call to the local police, just in case.*

"I think you're over exaggerating. Liz Carlson got flowers her first week," Tom shrugged. "Granted, they weren't dead when they arrived, but like Reggie said, someone probably just forgot to give them to you."

"You're probably right." Jill half smiled. "Well, I'm off to meet the big boys. Are you sure you don't want to come. It'll be fun."

"I met them both last year. Trust me, it's not fun." Tom's negativity usual put a damper on her mood, but today nothing was going to spoil her high.

* * * *

Ian Hamlin hadn't been home for almost an entire week and it was wreaking havoc on his already sour mood. After finding yet another deceased Jill Walker just west of Memphis, the other similar named women in the area were briefed and now either scared out of their minds or packing their bags to hold up at the safe house the FBI had rented in a small town in Kentucky.

After checking the department of motor vehicles records over the past three days, Agents Hamlin and Harrison had come up with only eight other Jill Walkers east of the Mississippi that fit in with the age group of the other victims. Eight he could tackle, but Ian wasn't even prepared to take on the west. The west was vast. Too vast and too much ground to cover on such a limited budget. He couldn't possibly fathom the idea that the killer would venture that far from home. This serial was still making his life miserable and he would gladly hand the case off to someone else if he hadn't still felt guilty for Jill –four's untimely death. It's not that he could have done anything to stop it. Nothing short of moving in with the woman and watching her twenty-four-hours a day would have saved her life. Furthermore, no one could have expected the killer would return after a two-year absence. Yet, the guilt still tore at his gut; making his heart race, his muscles clench and the anger inside him at times rage out of control.

He took out the files of the six victims and laid them out, one by one the bed. Starting with the first murder four years ago and ending with the latest victim who was killed in her bathtub.

He'd become a man obsessed with Jill Walker. Since the discovery of Jill- four, he hadn't shaved, gotten his unruly black hair cut, or even taken the time to examine just what it was about these women's deaths that had him so scared. Was it because the killer was being so off-the-cuff with his motive and means? Or was it just that he felt out of control, a feeling he hated? His life was all about order and people listening to him and doing what he says. If it were up to him, he'd take all the Jill Walkers in the world and lock them up to keep them safe. Something had to fall into place and fast.

Flipping the first file open, he finished his ham and cheese sandwich, chugged down some soda, and then began comparing even the slightest, most insignificant details;

anything that might link these women together besides just their names. There *had* to be something they were all missing and Ian Hamlin was making it his mission to find it.

Ian fell asleep on top of the files on his bed after watching the late movie, only to be woken by the obnoxious ranting of the screaming audience of the Today Show live in Time Square. The digital clock read seven thirty, and he knew it was time to start the day. His days had been long and drawn out and after staying up until four a.m. searching the files for any hint of a clue; daybreak seemed depressing.

Stretching one arm high over his head, he curled it over his ear to adjust his pillow and that's when he saw her. Sitting up with a start, he stared harder at the television and grappled for the remote under the piles of paperwork on the paisley comforter.

He pointed the remote at the television and turned up the volume to hear Al Roker on location from Seattle introducing the newest weather girl in the area...Jill Walker. His head throbbed from the lack of sleep and his eyes burned, but it was the gnawing in his stomach that had him jumping off the bed to get a closer look. Besides the fact that this woman on TV had the unfortunate luck to have the same name as the six victims, he couldn't shake the notion he'd seen her somewhere before. Her smile and that long dark hair seemed so familiar, yet he couldn't put a finger on it. Shaking his head from side to side, he muttered a few choice obscenities and called the New Haven office.

* * * *

"Well, I guess it is a small world isn't it." A deep voice boomed from over Jill's head at the Hilton Hotel in downtown Seattle. She looked more professional than ever this morning; her hair was pulled back into a tight French braid and even though she preferred bold, bright colors, today she was in a beige blazer and matching skirt. Her morning had been a dream come true and now she had a handsome blonde staring down at her with a wild sparkle in his eyes.

She flushed slightly and swallowed her bite of Caesar salad before wiping the corner of her mouth with her napkin. "Well, hello."

"Do you live here in Seattle?" He sat down across the table from her without even waiting for the invitation.

Jill stared bright eyed and leery at first, and then sipped from her glass of Chardonnay and smiled because it had just been one of those wonderful days that caused perma-grin.

"No," she replied. "How about you?"

He smiled and pointed out the window toward the large towering building to their right. "I live at the top of that building, so that puts you right in my backyard. What did I do to deserve this?" There was a special sparkle in his eyes again.

Jill smiled demurely and extended her hand.

The man took it and gave it a gently squeeze. "Elias Webber."

"Jill Walker." She smiled. "Elias, huh? That's an unusual name."

In fact, she had only heard that name one other time in her life, but she couldn't quite remember off the top of her head. Then she placed it. "Ah ha. Elias Howe," she mumbled and then blushed because she was mumbling in front of a handsome stranger.

"Excuse me?" He leaned closer and took a quick sniff of her perfume. *Beautiful*, he thought; the scent intoxicating him.

"Elias Howe. He invented the sewing machine."

"Oh," Elias chuckled. "So, is it Miss Walker, or Mrs. Walker?"

"Miss," She said, and then sipped more wine

because his gaze was not only making her nervous, but also making her flushed. Just slightly, and for the most part it was a nice, comfortable feeling. The waiter removed her plate and cleared the breadbasket from in front of her and Elias leaned closer. "Miss Walker, what brings you to Seattle?" He said as he got comfortable and waved to the bartender.

"Just work. I report the weather on Channel 12 in Vancouver. I was here this morning meeting some fellow colleagues."

"Oh, a weathergirl? I would never have guessed."

"I prefer meteorologist. *Weathergirl* went out of style in the late eighties." Jill said triumphantly. She didn't know why exactly, but she wanted to make a good impression. Especially since Elias seemed so perfectly put together. His tailor made navy blue suit looked to cost more than she made in a month, his hair was perfect, and with the large leather briefcase he carried, he looked as if he belonged on the cover of Gentlemen's Quarterly.

Elias stared hard at his prize and with a twinge of panic he wondered if perhaps Jill had recognized him somehow and what if she did? How could he explain the rare coincidence of running into her after all these years? But then again, they had only shared a couple of awkward moments over thirteen years ago and Jill did only live in the house for seven days. How could she remember him? Hell, she hadn't even been there long enough to meet his best friend Ian. *And boy had Ian been furious about that.* Elias sniggered to himself about Ian Hamlin and how badly their friendship had ended.

He finally snapped out of his temporary jaunt down memory lane and sent her an enigmatic smile. "So, in your expert opinion is the weather going to be nice for say...a picnic in the park tomorrow?"

"Well, the weather in Vancouver...where I will be...should be a perfect day for a picnic, but here....where you will be...I really don't know."

"Oh, I see." He said as he bent forward and reached out to tuck a strand of her long hair behind her ear. Jill didn't flinch, although she wanted to. It seemed fairly unnerving to have a strange man touching her face. Nice, but still unsettling. "How about this weekend? I might feel like taking a drive to, let's say.... Lewis River."

She thought long and hard about that. The man was offering to meet her just twenty miles north of Vancouver, for a picnic by the fabulous Lewis River. *Is this guy for real?*

"Saturday?"

"Perfect."

* * *

Jill was home by nightfall. The air smelled like mesquite and barbecue sauce. Plenty of kids were still shooting hoops in the street and the coolness of dusk was like a breath of fresh air. She had just pulled into the driveway when a car screeched to a halt in front of their house.

Ryan jumped out from behind the steering wheel and started for the door. Jill quickened her steps and cut him off before he stepped onto the front deck.

"Where is she?" he slurred, and Jill could smell the whiskey on his breath. "Come on Jill. I know she's here. I tried work, but they said she went home sick."

"Go home, Ryan. You don't want to do this."

He hung his head. "Will you *like* tell her I stopped by?"

"Yes, now go home and drive careful." Jill pushed lightly against his broad chest. "Go."

The tall, heartbroken young man sauntered back to his car and pulled away from the curb just before Anita peeked her head out the door.

Jill noticed right away that her friend was pale. "Morning sickness?" She followed Anita into the kitchen and tossed her purse on the counter.

"No, I just didn't think I could handle seeing him,

so I came home early. So far I feel pretty okay." Anita moved around the kitchen table and handed Jill a martini that she had just made her. "I saw it. You looked wonderful. Is Al as wonderful and funny as you expected?"

"Yep." Jill smiled and walked into the family room just beyond the kitchen. She kicked off her shoes and sank down on their new couch. She'd waited her whole life to buy a couch like this one; big, and so overstuffed that she felt as if she was sitting on a cloud. It sure beat the heck out of Anita's old one that unfortunately didn't make the move with them. "Guess who I ran into in Seattle."

"Uh, Gary Payton?" Anita joked.

Jill shook her head with a smirk. "Shorter-- and probably can't dunk as well?"

"Uh...I give up."

"The tall blonde from the other night. Remember him?"

"Are you kidding? You have the best luck. What the hell was he doing in Seattle?"

"He lives there, and we had drinks and—boy, does he ever remind me of someone. He looks so familiar but I can't place him."

"So, what's his name? Maybe I can help."

"Elias Webber. He's thirty, so I doubt we went to school with him." Jill replied. "It's really odd."

"It doesn't ring a bell," Anita said, and then sighed. "How did he look? Did he seem depressed?"

Jill shrugged. "I don't think so, he looked *fine*. So *fine*. In fact, we have a date on Saturday."

Anita's jaw dropped, and she shook her head. "I meant Ryan! Did Ryan seem upset?"

"He seemed drunk."

"Drunk is a good start," Anita said. "A date, huh? He must be something special. You never date strangers. Hell, you never date period. Is this guy the one?"

"Give me a break? I just met him. Besides. I don't believe in fate."

"Bullshit," Anita smirked. "You're still waiting around for mystery boy. You're such a liar."

"No," Jill said solemnly. "I'm refusing to believe in fate anymore. If fate were real, then somehow, somewhere, mystery boy would have surfaced by now and we'd be happily married with a baby on the way. Fate is taking too fucking long and the ticking gets louder every damn day."

"I'm sorry." Anita stood up and embraced her friend. "You can share my baby."

Jill let the tears stream down her face as she hugged her pregnant friend tighter. "Thanks, but it's not the same." She sobbed hard, and wiped the tears from her cheeks. "I really am happy for you."

"I know. I know." Anita rocked her gently. "Take a chance with this guy. You never know. He might be just like your dad."

Jill snorted with laughter before breaking away to send her friend a playful glare.

* * * *

Red-faced and flushed with rage would be an understatement as to how Ian Hamlin felt as he finished his conversation with his superiors at the New Haven Bureau. It had been another long, exhausting day going over more clues and more information they had gathered from the latest victims. The files were still strewn on the bed in his miniscule hotel room and the worst part was Jill Walker, the weather gal, had been on his mind all day. He couldn't get over how she looked so familiar and furthermore that he'd been told she was off limits. The killer hadn't gone that far west and his superiors at the bureau didn't feel that he would. Not anytime soon anyway, and that had Agent Hamlin strung tight with rage. He could feel the muscles in his shoulders tighten as he was told again and again that the weathergirl was off limits.

"Fuck that!" he shouted. "She was on the fucking news. You don't think this son-of-a-bitch watches television. It would be like hanging a bloody limb over the side of a boat just waiting for a Great White to come along and bite it off." He huffed and slammed his fist into the wall. "...I get that she's in Seattle and he hasn't moved that far west, but I guarantee he will. She fits the age group and she's very attractive. I have to at least warn her."

He listened intently to his superior on the other end of the line, and then threw the phone down on the bed and lifted a chair up over his head. With all his might and all the rage burrowing in his veins, he tossed the chair through the window, shattering it into a million tiny pieces. He hadn't done anything that destructive in twelve years and it felt great. He forgot how wonderful the sound of breaking glass was to his ears.

Finally, after a few long deep breaths, he reigned in his anger and picked up the phone again. This time he called Channel 34 in Seattle Washington and demanded to speak to Jill Walker.

"There's no Jill Walker at this station sir. I'm sorry." The nice friendly woman reiterated for the second time.

"No, I mean... I saw her, just this morning. On your station. With Al Roker and Willard Scott. I saw her," he shouted in frustration. This had been the third person he'd spoken to at the station and coincidentally, the third person that said the same damn thing.

"Sir, who did you say you were again?"

"Agent Ian Hamlin of the FBI."

"Hold on a minute."

Ian paced his miniscule hotel room and kicked the door a couple of times in frustration.

Three minutes later, he was finally speaking to someone who knew what he or she was talking about. "I'm sorry, but I can't give out that kind of information. But I assure you that there is no Jill Walker at this station. I've worked her for over six years. I'm sorry sir."

"Fuck." Ian slammed down the phone.

If there was no such woman at that station in

Seattle, then where the hell did she come from? My only shot is to actually go to Seattle and make those fucking people at the station listen to me. Someone had to know something. Suddenly, time seemed to be of the essence for Agent Hamlin, and come hell or high water, he would get to Seattle.

He sank down on the bed in resignation. *Seattle,* he thought. *Now there was a whole big can of worms I really don't want to re-open.*

Pulling the t-shirt off over his head, he tossed it in the corner, wishing he could do the same with his ever-growing frustrations. His muscled chest was still rising and falling rapidly from his bout of aggravation. He popped the top three buttons of his Levis before sliding them down his lean hips. It was summer, yet there was no sign of a tan; he lived in jeans and the pallor of his skin told the tale. Crawling across the king-size bed, he lay down, curled his hands behind his head, and stared up at the ceiling. *How did I get here? Maybe I should just try to let it go and stop dwelling on the past. Besides, I really didn't do anything wrong.* His dark eyes twinkled with the threat of tears as he blinked hard to regain control. Sleep once again eluded him for the most part, but around the four a.m. hour, he felt himself start to fade off to sleep.

* * *

The drive to Paradise Point on the Lewis River was nice Saturday morning. The traffic was light, the sun was bright in the sky, and she was feeling fairly optimistic about her first date in nearly a year. Jill left Anita alone with a box of saltine crackers, a couple of her favorite movies on dvd, and a pound of the best chocolates she could find so as not to feel guilty for leaving her emotionally drained friend to go off and frolic with a perfect stranger. The thought of spending the day with Elias Webber had its good points, but in no way was she ready to accept that this may lead somewhere. Sure, she had deluded herself into thinking that fate had done her wrong, but the thought of abandoning the idea that *he'd* never come for her had kept her up late into the night. Her last broadcast on Friday evening said temperatures might reach the upper eighties, so she packed extra bottles of water, her sunscreen and wore a very sheer and breathable sundress with just her one-piece bathing suit underneath. She preferred her pretty purple bikini, but it was not something she was prepared to wear on a first date.

As she pulled into the lot at Paradise Point, it was already crowded with day visitors, boat trailers and there were even a couple of tailgate barbecues already in progress.

It must be nice, she thought, trying to remember the last time she actually went on a real date. It was over a year ago when she lived in San Francisco and unbeknownst to her, the jackass actually expected sex after dinner. Times sure had changed from when she was in college and dated quite a bit. College men also expected sex, but usually not on the first date. They'd wait until the second date before getting her drunk and attempting to seduce her in their fraternity house study rooms. Of course Jill never fell for it. She kept her head most of the time, with a couple of exceptions when her hormones got the best of her. But still, in the back of her mind, she was always thinking about *him*, the boy on the beach.

Pulling her newer-model blue Honda into the parking lot, she took a deep breath before grabbing her beach bag and smiling brightly at Elias as he emerged from his bright yellow Porsche 911. The car gave her a hot flash, but the man...not so much.

"Hi, how was the drive? I still can't believe you drove all the way here just for a picnic." Jill rambled nervously.

"I drove all the way from Seattle for more than a picnic." His brow cocked upward. "I came for you, Jill."

She blushed, hoping he hadn't gotten it in his head

that sex would be had, or worse, that she would invite him for the rest of the weekend, so he wouldn't have to drive home tonight. *Shit. I hadn't even thought about that.*

She took the hand he extended and followed him down to the beach. They found a quiet spot in the shade of a large aspen tree and talked about the weather. To Elias it probably seemed like small talk, but to Jill, it was her favorite subject and it was the one thing that she knew. She did let him share a couple of his own stories, and as he did, she leaned back on her elbows and extended her long legs out into the warm sand. The sand tickling her calves had her thinking about *him* again, and that had her inching closer, almost as if he were the boy from the beach.

"You really are very good," he said with a smile.

Jill hadn't heard the last of what he was saying because she was daydreaming about that day at Compo Beach. She'd gone over it in her mind so many damn times and it just didn't make sense to her that the young man had not approached her. *He looked interested. He was only a few feet away and yet, all he did was narrow his eyes and stare at me as if I were the only girl on the beach.*

She fanned her face a few times and licked her lips as Elias reiterated what he had just said.

"You really are very good." He went on.

"What?" Jill shook her head and realized that she was just inches from the man's lips. She hesitantly moved away. "I'm sorry, I was lost in space."

He bent forward and caught her by surprise with a delicate, lingering kiss.

"I *said* you are really good at the weather. I watched you last night."

"Oh," Jill mumbled; still shocked from the kiss. It had been so long since she'd kissed anyone, she somewhat wanted to do it again. "Thanks," she said with a smile, and then leaned in to continue. He caught her bottom lip between his own lips and suckled it gently, and then opened her mouth with his tongue and delved deeply, carefully caressing the side of her tongue with his own. A low-grade fire burned low in her belly as he deepened the kiss, and she moved closer to his chest.

Taking a minute to realize that his hand was wrapped around her ass, she abruptly stopped and scooted away.

"How about a swim?" he asked with a wink.

"That would be nice." She let him help her to a standing position. She stepped out of her dress and was in the water before he had time to catch up.

Because the heat was so intense, the rest of the afternoon was either spent in the water, or sitting in the sand where the waves hit the beach. Jill felt downright comfortable and could envision doing this again sometime; that is if she hadn't blown it by demanding they take things slowly. She knew he was interested and so if she was going to do this, she was going to do it right. Elias had already pretty much admitted that he was a very wealthy, stable man. He was handsome, funny, and gentle. His body was beyond fabulous and yet, Jill still thought he was too perfect. It was if all the articles in Cosmopolitan magazine had come alive and every descriptive word to describe the perfect man was staring into her eyes. He was a perfect man. She couldn't have made him any more right for her if she tried. He said the right things, laughed on cue and pretty much enjoyed the same things in life that she did.

"I'm in town on Tuesday for a conference. Do you think we could meet for dinner?"

Jill wrapped her towel tightly around her waist and gathered up her clothes. "Actually I work until almost one in the morning. I keep pretty crazy hours."

"Lunch then?"

"Uh, I guess that would work. I usually don't have to be at the station until three, so we could do that." She smiled warmly and opened herself up to accept a small kiss on the lips. "That would be really nice."

"Great!" He kissed her again and wrapped his

broad arms around her shoulders. "How about noon at the Heathman?"

"Noon it is."

Chapter Four

Elias returned home frustrated, irate, and pretty damn pissed off that Jill didn't even have the courtesy to ask him to stay the weekend. He'd done everything perfectly; he was a gentleman, he was witty and yet somehow she seemed immune to his charm. He hadn't expected that she would be this much work. *Why hadn't she fallen into my arms and demanded that I marry her? So far, Jill Walker was the most difficult of all my conquests, which made it that much more challenging.* Although, he was rather put out that she hadn't fallen on her back with her legs in the air. Elias thought very highly of himself, after all, and who ever Elias wanted, Elias got. *Hell, I've even taken women away from their husbands in the past. I'm irresistible and I have Sara to prove it.*

"Hey baby," Sara cooed from the sofa. A bottle of his favorite champagne was chilling on the coffee table beside her. "Where have you been? I've been waiting here for hours."

Elias looked over at the tall, naked blonde on the couch. Now that's what he was used to. *Woman flocking to my side, falling at my feet, and just plain begging for my dick.* He dropped his shorts, fumbled with the buttons on his red Hawaiian shirt and was easily inside her within minutes. Hell, she hadn't even demanded an explanation as to why he had snuck out of bed in the wee hours of the morning--on a Saturday no less. *How could I have respect for someone like her? Sure, she'd been living in my place for the past two years, only because she was a constant reminder that I get what I want.*

But now, he thought as he howled and came hard inside her. *There's something else I want.* And his mind was once again on Jill Walker.

* * *

Agent Hamlin paced the floor at the Whitefish Montana Memorial Hospital just ten days after Jill-six had been murdered in Tennessee. Both he and agent Will Harrison were pacing the hall with tight lips. Steaming cups of coffee gripped tightly in their hands. Both their grim expressions grew unchanged as the doctor emerged to tell them the news.

"She didn't make it. I'm sorry," the doctor said with his head hung low.

"Fuck!" Ian slammed his fist into the wall behind the coffee maker. Nothing would have prepared him for this one. "Did she happen to say anything? Give you a clue as to what the guy looked like. Anything?"

"No, I'm sorry. By the time they brought her in, she'd lost so much blood that she never regained consciousness. We did everything we could, but it was too late. Do you want to see her?"

Both agents nodded and followed the doctor into the emergency room to examine the body. Jill Raven Walker, age thirty-three, was the most recent of the Jill murders, with the count now up to seven and stretched across the Mississippi. This time though, the victim had tried to escape by jumping out of a moving vehicle, and was found by a couple of young kids on their way home from a party in some nearby woods. The two teenagers told police that they had seen the woman fall from the vehicle and nearly swerved off the road to stop from running her over. The markings on her body were similar to the others, being that her midsection had been slashed into a number of times.

The room quickly filled with crime lab specialists. Photographers were snapping shots of the naked, mutilated corpse and after getting the information that he needed, Ian had to leave the room to escape the horror and the stench. He dialed Special Agent Pete Morrow at the New Haven office using his cell phone.

"She's a Jill all right," Ian began. "Her husband had called the police when she failed to come home after working late. He identified her when she was brought into the emergency room. *Now* will you let me do my fucking job?"

"You'll sit tight until we give the word. Is that clear Agent Hamlin?"

"Crystal." Ian hung up and waited for the examiners to finish before heading to the site on the rural highway where the young kids found Jill-seven's body. The drive took about twenty minutes on a long stretch of highway lined with tall brush and weeds. Both boys sat in the back seat, not saying much, other than to direct Ian to the crime scene. The morning chill was still evident in the air and had Agent Hamlin tightening his leather jacket around his chest. Ian and Will walked around the site, being careful not to disturb the forensic team that was already hard at work. Coffee was doing nothing as far as keeping Ian sharp. His brain felt as if it was swelling from exhaustion and a deep sense of petulance.

"She was right here." The young man named Carl pointed to the bloody spot on the asphalt. The sun had just started to rise beyond the mountains and the chill in the air was slowly evaporating as the sun began to warm the ground. "Is she okay?"

Ian shook his head sadly and thanked the young boys for all their help. He couldn't imagine what these poor kids were going through. All their clothes had been confiscated, leaving them both in old sweats that the Sheriff had given them. Hopefully, they could catch a break and some kind of trace evidence had made its way onto the fabric of their shirts when they lifted her body into their car. Their car had also been tagged, towed, and was now being inspected by the Montana Sheriff's crime unit. Not to mention the fact that both boys had never seen a dead body before. *Hell,* Ian thought. *They've probably never seen a naked women either.* His jaw tightened with rage.

Every detail was thoroughly checked out with a fine-tooth-comb. Ian hoped and prayed that this would be the last; that perhaps the killer had gotten scared and decided it was too risky to strike again. He actually prayed to God that it was true. Actually, he prayed a lot lately.

Needless to say, Ian hadn't been thanking God for much in his life lately. He'd been a spiritual man in his youth. Obeyed his parents, done his best to be a good person and yet, nothing ever worked out for him, so he'd pretty much given up on God and a life he once wanted. *Now was different.* He needed something to help with his grief and pain and he needed someone to show him the path to forgiveness. He prayed for his sanity and he prayed for the safety of every Jill Walker out there. *Mostly I pray that I'd have a couple of seconds alone in a dark alley with this son-of-a-bitch.* He knew it was unethical to think that way, but he couldn't help it. Anger management had helped with this in the past, but he still had a long way to go.

* * *

Three long and draining hours later, Ian sat across from Sheriff Kip Krause and finished briefing the room on the Jill murders. The Sheriff's white hair and big belly made him look like Santa Claus in Ian's opinion. All in all, there were three deputies, a couple local city police, and the big city boys whom everyone was watching carefully—Ian and Will.

All eyes narrowed on Ian and he again felt the guilt bear down on his shoulders. *If I had just been more insistent on staying with Jill-four, then I could have caught the killer and this wouldn't be happening.* "This is your turf. You tell me what to do." Ian said as an apology for not being able to stop these atrocious murders sooner.

"I want what you want. I want every Jill Walker between the age of thirty and thirty- four to be informed and put in either protective custody or under twenty-four hour surveillance. If this gets leaked to the press, we might as well turn in our badges, because there will be hell to pay for holding this information back from these women. We can't risk that now." Sheriff Krause said sternly and for the most part Ian agreed--And then he told agent Krause all about Jill Walker from the news station in Seattle.

"I don't have the authority to override your superiors, but if you're that worried about her, take a chance, son. The worst thing that could happen is you get fired for insubordination and brought up on charges." The old man's belly jiggled as he chuckled. "But on the other hand, you might just save her life."

"I'm counting on the second scenario." Ian finally smiled and stood up. Krause was right and Ian was that worried. *So worried, that I'm willing to fly to Seattle right this fucking minute and move into the babe's house--* but that would mean he'd actually be in Seattle again. His stomach churned at the thought.

* * *

"Damn, you're jittery lately," Tom said bitterly and handed Jill the latest weather reports. His bow tie actually matched his maroon sweater vest this morning. "Every time the phone rings, you jump a mile in the air. You might want to cut back on the caffeine."

"Bite me," Jill barked. Not only was it not funny, but also he was right. The phone calls at her house had become so unbearable that she and Anita decided the ringer should remain off until they get a new number, and thanks to a very sweet guy at the phone company, they would soon have that new unlisted number.

Jill finished her work, tucked her hair back behind her ears, and waited patiently for Elias to pick her up. The station was dark, most of the staff and crew had already gone home and the early morning anchors were still at home sleeping. The station was only quiet from one a.m. to three a.m. before the early birds got there. The parking garage was deserted and it was by far the worst part of her day. She loved coming to work in the warm sun, but lately, she had felt uneasy about even walking to her car that was just three slots down from the elevator--in a very secure parking garage--and yet, she still felt the tingle of tiny hairs standing on end that drove her crazy with fright. Tonight was no exception.

She felt a cool draft blow past her feet as she remained within inches of the door, just waiting to hear Elias pull up and take her home. He'd been in Portland for three days straight that time and had spent much of his time wooing the pretty meteorologist at the finest restaurants, concerts and had even taken her to the observatory to see the meteor shower the previous Monday night. Elias seemed more and more compatible with Jill's idea of the perfect mate.

Date number six was about to happen and to Jill, having six dates in a matter of two weeks was almost a relationship. She wasn't quite sure if she wanted it to be a relationship yet and she wasn't about to bring it up because that was a major faux pa according to Cosmo. *Women should never be the ones who bring up commitment.* It's the men who need to make that move and she was actually thankful about that and didn't really want him to bring it up either. She had still remained adamant about staying out of his bed and him out of hers, but tonight she had made the bold move of inviting him to her house due to the fact it was his last night in Portland for a while. Of course when she invited him, she insisted that he understand that no sex would be had. He had laughed and kissed her wildly, hoping to knock some sense into the woman.

The door creaked slightly, and Jill's skin crawled, only to realize she had been daydreaming again and accidentally leaned against it, causing it to sway lightly.

She could hear a car pull up and stop. The engine was still humming and she heard a door open and close. She pressed her ear to the door and waited to hear the footsteps. They got closer and closer to the door before Elias lightly knocked and called her name.

"Oh thank God!" Jill opened the door and nearly jumped into his arms. "What took you so long?"

He cuddled her closer and could feel her heart beating wildly in her chest. "Jeez, Honey, what's gotten into you?"

"I just hate it here at night. It's spooky. Let's go." She hustled to the car and got in quickly, letting the last shiver roll down her spine before getting herself together and shaking the feeling that someone was watching. Always--she felt that someone was watching. *Even when I go out to get the mail, I feel that someone is always watching.* She shuddered again and stared out the windows at the bright lights of the city.

Elias took them both back to her house in Wallingford Heights. It was the first time he had seen her house, and although it was pitch black outside, he could see that it was a large, older home with style and most likely termites. "Wow, you live here?"

"Yeah," Jill looked over at his agape expression. "Are you being a snob again?"

"No," he scoffed. "I just expected something smaller, perhaps newer."

"This is my house and I love it. I'm even thinking about buying it. The owners gave us the option just last week and since Anita's hanging out for awhile, I thought it would be a good idea."

Elias grinned at her and reached over to pull her to his lips after helping her out of the car.

"You have the subtlety of a rock, you know that right?" He laughed after he finished kissing her solidly on the mouth. She stared at him bright eyed and weary.

"I was just stating a fact."

"No, you were telling me, in so many words, that you don't intend on moving to Seattle any time soon."

"Hey, it's only been two weeks. I'm not ready to have this discussion." Jill said, trying to keep her voice from squealing. She moved quickly passed him and opened the front door. "Anita's a light sleeper so keep it down please."

Elias shut the front door and pulled her to him, pinning her against the door. He moved his hand up to cup her breast and lowered his lips to meet hers. The kiss deepened and even though she had reservations about sleeping with him, he made a good point with his grinding hips. *I do need to get laid.*

"You drive me mad. You know that, right."

"I know," Jill smiled against his lips. "But you're still sleeping on the couch."

"What are you so afraid of?" he whispered before kissing her again. "I have plenty of protection. I have a clean bill of health and I promise you that you'll enjoy yourself."

She pushed gently against his chest. "I like you Elias. You're a wonderful man and I want to do this right, so please respect my wishes and keep it in your pants."

"Fine." He sighed in resignation. "But the couch? Come on. I promise I'll behave."

Jill thought long and hard about that and for the most part, he'd been a perfect gentleman up to that point. He hadn't ever tried to go below the waist and he did smell rather good this evening; like apple pie and good cigars. "Okay, but you try anything and I'll never invite you back."

He just smiled and followed her into her bedroom.

The bed was large, but not a king size like where he normally slept. Which was fine by him-- *that just means that I get to be closer to her throughout the night.* She shed her dress, but turned and headed into the bathroom before he could see anymore than her bra and lacy panties. When she returned wearing a long green t-shirt that covered her all the way to the knees, he was sadly disappointed.

"Ducks, huh? Did you go to University of Oregon?" He smiled and stepped out of his Dockers.

Jill kept her gaze from going south and then slid her toes under the covers before looking into his eyes. She wondered if this is what it would be like once they were married. The passion just wasn't there for her. *The heat wasn't there, but everything else about Elias Webber was so darn perfect it was a pity to think about giving it all up.* "Yep, Anita and I both went."

"Really? I thought you went to the University of Connecticut." He slithered into bed beside her and wiggled his toes against hers.

"UCONN?" Jill blurted out and then narrowed her eyes. She had never even mentioned to him that she had been a nanny back east. *Where the hell did that come from?* "What makes you say that?"

"I thought you told me you lived in Connecticut."

"I never said that. I did live there for awhile, but I never told *you.*"

He felt her retract her toes from the sheets. He had to think of something to control the damage of his big mouth. "Sorry, I guess I got you confused with someone else."

"Oh." Jill let her feet slide back under the covers. Elias nestled his head against the pillow and closed his eyes tightly as he berated himself for almost blowing it. He was so close to getting what he wanted and like it or not, he was falling harder and harder every day. *Once I get what I want, will I be able to let her go?* He was beginning to wonder.

After a few slow strokes to her long dark hair, she was out like a light and he soon followed.

*** Ian's flight to New Haven took most of the day, but he was glad to be home. He stopped by his house for a quick change of clothes and to see if perhaps he'd won a million dollars in the Publisher's Clearing House sweepstakes. He dropped his duffle onto the floor, grabbed the pile of mail off the floor, and flipped through it to find the important stuff, like the mortgage bill and utilities. He showered quickly and stepped back into his Levis and black Nikes and then pulled yet another black t-shirt over his head. Raking his hand through his wet hair, he grabbed a green apple from the bottom of the refrigerator and bolted out his front door to meet Agent Morrow at the downtown office.

Pete was seated on the edge of his desk flipping through the latest Jill murder file when Ian finally approached.

"Nothing on the Montana Jill yet, huh?" Pete said to Ian

"Nothing. It's like the guy's a ghost."

"Look, I know how upset you are about these Jill murders, and I'd like to be able to send you out looking for this weathergirl, but I need you on this one and if you're out west playing bodyguard, then I won't have anyone here to take point."

"Then I'll resign." Ian said seriously.

Pete glared at him with a disapproving scowl.

Ian rolled his eyes. "I didn't mean from the bureau, I meant I'll step off point on the case. This is important to me. I feel like I let Jill-four down somehow and my gut tells me that there's something to this woman. I know you don't think there's anything to this theory of mine, but I do. I feel it and I have to take a chance," Ian said sternly and went on. "I can't have any more regrets."

Pete inhaled sharply, and then let out his breath. *What can I say to that? Ian Hamlin had been a godsend to this team. I was lucky to get him and I'd do anything to keep him.* "Are you sure you want to do this?"

"I've never been more sure."

Pete smirked and shook his head. "You're kind of a stubborn bastard, you know that, right?"

Ian actually smiled as he felt the weight lift from his shoulders. "That's what I've been told."

Pete pulled a piece of paper from his back pocket and hesitantly handed it over to his top agent. "She works at Channel 12 in *Vancouver.*"

Ian's eyes appeared wider in appreciation of Pete's helpfulness.

"I'm giving you two weeks to either watch her carefully or tell her the truth, but if one word of this ends up in the media, then I'll have your head *and* your badge," Pete said sternly, and then unfurled two fingers into the air. "Two weeks, and then I want your ass back here."

"Yes, sir." Ian gathered his paperwork, taking the next hour to type up a couple of reports that needed finishing and then called his mom in Darien to set up an impromptu visit.

     * * *

Within three hours, he was seated beside Lily Hamlin in the house he grew up in. "I'm going to Washington for a couple of weeks."

"Oh," his mother said with a weary tone. She knew things had been tough since he left the west coast. Sometimes she feared that he'd never get passed it and he'd end up a bitter old man and she'd be without grandchildren "Are you planning on popping in on any old friends?"

"No Mom, I'm going to Vancouver," he snapped. Ian felt his pulse rocket at the thought of how badly his friendship with Elias ended. How could they have let things spiral that out of control? "Hell, Mom, he's not my friend and I'd rather eat a bullet than step one foot in Seattle again." His face tightened with righteous indignation.

"You keep this up and that anger is going to eat you alive. You have to let it go," his mother said.

"Thanks. I know you worry, but I'm fine. I've moved on." He stood up and took a couple deep breaths as he stared out the window, to the house next door where Elias Webber grew up. "Do you ever hear from Donna?"

"We talk a couple times a year." Mrs. Hamlin knew better than to go into detail about what her and Donna Webber talk about. Ever since the boys graduated from high school, Ian demanded that his parents stay out of it and never say the name Elias Webber in his presence. Ian had always been a volatile young man. Even as a teen, his mother saw the rage in his eyes. She'd never seen him do anything about that rage and it didn't surprise her at all that he ended up in law enforcement. Sure, she'd heard a rumor or two; actually a terrible rumor about something that her Ian had done after graduation. She chose not to believe the vicious lie and had never brought up that night because she really was afraid of knowing the truth about her boy.

"Where's Dad?" Ian continued staring at the old house next door. Suddenly, as if a light had been turned on inside his head, an idea flashed in his memory. He shook his head to clear the fog. It had been so long ago and yet, her face was forever etched in his mind. *How could I have not put it together? She's all I ever thought about at times.* His shoulders tensed as he turned to his mother. With narrowed eyes and a racing pulse, he sat back down and gazed into his mother's eyes as she explained that his dad was fishing and he'd be home later.

"Honey, are you okay?" she asked and pressed a palm against his forehead because his cheeks were suddenly so flushed.

"Do you remember when Donna married Dick Swenson?"

"Sure I do." Mrs. Hamlin tensed at hearing his name. She shivered and wrapped her hand up around the back of Ian's neck. "You look awfully flush, Ian. Do you want a cold lemonade or something?"

He caught his mother's hand as she got up to leave. "No, I want to talk about Dick and his daughter Tanya."

"What about them?" She nearly cried as she sank back down. She hadn't thought about that day in many, many years.

"Do you remember the name of the nanny that lived with them? She was only there for like a week. She was really pretty. Long dark hair." He went on as he described her, and the more he thought about it, he was positive that the weathergirl and the nanny were the same person. "Do you remember her? She left right after the accident, I think her name was..."

"Jill."

Ian stood up and began pacing. He was right! *Unbelievable.* His Nikes scuffed the hardwood floor as he made each pass in front of the indigo couch. "Jill Walker?" He looked at his mother. "Was her last name Walker?"

"No, no." His mother brushed off the words with a wave of her hand. "She had a strange last name. I think Donna told me she was Polish. It was something that started with a *W* and ended with an *owski.* You know, one of those Polish names."

"I don't remember. I never even met her. I saw her a couple of times, but Eli..."He caught himself before he let that name slip from his lips. "*He*...was really weird about letting me meet her, and then she was gone...." The words slipped slowly from his lips. "I saw her again--that summer."

Mrs. Hamlin's eyes lit up with the sparkle of imminent tears. "You never told me that."

"It was the summer after the accident. I saw Jill at the beach--at Compo Beach in Westport. I just stared at her. I didn't know what to say. I remember you telling me about how much little Tanya meant to her and I just didn't want to bring up the horrible memory, so I just stared into her eyes and then walked away like a coward." He looked down and fidgeted with his thumbs.

He couldn't believe that this was happening. *After all these years and out of all the names, why did she have to be a Jill Walker?* And now it looked like he was finally going to have that chance to meet her. After all these years and those seven nights that he sat watching her through his bedroom window, he was finally going to get the chance to say hi. Despite the fact that his mother had disagreed with him about her last name, he was positive that the weathergirl was *Jill the nanny.*

Ian's father arrived shortly thereafter and just in time for dinner. After filling up on his mom's pot roast and mashed potatoes, he watched a tennis match with his father, talked about some tough times that he'd recently been through and solicited a little advice from his dad about women. Ian actually laughed a couple of times and wished his father had given him that advice before he married *The Bitch*. The Bitch had turned him off women and now he didn't even know how to approach one anymore, so he just gave up for the time being and concentrated on his job and keeping himself in shape.

Ian never thought of himself as a good-looking guy. His nose was slightly crooked from years on the football field; he had one dimple on his left cheek and to him, his eyes seemed too blue. A girl in college once told him that he had *scary eyes* and she hated looking into them because they were so crystal clear. That didn't do any good for his self-esteem, so he worked on what he did have control over and did the best he could with what he had. And what he had was a great body that he worked on constantly. He didn't make that much money and he definitely lacked charm and grace under pressure. All in all, he was a big, burly ball of pent up frustration and his scowl was just about as intimidating as his bite. His hair had remained jet black and it wasn't until his thirtieth birthday a couple months before that he actually saw his first gray hair. In fact, now he had seven of them. One for each of the *Jills* that had been murdered. He didn't want any more gray hairs so he was anxious to head to the airport for his red eye flight to Portland, Oregon.

He knew he'd probably have just enough time to rush to the station where Jill Walker worked once he reached Portland because his flight was due in around midnight. That meant he didn't have a lot of time to rehearse just exactly he would say to her, so he practiced on the flight. He went over it in his head repeatedly and even practiced in front of the mirror in the john because the last thing he wanted to do was end up tongue tied like a blabbering moron. He wanted to be smooth, articulate and to the point. The faster he wrapped this up, the faster he could get back to work, and finally catch this guy once and for all.

Once he was sure about his speech, he closed his eyes and tried to think about anything other than losing yet another Jill.

* * *

The new phone number seemed to be working like a charm. In fact, it worked so well, that the phone never rang and Anita was constantly picking up the receiver to see if it was working. She checked the ringer button a number of times, but to her dismay it was in the on position.

"Shit," she said hastily. The phone was working just fine. She broke into tears because it had been two weeks since Ryan at least tried to make amends and although she tossed him out on his ass, she still wanted him back. She knew she loved him and feeling his child growing inside her just confirmed her feelings that much more. She didn't want to go through a pregnancy alone and no matter how many times she yelled at him that it was over, he usually kept coming back for more punishment. The big man definitely   scored points with his honesty and lack of humility, but as of lately, his follow-through had been fairly lame.

Anita tried the phone one more time and then ran to the bathroom to experience the joy of morning sickness once again. She curled up over the toilet and let it all out before crying herself to sleep on the furry bathroom rug.

Jolted awake by a strange noise, Anita lifted her weary head slightly and heard the flapping of the screen door. Carefully she got to her knees and peered out through the doorway. The old house always creaked, but every so often, it was as if she heard footsteps. She chalked it up to being pregnant and deranged. She still hadn't told Jill about the dead rats that she keeps finding on the front porch. It was most likely just the cat next door, leaving them as a peace offering and trying to get in good with Anita's cat, Whiskers, but it was still unnerving. Both the women got good laughs out of the cat theory and then both vowed to stop watching scary movies because they were on the path to becoming paranoid old ladies. Anita had even begun talking to her cat on a regular basis because she was alone a lot and well... *pregnant and hormonally imbalanced.*

Nothing seemed out of place as she peered into the living room, but she could still hear the flapping of the screen door. Positive that she locked it before getting ready for bed, she slumped down onto the floor and waited an extra half an hour or so before crawling on her hands and knees into her bedroom and barricading the door closed with her dresser just to be sure nothing was amiss. For a second, she thought about calling the police, but they would most likely laugh and tell her that she's delusional, but she knew she wasn't. She knew the sounds of that old house pretty well. So instead, she compromised and called Ryan. After all, he was a firefighter and an impressively large man. He could handle an emergency, and even if it were just her imagination, she would benefit highly from seeing his face again.

        * * *

Ten minutes after the call was made, Ryan was screaming her name from the front porch, afraid to go in because of the blood that was trickled down the door. He pulled his cell phone out, called the police and then screamed out for Anita once again.

She finally heard the cries and opened her bedroom door. Ryan was on the front porch, pale as parchment and shaking.

"What?"

"Oh God," he shouted through the door but didn't dare touch it. "Stay where you are. The police are on the way."

"What?" Anita whimpered. "What is it?"

"Meet me at the back door," he said, and took off around the house. Anita was pretty shaken and pale herself by the time she reached for the door handle on the backdoor.

Ryan immediately pulled her into his arms and held her tightly, rocking her back and forth. "Jesus, you scared the shit out of me. What the fuck happened here?"

"I told you, I thought I heard the screen door flapping and I'm positive I locked it," Anita explained, enjoying his warm arms around her shoulders. "What was it?"

"Blood," he said and then kissed her temple. "*Like*, lots of blood."

Anita's knees buckled, but he caught her before she went down on the hard floor. Soon they heard the sirens in the distance. Ryan helped Anita out the back door and met the officers in the front yard.

"What does it mean? Is it human?" Anita was clearly shaken as she watched the officers inspect the mess on the front porch. The blood had dripped down, but as far as anyone could tell, whoever did it drew a large number nine on the front door and had done it from inside the house due to the fact that there was also blood dribbled on the hardwood in front of the foyer.

Anita stood in awe. "I locked it. I know I did." She trembled and reached out for Ryan again.

Two more police cars pulled in with lights and sirens blazing, making the total six. Six policemen, shaking their heads in wonderment, sipping coffee, and creating quite a spectacle for the neighbors.

"We have to take this to the lab. We won't know anything until it's analyzed, but my feeling is that it is human blood. Can you come down to the station with us? And we'll also need to call your roommate." Officer West said.

Anita only got as far as the driveway when she puked. She was hoping to make it to the rose bushes, but it was just impossible under the circumstances.

"Babe," Ryan caught her around the waist, his gaze unwavering. "I'll take you."

"Jill's on the air right now." Anita went into detail about Jill as Officer West jotted down the data in his little black notebook. "She's unreachable, but at eleven thirty, you should be able to get through. Please don't let her come home to this. Please, make sure you catch her at the station." Anita explained.

"We will, ma'am. We will."

* * *

Jill finished up the late news broadcast with a smile. She'd hadn't been sleeping well lately because she was still pondering the idea of jumping into bed with Elias and possibly taking their relationship to the next level--*whatever that may be.* Her eyes were heavy with indecision and some minor sexual frustration from spending a couple of nights curled up to a man, without the benefit of penetration or even a little heavy petting. Elias was pretty much a perfect man and she wondered how he kept his cool about being denied time after time again. She just chalked it up to the wonder of masturbation and figured he spent a lot of time alone in the shower after their dates.

"Goodnight Irene!" Tom yelled out with finesse. "Man, I love *hump-day.*"

"You would," Jill chuckled at Tom, who had really started growing on her as of late and went to the makeup chair to get *de-caked*-as she called it. She couldn't believe just how much freaking makeup she had to put on nightly just to hide the tiny imperfections of her skin. A couple of moles that she thought were distinguished were always concealed, along with her laugh lines and lately, the big bags under her eyes. She looked in the mirror and pretty much decided right at that moment that she best just bite the bullet and sleep with the man before she turns into an insomnia zombie. "See you tomorrow," Jill yelled.

She expected the door to close tightly behind him, but instead two uniformed police officers and one plainclothesman entered the studio and looked in her direction.

Jill thought the worst and sank down in her chair, waiting for the news of someone's death or dismemberment. It didn't happen.

Instead, the officers escorted her to their awaiting police cruiser and took her a couple blocks away to the downtown station where she was questioned and informed of the bloody nine on her door.
* * *

Ian had just one bag to wait for at carousel B at the airport in Portland, Oregon. The temperature was still in the high sixties, but it wasn't the least bit humid like back home. The air was clean, the stars lit up the sky, and he felt uncomfortably close to --*Seattle.*

He'd packed fairly light for his trip; a couple of t-shirts, two pairs of jeans, and some underwear, and of course, his bag of toiletries, but again, he left his box of condoms safely in the bathroom of his house.

He hadn't put two and two together until he had already packed and then left straight from his parent's house, but if he'd known that he was about to meet *Jill the nanny*, he'd have brought the entire box, and he'd have given just about anything to actually use them. It had been a long time since he'd fantasized about what it would be like to love a girl like Jill, but he was older now; wiser and much more skittish about beautiful women. Beautiful women reeked havoc on a man in more ways than one -- but still, he couldn't help the slight tightening in his groin at the thought of seeing her again.

He rented a moderate sized SUV and drove to downtown Vancouver and made it to the Channel 12 building at exactly 12:01a.m. He changed the time to Pacific Standard Time on his silver Timex. Then pulled out his cell phone and punched in the station's phone number so he could get clearance to enter the secure building.

"I need to see Jill Walker," he said as he flashed his badge to the security agent, once he was in the door.

"I'm sorry, but Miss Walker has left the building. Just about ten minutes ago."

"Fuck." Ian's temper reared its ugly head. He turned abruptly and knocked open the double doors with both fists before sliding behind the wheel of the SUV he rented at the airport.

He took off west and followed the map of Vancouver until he pulled onto Elm Street just a few miles north of the station. Elm Street led him down through a quiet residential neighborhood where he took a right onto Wiley Ave. Police cars were assembled in the driveway just beyond the rose bushes that lined the street and three uniformed officers were milling around on the front lawn.

He looked down at his file and made double sure that this was Jill's address.

"22445 Wiley Ave. Yep, this is it," he mumbled

under his breath and pulled behind the police cruiser. He got out with his badge in hand and waved to the officers on the lawn.

"What can we do for you, *Agent* Hamlin?" one of the beat cops said with contempt.

"What the hell happened here?"

"Don't know yet. Might just be a prank," another officer replied. "I'm Dave, that's Ben. Don't mind him, he's just a cranky old coot."

"What's it to the FBI?" Ben replied with a frown.

"Do you know where I can find Miss Walker?"

"I believe she's still at the station. Downtown, a block north of Franklin and 13ᵗʰ," Dave said.

"Thanks," Ian tightened his jaw and re-entered his vehicle to find Jill.

The scene on her front porch wasn't something he'd expected. He was actually hoping that this mess was all behind him and he could just ask her to dinner and that would be that. He'd tell her of the potential danger and be on his way, but that wasn't the case, and perhaps it had nothing to do with the Jill murders. *Perhaps it was a stupid kid, or someone who was upset with her because it rained when she said it was supposed to be sunny.* All sorts of scenarios ran through his mind until he finally found the Vancouver police station and got out to investigate for himself.

* * *

When Jill had first arrived at the police station, Anita was still pretty shaken and was nibbling on a cracker with Ryan right by her side. At first, she was happy to see them together, but then cringed because he still knew nothing about the baby that was now growing bigger everyday inside her best friend's womb. She tried to think of anything to distract her from the horror of being told that some sicko had invaded her privacy, marred her door with a bloody symbol and frightened her dear friend within an inch of her life. She'd never seen Anita rattled. Anita never got rattled. She was the strong one. *The one who told solicitors to get fucked. The one who yelled at the paperboy for missing the porch, but nevertheless, Anita was white as a ghost, being consoled by her cheating ex-boyfriend.*

Jill quivered and sank down next to Anita and gave her a hug. "Did they tell you anything? Has this happened to anyone else in the neighborhood?"

"They haven't said, just that they'd never seen anything like it. I'm taking that as a bad sign." Anita watched Ryan get up and saunter over to question the cops. "He's so fucking sweet. He's being such a doll," she said as she clutched her chest and sighed.

"Are you going to tell him now?" Jill asked.

Anita shot her a look of desperation. "I can't," she wailed. "If I tell him, he'll run for the hills and I just want him back. I miss him." She stopped talking when he came back over and pressed a kiss against her hair.

"I can take you home with me--if you want." Ryan batted his big, brown doe eyes at Anita, who only sobbed harder and pulled him closer.

"I'd like that, but I can't leave Jill here." Anita said looking over at her friend. "You want me to call Elias?"

Jill shook her head. "He's in Nevada."

Chapter Five

The officers at Jill's house were tired of hanging out in her yard but at least they had things to do, like interrogate strange men who came looking for the Walker woman. The first guy had been FBI, so they cooperated, but the latest guy had gotten a bit rough and had talked himself right into a pair of cuffs when the cops insisted that he step away from the house. The large man had actually put his hand on one of the officers, and that was a big no-no.

"Where is she?" The man screamed as two officers tucked his head and pushed him into the back of one of the police cruisers. "Where the fuck is she? Where's Jill? *Come on.*"

The officer who had been slugged in the jaw shook off the pain and read the man his Miranda rights before slamming the door of the police cruiser.

* * *

Ian entered the police station in Portland with the intent of walking straight up to Jill and telling her the entire truth. *If I have to scare the fuck out of her to make her listen, then so be it.* He was ready. Adrenaline surged in his veins and although he'd never even met the woman, his protective instincts for her tightened his muscles and sent him into warrior mode.

The door swung open a few feet from where Jill was sitting and, because of the tears in her eyes, it took her a minute to actually focus on the face of the man who was coming through the door. She'd been startled by the rattling sound of the glass doors, but not as startled as when she finally focused solely on the man's deep blue eyes. *His eyes.*

Her breath caught in her throat as if someone had a stranglehold around her lungs. For a minute she thought she was dreaming. *It has to be a dream. Why now? Why would fate intervene at this very moment in time?* It made no sense, but there he was. She was sure of it. It was *him.* Right down to the jet-black bangs that lightly brushed his dark brow. The same contorted scowl was present on his rugged face and even through the confines of his tight black t-shirt, she could see the outline of his muscled chest.

Her face flushed slightly as she looked south and took in the entire package. The man was oozing testosterone and with just a glance her vagina clenched spasmodically. *It was him.* She reached over and grabbed Anita's hand, giving it a tight, painful squeeze.

"Yeow," Anita grumbled and rubbed the spot where Jill's fingernails had dug into her flesh. "What is it?"

"It's *him,*" Jill muttered breathlessly and felt the air

around her electrify. Every tiny hair on her neck was standing on end, as were her nerve endings that sparked with excitement. Never before had she felt so alive looking at a man. *This is what I've been dreaming of my entire life; this feeling of complete stimulation.*

Anita followed her gaze to the man who walked over to the counter and demanded to see the detective in charge.

"Not now, okay?" Anita grumbled. "We can talk fantasies later. Right now, you need to concentrate and think about anything that might help the police make sense of our front door. Can you please concentrate?" Anita said as she dropped her head onto Jill's shoulder and inhaled loudly.

Jill could tell that Anita was attempting to either hold back another bout of projectile vomit, or she was doing her best to remain panic free. Either way, she snapped out of her erotic fog and closely cuddled her friend as the man disappeared into the inner office.

"I need to speak to someone in charge," Ian unfolded his badge and, through the window in the door, kept one eye on Jill. He'd expected her to be pretty, but not like this. She looked exquisite and way out of his league. Flawless skin, perfect hair, and she looked tall. Probably almost as tall as he was from the looks of those long legs that seemed to never end. *Damn, I'm having a lust attack in the middle of a crisis here.* He needed to get hold of his emotions before he completely broke down like a tongue-tied teenager and did something stupid, like make her touch his boner. He had no control over the thoughts that were rushing through his mind. "Please, just hurry," Ian became irritated and then was escorted behind the counter to a private office where detective Jake Whitney was waiting.

"Agent Hamlin." The detective stood and extended his hand. He sat down behind a dark mahogany desk lined with photos of his kids. The walls behind him told the tale of the detective's career: awards, diplomas, and commendations. Detective Whitney looked no older than forty-five, so his wall was quite impressive.

"Just Ian is fine. What can you tell me about the Walker woman's house?"

"You mean Wallokowski?"

"Wallokowski?" Ian mumbled. "Polish?"

"Yeah...." Detective Whitney cocked an eyebrow. His hair was a shade lighter than Ian's, and he was much taller. "Anyway, not much to tell. We're having the blood analyzed right now to see if it's human. We know that the intruder was actually inside the house, but we don't know the significance of the number nine. This is pretty much stumping us, and the ladies aren't much help at this point," the detective explained.

Ian took in all the vital components of what he said and it really didn't make sense to him either. "Is there somewhere private where I could make a call?"

"You can use my phone. I'll be right outside," Detective Whitney stepped out to leave and then poked his head back inside. "What's the FBI's tie-in here? Is there something we should know?"

"When I know, I'll let you know, but for now...we've never met."

The detective nodded and was out the door.

Ian called the New Haven office and although it was only four a.m. back east, he was sure to get someone on the line. After getting bumped around between receptionists, Agent Harrison ended up being the lucky one on call. "Harrison," he said. "This better be good," he mumbled sleepily.

"I'm in Vancouver. Someone tagged Jill Walker's door with a bloody number nine. Any thoughts on that?" Ian skipped the usually formality and got straight to the point.

Harrison sat up straight in bed and slid his glasses

onto his nose. He flipped on the lamp by his bed and lit up a cigarette as he let Hamlin's words really sink in.

"Bloody nine? Maybe it's a gang symbol and they just got the wrong house. Is it human?"

"Don't know yet, but I highly doubt Vancouver, Washington, has been over run by Bloods. Next idea, please." Ian growled.

"I don't know, man." Will scratched his light brown hair and exhaled another cloud of smoke. "It might have nothing to do with our guy, or our guy could be living in her basement. Like you've said a hundred times, he isn't playing by the rules. Anything is possible, but I do know this ..." Harrison exhaled another line of gray smoke. "If it is our guy, you've got the edge. Well, that is if you haven't done something stupid, like flashed your badge in her front yard."

"Fuck," Ian grumbled.

"You flashed your badge in her front yard?" Harrison chuckled.

"I needed to know where she was. It was just a couple of beat cops."

"Keep a low profile and you might just catch the son-of-a-bitch. She's the bait and obviously he's nibbling. Did you introduce yourself to her yet?"

"No, I saw her in the lobby and I called you. She knows nothing."

"Keep it that way. I'll be there tomorrow afternoon if Morrow approves and we'll get this sick fuck. You and me- — Tarzan and Jane- — Lone Ranger and Tonto." Harrison chuckled lightly. "Stay on her, man. Hell, move across the street from her house, but don't let her out of your sight."

"Are you kidding? I can't keep my eyes off her. See you tomorrow afternoon." Ian disconnected and took a minute to collect his thoughts before stepping from the office and making a beeline for the outer door.

He actually liked the idea that Jill was safely held

up in a police station for the time being. *Maybe I could frame her for drug possession and then get her locked up for a good month or two? But then again, this could be the perfect opportunity to watch from afar and find the bastard before he strikes again.*

* * *

"Miss Walker," Detective Whitney approached the women and extended his hand.

Jill took it and gave him a worried, partial smile. "I'm sorry to keep you here so long but we just got word that a man was arrested in your front yard. He claims to be your boyfriend."

"My *boyfriend?*" Jill choked on her words. She'd never called him that before, but it seemed fitting. "... is in Nevada." Jill stood up and shivered. "Where is this man now?"

"We're holding him at the jail across the street. His name is Elias Webber. Does that ring a bell?"

"Are you sure?" Jill's voice squealed.

"We're positive. We have his identification. Tall guy, long blonde hair. Too bad, he can't control his temper."

Jill felt a twinge of fear and clenched her jaw. *This night couldn't possibly get any worse.*

"What did he do?"

"Apparently he hit an officer when they refused to tell him where you were."

"Crap," Jill muttered. "Can I see him?"

Across the street in the detention center, Elias had been booked for assaulting an officer but was being released now that Jill had positively identified him and convinced them that he wasn't a menace to society.

Ryan took Anita home just as Elias was released on his own recognizance and five hundred dollars bail.

Jill met him with a confused frown, just outside the police records office on the ground floor.

81

"Oh, baby," he muttered against her hair while pulling her close. "I was so worried about you." He pushed back from her embrace and looked her over. "Are you okay?"

"I wasn't even home. I'm fine." She mumbled against his chest, but couldn't keep her mind off *him*. The man in the police station. It was *him*. She was positive. "What the hell were you thinking? You hit a cop?"

"I was out of my mind. I saw the door and all the blood and they wouldn't tell me anything. I was freaked out." He kissed her hard and long and raked his fingers up and down the backside of her arms and then back up into her long hair. He held her there while he deepened his urgent kiss.

Jill stepped back and glared at him. Her pulse raced. "You said you were in Reno. What the hell were you doing in my yard in the middle of the night?"

"I got home early. I flew into Portland so I could see you."

Her eyes relaxed, as did the white knuckled grip she had on her sundress. Unclenching her fists, she pulled him closer and nuzzled against his chest. "I'm sorry. It's been a really long day." She didn't want to take her fright and anxiety out on him, but it was hard to control her wild imagination. *Then again, what would Elias have to gain by scaring the wits out of me and painting my door with a bloody nine? I know he wants more from me than I'm willing to give, but why am I so skeptical about his motives?*

"Would it be completely inappropriate of me to take you to a hotel?"

"I'm not sleeping with you... not tonight anyway," she barked. Her eyes meant business. "But yeah, can we stay at a hotel? I don't want to go home."

Elias rolled his eyes, but tried to keep his anger from rising and showing in his eyes. *It's almost not even worth it anymore, but I never give up.* He'd tried everything to finally get her to yield to his sexual advances, but the woman was more stubborn than he could have ever imagined. Once again, he set his sights on his goal and kept his chin up. Someday she would be his. Because Elias Webber gets whatever he wants.

From across the street, Ian had watched the big man take the tiny blonde and get her nestled in the front seat of his flashy Mustang, and later he watched Jill emerge. She waited on the curb until a cab pulled around. She got in and a few seconds later, a tall, longhaired, blonde man followed her and entered the same cab. He didn't want to speculate about who the man was and, up until that moment, it hadn't even dawned on him that Jill might be married, engaged or even steadily dating anyone. *I just hope that fate won't do something that fucking cruel, but then again, I've always been dealt the lousy hands.* He was used to it by now, but it still creased his brow and kept his bitter scowl in place.

Ian followed that cab closely as it wound its way down Interstate five and into Portland. He stayed on it until the cab pulled up in front of a hotel in the downtown area. The cab stopped in front of the Heathman Hotel and Ian knew he could do nothing to keep her safe tonight. He just had to pray that the blonde guy could keep her safe for the time being. There was no curbside parking near the hotel and he was certain that a high class place like this wouldn't let him crash in the lobby. He didn't want to take the chance of getting a room himself and then missing her in the morning, so he pulled around the side of the hotel and leaned up against his window, closed his eyes and let the sandman take him back to the beach he remembered from so long ago.

In his dreams he relived that day twelve years ago when he had wanted so badly to approach the young nanny and extend a kind word or two to make her loss that much easier to take. But he hadn't. If he had, perhaps the course of events may have changed dramatically, and if he had just said those two little words, "I'm sorry," perhaps they would have developed that encounter into a friendship or perhaps something more.

Fate had a sick way of working out and somehow Ian felt that he was meant to be here now. Something in his gut told him that everything up to this point in his life had been leading to the moment when he could finally walk up to her and say, "Hi." Just like he had wanted to do that day on the beach. His thoughts and dreams were on Jill all night as he slept in his car.

* * *

Jill woke up curled into the chest of Elias. His cell phone was chirping in his coat. She sat up to grab it off the end of the bed.

"Hello," she said into the receiver. She probably shouldn't have done it, but she answered the man's phone and heard the hiss of a high-pitched voice. It sounded like a snake, but Jill concluded that it was most likely a woman. She flipped it closed and leaned over to see Elias bright-eyed and narrowing his gaze on her.

"Who was it?"

"They hung up."

"Come back to bed." He demanded and she didn't like demanding. Demanding was demeaning and made her blood boil. He patted the bed and it bounced beneath the strong pounding motion of his hand. He softened his glare and sat up. Entwining his fingers into the back of her hair, he bent to kiss her, but she turned away. He growled in frustration. "What did I do?" His head flopped back onto his pillow.

"Nothing," she said quietly. "I'm just stressed. I really need to get home."

"Are you sure you don't want to come back home with me? Just for a few days. I have a really nice place on the peninsula. It's quiet and secluded and no one will bother us."

"I can't miss work. It sounds nice, but I just can't."

84

"Fine," he growled again. Grabbing his pants off the floor, he pulled them on and handed Jill her purse. Jill didn't take it from him; she just glared and wondered why he was being such a big baby.

"I can't believe that you are acting like a spoiled rotten little brat about this. I've just been through something extremely traumatic and you're sulking cause you didn't get laid last night. Well, I'm sorry, but big bloody numbers on my door don't make me horny. They make me scared." Jill shouted and stood up. Normally, she didn't have a temper, but when she blew, she blew big and loud. "You're infuriating!"

Elias kept his rage to himself. "Hey, I was supportive and I'm sorry that this happened to you, but I will not be sorry for wanting to make love to the woman I love. It's not going to happen."

Jill's jaw dropped. "Uhh." She couldn't think of what to say. *I don't love him. Sure, in time, I could probably learn to love him, but I can't lie to the man.* So instead, she buried the thought of her non-existent feelings and moved around the bed to embrace him warmly. "I'm sorry I yelled. I'm just so scared."

"I know, but I'm here. Nothing is going to happen to you."

"I would like to go to the beach, but it would have to be on a weekend."

"That sounds great. I'll set something up and I'll let you know." He kissed her warmly and clenched his jaw, trying to keep a smile on his face.

* * *

When the first rush of people walked by his car, Ian jolted awake and wiped the sleep from his eyes. He was disoriented at best, but quickly got a handle on his surroundings and realized that he was in a rented Ford Explorer in downtown Portland. His cell phone was already plugged into the cigarette lighter, getting a well-needed charge. It chirped just as he turned on the radio.

"Hamlin," he rasped.

"I heard you might have a lead." Agent Morrow said. "I want you to assemble a team and keep a close eye on the woman. I've contacted the bureau there in Portland. They're expecting you today at three. Obviously, I'm granting you all the time you need. Forget what I said about the two weeks. Your gut was right."

"I don't get it," Ian was sure his ears were deceiving him. Pete Morrow rarely did an about-face about anything. His decisions were usually final and here he was changing the rules. "We don't even know if this connects us to our guy. It may just be some stupid prank."

"No, it's our guy all right," Pete said through clenched teeth. "We just found Jill Eight in Reno, Nevada. Your girl makes nine."

The air left Hamlin's lungs in a half-moan half-gasp. He had been somewhat hoping he was barking up the wrong tree. What he wouldn't give to be wrong every once in awhile.

"I'll find the fucker." Ian said with certainty. "Have we checked to see if there are any other Jill Walkers in the area?"

"There are three, but I think we should concentrate on number nine. All clues lead to the weathergirl."

* * *

Ian popped a couple of Rolaids into his mouth after disconnecting. So, his gut was right and all clues led to the weathergirl. He pondered the thought of telling her, but then again, what good would that do? Sure, it would make him feel so much better about the fact that he was using her as bait to catch a serial killer who doesn't play by the rules, but he wanted this to end. His nemesis was here. So close that he was probably lurking behind the rose bushes in Jill's yard.

If only he had an in. Someone he could talk to about keeping the woman out of harm's way. Someone who could ingratiate himself into Jill's life, or even her roommate's life. He needed an inside guy and hopefully that inside guy was on a plane headed his way.

Ian hadn't wanted to leave his post outside the hotel, but a little matter of nature calling had him running into Starbucks and that is when Jill and Elias emerged hand-in-hand and entered a cab that took them back to her house.

Ian finished up his jaunt to the restroom, grabbed a cup of coffee and a scone and went back to the SUV to wait it out and hope for a sign that no one would die on his watch. Not today. Hopefully not ever.

* * *

Anita rolled over and punched the snooze button for the third time. Ryan was already up, dressed and tossing her clothes onto his futon.

So much for getting my man back.

"Are you trying to get rid of me?" Anita whimpered and held back the tears. Hormones were most likely to blame for her common outbursts these days because the woman usually kept a pretty good poker face most of the time.

Ryan sank down on the queen-size futon bed, but couldn't quite look Anita in the eye. "I'm just not ready for this. I'm sorry, but I'm too young to be with *like* one woman and I don't want to hurt you. I really don't."

"Well," Anita sucked back a tear. "At least you're honest." Then of course anger emerged, followed quickly by denial. "But last night you were there for me. You made love to me and you made me soup...I just don't get it."

His head shook solemnly and he leaned in closer. "I like you....a lot, Anita. In fact, I'm pretty fucking crazy about you, but I don't want a commitment. I want my freedom, I want..."

"I know. You want to chase pussy and see the world." She finally let the tears stream out. Anger slammed into her hard and had her body tensed in rage and sadness that she'd gotten herself into this mess and was now saddled with this Casanova's baby. "Take me home."

She hadn't thought about what triggered her bouts of morning sickness until they were halfway to her house. Most of the time it was either hunger or an aversion to something she ate. Right now, it was hunger and as she felt the first pang of her rumbling stomach, she grappled with the door handle, but was too late and she ended up vomiting all over the dashboard of Ryan's new Mustang.

"Fuck me!" Ryan screeched to a halt alongside the road and all Anita could do was sob hysterically and then suddenly she was laughing hysterically. Mixed in with her tears of humiliation were the hiccups of absolute delight. He glared and she got out. Huddled around her purse, she eased herself onto the curb and slammed the door in his face.

"Serves you right, asshole," she yelled and began walking the rest of the way home.

He drove slowly, following her as she walked down the street because he wasn't that big of a jerk. Once he could see Jill and Anita's house and the cab pulled up in front of it, he honked and sped off.

"Fuck you." Anita screamed and quickened her steps to meet Jill, who was emerging from Elias's car in the driveway.

"So much for wanting him back. Are you okay?" Jill took in the sight of Anita's tear-stained face, the gunk on her chin and of course the smudged mascara under her eyes.

"I'm fine," Anita said with pride. "He's crazy about me, but doesn't want a commitment, so I puked on his dash."

Jill smirked. "Nice going."

"Hello, Elias," Anita said when Elias returned from the front porch where he was inspecting the door to make sure that all the blood had been removed. He tugged at the yellow police tape and gave Anita a little wave.

"How was your night?" Anita asked Jill.

"I barely slept," Jill said with a yawn.

Anita gave her a quick hip bump and a wicked smile.

"No, I meant I barely slept because I was scared out of my mind." She hugged her friend and then followed Elias back to his car still parked in the driveway.

"I'll see if I can get the beach trip set up for next weekend." Elias kissed her lightly and gave her cheek a squeeze. "Would that be okay?"

"I'd like that," Jill said sweetly and returned his kiss. "I'm sorry I yelled at you. I really am."

"Don't worry about it. I'm over it." He winked and gave her one last kiss that deepened and had her clutching his white oxford shirt. "I meant what I said...."

He hadn't had enough time to finish his sentence when Anita yelled out the door that Jill had received a phone call.

"I'll see you next week sometime. I don't know when, but I'll call you," and he was off.

Jill waved from the front porch and picked up the phone. "Hello...yes this is Jill Walker."

"You're dead, do you hear me. Fucking dead." The shrill voice screamed at her.

Jill dropped the phone, looked over at the ID and saw that again it was a blocked number. *So much for making my phone safe from pranksters.*

"Who was it?" Anita had already pulled out the box of soda crackers and had one en route to her mouth.

"Some woman. She said I was dead — fucking dead and then she shrieked and hung up."

"Ooookay." Anita paled. "Maybe it's time you told the cops everything. The flowers, the phone calls, the feeling that you're being watched. Maybe you aren't paranoid. Maybe this shit is real." *I hope it's not true, but being on television does invite the sickos to come out of the woodwork.*

"I don't know," Jill shook her head and sank down at the table across from Anita. "It's probably normal." She fiddled with the cracker box and Anita noted her trembling hands. She reached out and held Jill's hand until it stopped wavering.

"What's the worst that could happen? They could balk and tell you to lay off the caffeine? I'll go with you if you want."

Jill thought about being in a police station again and that had her thinking about him. She attempted a smile. "I saw him last night. It really was him. I'm not delusional and it wasn't a fantasy. It was *him*."

Anita rolled her eyes. "There's probably a couple million men with jet black hair, deep blue eyes and a perfectly ripped chest. It was twelve years ago, get over it. You have a wonderful handsome man who dotes on you left and right and you are still holding him at arm's length. What the hell is wrong with you?"

Jill didn't like her friend's tone, but Anita did have a point. She shrugged miserably. "I don't know. He said he loved me this morning and all I could do was sit there and stare at his handsome face and yet, nothing. Absolutely nothing happened. I didn't feel happy, I didn't feel excited. Hell, I didn't even smile. He just doesn't do it for me. There's no fire. No spark, no chemistry."

"And now you've convinced yourself that mystery boy is back. Nice timing, Jill." Anita stood up and reached for the herbal teabags once the kettle on the stove whistled loudly. "It sounds to me like you haven't given up on *him* and now that you have someone stable and perfect- — who loves you no doubt- — you are going to sabotage it because you're seeing ghosts. You really should get your head examined."

Jill dropped her chin to her chest in resignation. Her heart sank low and she thought about it until she was sick of rationalizing a relationship with the perfect man. *Elias is real, he is in love with me, and hell, the man is rich, gorgeous and very well mannered. What the hell is my problem anyway?*

"I hate it when you're right," Jill said. *But he seemed real. It was him, I know it was.* She decided that perhaps keeping her ideas about her mystery man now would save her a lot of heartache and lectures later.

* * *

Agent Ian Hamlin had waited long enough outside that hotel in Portland, and after three cups of coffee, he threw in the towel and headed to Jill's house in Vancouver. His red Ford Explorer fit in well with the other SUVs in the neighborhood, so he parked across the street, just kitty-corner from the weathergirl's house. He sipped the last of his fourth cup of coffee and got comfortable. Through his binoculars, he could clearly see the two women sitting at the kitchen table that was just beyond the front room of their house. Thank goodness, the women weren't that paranoid and kept their blinds open to let the early morning sunshine in to brighten their home.

Ian's heart skipped a couple of beats at the sight of Jill as she wandered out the front door and retrieved the mail from the mailbox at the curb.

She looked beautiful, even in her day-old clothes with her hair tied tightly into a bun on the back of her head. Her smile seemed easy as she waved to the neighbors and went about her business as if nothing strange had happened. *Perhaps she's used to people writing strange signs on her door, or perhaps the terror of it all hasn't quite sunk in yet.* Either way, she seemed completely relaxed in her front yard and that was a good thing. That meant that Jill-nine would go about her life and hopefully lead the killer right into Agent Hamlin's sights.

His phone chirped on his hip, taking him out of his momentary daze.

"Hamlin."

"Agent Hamlin, this is Detective Whitney of the Vancouver Police. We met last night in my office."

"Do you have any news?" Ian sat up straighter and waited for the results as he peered through the high-powered binoculars and felt a surge of panic when he could no longer see Jill through the front windows.

"The blood is human and there was enough of it that we're sure it wasn't the perpetrator's. Any thoughts on how the son-of-a-bitch got his hands on that much human blood?" Jake Whitney was fishing at best, but the thought of having something this sick happen in his backyard turned his stomach and set his mind reeling.

"Fuck," Ian muttered under his breath and dropped the binoculars into his lap. "I have a thought or two, but we've got it handled. I think it might be best if you don't inform Miss Wallokowski that it was human. We don't want to scare her any more than she already is."

"I don't know if I can do that. She just called my office and wants to talk about a couple of instances that might be of relevance. I don't think it would be ethical of me to lie to her about something this serious. Do you?"

Ian let out his breath with a hiss. "I guess not. When is she coming in?"

"In about an hour."

"I'll be around." Ian hung up and muttered his usual string of obscenities before calling in the findings to the New Haven office.

* * *

Jill didn't like the fact that she was now scared to even walk out her own front door. Nor did she like the fact that again she felt as if eyes were on her and not in a good way and furthermore, she didn't like the fact that when she walked upstairs to check her email, she saw a man sitting in the front seat of a Ford Explorer and he hadn't taken his eyes off her house for the past ten minutes. Sure, it was probably nothing, but she could clearly see that he was on the phone and she could clearly see that, at two different times during the few minutes that she watched him out the tiny window, the man actually had the nerve to use binoculars.

Fearful shivers raced up her spine and had her gasping for breath when she in turn decided to get a better look. She mumbled a couple of not so ladylike words and shuffled around in her cedar hope chest. Sweaters were tossed aside, as were her old high school yearbooks and a couple of old tennis trophies. "Ah ha," she said wickedly and pulled her old binoculars out of the bottom of the chest. Her father had given them to her so she could study the clouds when she was younger. Now she had satellite systems that helped her study the clouds. When she finally got the sights adjusted, she gasped at the sight of him. It was *him*. The same man from the beach in Connecticut and the same man she saw at the police station just last night. She wasn't going crazy. This wasn't some trick her mind was playing on her. It was *him*.

What if he was the man who tagged her door with a bloody number? What if it was him who had made all those phone calls? What if this man had been stalking her for the last twelve years? Jill giggled nervously and bit down on her nail before realizing what she was doing. She quickly dropped her hand from her mouth and paced the floor, before finally showering and taking half an hour to try and make sense of it all.

Well, whatever the hell he was doing, it was going to stop. Right then, she was pretty pleased that Anita had been so adamant about her telling the police everything and that meant that she'd also inform them of the mysterious stranger that morning.

* * *

"Did you happen to get a license plate number on the vehicle he was driving?" Detective Whitney asked Jill when she informed him of her mysterious stranger. He took out a notepad, made a few notes and then sat back in his office chair and listened to the beautiful weather-gal.

"No, I didn't even think about it. I'm sorry." Jill said remorsefully. Hell, it wasn't her fault that she didn't think like a cop. She was too intrigued by seeing *him* again to even look at the kind of car he was driving. She could just explain his eyes and that scowl that was again present on his face. She knew he wore a black leather jacket, black t-shirt and he had hair that matched his clothes. Other than that, she didn't care. He could have been driving the bat mobile for all she knew.

"Had you seen this man before?"

"Yes. Here. Last night," Jill said and then crinkled her forehead in question. "Is he a cop? He was here last night. I saw him right there," she pointed toward the exit, "outside that door."

Jake didn't know what to say. He wondered why Agent Hamlin was so interested in a small town weathergirl and why he was apparently camped out on her street. He didn't like this one bit but Ian Hamlin had made it perfectly clear that they had never met. "I'm sorry. I don't know who you are talking about, but if you fear that this man might be the perpetrator, then I can put out the word to watch out for a man fitting that description. Is there anything else that might be of significance here? You said you had a couple of things to tell me."

"There had just been some phone calls. Most of the time, they just hang up, but once or twice, a man has said I was purty. I got flowers on my first night on the air and then....oh yeah. I got more flowers: Dead roses with a card. The card had a number nine on it too. Could that mean something?"

Jake had no clue what it meant, but he intended to find out what the significance of the number nine was. He had some phone calls to make and an FBI agent to get some answers from. "There might be something there. Can you tell me when this was?"

"It was the day before I met Al Roker." Jill said as if Detective Whitney would know what she was talking about. "July 8th," she explained further.

"Thanks. We'll check into the phone calls. Do you

have caller ID?"

"Yes, but the calls always came from an unidentified number and the one this morning was also blocked."

Jake's brow cocked upward. "This morning you got a call?"

"Yes. A woman screamed at me and said I was dead. 'Fucking dead' she said and then she hung up." Jill still hadn't been rattled too badly by the call. The one a month ago, by the strange man who said she was puur-rrty had been much more frightening than the hysterical woman.

* * *

Anita waited for Jill to return from her meeting just outside the office of Detective Whitney at the Vancouver Police station. She had some more crackers, nibbled on some Tums to get her calcium, and watched the door, waiting patiently for her friend to emerge, so she could get home and get ready for her shift at the bar.

Jill finally emerged from Detective Whitney's office more relaxed than when she first arrived at the police station.

"Everything okay?" Anita stood up and shook the crumbs off her tight black skirt. She probably only had a few more weeks of being svelte, so she was taking advantage of her figure as long as she could. Everything was tight and showing every curve of her thin physique. Anita flipped her blonde hair over her shoulder and looked up at Jill. She'd always envied Jill's height because she stopped growing when she hit five-foot-five and Jill kept on going until she hit five-foot-ten.

"Fine," Jill said with a shrug. "He said it wasn't uncommon for this sort of thing to happen to a new local celebrity. The woman was most likely a crazy fan who is jealous and they think that the nine on our door was a case of mistaken identity." Jill smiled. "I guess there's nothing to worry about."

"Phew," Anita smiled, then took a long whiff of the air and paled slightly.

Jill looked concerned. "What is it?" she asked.

"Tuna fish. Someone's eating tuna." Anita gagged and ran for the bathroom.

Jill cringed and ran after her. *Morning sickness shouldn't be called morning sickness at all; it should be re-named all day sickness. Poor Anita.* Her food aversions had made cooking a difficult chore lately.

As Jill helped Anita to the car she explained further about what the detective had told her. Of course, Jill didn't dare bring up the fact that she had seen *him* again. That would just result in another lecture about how she's poisoning a perfectly good relationship with a man who actually wants a future. Jill shivered at the thought, but it did have its appeal. Hell, the thought of marrying a perfect man like Elias Webber actually made her heart fill with elation. *Yet it wasn't Elias; it was more the idea of Elias that was appealing.*

Chapter Six

Will Harrison walked into the FBI building in downtown Portland just about the same time that Ian Hamlin sat down and took point on what he was calling Jill-nine. He explained the situation about the other eight murders, and about the inconsistency of the killer's method of operation. The killer's lack of leaving anything solid to go on and how the killer seems to have targeted Jill Walker of Channel 12 news just over the bridge in Vancouver. The blood sample that Hamlin solicited from the Vancouver police was currently being typed and cross-checked to see if perhaps it matched any of the other four victims who had been murdered in the past couple of weeks.

The agents in the room were stunned by the information that was given to them. Will snuck in past the other agents, gave Hamlin a small nod and quietly listened along with the rest of the local Portland agents who had been chosen to help on the case.

All in all, two agents from the Portland bureau had been assigned to help Agents Hamlin and Harrison in their quest to keep Jill-nine safe and also attempt to get a handle on the killer.

"Any questions?" Hamlin said between sips of steaming coffee.

"Are we informing Miss Walker about the potential danger, or are we being sneaky bastards?"

"Sneaky bastards," Ian said sternly. "In no way are you to confront Miss Walker, talk to her, let her see you, or let her out of your sight. We'll take shifts starting tonight. I'll get with Agent Harrison and set up a schedule that's consistent with her habits. All we know right now is that she works odd hours, and our man, at least in the past, seems to do his killing in the wee hours of the mornings. In most cases, the time of death was pegged at or around three a.m., but that doesn't mean that he didn't abduct them during the day. At this point nothing he has done has been repetitious with the exception of the time of death. That's the only constant that we have to go on."

"So, there's no motive here, other than some sick fuck fixated on the Jill Walkers of the world." Agent Hardy of the Portland bureau asked with a tight jaw.

"That's correct. We aren't talking about the normal serial stalker here. Sometimes we are sure that the victims knew the killer, sometimes it seemed completely random. Even more disturbing is that it looks like he had one Jill in his sights for more than three months before he actually went in for the kill. He's completely unpredictable, but now we have an edge. Now we have Jill-nine and he's already made his intentions clear, so we know he's in town." Ian stopped to sip his coffee and engage every man with his scowl. "I'm holding each and every one of you completely responsible for this woman's safety. Her life is in our hands and there is no margin for error. Got it?"

"Got it," the other agents said and then were dismissed from the conference room.

Will approached his old friend and partner with a grim smile.

"I know this one, Will." Ian said.

"What do you mean, you know her?" Will sat down on the corner of the desk with a very disapproving scowl.

"I don't mean it like that," Ian said, dodging the sexual implication of saying he knew her. "I've never actually met her, but she lived next door to me for about a week when I was seventeen."

"Oh, then you technically *don't know* her in the biblical sense." Will let out his breath. "You look like you could use a good night's sleep, a shave and a shower."

"Don't I know it? You want to take the first shift so I can get cleaned up?"

"Sure. Where's she at now?"

"I followed her to the news station at two and then I came right here. Her friend dropped her off...." Ian grinned. "I have a very special assignment for you."

"Oh yeah? I hope it won't get me killed." Will scoffed.

"Nah, but it probably won't do any good for your marriage. I'm sorry." Ian said with a grin.

Will perked up. "Do I finally get to seduce a hot babe?"

Ian uncharacteristically laughed aloud. "Sort of. Come with me and I'll tell you all about it."

* * *

Reporting the weather in mid-July in the Pacific Northwest was almost as monotonous at listening the same songs every morning on her favorite radio station. Nearly every day, Jill reported that it would reach the high eighties with a low of fifty-eight after sundown, which was a good thing because the house that she and Anita shared lacked air conditioning and nights were excruciating unless the temperature dipped down below sixty-five. It hadn't dropped the last two days, so tonight Jill was looking forward to going home to a cool house, *that is if Anita remembered to open all the windows and turn on the fans.*

Jill left the station at around one a.m., stopped by 7-11 for a Diet Coke and some Pringles because she had PMS and that always ignited her lust for salty chips. It also ignited her hatred for red lights and, as of lately, ignited some pretty fierce envy that Anita was pregnant and yet she wasn't even close to the joy of motherhood.

Elias had called every morning, but after six weeks of dating the man, she still didn't have his home phone number and sometimes that made her uneasy because she considered him her boyfriend now and sometimes she just wanted to talk. Most of the time, she wanted to talk at three a.m. when she couldn't sleep because of the heat, or because she was scared to close her eyes because she would see *him*. She'd seen *him* everywhere lately.

Her body ached from either extreme fear or a heightened sense of sexual frustration because she was just that damn attracted to the strange mystery man. The more she thought about it, the more she was convinced that he was watching her, but it didn't seem to bother her the way she expected it would. It was nice to see his face at Starbucks in the mornings, or outside of the station when she looked down at the street in the middle of the day. He always wore that damn leather jacket and faded Levis, even though it was eighty-five degrees out.

She even wondered if he watched her on the news every night. *Does he sit on his bed at eleven at night and think about me naked while I read the weather reports?* She hoped he did, because she was having quite a few fantasies of her own. Every once in a while she would dream of the dark stranger. Sometimes they would end up sweaty and satisfied from hot sexual encounters and other times he would throw her against the wall, or point a gun at her head. She still didn't know why he was watching her, or whether or not he was a good-guy or the one who'd been tormenting her with bizarre phone calls. Either way, she still fantasized that fate had brought them back together after all this time.

Jill finally pulled up in front of her house. The street was dark and quiet, just like every other night. Cats shrieked from behind the garbage cans, frogs croaked loudly from the gutters and sometimes she heard sirens from afar. Tonight was no exception and that sent shivers up her spine. She stayed put behind the driver's seat as the garage door lifted and she slowly pulled inside. She immediately hit the button again and watched the automatic garage door slide down behind her. It wasn't until it was tightly shut that she got out with snacks in hand and padded into the house, carrying her uncomfortable high heels in one hand and her bag of sinful goodies in the other.

Anita was on the couch, watching *Nine Months* for the third time in two weeks.

"It's just not fair," Anita bellowed and looked over at Jill. "He's crazy about me, but he doesn't want a commitment. What kind of messed up shit is that? Why couldn't I meet a nice handsome thirty-year old? Huh..." She sobbed into her Kleenex and blew her nose loudly. "Tell me why?"

"I don't know," Jill sighed, handing her the canister of Pringles. "Why don't you tell me why I can't bring myself to sleep with the man I should probably marry? Tell *me* that." She sat down on the couch beside her friend.

Anita's sobs turned to laughter as she patted Jill's knee and helped herself to some   reduced fat Pringles. "Maybe this trip to the beach will end your obsession with celibacy. It's hard to say no to a man while he's holding your hand and walking you down the beach. Trust me.

The ocean is one big, wet aphrodisiac."

"With my luck, I'll finally decide to do it and I'll start my period a couple days early," Jill laughed, but it wasn't really all that funny. *Stranger things have happened.* "Have you heard from Ryan?"

"No," Anita said sternly. "And I've moved on. I actually have a date with a very handsome older man I met last night."

"Oh man, you are playing with fire, aren't you?"

"No. I'm getting back at the son-of-a-bitch," Anita explained further, then stared intently at her friend and sighed. "Who am I kidding? I don't want anyone else. Hell, right now is not the most ideal time for me to start dating. I actually had to buy some elastic-waist pants yesterday. I'm going to be huge soon and no man will want to come within miles of me. I'm the poster child for Save Me From The Hell Of Single Parenting dot com."

Jill laughed, sputtering bits of Pringles from her lips. "You need help."

"I need Ryan." Anita said sadly.

"I need a new bathing suit." Jill smiled.

* * *

At ten a.m. the next morning, Jill was awakened by the sound of laughter and the deep booming voice of a man she didn't recognize. Pulling her pink satin robe around her, she skittishly opened her bedroom door and saw Anita slouched over the counter, sipping tea and engaging in what looked like blatant flirting with the cable-guy.

"Oh," Anita stood up and smiled at Jill. "This is Will. The guy I told you about...you know..."Anita bobbed her brows.

Jill narrowed her eyes and then realized what the hell she was talking about. *The guy.* The guy she has a date with. *Poor man.*

"He's giving us a free upgrade."

"Oh," Jill could have cared less. The most TV she

101

watched was an occasional old movie on PBS during the wee hours of the morning if she couldn't sleep. "That's very nice of you, Will."

She moved around the giddy Anita and poured herself some coffee.

"I should be out of your hair in about half an hour." Agent Will Harrison smiled at the women and continued doing what he was doing, which wasn't giving them extra channels. He was bugging the house with tiny listening devices, so he and his partner could listen in on the their lives and keep them both out of harm's way.

Ian was handling the outside phone line tap, but Will was responsible for the inside, so when Anita finally left him alone, he grabbed up the phone and placed a tiny bug into the mouthpiece. He placed one inside the television remote and another behind a photograph in the kitchen.

Then he casually walked to the front window and waved to Ian, who was safely hidden in the FBI surveillance van across the street, letting him know that his mission was complete. Will then fiddled with the television and waited for Anita to emerge from her room.

"You're all set." He rocked back on his heels and smiled. "So, tomorrow night," he grinned. "Dinner and a movie?"

"Tomorrow night." Anita smiled, then excused herself to puke up her breakfast.

    * * *

Elias promised to meet Jill at the park by Vancouver Lake and when she arrived, she could clearly see his bright yellow Porsche at the end of the lot. She was actually looking forward to seeing him after having a nice conversation with her mom about how her mother wasn't all that attracted to her father when they met, but he was a good man. A moral man who was handsome and well to do and he treated her like a queen so she knew that she'd found her prince.

Jill hadn't ever heard the story of her parents quite like that before, so it made her feel somewhat less hesitant about taking the next step with Elias, despite the fact that the man still hadn't made her panties drop. *Or even moisten them for that matter.*

She smiled as he approached.

"Hi," Elias hit her with his killer smile and enveloped her in his arms. "God, I missed you. Are you ready for this weekend? I have everything set. Here's the key and directions," he handed her a manila envelope. "I won't be able to meet you until late Saturday night, but you just let yourself in and make yourself at home." He kissed her passionately with a promise of so much more as he nibbled her bottom lip and pulled her closer. "What's mine is yours...You know that right." *I have her just where I want her and although my little game of seducing her and finally getting what I want is taking a bit longer than planned, I'm actually enjoying myself.* Jill Walker had been by far the most difficult of his challenges. *Hell, it only took one afternoon to finally get Sara into bed, and she still remained in my bed.* Elias was now seriously pondering the idea of tossing the blonde bimbo overboard and concentrating his sights more on keeping Jill around longer than he first intended. *This game is just getting started.*

"Thanks," Jill returned his kiss.

They enjoyed the beginning of the afternoon under the shade of a large maple tree, but Elias was called away a little before two and since Jill was already prepared for tonight's forecast, she gave him a nice kiss and stayed behind to soak up more sun and relax in the cool grass.

She took a walk along the sandy shore of Vancouver Lake, with a bright smile and her shoes held tightly in her hands. She thought more about what her mother had said and realized that maybe she couldn't have it all. Perhaps she needed to give up the fantasy and take what she could get before Elias got sick of her subtle brush-offs and flippant attitude about his love for her. It could only be a matter of time before a man like that cuts his losses and moves on.

Kicking a small rock with her bare toe, she glanced down at the white rock and smiled. She bent to pick up the small agate and started to feel those familiar prickles up her spine like she was being watched again and when she straightened and turned around, she saw *him*. There he was again, on the other side of the lake, skulking behind a picnic table, yet almost daring her to finally approach him. *He'd been more blatant about his whereabouts as of lately.* Jill had noticed that the other day. *Did the man really think I don't pay attention to my surroundings, or did he want to get caught?* Maybe, just maybe he wanted to walk up to her and say Hi. Jill hadn't a clue, but she watched him intently as he sauntered into the grass and then disappeared behind a couple of skateboarders in the parking lot.

As she left the lakeshore for the parking lot, her mind was on nothing else besides the fact that she'd seen him again and her body had responded like it always had. She was shaking, but not from fear or anxiety. She was trembling from the surge of sexual energy that this man induced with just a glance. Paying no attention to where she was walking, she hadn't even noticed the condition of her car until she went to insert the key in its hole in the door.

She stepped back and frowned.

"What the hell?" She looked down at the tires and saw both flattened to the ground, the side panel had a large scratch all the way down the side. As she walked around to the other side, she noticed the other two flat tires and the scratches were actual words on that side. The words "Die Whore," were scratched into the side of her bright blue Honda.

"Damn it to hell," she shouted and quickly pulled her cell phone out, called AAA and the police and then begged a ride from Anita so she wouldn't be late for work.

* * *

"I love that car." Jill said to Anita when her friend finally picked her up in the park. "Damn it!" She looked back over her shoulder at the tow truck and the policeman who was still lurking around the parking lot.

"You need to start being more careful. This is getting spooky. First the phone call from the hysterical woman and now this. Please tell me you will be more careful. Have Scott the security hottie walk you out to your car from now on and, just to be safe, let's stop leaving our windows open. I'm starting to get a bad feeling about this." Anita explained with a shiver.

"You're right," Jill said and thought about the mystery man. So far, he'd been there the night of the door debacle. Now he was there when her car got trashed. "I'll be more careful. I promise." She didn't want her friend to worry. Most likely nothing sinister would come of this, but she wanted to keep Anita as calm and worry free as possible. After all, she had a pregnancy and a potential godchild to protect.

* * *

"You look amazing," Will said as he stood to meet his date for the night. Anita was dressed appropriately for a first date. Long flowing skirt, and not too much cleavage up front. Agent's Hamlin's instructions were for Will to somehow get in the good graces of the women, any way that he could. Originally, he started out at the bar where Anita worked, hoping to hit on Jill, but when Jill failed to surface a couple of nights ago, Will started in on Anita and the woman bit quickly. Actually, he couldn't believe that after being off the market for the past fifteen years, he could turn on the charm and, more surprising, that it worked. He'd already been inside their house and hopefully tonight wouldn't be much different. Even if it was just for coffee, or some platonic conversation. Hamlin was insistent that Will stay closer than ever since the news of Jill's latest encounter with someone who wanted her dead.

"Thanks," Anita said with a smile. She'd picked this particular restaurant because Ryan's sister worked there as a hostess and she knew word would eventually get around that she had dinner with a tall handsome older gentleman. Will wasn't quite as big and burly as Ryan. Will's hair color was about the same; exception Ryan bleached the tips of his mousy brown hair, making him look like a surfer-boy. She also liked Will's kind, brown eyes that were always hidden behind his glasses. *He looks like such a nice guy.*

He immediately rose and pulled her chair out for her. She smiled, sat down and he returned to his seat, reached over and attempted to pour her a glass of wine.

"Oh, no thank you," Anita said as she bit her lip. "I...I don't drink."

"Oh, how about some tea then. Or coffee?"

"Water's good." Anita sipped it carefully because her stomach was once again on the fritz and nothing was staying down.

"This place is amazing, and you look beau..." Will looked over at the pale and very frail looking Anita. Her long blonde hair was gently tucked behind her ears, and her face was sunken as if she hadn't eaten anything in a week. "...You okay? You look a little pale." Will asked with concern, forgoing his near-compliment.

"I'm fine," Anita swallowed hard and made a face that Will recognized right away.

"Oh god, are you going to be sick?"

Anita shrugged and tried to laugh it off, but wound up running for the ladies room instead.

Once she returned, Will stood up to greet her and let out a chuckle. "You looked exactly like my wife used to look when she was pregnant." He gingerly took her hand and helped her to her seat again. Then he realized his mistake and felt his face flush.

Anita shot him a look of horror. Not sure whether she was more horrified that he thought she was pregnant, or that he was married. "Wife?" She struggled with the words.

Will flushed slightly and hoped that the indentation on his ring finger hadn't already given him away. "I meant... ex-wife."

"Oh," Anita calmed down a bit, and then berated herself for being such a manipulative bitch. *This man had been so damn nice to me and yet, I'm not being honest with him and now I just about jumped down his throat for being married.* Her conscience couldn't handle it anymore. She placed her napkin on the table and deeply inhaled.

"I'm so sorry. I can't do this."

She felt compelled to explain further when his eyes widened and he looked mortified. "The thing is, is that you're a really nice man and I'm a horrible, horrible person for using you like this...." She continued on and explained about her situation with Ryan and about the baby and how this was just a big plan to get him to snap out of his fear of commitment.

Will listened and lent her a friendly ear. His mind reeled about how he was going to stay in her life and hopefully be invited back inside her home. *I have to think of something fast, or Ian will skin me alive.*

"Wow," Will smiled and grabbed for her hand. He patted it gently, like a friend would do. "Thanks for telling me the truth. That took a lot of guts." He smiled and remembered his mission. *Failure isn't an option.* "Do you still want dinner?"

"I have no appetite, but you go ahead. I'll just be on my way."

"No." Will practically shouted. "I mean, no. I like your company and I want to hear more about the baby plans. I have three kids of my own, maybe I could give you some pointers."

Anita actually smiled and sat back down. *This man is just one big breath of fresh air.* She had no idea why the man was being so nice to her, but she liked it. She liked it so much that after dinner she invited him over for some platonic conversation and a big bowl of popcorn.

* * *

Ian sat in the van, watching as Will followed Anita's car into her driveway. He had never been prouder. He listened in when they entered the house, and he couldn't have asked for a better scenario.

The two laughed, played cards and watched the Late Show together. From what Ian was hearing, Will could have access at any time because he had just come up with a perfect way to stay in Anita Long's life and not damage his marriage.

"Are you sure, you don't mind?" she asked as she went to the hall closet and opened it. "I can't believe you're willing to do this for me, out of the kindness of your heart."

"It'll be fine," Will said sweetly. "Kids should have both their parents, so if my sleeping on your couch helps him see the light, then the back cramps will be well worth it."

Anita loved the idea of making Ryan jealous and handed him a blanket and a pillow as he curled up on the couch and listened to the soft moans of her cat.

After Jill returned home and was given the Reader's Digest version of why the cable man was sleeping on the couch, she laughed and drank a big glass of wine before heading to her room to pack for her weekend away. At least she felt less guilty about leaving Anita for three days because apparently Anita had made a new friend and the guy was cool about being her pawn to get the father of her baby back. It actually was an ingenious plan and Jill liked the idea that, at least for tonight, someone male was in the house. Someone big, strong and capable of keeping the boogey man from sneaking in and hacking her and/or her roommate into a million pieces.

After Jill's bedroom door shut tight for the night, Will grabbed the remote and gave Hamlin the information he'd learned earlier that evening at the restaurant.

"She's going to the beach tomorrow morning. Someplace called Sequim, up towards the Olympic Peninsula." Will said under his breath into the television remote control.

Ian knew the place well. After all he had lived in Seattle for years before his wife left him. He listened more and chuckled lightly about Will's conversation with Anita and how she and Jill had been best friends since high school. He learned a lot more about Jill Wallokowski that night and, at daybreak, he watched the second team of agents pull in behind him.

He got out and told them to stay on the house for the weekend, but he was headed north to make sure Jill was safe on her weekend away from home. Every minute of her life the past few days had been under the guard of eight men, and just because she was headed out of town in no way meant that she was safe. As far as Ian was concerned, *Jill isn't going to be safe until the killer is pronounced dead.*

* * *

The drive to Sequim took just three-and-a-half hours from her house in Vancouver. The directions that Elias had given her were perfect and, just past the local bank in town, she took a right-hand turn toward the lavish spread of Elias Webber near the small community of Dungeness. Her car still hadn't been repaired, so she drove a convertible Sebring that her insurance company had rented in her name. It made the drive to the beach just that much more enjoyable. After driving slowly through the small coastal community, she pulled up to the large gate. She punched in the alarm code that opened the large wrought iron gate at the entrance to the ten-acre spread that Elias called home. It was beautiful and elegant and took her breath away. The house was just a block from the water and yet, it was like no beach house she'd ever seen. It was more like the homes she'd lived in during her time spent in Connecticut. It somewhat reminded her of a house she lived in during her senior year of college in Cape Cod. She'd been lucky enough to get a job with a family who only needed her in the summer, and for two consecutive summers she worked for the Mayer family and spent time in Boston and the Cape.

Most of the jobs she took as a nanny were for the summer. Once or twice she'd taken a term off school to stay and make more money and one particular family had made a lasting impression on her. The little girl was just seven years old when Jill went to work for them. She'd taken spring term off and had moved in with a kind widower and his young daughter. Jill couldn't for the life of her remember how she'd been lucky enough to find such a smart and wonderful little girl to watch. Most of the children she watched were spoiled rotten little brats. But not Tanya. Tanya Swenson was every nanny's dream-come-true. It probably had to do with the fact that Tanya's mother had passed away when she was very young and had been raised solely by her father, Dick, and a myriad of nice nannies that had taught her at an early age to be polite and be respectful of others.

Jill just about slipped when she entered the house, which brought her out of her saddened thoughts of Tanya's death and into the present. *The present looks promising.* The house was so much more than she had expected, yet it didn't feel like home. The little simple things that make a house a home were missing from the walls, the mantle and even the tables beside the couch. Plastic still hung over the furniture, but the tables were cleared of all knickknacks, photos and anything else that told the story of the man who was frontrunner in her quest to marry and raise a family.

She kicked off her white leather sandals and took the stairs two at a time to see if she could find anything to unravel the mystery of Elias Webber. Jill found the bed first. Curling up on it was her utmost priority and that's just what she did.

Her dreams took her back to Connecticut again. She was reacquainted with Tanya and relished their time spent together in her mind during her erratic dreams. *They played on the swing set in the yard, and her little face was so sweet and innocent, it took Jill by surprise at how vividly she remembered the young girl. Her long red hair. Those cute little dimples and that same red and white dress that she wore constantly,- even though it was way too small.* Jill's dream continued and got more and more confusing. *Tanya was with her that day on the beach. That day the boy was there. He wasn't scowling this time though, he was laughing. And then he wasn't anymore. He was frowning and coming toward her with fire in his eyes. Jill pushed Tanya around behind her to protect the girl from the aggressive stance of the young boy. He got closer and closer and his face changed in her mind. His hair lightened. He became taller and broader around the shoulders, then he grinned, and it was Elias.*

Sitting straight up in bed, Jill shivered and pulled the comforter around her bare shoulders. Tears stained her eyes. *It's just a dream. Tanya couldn't have been with me on the beach because Tanya had already been dead for six months and why was Elias there?* Jill had a hard time deciphering her bold and dramatic dream and brushed it off as she headed downstairs.

Elias called at two o'clock to say that he may even be later than he had originally anticipated. Jill didn't mind. She had plans to camp out at the beach and make the most of her time away from the hustle and bustle of the city. She packed up her striped beach bag with snacks, a bottle of water, sunscreen, and her beach towel. A smile tugged at her lips as she walked across the grass toward the cool water. For the first time in weeks, she felt relaxed. There was no one there to remind her of her painted door, or her vandalized car. No one around to remind her that some woman out there potentially wanted her dead or that some silly little man thought she was *puurrty.* No telephones to dodge. No sound of Anita puking in the bathroom. Just the beach. The sand and.... *him.*

    * * *

The trail that led down to the beach is the route he took to saunter out onto the sand. Ian seemed more at ease outside of the city. His shoulders relaxed more. He took off that obnoxiously hot leather jacket and even left his shoes in the car because it was just that hot and to him this was almost a vacation. He'd followed Jill from the large house and in no way feared that either of them had attracted a tail, so he slipped his sunglasses over his eyes and headed onto the sand. He'd lost sight of her near the dunes, but wasn't that concerned. He was more concerned with the thorn he'd just stepped on. Standing on one leg, he pulled the thorn out and continued on. The sight of the ocean almost made him smile. The beach was somewhat crowded with families, women in bikinis and kids playing football. He looked around, trying to get his sights on Jill. He hadn't walked more than a couple of feet onto the sand, when much to his dismay he literally bumped into her.

"Excuse me," Jill said and then snapped her jaw shut and took two steps back because she really couldn't believe it. This frightened her beyond words, but his hand was hot on her upper arm and sensations that she'd never experienced before raced up her spine and set her blood on fire.

"Uuhh." Ian stuttered and released her arm. It was like trying to peel wet flesh off a frozen pole and it hurt him just as much, to be touching her and then have to release her just as quickly. He hadn't wanted to release her. He'd wanted to pull her into his arms and keep her close so that nothing could happen to her. *She'd feel amazing in my arms.* He was sure of it. But that wasn't possible. "Sorry," he muttered with a scowl and hurried around her.

Jill wanted a goddamned explanation, but it wasn't her nature to chase down strange men and demand to be told the truth. *The truth might not make me feel any better. Perhaps the truth at this point would make matters worse. But, damn, that man set a fire inside me that I've never felt before — ever.* She had been so close to him that, for the first time, she noticed the tiny scar on his upper lip. And he had a mole on his left cheek, and his lips... *God, they were fuller than I ever imagined. Almost calling out to her as he mumbled his apology.* His hand had been rough, his skin calloused. *He's obviously done manual labor once or twice in his lifetime.* As opposed to Elias's baby-soft and delicate hands, with perfect nail beds and probably a manicure on a weekly basis. *Ugh.*

Trembling in the hot sun, Jill couldn't help but close her eyes and imagine those rough callous hands grazing her skin, her breasts, the delicate flesh of her neck and the inner part of her thigh and... higher. She moaned aloud and shivered again.

Opening her eyes, she looked down the beach, but the man was gone. She'd lost her chance at making him talk. Making him explain why he'd come back at this point in her life and then suddenly, something became all to clear and set her heart into an arrhythmic flutter.

He touched me. He'd actually had his hand wrapped tightly around her arm and it was real. She could feel it. *He was real. He wasn't a figment of my imagination or a ghost that had come back to sabotage my relationship with Elias.* That man was flesh and bone and she wanted him. More than she'd ever wanted anything in her whole life.

* * *

Ian berated himself for the zillionth time about not being more careful. Hell, he'd practically skipped onto that beach without a care in his head. Without a thought that perhaps she'd recognize him. He wasn't that delusional to think that she'd remember what he looked like after all these years, but he knew that they had made eye contact on the beach that day twelve years ago, just like they had just moments ago. Their gazes had locked for a good solid minute before he chickened out and made a beeline for the concession stand back when he was eighteen. *Hell, she was a beautiful girl. She probably had lots of guys staring at her. Why would she have remembered my face?*

He shook off the notion that he'd just ruined his cover and sank down in the sand just above the dune where she had laid her towel and was now dozing in the heat. That skimpy bathing suit was doing nothing for his self-control and, sooner rather than later, he had removed his shirt and wiped his brow clean of sweat. His black hair was much shorter now that he'd taken time to get a cut before heading out of town, but the heat was still frying his brain and causing him to fantasize about a woman that he could never have.

Not even in my wildest dreams could I have a woman of that caliber. Hell, he'd seen her without makeup, just out of the shower and even late at night and the woman was naturally beautiful. Her lips were plush and moist. Her skin flawless and her body was downright sinful. She didn't have much muscle tone, but she was slim and tight and he knew by her usual workout routine that she paid attention to her body. He had to admire the time and effort she took to look that damn good in that bikini that barely kept her breasts concealed. *Damn, it's hot outside.* He wiped his brow again and retreated behind the cover of a tree to keep his mind clear and out of the gutter.

Out of the sun, Ian regrouped his thoughts. He'd been with a beautiful woman before and she had destroyed him. She'd taken his heart and dumped him in the worst way. The worst way possible and it still stung deep. The love he once felt for his ex-wife had been long gone, but the pain of how she left still haunted his dreams and kept his muscles tight with unrelenting fury. Ian had worked hard for the love of his wife and with one conversation and a glass of wine; she had been whisked away by a spoiled man with great hair.

* * *

Jill's afternoon on the sand was interrupted by the thunderclouds that came rolling in around four o'clock. The sky began to darken above her. The first clap of thunder had the beach inhabitants rolling up their towels and heading back to their beach houses and Jill was no different. The rain hadn't begun beating down until she reached the front lawn. Her hair and clothes were soaked through by the time she reached the front porch.

She opened the door and immediately stripped down to her bare skin before reaching down to grab the pile of wet clothes. Thunder clapped loudly, followed by a strong and bright bolt of lightning. Jill loved lightening. Lightening was fascinating to her and had her opening the door to listen for the clap of thunder that she knew would follow. It did clap, and louder than she had expected. She jumped slightly and let out a giggle. Her nipples puckered tightly from the cool air against her skin. A second bright bolt lit up the sky and the yard and before she had time to register what she had seen, a black figure streaked in front of her eyes just twenty feet in front of her, out on the lawn, between the tall hills of lemon grass.

"Shit," Jill jumped a mile in the air and slammed the door. Her heart beat loudly in her chest and it hadn't dawned on her that she had been standing in the doorway completely naked. *Whoever is out there had just gotten an eyeful.* The thought of that someone being her mystery man sent a wild shiver up her spine. The thought of his eyes...those eyes getting a free shot at her body, naked and vulnerable, had a strange effect on her knees. They shook and weakened at the thought. It was intense. So intense that she walked not so modestly into the living room and stepped closer to the window. With no clothes on, just an unbridled feeling of empowerment and lust, an overwhelming sense of want and pure animalistic need.

"I need to see a shrink." Jill giggled and quickly

pulled the curtains. She sank down on the couch and pulled the quilt over her naked and quivering body. She laughed some more and shook violently from the air-conditioned breeze.

* * *

A hot bath and a warm pair of pajamas were all it took to take the edge off her shivering and put her in the mood for food and some wine. She still had plenty of time before Elias was due home and wine seemed like the perfect way for her to get over her fear of sleeping with the man. She poured herself a nice glass of chardonnay and once again went in search of clues about Elias's life. She'd never considered herself a nosey person, but the man never even told her where he grew up. What college he went to or how he had become a banker. An international banker is what he had told her that first day that they met. His work had him traveling a lot and therefore it had never given him much time to date or hold down a serious relationship.

On their third date, he was already convinced that he'd been waiting his whole life for her and that fate had just dealt them both a royal flush. Every time he'd get to her with his killer smile and some story about how he was such an angel and Jill believed every minute of it. Still, she was snooping around his house because she was curious and she wanted to know as much about him as she could before taking the big step and letting him into her bed.

She started in the master bedroom. It was eloquently decorated with paisley and large stripes of burgundy and navy blue. The curtains matched the comforter and large area rug on the hardwood floor. A large king bed sat dead center against the back wall. Tall picture windows surrounded her. A gas fireplace sat directly across from the bed and a tall armoire was in the corner, two leather chairs sat on each side of it.

Under a big stack of old newspapers on the armoire, Jill found a couple of photos that she found interesting. One was of Elias with a very pretty older lady. He looked younger in the photo, perhaps early twenties. Jill brought the picture closer and stared longer until recognition slapped her in the face like a cold dead fish.

"Shit." Jill stood up and began pacing, then rummaged through the rest of the photos and then unlatched the cabinet and tossed everything out and onto the bed. She rifled through photo after photo and the more she saw, the more she was convinced. She remembered the woman in the photo from her year spent caring for Tanya Swenson. Dick had met Donna Webber at a fundraising gala and after courting her for months, he finally proposed and shortly after, moved herself and little Tanya into the Donna's house in Darien. During that time, Jill had gotten to know Donna fairly well and now, after all her time spent with *Elias*...

Tears streamed from her eyes as the truth became clear. She still hadn't known what it meant, but by god, she wasn't going to waste time. She pulled the phone to her and began punching buttons. The speed dial list was short, but when she saw the button she wanted she punched it and wiped the tears from her eyes.

"Hello," the distinguished voice of Donna Webber said after a few short rings.

"Donna?" Jill said, feeling her lungs seize up. It had been years, but she recognized her soft voice.

"Who is this?" Donna Webber replied. "Hello. Are you there?"

"Donna Swenson?" Jill's voice quivered.

Donna stilled at hearing someone call her that. She hadn't been called by that name in thirteen years. Tears stung her eyes and her tone turned venomous. "Who are you and what do you want?"

Jill didn't know what to say, so she quickly hung up. She sat, completely dazed by her findings. The phone immediately rang again and she looked at the caller ID. It read Donna Webber and had a Boston area code. "Damn it." Jill sobbed into her hands and that is when she heard his voice.

"What the hell is all this?" Elias tried to remain calm, but keeping his cool was hard with Jill sitting on his bed surrounded by family pictures of him and his mom and his phone continually ringing just out of Jill's grasp. "Jill?" he said a bit calmer once he saw how upset she was. He picked up the phone.

"Hi Mom, No everything is fine. It was just my girlfriend...No. I'll call you tomorrow and explain everything. No mom...it's fine." He hung up and bent down on one knee in front of the tearful Jill.

"How the fuck could you keep something like this from me? Are you sick?" Jill jumped up and scrambled out of his reach. "Tell me. Tell me that this isn't what it looks like. Tell me." She shouted again.

"Oh god, honey. I know this looks bad." He moved toward her, but she flinched and cowered behind a chair near the fireplace. "Come here, Jill."

"No. I don't even know you. How could you not tell me?"

"God, Jill. I didn't know what to say. I saw you in the bar and at first I didn't even recognize you. I thought you looked familiar and it wasn't until our first day at the lake that I knew who you were, and then I just didn't know what to say. I thought it would be too painful for you if I brought up such a sad memory, come here."

"No," Jill wiped her cheek dry. He made sense, but she was still coming to terms with the fact that she lived with Elias when she was nineteen. She'd actually shared a bathroom with this man when he was a teenager. She'd eaten dinner with him and watched him eat popcorn on the couch. She remembered things clearly now. Dick had married Donna and in December, they moved into the house in Darien, Connecticut. Donna and Elias's house, and she remembered now. Elias. *Elias. How could I forget a name like Elias?*

"How did you remember me? I only lived with you for a week. Dick hadn't even finished unpacking and Tanya..." Jill's eyes filled with tears again. "Tanya hated it. She hated living there and she cried. Oh god, she cried every night and begged me to take her away from there...." She bent forward and sniffled loudly, giving Elias just enough of a window of opportunity to pull her into his arms. She was mad as hell, but enjoyed the comfort for the most part. "God, that day was the worst day of my life. When the police showed up at the door and told Donna that Dick had been killed in a car accident, I felt the floor fall out from under me. I knew Tanya had been with him that morning...and, oh god, I was so sad. She was like my own daughter. I'd been with her and Dick off and on for almost a year."

"I know," Elias swayed her gently is his arms. "You were everything to her and I knew that bringing this up would just make you miserable. I wondered if somehow you had chosen not to remember me because it reminded you too much of the pain. I really never meant to hide it from you. I thought I was protecting you."

Jill looked up into his eyes. "How is your mom? I felt so bad leaving like I did and she was so destroyed. Did she ever remarry?"

"No, but she and my father reconciled, for a few years anyway. To be completely honest, I think she was more worried about you and how you were handling Tanya's death."

"I should really call her and explain why I just did that. Oh god, she probably thinks I'm a wacko." Jill chuckled lightly against his chest.

Elias looked down at her tearful eyes and gave her a gentle kiss. "I really am so sorry."

"It's okay. I guess it was just sort of unnerving seeing these pictures. Were you ever going to tell me?"

"Actually, I had thought a lot about it. I was just going to wait until you remembered me. I knew it wouldn't

119

have taken long. Like I said, you probably blocked it out because of the trauma."

"You're one smart banker." Jill smiled and eased back into his arms.

Jill remained calm and listened to the story of Elias's life, now that he was able to tell her the truth. Of course, he didn't tell her the entire truth. The entire truth would have her running for the hills instead of curling her toes under the covers and raking her fingers up and down his naked back. He relished every minute of their lovemaking as he kissed her again and again and, finally after all his hard work, got what he wanted, and it was more than he ever expected. A new, unfamiliar feeling of love swept over him. This wasn't just possession, like he'd felt in the past. Jill was much more than just another challenge, she was *the one. The one I'm supposed to be with — forever.*

* *

Ian remained out of sight after he saw a bright yellow Porsche pull into the driveway. It was dark, so he couldn't see the man that got out and entered the house, but the man apparently had a key and from the size of him and the long hair he realized that this man was the same man that had walked out of the detention center and entered the cab with Jill that first night he was in Vancouver. This man he presumed was her boyfriend, lover, or someone else she felt comfortable with.

The lights all remained off in the house except for the one that Ian had been watching all night. It was a second floor bedroom he assumed, but couldn't tell by the angle he was looking at it from. Shortly after the man entered the house, the lights dimmed and remained off for the next hour or so, so Ian curled up in the front of his Explorer and closed his eyes, trying to keep his mind from wandering back into that bedroom because he didn't want to think about Jill with any other man. He only wanted to think of Jill with himself. Before closing his eyes, his last thought was on Jill. The naked Jill that he had seen when the lightning lit up the sky. The same Jill that stood in front of that window without a care in the world. Her body had already been forever engrained in his memory from his teenage years, but it was nice to see her again. She hadn't changed much in the past thirteen years. Perhaps she lost a little weight, but she still looked like an angel sent from above. All he had to do was close his eyes and imagine himself naked and aroused and slowly, finally after all these years, sinking into her. That sweet spot between her legs that he could only imagine was just as perfect as she was.

Chapter Seven

The morning after, Jill woke up feeling pretty okay with the way they had left things the night before, but not for long. Elias was hogging the covers, wrapped up in the majority of the sheets. Every muscle in her body ached from making love. It had been a long time and her body was feeling it this morning.

He grumbled a couple of times and she was certain that in the middle of the night he had tried to have his way with her again, but her body just wasn't as into it as she would have wanted it to be. She'd wanted pure passion, an orgasm that rocked her soul. But all she had gotten was a selfish man who left her frustrated and sore from the friction and, so to speak, never found the correct button to push.

The phone rang and she quickly grabbed it up before Elias lifted his head off the pillow. "Hello," Jill said quietly.

"Hello," the woman said, false sincerity tainting her greeting.

Jill's hand clutched the phone tighter. "Can I help you?"

"For starters, you can get out of my bed and never see my fiancé again." The woman's voice on the other end was eerily calm and that sent a shiver of panic up Jill's spine.

"Excuse me? You must have the wrong number." Jill said, hoping it was true.

"I don't think so, sweetie. I know my own phone number and I know who you are *little miss weathergirl.*"

Jill immediately hung up and swallowed hard. She nudged Elias in the back a couple of times. He rolled over, mumbled something to the effect of, "*Shut the hell up, Sara,*" and then sat straight up in bed with wide eyes.

Jill stared at this man; this man that she really didn't know at all. She hadn't known what surprised her more. The fact that Elias had again lied about something as important as being engaged, or that the woman's voice on the other line sounded frighteningly close to that of the woman who had called her house. It did dawn on Jill that it was possible and now it all made sense. Of course the woman would want her dead and would have access to her home phone number because Elias called every day from his cell phone. All of this registered in her mind as Elias came to his senses and tried to backtrack out the latest disaster.

And to top it all off, Jill was naked in bed with this man who was still a great big mystery to her.

"That was your fiancé." Jill said, resisting the urge to scream. She couldn't really think of anything better to say at the time.

"I don't have a fiancé."

"Then you should tell Sara that." Jill said with disdain and brought up the name she had heard him mumble in his sleep because she figured it would rattle him into telling her the truth for once.

He stared bright-eyed like a deer caught in the headlights. "Sara? She's my ex-girlfriend. Very ex in fact. That was her...on the phone?"

"Yes. She warned me to get out of her bed and leave you alone. She knows who I am, Elias, and she's probably the one who messed up my car. She could have followed you to the lake that day. Hell, she could know where I live." Jill shouted and grabbed the sheet, wrapping it securely around her bare breasts. "Damn it, Elias. You better be telling me the truth here because my trust in you isn't really rock-solid right now." Jill's bravado surprised even herself and her emotional stability at this crucial juncture was yet another reminder that she wasn't in love with this man. If she loved him, she was sure that she would be in tears, or beating him over the head with a lamp.

"Jeez," Elias raked a hand through his thick golden hair. "I'm telling you the truth. She's always been a bit unhinged, but I never imagined she'd actually come after you. I'm so sorry, Jill," Elias said in a state of panic. Now that he was certain he wanted Jill forever, he was going to have to do something about Sara.

Jill slammed the door to the bathroom and got dressed in private. Her emotions were all over the place about this one. Sure, Elias seemed too good to be true at first and of course she was going to find faults sooner or later. It was now just a matter of deciding if she could live with a dishonest man. A man who might not be telling her the truth. This time what she needed was time. Time away from Elias's perfect smile and silver-tongue.

"Honey," Elias rapped on the bathroom door lightly. "Please come back to bed."

"No," Jill shouted and stepped into her sundress. She pulled open the door and glared. "I need to go home."

"What?" He glared and grabbed for her wrist. After all the time he had spent wooing her and convincing her that he was Mr. Perfect, he couldn't let her go now. "I just told you the truth. We still have two days here. Why do you want to leave?" His brow fluttered in a menacing fashion.

"After last night, I don't know if I trust you or not, so there's no point of staying here and pretending that things are fine. She threatened me, Elias. She probably damaged my car. I'm going home and I'm calling the police."

"Don't." Elias said sternly as a warning. Jill winced at the harsh tone of his voice. "I'll handle Sara. I'm sorry." He lowered his voice and drew Jill into his arms. That's all he could say. Forcing her against her will wasn't something that he'd ever do. Right now he needed to take care of Sara and then he'd concentrate of winning back Jill. After all, she'd become a lot more important to him than he had ever imagined. "I love you, Jill."

Jill turned with a suspicious gaze. "If she calls me again, I'm calling the police," she said, and was out the door without another word.

Elias stood naked in his bedroom, engorged with need, and enraged with a sense of impending loss. For once in his sorry life, he had something that actually mattered to him and now was not the time for Jill to start walking away from him. Women don't walk away from Elias Webber. *I get what I want and, by god, I intend on seeing to it that Jill will never walk away from me again.*

* * *

Jill, who wanted to talk on the long drive back home, had called Anita for a quick gut check. Anita hadn't been doing anything besides hanging out with Will, watching a movie and eating soda crackers. Will had concocted a wonderful cocktail of soda water, bitters and lemonade that was working wonders on her gurgling stomach. He also suggested that she keep soda crackers by her bed to nibble on first thing in the mornings before getting out of bed. The man really was a godsend and if Anita hadn't been so head over heels in love with Ryan, she would have snatched him up before he escaped.

"I can't believe he never told you that." Anita was astonished that Elias would have the nerve to hold something that important back at the beginning of a new relationship. "I think that's a really bad sign. He should have told you right up front that you used to live together. That's some pretty deep shit." Anita said when Jill called from the road and told her the latest news.

"I don't think I can trust him now. He says that he's not engaged to this woman, but how else would she have access to my phone number and she must have followed him to the lake. I think he's lying to me. In fact I don't even think he's a banker. He never talks about his work and he's never once given me his home number. Why didn't I see these signs earlier? Am I that stupid?"

"You aren't stupid." Anita said and sent Will an apologetic smile for making him pause the movie for so long. "How was the sex?"

"Horrible. He was selfish and I wasn't even the least bit turned on. It sucked."

"Dump him!"

"Hey, weren't you the one who said he was Mr. Perfect and that I'd be a fool to let a little thing like chemistry stop me from finding a good man. What happened to you?"

"Hey, I have a woman's prerogative to change my mind. Look at my situation with Ryan. For the most part on paper the guy is all-wrong for me, but my knees buckle when I see him and with one kiss, I'm on my back with my legs spread. Chemistry *does* matter. And the guy lied, probably twice, and if the sex is bad, then the sex is bad.

It's not going to get any better. I'm sorry. I shouldn't have pushed you into this. You were right. I'm a big boob." Anita felt true remorse and sad for her friend.

"He was sort of growing on me. I mean the guy's a big teddy bear and it's sort of nice having someone doting on me all the time. Hell, I don't know."

"Well, you have a long drive home, so just make a mental pros and cons list and drive careful. I love you."

"I love you, too," Jill replied. "How's Will? Do you think word has gotten around that you have a new man yet?"

"I hope so. We went to Starbucks in our pajamas this morning. Shit will most likely hit the fan by nightfall." Anita laughed.

"You're so bad." Jill chuckled.

"No, I'm pregnant and getting bigger every day. If this doesn't work. I don't think anything will."

"Yeah, but if he comes back you're going to have to tell him about the baby eventually. Why don't you just be a man about it and call him up, invite him for tea and say 'by the way, in six months, you're going to be a daddy, so you best grow up and learn to deal with it'."

"I'm not that desperate. Drive careful." Anita disconnected and went back to her movie.

* * *

Ian was happy that Jill was now back in town under his watchful eye. He'd followed her home around eleven and then had gotten some overdue sleep while the day guys took over. Nothing of importance had happened during the day shift, which was a good thing because Ian was asleep in his hotel room.

The lights had been off for hours. His shift had begun at midnight and he had already finished two crossword puzzles and a letter to his mom. The digital LED readout in Ian's SUV had just hit the three a.m. mark. The street was quiet, even for very early Sunday morning. The neighborhood bar traffic from down the street had already dispersed after it closed up for the night and nothing seemed out of the ordinary. Ian had just finished his letter and had already read the entire Sunday morning paper that he'd "borrowed " off Jill's neighbor's porch. He felt somewhat relaxed that Will was asleep inside. Actually he was jealous as hell, because right around two a.m. he heard Anita's voice insisting that Will actually get some good sleep and she invited him to share her bed.

Will willingly agreed because he was a good agent and Anita was a pretty little blonde. Not that he'd ever do anything to hurt his wife. He kept his hands to himself and had just closed his eyes when he heard the banging sound that jostled him out of his quest for a good night's sleep. He sat straight up in bed and grabbed under the mattress where he had left his gun. Gripping it tightly, he went to investigate. In the back of his mind, he ruled out anything suspicious and thought it was most likely just Jill, who had maybe dropped the jug of milk in the kitchen. Although he wasn't taking any chances.

He heard more scuffling when he entered the living room, but couldn't quite get a fix on where the noise was coming from. It sounded like the kitchen window, which he could see clearly now. Getting on his hands and knees he crept around the couch and whispered into the remote control that coincidentally housed a tiny microphone that led right into the receiver in Agent Hamlin's SUV. "Someone's at the back window."

That's all Ian needed to hear. He was out the door with his gun gripped tightly in his grasp. Heart pounding loudly in his chest, he tried to reign in the surge of adrenaline that had just taken over his thought process. He was strictly in cop-mode right then and it didn't take him long to jump the backyard gate and see the last of the leg that had just slid into the back window. His heavy tennis shoe splintered the doorjamb as he rammed it hard with a swift and powerful kick. Glass shattered as the door flung open.

Will had done his job and was standing between Jill's door and the man sprawled on the kitchen floor. Within seconds, Ian was on top of the man, gun rammed tightly against the back of the large man's neck.

Anita was the first to come see what the ruckus was about. She flipped on the hall light and froze at the sight of Ryan being manhandled on the floor. "What the hell?" she shouted.

Will stood speechless holding his gun pointed directly at Ryan and looked wide-eyed at Anita.

Anita dodged the arm of Will who was trying to keep her securely in her room. "Get off him!" Anita yelled at Ian, who had now had a stranglehold on Ryan's throat, attempting to cuff him. "Get the fuck off him," she screamed and was lifted in the air by Will who was trying to keep her calm and out of harm's way.

Jill came out of her room just as Ian finally secured the cuffs around the man's wrists and rolled him over to look him in the eye.

Seeing Ian on the floor took her completely by surprise and it hadn't dawned on her that he was armed. She just stared at him with a dazed expression. Her breath caught in her throat as he looked up with those eyes. "It's him," she breathed.

Anita shot her a horrified glare. "Well your *him* has my *him* on the floor. Your *him* has a gun. He-llo, do you *not* see that the man has a gun?" Anita screamed at her bright eyed, dazed friend. "And you.... what the hell are you doing?" Anita snapped at Will who was still armed and looking rather dangerous, while holding her firmly around the waist. "That's my Ryan," she yelled and struggled from his grasp. She swiftly moved past the surprised agent and went to Ryan. The room remained quiet, except for the heaving breathing of Ryan, the tears of Anita, and the loud thumping of Ian's heart. Jill still hadn't blinked and neither had Ian. It was if they were both transfixed in each other's gazes and it wasn't until Jill moved toward him that he lowered his gun and realized his mistake.

She was moving closer, taking each step as if being drawn by a magnetic force. Jill didn't stop until her hand was splayed flatly against his chest, which was rising and falling raggedly.

Ian looked down at her hand on his chest, felt a ripple of some unexplained force and then stepped back and scowled hard. "You know this man?"

Jill nodded but remained placid. "It's you — you're here."

"Jesus fucking Christ," Anita shouted and wiped the sweat off Ryan's brow. "What the hell is going on here?" she shouted at the two men with guns, then turned her venom on Jill. "Jill...snap the fuck out of it. Get a grip. Focus, woman."

Ian and Will both held up their badges and, since Ian was still awestruck by Jill in her fabulous short nightie, Will stepped forward and released Ryan from the cuffs.

"Thanks," Ryan said to Will and then sat down at the kitchen table. Only a few dishes had been broken in the scuffle, so Will picked them up off the floor and nudged Ian out of his daze.

"I think now would be a good time for you to explain to me why you've been following me," Jill said quietly and a bit breathlessly. *So he was a cop and not some psycho stalker.* "Why are you here?"

Will moved around everyone, put on a pot of tea, and made coffee for himself and Agent Hamlin. He figured it was going to be a very long night.

"What the hell are you doing here?" Anita said to Ryan once the poor man could breathe again. *It's not every day that he gets tackled to the ground and cuffed like a common criminal.*

"What are you doing with this guy?" Ryan yelled out in frustration. His cheeks were still flushed from the scuffle and his eyes were wide with confusion.

"None of your business," Anita said haughtily. Now seemed the opportune time to try out her flippant attitude about why the love of her life was breaking into her house during the wee hours of the morning. Her plan was working wonderfully. "You said you didn't want a commitment — well two can play that game, Mister."

"Jesus, Anita," Ryan groaned and placed a big hand around the back of her neck. "That's not what I meant. I love you, for fucks sake. I was scared. I wasn't ready for you. It's like I'd been trying so hard not to *like* fall in love, and then bam. You had to come along with those sexy hips and that great smile and I just got scared. I love you, baby. Don't you get that by now?" He looked lovingly into her eyes and Anita's heart melted. And then she ran for the bathroom.

Will was trying not to eavesdrop on Anita and Ryan's conversation but it was difficult so he left the kitchen and sat down on the sofa across from Jill, who was still watching Ian as if he were surrounded by an aura of angelic proportions. Will had never seen anything like it. The sparks in the room were enough to light up an entire football stadium in the dead of night.

"Well. Speak!" Jill demanded after the silence became unbearable. Her mystery man was seated across from her, in her house, and now was the time to get that explanation. Although, when she looked at his full lips, all she could think about was how good they would feel pressed up against hers. She swallowed hard and strengthened her resolve for the truth.

"We're following up on the incident that happened with your door." Ian told only part of the truth. The whole truth wasn't going to happen .Not tonight anyway. "We believe that the members of a Ukrainian gang might have targeted your house by mistake and we were watching to see if they came back," Ian lied through his teeth. Which he hated doing, but he didn't have much choice in the matter. *I've blown it big time tonight.*

"Bullshit," Jill's voice seemed much deeper when she was perturbed and overly tired, not to mention incredibly turned on. "I've had just about enough lies for one weekend. What the hell is really going on?"

Will and Ian exchanged glances. Will got up and tended to the beverage making just as Anita emerged from the bathroom. "You okay?" he wrapped his fingers around her wrist gently and pulled her aside.

"I will be when I tell him the truth." Anita said with a smile, and took Ryan by the hand and led him into the bedroom with full intentions of reciprocating his love and finally telling him the truth about the baby on the way.

Jill shivered from the cool stream of air that was flowing through the kitchen and right into the front room where she was patiently waiting for a better explanation as to why an FBI agent and his partner were wrestling Ryan in her kitchen. The feeling of her nipples puckering tightly unnerved her because she wasn't sure what caused the effect. *Was it the cool blast of air, or the very sexy man?*

She had a damn good suspicion that their being there had nothing to do with the bloody nine on her door, because Ian hadn't looked her in the eye during his rehearsed little speech, so Jill wasn't buying any of what he was dishing out.

Ian looked overwrought at best. Completely disheveled and sweaty from his brawl on the kitchen floor. He did his best to regain his composure and do a better job of lying to the pretty lady. "We have reason to believe, Miss Wallokowski, that you have been targeted by a stalker, and in Washington we take that very seriously." Ian tried again and this time he actually looked into her amazing dark eyes. His heart thumped a little faster and harder in his chest. He rose off the chair and paced the floor in front of her, doing his best to busy his hands in the thickness of his hair so he wouldn't do something crazy like reach out and rake his finger across her pouty lips. *God, her full lips are a thing of beauty.* Everything about her was a thing of beauty and suddenly it was if someone had turned up the heat to a scorching hundred degrees. A bead of sweat dripped off his brow. He didn't flinch or attempt to keep it from running into his eyes for he was too busy gawking at her heaving chest.

Jill's breathing grew ragged just looking at the man and, of course, she was now frightened that he was telling the truth. That made a lot more sense because she'd also felt that someone had been watching her. A minute or two seemed to pass before she got herself together enough to take a deep breath and that is when she noticed his gaze drop to the opening of her gown. She didn't attempt to close it; she just shifted positions and bit her lip to refrain from pulling him down on the couch and wrapping her lips around the soft contour of his neck. It was calling to her. Strong pulses of desire swept over her. She felt the flush, but remained cool about the feverish twinge that her cheeks felt.

"Is that all?" she finally spoke quietly. "Is there anything else that you want to say to me?" She was hoping for an explanation of his Peeping Tom routine at Elias's house at the beach, but he simply shook his head and extended his hand.

Jill looked him deep in the eye and then she took the extended limb and for the life of her she didn't want to let go. This man was brought back to her to watch over her. *To protect me, and nothing, absolutely nothing is sexier than that.*

"I'm sorry for the ruckus tonight," Ian said as he firmly shook her hand. "Are there any other men who might be sneaking in on a regular basis?"

Jill chuckled lightly and remained holding onto the rough hand of Agent Hamlin. "I don't think so... Ian -- was it?"

Ian nodded and sent her a small smile. It was nice.

Totally unlike the scowl that she was used to seeing on his face. "I'll call you in the morning and I'll explain things further..." Ian stopped short when he heard the ecstatic whoop that came from Anita's bedroom.

To Jill, it didn't sound like Ryan was upset at all that he was about to be a father. In fact, Jill thought he sounded pretty damn happy. "They're having a baby." Jill smiled in explanation.

Ian gave her a wink and gathered up his gun and cuffs. "I'll fix that door in the morning. You don't mind if Agent Harrison sleeps on your couch again, do you?"

Jill shook her head and cautiously stepped toward him. "Don't you want to stay too?" She couldn't believe she just blurted that out like that but she did. Her cheeks flushed to a deep shade of crimson, but it was dark in the room. Still she smiled to mask her embarrassment.

Ian's heart stopped dead in his chest. He wanted to stay, oh boy, did he want to stay. God, it was hard to walk out that damned door, but he did it anyway. With just a wave, he was out the back door and back in his SUV within minutes.

* * *

The morning light woke Jill up before she wanted to open her eyes. The slight pounding at her back door was hindering her desire to fall back to sleep. Uncurling her toes from the sheets, she stretched and peeked out the window. Will and Ryan were working side by side, fixing the door and Anita stood by smiling and sipping tea. Jill pulled her curtains back further to see if Ian was in the yard and, to her dismay, he was not. She saw Ryan waltz over and give Anita a pretty impressive kiss and then quickly got back to work.

The phone rang by her bed. She picked it up hoping for a chance to speak to Agent Hamlin again. "Hello." Her voice seemed bright and friendly, but she was exhausted beyond words.

"Hi baby," Elias said wearily. "How's my girl this

133

morning?"

Jill sat up straighter in bed and pulled the covers to her chest. Leaning back against the oak headboard of her bed, she took a deep breath. "I'm good. How are you? Are you still in Sequim?" Her tone was light and sleepy. She was still leery about Elias's ability to hide the truth, but it was nice to hear his soft voice.

"No, I'm in Seattle. I was worried about you and then I started thinking," he said. "I'd like to come see you this week. I'll be in town on Wednesday. Maybe I could pick you up after work and we could talk."

"I guess Wednesday would be fine," Jill said.

"I'll see you then," Elias disconnected and turned to see Sara emerge from the bedroom. Tears streaked her face. Her bags were packed and there was nothing left to say to the man.

Elias glared and turned to look out the window and over the tall buildings in downtown Seattle. He no longer needed Sara as a reminder that he could get whatever he wanted. Now he had Jill. *Jill is all mine and I'm not about to let her go now.*

* * *

Sunday night around six thirty, Jill finally saw the agents exchange cars. Ian emerged from the front seat of an unmarked gold Crown Victoria. He stretched, raked a hand through his hair, and gave the departing team a farewell wave as they drove off, leaving him on his own to watch over Jill. She'd stayed in most of the day because she was exhausted, and Ryan had demanded that Anita go home with him, so Jill caught up on emails to her family and finished the giant jigsaw puzzle that she had started the day before she met Elias Webber.

She liked watching Ian out the window. Every couple of minutes he would change position but his eyes remained continually focused on the house. In a very bizarre and twisted way, it made Jill feel as if she were the most important woman in the world. She had Agent Ian Hamlin watching her and her alone. If anything, it was a boost for the ego. *Not that I need it.* Jill had always known that men wanted her, but she remained grounded for the most part. She liked the attention, that was a given.

Just watching Ian, she got the feeling that somehow it was fate intervening. *Like perhaps I'm not supposed to be with Elias. Fate had stepped in at just the right time.* She smiled and ran downstairs to make the best of the hand that fate had dealt her.

She made soup and had just sat down on the couch when she saw the business card on the coffee table. She dialed the number and was elated to hear his husky voice.

"Hamlin."

"It's Jill," she said, but then couldn't think of a good reason for calling him. And then her mind took her back to that day at Compo Beach and her resolve was strengthened. *I need to know. Why now, what could possibly be the reasoning for him coming back for me now? Does this mean we're meant to be? What about Elias? Am I analyzing this to death? Yes!*

"Is everything okay?" Ian rustled in the front seat of the surveillance van parked on the corner. "Are you all right?"

"I'm fine." Jill said. Her heart raced. "I just wondered if you wanted dinner. I made soup. It's homemade minestrone."

"I can't.... but thanks." Ian said with feeling.

"Well if you change your mind, I'll be here." Jill said, but wasn't really ready to disconnect from her mystery man. She had so many questions.

"No hot date tonight?" Ian tossed that out there with a wince. He watched her through his binoculars and saw the frown furl on her face.

"No." Jill said and then bit her lip as she fumbled with the buttons on her sundress. *He obviously knows I have a boyfriend. Damn, fate sucks.* "You saw me... in

Sequim... didn't you?" she said quietly, with a hint of mischief.

Ian blew out his breath and had to lower his binoculars before he got himself worked into a state. "I'm sorry about that. But if it makes you feel any better, you are very beautiful." He smacked his palm against his forehead, and then focused on her face again through the binoculars. It was hard to see, but he was sure she was blushing. She was most certainly smiling from ear to ear.

"It's a bit intimidating, having you know what I look like naked." The bright smile remained on her face.

"It wasn't the first time," Ian said without regard to what the fuck he was talking about. "Shit," he grumbled under his breath and regained his composure. "I mean... I've seen naked women before. It's not really that much different." *But, oh, god, it was different.* It was different because at the tender age of seventeen, she was the first woman he ever saw naked and uninhibited. Sure, he'd had sex when he was seventeen, once, with a timid teenager who refused to let him get a good look. But watching Jill dress and undress through his bedroom window was a defining time in his life. From that day forward, every woman's body he'd ever seen had been compared to Jill's perfect tight body. Her high tits and the round suppleness of her backside. Those two dimples just above her ass. God, he'd longed to kiss her there when he was a horny teenager. Hell, he still wanted to kiss her there. *Some fantasies never die.*

Jill chuckled lightly. She walked to the window and knew that he was looking. It was almost a turn on, even fully clothed, to know that he was watching her every move.

"You really should keep those blinds closed," Ian said breathlessly. "In fact, why don't you do it now."

He watched her lean over and pull the chord, and then suddenly she was out of sight, hidden behind the mini-blinds.

"Is that better?" she asked and then appeared in

the adjacent window and did the same. The blind lowered and Ian felt disappointed.

"Much better," he lied. "Did you lock the back door?"

"I think so." She started toward the kitchen, just to make sure. She didn't like his tone of voice. He seemed different now. Guarded. He sounded like a cop. "Is Will staying here again tonight?" She asked as she flipped the lock on the back door.

"No. Would you like him to?"

Jill's heart raced again and flip flopped in her chest. Taking a moment to calm her breathing, she smiled into the phone. A rush of unadulterated need washed over her body and had her flushed from head to toe. "Anita isn't coming home. It would be nice if *someone* was here."

Ian's eyes rolled back in his skull. He scooted down in his seat and felt his jeans tighten in the groin. "He'll be there."

"Thanks," Jill said a bit disappointed. "I'll save you some soup. Maybe tomorrow night, okay?"

"Fine." He disconnected without another word. *Damn if she didn't know just the right buttons to push.*

* * *

Two days passed without incident, which was fine by Ian. It didn't cause him to sit any less at attention, but he preferred the quiet time to get to know Jill and watch the curves of her hips while she watered the roses. He'd been a bit more careful and guarded about watching her, and had been insistent that she stick to her normal routine. He hated lying to her and telling her that things were fine and not to worry. He hated it so much he thought an ulcer the size of his fist was most likely growing inside his stomach, ready to erupt at a moment's notice.

He hadn't slept much because it was hard to sleep in the middle of the day and he still preferred to be the one who stayed up into the wee hours of the night. He didn't have much trust in these Portland boys. Control freak?

That was putting it mildly.

Jill's car had been returned to her by the body shop. It looked good as new and as Jill slid into the driver's seat and pulled out into the street, Ian gave up control and let the other boys tail her to the television studio. He had a date with a pillow and a hot meatball sub.

* * *

Jill was still unsure about the FBI sitting across the street and wondered if there was more to the story than they were letting on. She'd tried a couple of times to get Ian to open up to her the last couple of nights on the phone, but the man had surrounded himself with a firewall and said nothing about the details of her case. She enjoyed their conversations immensely, especially because she knew that he was watching her. When she asked direct questions, she got no answers, but she could hear the gnashing of his teeth. Sure, he'd told her a number of times not to worry; it was nothing serious, but she wasn't stupid. She had around-the-clock agents sitting across the street or behind her at traffic lights and a number of times during the past two days at the station, she'd seen the same two men, dressed casually, yet they looked high strung and on guard at all times.

Will was a different story entirely because she saw him up close and personal nearly every day. The man had made her couch a home and yet he wouldn't even look her in the eye. Jill had tried bribing him with donuts, homemade chocolate cookies and had even attempted to get him drunk a couple of times, but the man was a tough nut to crack and continually passed her up on her double martinis.

Anita hadn't been home much. Just a couple of times here and there to exchange clothes and talk about how wonderful Ryan is. *Ryan is wonderful,* Jill had to admit that. The young man far exceeded her expectations in the maturity department and had even asked Anita for her hand in marriage. Anita said she'd rather wait until the baby came to make a decision like that, and then the next morning she changed her mind. She did have that prerogative, being a woman and all. Being a pregnant woman at that just made it that much more fun to be around the wishy-washy gal. Jill couldn't be happier for her giddy friend and it saddened her that her own love life was still such a jumbled mess.

Elias had called a number of times. Sent flowers to work and left cute messages on her machine. The man was making the right moves and saying all the right things. Jill just wasn't sure that he was the right man. *Not for me anyway.* Not entirely sure what she was going to do, she sighed hard as she glanced out the back window of her Honda and watched Ian pull away from the curb in his cop-mobile.

The Hardy Boys were now her chaperones for the day and what a day it was. The sun was shining bright, the temperature was just a degree hotter than she said it would be that afternoon and rain was out of the picture for a good three days at least.

When she arrived at work, the parking garage was filled with police cars, men in uniform and a couple of plainclothesmen that she recognized as Detective Whitney and his sidekick. She parked in the first spot she could find that wasn't roped off by security, because her own reserved spot was cordoned off by yellow police tape.

To her astonishment, Ian was one of the men leaning over the mess that was all over the cement floor of the parking structure. He looked up and caught her eye, nodded and then went back to what he was doing. Men were taking snapshots of the ground, and of the footprints that surrounded the mess, being careful as to where they were stepping. Jill's face paled slightly when Detective Whitney and Ian Hamlin finally sauntered over to where she was impatiently waiting. It was if her shoes had somehow become one with the concrete, she couldn't have moved if she tried.

"Miss Wallokowski," Detective Whitney took her arm and helped her over to the elevator. "Can you come with me?"

Ian stepped in behind them and no one said a word to her until they reached the studio entrance. She was quickly shuffled aside and taken into the producer's office.

Fear wasn't the only emotion taking a toll on her body. A dizzy wave of nausea had her sinking down into the chair in the corner of her boss's office. She wanted answers and comfort and a warm hand to hold. Ian hadn't as much as even given her a weak smile. *The man knows nothing about sensitivity. He is one hundred percent cop one hundred percent of the time.* God, what she wouldn't give for a warm arm to be wrapped around her. *I want Elias. I miss Elias!*

"What is it? Just tell me," Jill sputtered and shivered. She'd seen the pools of bright shiny liquid. She just didn't want to speculate what it was. *Hopefully the engineers had just spilled some red paint.*

"I'll let him explain," Jake Whitney took a step back and motioned to Ian Hamlin of the FBI. "This is your show."

Ian had been on his way to his hotel when he got the call. Boy, that had pissed him off. Not so much that sleep was once again put on the back burner, but that the son-of-a-bitch had left yet another sign that Jill was in imminent danger. He looked at Jill, searching her eyes for... something. "I need you to be completely honest with me here," Ian demanded and Jill's temples throbbed. *Hell, I could say the same thing to you, pal.*

Detective Whitney cleared his throat due to the tension in the air. Clearly, he was out of his mind to get himself in the middle of whatever they had going on between them. The air around them was electrified and had Detective Whitney's shaggy brown hair, standing on end. "I'll be outside."

Jill squirmed in her seat and kept her piercing gaze

on Ian's deep blue eyes. "I'd like to say the same thing to you. What the hell is going on? And don't give me some cockamamie story about stalker-laws in Washington." She glared hard and stood up, inching closer to his taut physique. "What aren't you telling me?"

Ian reached out to her because it seemed like the right thing to do at the time. In his mind, he'd honestly expected her to slap his hand away, but she didn't do any such thing. When his hand wrapped around the soft curve of her neck, she stepped toward him and moaned in approval as she laid her head against his shoulder.

His breathing was tattered. She noticed that right away as she relaxed slowly and took in every conceivable scent that lingered around him. Mostly he smelled like a man. Musky and sweaty, with a hint of Old Spice and...meatballs and marinara. Jill closed her eyes and shuddered to keep from completely losing control and weeping against his shoulder. Her hands remained at her sides, but she could feel his body against hers and it felt wonderful. Even with clothes on, in her producer's office of all places, he felt damn good. She could barely stand the thought of how he might feel, perhaps naked in bed, or in the back of her car, or hell, right here on the desk. Her mind raced and her vagina clenched at the thought. The man had gotten her wet with just his scent. By god, she wanted him.

Ian was only two inches taller than she was, so when she pulled back, he countered the movement and kept his face close to hers when he finally spoke.

"I'm not going to let anything happen to you. Just know that right now." His hand closed tighter around the back of her neck. He raked a thumb over the pulsing artery in her neck, over and over causing the blood to sing in her veins. "I'm not telling you anything until you trust that I'm not going to let anything happen to you." He gazed into her eyes, bringing her face within inches of his lips as he spoke.

His breath was hot against her lips. And she was right about the meatballs, she could smell the Italian spices on his breath. "Do you trust me, Jill?" he asked breathlessly.

Jill wanted nothing more than to stumble forward against his lush lips, but she just blinked and nodded. "Yes."

"Good." He finally returned to the guarded cop that she knew so well. His eyes narrowed. "Tell me about the flowers you received." He leaned back against the desk and crossed his arms in front of his chest. Again, he had donned faded Levis, a navy blue t-shirt, and a black leather jacket.

Perhaps if the man just wore khaki sometimes, he might seem less intimidating. She shook her head and retreated to her chair. She guessed his moment of weakness was up and that was all the comfort she was going to get. "Like I told Detective Whitney. I came to work that morning and there was a bouquet of dead roses on my desk. The card simply had a red nine on it. I'd been getting some strange phone calls, so I just chalked it up to a secret admirer." Jill's skin crawled as if something just clicked into place. "In fact..." She sat up straighter. "My first night on the air...there were flowers sent to the station for me. The card was signed from a secret admirer. I just didn't think anything of it at the time? What does this have to do with the number nine? And what happened in the parking garage?"

"Looks like someone painted your parking spot with a big red nine. But I'm more concerned with the phone calls. When did these start and did anyone ever talk?"

"I heard breathing a couple of times. I think the first time it happened was the night of my first on-air broadcast. In fact I know it was. Then they got more frequent. We moved into the house and then one of the first days at our new place, I got a call and the man just said, 'you're puurrty.' He sounded like a little man with a high squeaky voice; kind of perverted and whiney. I think he said that one other time, but I can't remember. Do you think it's relevant? Could this all be connected?"

"Okay, after you get home tonight, I want you to try to remember everything." His eyes narrowed on her once again, and his scowl was back. Fear rippled up his spine, a deep fear that Jill would want answers that he wasn't prepared to give. Somehow, he had to make it better for her without scaring the fuck out of her, not yet anyway. Jill was not only his best chance at nailing this son-of-a-bitch, but to his dismay, keeping Jill safe seemed more important than finally nailing the sick fuck. His heart was definitely wreaking havoc on his career. "I'll be taking you home, by the way, and I want you to write down these exact dates for me. Every phone call you can remember. The date of your first broadcast. I need it all. Can you do that for me?"

"Sure, I guess I can do that." Jill bit her lip. "Can I go now?" She had work to do and a new sense of urgency to escape his intense gaze before she felt compelled to rip off his clothes and beg him to make her scream out in ecstasy.

"Stay on this floor. Reynolds and Hardy will be here until I get back. Don't go for coffee. Don't answer the phone. Don't do anything until I get back. Got it."

"Yes *sir*!" Jill said with a hint of irritation. Her impulse to do *the nasty* with him was quickly demolished by his cop-tone. Needless to say, demands didn't sit well with her.

Ian shook his head with a smirk and stared at the ground. "Are you taking this shit seriously or am I going to have to cuff you to the closet in my hotel room?"

Jill sucked in her breath. That did have a certain amount of appeal, *but then again...*

She yanked open the door and got to work.
* * *

The ride home at one a.m. was unbearably

uncomfortable for both Jill and Ian. Ian had managed to sleep about five hours while Jill was playing weathergirl but his well-needed nap did nothing for his demeanor this evening. He knew it would be a long night, but what he hadn't expected was Jill's snotty attitude when he came around to pick her up and take her home. *I haven't been that big of an ass,* or at least he didn't think so. Jill might have thought otherwise, but she hadn't said a word about it. He sensed that something was amiss, but he couldn't quite put a finger on exactly what he had done that had set her off.

Perhaps it was something that happened to her earlier in life that made Jill despise being barked at. That demanding tone of voice that men sometimes used always set her into bitch mode. And at this particular time, Ian deserved the fierce glare that she was still sending him. He'd marched right up to her in front of her producer, her assistant and even the vice president of the television station and grabbed her elbow and said, "Let's go." With a tug and a scowl, he dragged her out the door with a caveman attitude and a groan to match when she demanded to drive her own car home.

"You can follow me. What's the big deal?" she had asked with one hand on her hip, the other digging into her purse for her keys.

He had moved closer and pinned her against the door of his SUV. The moment was nice and extremely arousing for about ten seconds until he spoke. Breathing heavily, he grunted and mumbled a few not-so-nice words and simply said, "I said ... get in."

Okay, so any woman would be mad about that. That's why when he pulled into her driveway, she got out and ran into the house and slammed the door in her wake.

"Fuck you!" she screamed at the closed door and then turned around and shrieked wildly, because Will was on her couch and she hadn't expected him this evening. "Jesus Christ!" She clutched her chest. Her purse dropped heavily to the floor and her belongings scattered across the hardwood floor. "How did you get in here?"

"Anita let me in. She's at Ryan's again." Will moved off the couch to help with the clean up.

"Fucking, fuck, fuck." Jill, who rarely cursed aloud, rammed her open palms against her forehead and groaned. "I need a drink," she said as the last of her stuff was back in her purse.

"Bad day?"

"Didn't you hear? Another mysterious red nine ended up in my parking space. I'd sure like to know what the hell is going on." Jill said flippantly and sank down next to Will, who squirmed toward the other end of the sofa. "Why don't you fill me in on the details while I fix us a couple of cocktails. You look like you need a martini." She stood up and moved into the kitchen.

Ian, who was already in the surveillance van listening in, heard his partner mumble, "Help me," in a high-pitched squeal.

Ian chuckled under his breath. "Better you than me, pal." He eased back into his seat and heard glass clinking together. The blinds were still shut, so all he could do was listen and calm himself after being so antagonized by Jill's hissy fit.

"Okay, so while I was at work tonight, I did a little research." Jill's tone was playful, but she was pretty serious. She shook the tin shaker full of vodka and dry vermouth and then poured the chilled cocktail into a crystal martini glass. "I know that both you and Ian are agents from New Haven, Connecticut, and that means that there's no way that you are chasing a Washington stalker." Before leaving the kitchen, she dropped two olives into the glass and made her way to the couch. She glared fiercely as she handed him a drink, ready to finally hear the truth. What she got instead was Will's pleasant smile.

"Thanks for the martini." Will gulped his down in five seconds flat then yawned dramatically. He usually wouldn't drink on the job, but her hostile gaze was making him anxious.

Jill narrowed her eyes. "This isn't over," she mumbled when he feigned another yawn. She headed for her room and slammed the door to make a point.

Ian closed his eyes tightly and listened to the silence in the house. That is until Will turned up the television and laid into him about making Jill so bitchy this evening. Ian, of course couldn't respond to his partner's harsh words, or even defend himself, so he sat back and shook his head. *Maybe having Will in the house wasn't a good idea after all.* Ian wanted to be the one sleeping on her couch. He wanted to be the one witnessing her making coffee in the morning, or walking into the bathroom in her pretty nightgown. *Damn, I need to get a handle on my libido. It's causing such misery.*

Both Ian and Will assumed that her little tizzy fit was over, but they were wrong.

Ian jolted out of his fantasy when he heard her high pitch shriek.

"Tell me the goddamn truth or I am marching out that fucking door and I'll blow your cover right this second. I can make your lives a living hell — or you can tell me the truth." She screamed and Will thought she looked pretty cute in her short nightie that showed the majority of her sculpted legs.

Will chuckled lightly and called her bluff. Hell, his wife was queen of bluffs and he knew the signs. Hands on hips. Lips pursed tightly and a scowl that could make a baby cry.

Jill eyeballed the door and wondered how long it would take Will to untangle himself from the blanket that was wrapped around his legs. *He'd probably trip on the coffee table and that would give me just enough time to get out the front door. I can do it.* She psyched herself up and let out a deep grunt. "Fine. You won't talk. I'll just go ask Ian. Ian will be happy to see me out in the street screaming my lungs off. Is that what you want?" Jill goaded him further but he wouldn't budge.

Ian heard the threats and he too didn't believe that she'd do something that bold, so when he heard the muffled scream and a couple of loud thuds, he was stunned and rightfully so.

"Get off me. Let me go."

He heard Jill's shouts, then a grunt, another loud thud, and a deep groan. "*Help.*"

That was the last thing Ian heard before he saw the door fling open. He ran as fast as his feet could carry him and had her inside and pinned against the now-closed door before she had time to blink.

"Jesus Christ," Ian looked down at Will writhing on the floor. "What did you do to him?"

"What did *I* do to him? He grabbed *me.*" Jill looked over at Will, completely unremorseful for what she had done. She got him right where it counted and she couldn't be happier about it. *That would teach him for laughing at me.* "He deserved it. He laughed at me."

Will finally made it back to the couch, mad as hell and clutching his groin.

Ian pulled Jill by the arm and into her room to protect her from the wrath of his partner. "Sit." He slammed the door to her room and stepped closer to her, his jaw clenched.

Oh, fire burned in her belly. Sparks shot from her fingertips and if Ian hadn't already been hopped up on adrenaline, he wouldn't have been fast enough to dodge her fist, but he was, so Jill was once again pinned up against the wall, breathing heavily with tears already streaming down her cheeks.

Ian couldn't help it. The only thing between them was the sheer fabric of her silk nightie and the faded denim of his jeans.

Jill's tears kept her from realizing that Ian was growing hard between his legs. All she concentrated on was the feeling of desperation and fear that had washed over her in the past ten hours. She struggled to free herself and inhaled deeply.

Ian wiped her tears dry with the hand that wasn't holding her captive against the wall. "Shhhh," he finally mumbled under his breath and lifted her chin with his rough fingers. Nudging closer to her, he wiggled into the space between her legs and heard the small, delicate moan erupt from her lips. He couldn't believe that he was here, in her bedroom, holding her against the wall with every part of himself. Every hard part that ached to be caressed by her full lips, her smooth fingers and, of course, he wanted to return the favor. He breathed deeply. *She must taste amazing,* he thought, *because she smelled amazing and it was only fair that she would taste as sweet as she smells.*

Jill knew now. She could feel him hard. Everywhere their bodies touched, she felt him hard. *This was more like it. This is what passion inspires bodies to do and it feels wonderful.* She was certain that he was about to kiss her. She could feel the tension in his muscles, and saw the rigid set to his jaw.

The last lucid thought in Ian's head had been that Jill had just done something so incredibly stupid. She'd almost made a spectacle of herself in the street. *Hell, that would have blown my best shot at getting this fucker right out of the water. What if the killer had been out there, watching from the bushes? What if we've just blown our chance?* That would mean that it would take that much longer to finish this case and be that much longer before he could get far away from this woman who seemed to continually knock his world off its nice, controlled axis. Anger replaced desire and he stepped back, but held her hand tightly so she wouldn't take another swing at his jaw.

The reaction this induced in Jill wasn't a pretty one. Her body felt his withdrawal and that's not what she wanted. God, she wanted him to lift her against the wall and take her in a way that no man had ever done before. Clearly he wanted her just as badly as she wanted him. *What is his problem?* Anger and fear returned to replace her yearning to have him thrusting hard inside her.

Jill felt the room spin after realizing that her growing feelings of attraction for Ian were the least of her troubles. She had a little problem that seemed to be getting worse every day and she felt it was high time for some honesty. "Does he want me dead?"

Ian didn't respond, but he did let her go as he stepped back.

Jill rubbed her wrist and sank down on the bed. "What's with the nine? Is he a serial killer or something?" Jill asked with wide eyes.

A muscle worked in Ian's jaw. His eyes dilated further as his brows furled.

"That's it isn't it? I'm expected to be the ninth victim." The color ran completely from her face and all Ian could do was ram his hands into his pockets and shake his head at the floor.

"I was sort of joking." Jill said quietly. "But that's it, isn't it?"

Ian said nothing. He just looked her in the eye. He didn't have to respond; Jill knew from his body language that she had hit the nail on the head.

"When did the first phone call come?" Ian asked sternly and then sat down on the edge of the windowsill across from her bed. "Let's take this day by day. I need to know everything that happened and I need dates."

Jill wept quietly on the bed, burying her face in her hands. God, she wanted him to console her and hold her close, not interrogate her in this manner. She yearned to hear him tell her that everything was going to be okay. But he didn't. He just sat there like a lump on a log, staring at her, waiting for an answer to his question. An answer that he was not going to get, not right now, anyway. Jill couldn't recall any details at that time. All she knew was that some psycho wanted her dead and she didn't even rate a warm pat on the back. *The bastard! The cop without feelings.* "Get out!" she screamed with a snarl. "Get the fuck out of my house."

Chapter Eight

Will woke up with a start just about the time that the sun peeked through the living room blinds. He stirred slightly and then jolted upright as he stared at Jill's long dark hair. Somehow in the middle of the night, the frightened woman had tiptoed out and curled on the corner of the couch next to him. If his balls hadn't ached so much, he might have laughed about how sweet and innocent she looked when she was sleeping, but hell, that girl could pack quite a punch.

"Hey," he whispered when her eyes fluttered open.

She pulled the quilt tighter around her body and struggled to sit up.

"Hi," she said with a twinge of humiliation. At least she had put on long sweats and a t-shirt before crawling into bed with the married man. "I'm sorry for kicking you."

"I'm sorry for laughing at you." He winked and stretched out the kink in his back. He didn't blame her, not in the least. In fact, under ordinary circumstances, he might consider her a friend. After all, she did cook for him, clean up his dishes, and she was fun to talk to — most of the time, anyway.

Jill sat up and wiped the sleep from her eyes with the back of her hand. She hadn't even taken off her makeup last night, so dark patches of mascara were smudged under her eyes and it looked as if anxiety had aged her ten years overnight.

"Is your partner always that big of a jerk, or do I somehow suck the empathy right out of him?"

Will didn't know how to respond to that, especially since he knew the room was bugged. "He's.... well. Let's just say he's one tough cop."

"Yeah, but even tough cops can crack a smile or offer a shoulder to cry on. The man's a real piece of work."

* * *

Ian heard the entire conversation and it pained him that his anger and rage was the only thing that woman saw in him. He had a kind side. A warm cuddly side, he just couldn't show it right now. He had Jill to protect, not to coddle. *If she wants a shoulder to cry on she can call her friends, because that just isn't my cup of tea.* He'd been nice before. He'd opened up and left himself wide open for the stomping, not once but twice. Two times it had happened, and never again was he going to work that hard for something just to have it taken away. *No woman was worth that.*

Ian growled as he listened to Jill go on about how insensitive and infuriating he was. Hell, at least she was concentrating on what a big jerk he is instead of concentrating on the fact that she's the target of a psycho. He grimaced as he added knowledge she didn't have — a psycho who undoubtedly wants to mutilate her body and leave her to die in the bushes.

"It'll hit her later." Ian scoffed and watched as his relief pulled in behind him.

* * *

It did hit Jill later. The minute she walked out the door and realized her car was still at the station, it hit her like a ton of bricks. Her knees buckled under her and it wasn't because the temperature had reached ninety-six degrees. It was fear. Even in her own front yard, with a couple of FBI agents just a couple hundred feet away, she still didn't feel safe.

"Damn," she muttered and went back in to call Anita for a ride. The minute she picked up the phone she heard a light rap on the door that sent her out of her skin.

"Jill, it's me."

She heard Ian's deep husky voice. She was still mad as hell, but at least she felt safe with him. *Comforted — not so much. But safe — unequivocally.*

She opened the door just enough to stick her perky upturned nose out. "What do you want?"

"You need a ride... right?" Ian tried to smile, but it was much more natural for him to furl his brows and tighten his jaw.

"Fine," Jill slammed the door in his face, grabbed her purse and then let herself out, locked the door tightly behind her and was escorted by the tough cop to his SUV. She wasn't going to pretend that she was okay about what transpired the night before and, even more adamantly, she wasn't going to admit that she liked being with him. She preferred to keep her feelings to herself.

"Did you happen to write down everything I wanted from you?"

The man is all business all the time. "And when was I supposed to have time to do this? I was a bit preoccupied with the fact that I'm about to die at the hands of a serial killer. I'm sorry if I didn't get my homework done." Jill said haughtily and stared out the window. She kept the tears at bay, but they were most definitely welled up behind her pretty brown eyes.

"Can you do it for me tonight? It's important, Jill."

She nodded and remained focused out the window.

He headed toward the station, keeping a comfortable speed and trying not to look down at the slit in her beige skirt. *She has amazing legs,* he thought and then looked up to see her sullen expression as she stared out the window. Ian felt like a first class cad, but what more could he do? Every fiber of his being was screaming out to him to wrap his arms around her and tell her that she had nothing to worry about. His lips ached to press tenderly against hers and caress the soft skin of her neck, but that wouldn't do a damn thing to help him find the killer. *That would just be a disaster in the making. Getting emotionally involved with this Jill Walker would be detrimental to my quest to stop a killer.* "Thanks," he said as they pulled up in front of the station. "Don't go anywhere tonight. No running for coffee, no sneaking out for dinner. I'll be back at one to pick you up."

"You're a real piece of work, you know that?" Jill's lips pursed tightly.

"So I've heard," he replied and winced when she slammed the car door with a vengeance.

He would have liked to go back to his hotel and sleep, but he had to make a call. He punched in a couple of numbers and got whom he wanted on the third ring.

"Whitney here."

"It's Hamlin." Ian said seriously. "Did we get word on the blood yet?"

"It's human, but it doesn't match the blood from the door. Any ideas you'd like to share?"

Ian let out his breath with a groan. *Okay, so the blood from the door came from Jill-eight in Reno, we at least know that much. So, where the hell did the guy get more blood?* "I'll be in touch." Ian disconnected and called the lab in New Haven. "Hey, it's Hamlin. I need you to send blood workup matches on the last three Jill's that were found. Send it to the office here in Portland. And I need the results quick."

So, that was a good place to start. It's conceivable that the man had made another kill, but not probable, so Jills six and seven were his best bets. *Time was running out,* or so he hoped. Ian hoped that the bastard would just make a move and get it over with so he'd have a chance to put a bullet in his brain. He was so ready he could taste it. Since he'd vowed to keep Jill safe, he felt confident that she'd survive unscathed and he could go about his life and finally stop thinking about Jill once and for all.

* * *

A woman in love would have been looking forward to seeing her boyfriend after hearing the news that she'd been targeted by a serial killer. A woman in love would have counted the minutes before she got to see him again. Clearly, from the look on Jill's face when she saw Elias's smiling face as he walked toward her, she was not a woman in love. In fact, she had been concentrating so much on trying not to cry, or not imagining making love to Agent Ian Hamlin, that she had completely forgotten that it was Wednesday.

"Hi," she attempted to keep the surprise out of her voice and was pulled into his arms. It was surprisingly nice to be comforted and held by a man who loves her and wants her. *Who cares if the sex is bad?* Elias was there and his arms felt wonderful around her bare, shivering shoulders. She eased back and straightened her black silk tanktop. Her high heels had already been kicked off under her desk and her beige skirt was wrinkled around her butt from sitting for so long. "I'm just about through." She looked up into his eyes and gave him a warm smile. Enough staff members had already left the studio, so she felt comfortable enough to lean in and meet him halfway for a kiss. Her mind was so jumbled with the news of her imminent death that she'd completely forgotten why she was having second thoughts about this man.

"You're shaking. Are you okay?" Elias pressed a kiss onto her temple and held her closer. "God, I missed you."

"Me too," Jill said and then she tensed in his arms when she saw the dark figure that stepped off the elevator. Now she remembered why she was having second thoughts. "Damn," she muttered under her breath and moved back out of Elias's arms. "Excuse me for just a minute, okay." Jill hurried over to Agent's Hamlin's side and just as Elias turned around and watched her approach the dark-haired, stern-looking man, the men's gazes locked in a fierce battlefield stare of surprise that quickly turned to fury.

"What the hell are you doing here?" Ian was the

first to speak after recognizing his former best friend, more recently his worst enemy. He looked from Jill to Elias and raked a hand through his hair. He recognized him now as the man whom Jill spent time with. Muscles clenched tightly in his arms, his nostrils flared and he took two aggressive steps toward the tall blonde man, putting himself between Elias and Jill.

"Stop it. This is my boyfriend." Jill grabbed Ian by the back of the arm, feeling pretty damned awkward standing between the two men who looked as if they were going to throw down in the middle of the television studio.

Elias glared, looking smug as ever and pulled Jill into his arms. "What the hell are you doing? And how do you two know each other?" Elias demanded an answer from Ian.

Ian felt control slip from his fingers as he hauled his fist back, and let it fly. Elias was knocked silly; his lip instantly swelled and blood dribbled onto his chin.

Without regard for herself, Jill quickly jumped between the two men and grabbed Ian's fist as he raised it again. "What the hell is wrong with you?" she gasped in horror. "I just said he's my boyfriend!" she snapped savagely and gave Ian a hard shove.

Ian inhaled sharply and dropped his fist. *What have I done? I lost it again -- but damn, it felt good. After all these years, it felt wonderful to make Elias feel pain.*

Elias looked a bit different since the last time their paths had crossed just two years ago at their ten-year high school reunion. His hair was noticeably shorter although it still grazed his broad shoulders. The painful recollection of their last meeting stung deep. He felt his teeth gnash and a jolt of pain ripped through his chest, tightening the muscles that surrounded his heart. "Why don't you ask him?" Ian snapped at Jill. He glared hard and watched Elias lick the blood from his lip.

Jill watched Ian's eyes and, for a split second, she saw a certain amount of vulnerability behind them. He almost looked human, like he might burst into tears. It was rather endearing, but the sight of Elias's bloody lip enraged her. "You've got some serious problems," she huffed and then was forcefully pulled aside by her bleeding boyfriend. "Are you okay?" she asked Elias with tight lips.

"I'm fine." Elias glared over her shoulder at the irate cop. "How the hell do you know Ian? What is he doing here?"

"It's a long story, but do you remember the bloody nine on my door? Well, it's not a prank and he's... well..." Jill looked over her shoulder at Ian. "I guess he's sort of my bodyguard."

"Oh, hell no," Elias began. "He's a fucking maniac. The guys a rage-aholic and I don't want you anywhere near him."

"Wait a second," Jill said with wide eyes. "How do you know Ian?"

"He *was* my best friend, that is until he went psycho. The guy is out of control and I don't want you anywhere near him." Elias suddenly became quite nervous about the situation. Everything could get shot to hell if Jill were to find out the truth. He tightened his grip on her bare arm. "Don't believe a word he says. He can't be trusted. In fact..." Elias pulled her toward his chest. "I'll make a call first thing in the morning and straighten this mess out. There's no way in hell I want you anywhere near this guy."

Jill pushed back from Elias and watched his eyes. They were glazed over with something she'd never seen in him before. An indescribable feeling flittered across her delicate skin, sending goose-bumps up and down the backs of her arms.

She turned and watched Ian out of the corner of her eye. He did seem a bit unglued by Elias's presence, but damn, she wasn't about to lose him now. Not before she had a chance to straighten out her feelings and find out why fate had brought him back to her at this particular point in time.

"It's fine, Elias. I'll tell you everything that's going on when we get home. Let's just go."

"Fine, but tomorrow I *am* making that call."

"I think you're overreacting. Please, just calm down and get the car. I'll be right out."

"Don't trust him, Jill." Elias snapped, conceding for the moment.

Jill rolled her eyes and left Elias alone for a minute so she could have a chat with her mystery man. She approached Ian cautiously while Elias went to pull his car around to the main entrance by the elevator doors on the main level. "Do you want to explain yourself?"

"It doesn't matter." Ian said with a grumble. He looked resigned. "You're going straight home I presume." His gaze narrowed. "Is *he* staying the night?" Ian felt as if the bottom had just dropped out. Sadness and a sense of sudden loss enveloped him fully. He could deal with the fact that Jill had a lover, a significant other, a man who shared her bed and her life, but what he couldn't deal with was the fact that the man was none other than Elias Webber — the man who got whatever he wanted. It was sickening to Ian and the pain was clear in his eyes.

Jill swallowed hard as if she were being unfaithful to Ian in some way. Like this was fate trying to tell her something. She was somehow choosing to ignore it and now felt guilty about the fact another man was taking her to bed. "Yes," she said demurely. "I guess I don't need Will to stay on the couch then."

"I'll make the call." Ian said and was out the door.

He watched Jill get into Elias's big expensive Cadillac Escalade. He couldn't believe the odds of this happening. Of all the women out there, why Jill? Why was Elias so damn insistent on making Ian feel inferior and not worthy of a good woman? The pain slashed at his heart and strengthened his resolve to remain emotionally unattached to Jill-nine. Hell, if he just kept calling her that, he might just believe that she was just another potential victim that he had been sent to protect. Sure, he'd try to convince himself of that, but deep down he knew better.

Ian followed the happy couple back to Jill's house in the dead of night. The street was again quiet, except for the croaking of frogs and the quiet hum of the tape recorder in the surveillance van. The women hadn't gotten too many phone calls, but Ian did learn that Jill loved Chinese food. The night was long and painful for Ian, who had to sit alone in the van listening for sounds that he really didn't want to hear. At first, he feared that Jill and Elias would go home and go at it on the couch and he'd be forced to listen, and then he just feared ... his heart began hurting at the mere thought of it. Ian closed his eyes, clutched his aching heart, and hummed a couple tunes to try and forget who was in Jill's bed.

* * *

"I just don't get why you won't let me hire a professional." Elias insisted the next morning after Jill quickly made her bed and followed him into the kitchen. He was beyond outraged that she had denied him entrance to that soft sweet spot between her legs yet again. He chalked it up to exhaustion and fear and tried not to take it personally that his girlfriend didn't want to make love to him last night. "I'll find a private company and I'll have an army around you at all times."

"I told you, I don't think that would work. I don't want a constant reminder. Just let him do his job and try not to worry." Jill said with a false sense of bravado. She enjoyed his company, liked having a big man around to keep her warm at night. Elias was a big cuddly teddy bear; unlike Ian, who was a raging lion. She'd rather have Ian keeping watch over her any day of the week and twice on Tuesday. "Please, just let it go. I barely have any contact with him. He's usually outside in the van." Jill said and poured the coffee, stirred in some non-fat milk and sank down onto Elias's lap.

He wrapped his arms around her and sighed.

"So, what happened?" Jill glanced over toward the street where she knew Ian was watching. "Why isn't he your best friend anymore?"

"It doesn't matter." Elias didn't want to get into it, he wanted in her pants. His hand slid down the edge of her silk robe. With a sultry gaze, he continued down her thighs and settled there between her legs while he watched her dazed expression.

Her hand grasped his wrist and brought it back up to the table. "I'm trying to talk to you." Jill said with disdain and frustration.

"What is it now?" Elias groused. "Are you not quite over what happened in Sequim? I'm trying to be patient with you, but you aren't making it very easy on me. Why won't you make love to me? What's standing in our way?" Elias asked quietly.

Jill rose and paced the floor, keeping her eyes focused on the van across the street. Was it really her obsession with the boy on the beach keeping her out of Elias's bed, or was it something more? She honestly didn't know. She only knew that something just wasn't right, but she didn't have time to dwell on it now, she had work to do. At that very moment she decided that she wanted to help in any way possible to save her own life, and that meant giving Ian full access to her life. A ripple of excitement raced up her spine. The idea of giving herself fully to Ian certainly had appeal.

"I don't really know what to tell you, Elias. I just have a lot on my mind and I can't concentrate on anything else right now. Please understand. It's not you. It's me." She kissed him lightly. "You've been amazing to me and I thank you for that."

"But you don't love me, do you?"

* * *

Ian wasn't trying to eavesdrop on their

159

conversation, but he couldn't help it. The house was bugged and it wasn't an option to turn off the listening device, besides it was kind of intriguing hearing that Elias wasn't getting what he wanted. In fact it was a hoot. A broad smile actually lit up Ian's face. That is until he heard silence, a couple of giggles, followed by a deep groan. His lips pursed tightly and he had to plug his ears to escape the horror of what he thought was going on inside the house. Thank god, the front door opened and Elias stepped onto the porch, fully clothed, and with his head hung low like a puppy that had peed on the carpet.

Ian couldn't hear the words that were exchanged, but the man looked as if he had been denied once again. Ian watched as Elias leaned forward, planted a kiss on the tip of Jill's nose and entered his vehicle.

Ian smiled and focused harder on Jill, who was still standing on the porch, holding a cup of coffee, and gazing in his direction. She disappeared into the house and his phone chirped on his hip. "Hamlin," he said quickly.

"Can you come in, or is that against procedure?" Jill asked.

"I need to stay put. What's up?"

"I..." Jill looked around for some excuse as to why she was calling. She bit her lip and decided to tell the truth. "I just don't want to be alone, I guess."

Ahhh. His heart ached at hearing that. He thought hard about a solution to that problem. Nothing doing. Not until the backup agents arrived to watch the house, because Ian couldn't watch the house from the inside. That would be career suicide and could potentially endanger her further.

"I want to go for a run. Will you be following me?"

"I'd rather you didn't do that." Ian said sternly. "I know I said I wanted you to follow your daily routine, but this guy is unpredictable and I don't have the manpower to follow you right now."

"Can you just talk to me like a human being for

once?" Jill said holding back her tears. "This would be so much easier if you'd just be straight with me. I think I deserve the truth about... everything."

Ian blew out his breath and stared at the now closed blinds. He could hear her quiet sobs over the sudden silence. She must have not wanted him to see her cry. "Did you do your homework?"

"I'm working on it." Jill sniffled lightly. "Anita's coming home to help me and it shouldn't take long."

"We'll talk when you're finished. Do you want a ride to work?"

"Please." Jill wiped her eyes dry, disconnected from Agent Hamlin and headed for the bathroom.

Whiskers skittered at her feet, surprising her as she let out a shriek. "Jesus," she groaned and showered thoroughly. Taking time to wash her hair under the heavy trickle of water that was heavenly compared to their last apartment. While in the shower, she went over every detail in her head about the first phone call that Anita answered. Then she thought about the flowers and the phone call from Sara. Her car getting keyed. Then she thought about Elias and tried to decipher her feelings about whether or not she actually trusted that he was telling her the truth about Sara. And she prayed to god that it was Sara who had threatened her. *An irate female seems a lot easier to handle than a serial killer.*

The suds had just trickled down her face when she heard the creak of the bathroom door. Quickly rinsing the soap from her eyes, she peered at the door that was slightly ajar and tried to reign in her fear. Shivering in the cool air, she pulled the towel from the rack and wrapped it around her breasts without the benefit of drying off first. She stepped from the shower stall and called out for Anita. "Anita? Is that you?" Listening intently, all she heard was the pitter-patter of cat feet on the hardwood floor. She opened the door and saw the tail of Whiskers coming out of her room. "Damned cat," she giggled to herself and took a couple of deep breaths to get a handle on her racing pulse and heightened sense of terror.

When she stepped into her bedroom, which was just left of the bathroom, she stopped and pulled her towel off her breasts and wrapped it tightly around her damp head. The blinds were drawn, so she felt okay enough to cross the bedroom naked. She glanced down at the red spot on her bed and shrieked wildly at the top of her lungs.

What seemed like maybe a second later, she heard the cracking sound of the door being kicked in and Ian was standing in her bedroom doorway with gun drawn, ready to take down the bad guy, or in this case, the dead rat on her bed. "Jesus," Ian quickly turned away at seeing Jill completed naked yet again. "What the fuck?" he groaned and raked his hand through his black hair. His hand that was holding his gun dropped to his side.

Jill's breath finally returned as she grabbed the towel off her head and once again wrapped it around her breasts. "Sorry, It's just a dead mouse." Jill shivered and made a mental note to have the cat killed. She stepped around the bed and stood sternly in front of the man. "Hey, how did you hear me? The windows are all closed." She narrowed her eyes as he turned a deep shade of red. "Oh, hell no!" Her gaze hardened when she realized what had just transpired. Private moments that had been heard by the FBI, her disposition to singing along with the radio, and even the notion that every phone conversation had been eavesdropped on, made her face flush. Anger rose in her belly and she felt more violated than when a bloody nine was painted on her door. "Isn't that a bit unconstitutional, even for the FBI?"

Ian just shrugged it off and kept his eyes focused on her face in fear that he'd actually rip that towel off her breasts and have his way with her like he'd wanted to do since the first day he ever saw her. He stepped around her maddened gaze and grabbed a handful of tissues. Carefully he picked up the rat and disposed of it while Jill quickly pulled on a pair of black shorts and a flowered tank top.

"Hey," Jill stopped him at the front door. "As long as you're here..."

"As long as I'm here, no one's watching the house. I'll be back in half an hour. Be ready." He slammed the door behind him. It flapped a couple of times and he peeked his head back in. "I'll fix this," he said sheepishly and was back across the street before she had time to digest just how damned good he looked today. *Hell, every day.* Jill sighed and went to work on her timeline of creepy events.

Anita arrived ten minutes later and between the two of them, they carefully chronologically defined all the strange happenings down to the last weird phone call.

"Should I mention what happened with Sara?" Jill asked her best friend, whose tummy had just started to pooch slightly. Jill's hand was lightly splayed across the bulge just south of Anita's navel.

"You aren't a hundred percent sure it was the bitch who keyed your car, so I don't think you should accuse the woman. Although, you should mention the phone call she made to you and they can take it from there."

"Okay," Jill added those instances to the long list. "Oh, by the way," She leaned forward and whispered in Anita's ear just in case her bedroom was bugged also.

"They can't fucking do that." Anita was outraged. "Bastards." She yelled out at the ceiling and then squirmed uncomfortably. "Ryan wants me to move in with him. Especially since the door incident. I know you told me not to worry, but hell, I'm scared out of my mind whenever I pull into the driveway and I really don't need the stress, but I don't want to leave you. I really don't. Why don't you come stay too? Ryan said he'd kick out his roommate to make room."

Jill held out her hand to her friend. "I'm fine," she said with a smile. "I want you to move in with him. You two need to start your life together and go shopping and make baby plans. I'm fine. Besides, Will is sort of growing on me. I'm fine."

"You're not fine," Anita growled at the fact that Jill had just said, "I'm fine," three times in the same breath. "You look like you haven't slept in two weeks and you're keeping something from me, aren't you?"

"Okay, so I haven't been sleeping. I'll take a couple of Tylenol PM tonight and I'll be okay."

"I wish you'd tell me what's really going on." Anita begged.

"The walls have ears..." Jill bobbed her brows playfully. "I'll stop by the bar on Friday night and we can talk then. Please don't worry about me. I've just got a lot on my plate right now. "

"Tell me about it." Anita sighed and they embraced tightly.

* * *

Jill waited for Will to come back, said hi, and grabbed her tablet off her nightstand. She had less than two hours before she had to be at the station, plenty of time to get the answers she wanted. Ian was already in the driveway patiently waiting for her to get into his SUV. He thought she looked especially pretty today, but her eyes looked heavy and desperately in need of a good night's sleep. He could relate.

"This is all of it?"

He hadn't even been cordial enough to say hello to the pretty woman.

"I think so." She slid in beside him and gave him the serious look that women often give men when they've forgotten anniversaries or perhaps blown off Valentine's Day. "We need to talk."

"I know. I know." He tossed the notepad onto the dash and grumbled as he headed toward Vancouver Lake just a few blocks from her house. The sun was beating down from the bright blue sky. Not a cloud was in sight today, just like Jill had mentioned on the news the night before. The lake was already packed with people. Kids were splashing in the shallow waves and the air smelled like summer.

She got out first and fastened her hair up in a clip because it was slightly windy down by the water. Ian cased the parking lot before getting out and sliding his gun into the waistband of his denim shorts.

"What do you want to know?" He kicked a rock with his toe and kept his eyes peeled on the myriad of people camped out on the shore.

"Why me?" Jill wondered and felt the panic race through her veins. *This is beginning to feel very real.*

"There have been eight woman killed in the past four years. All those women were between the age of thirty and thirty-four and all those women were named Jill Walker."

Jill almost laughed. *Of all the names I could have chosen as an on-air persona, I had to pick Walker.* "But that's not even my real name. I don't get it. There's nothing else that these women had in common, besides their name?"

"Not that we have been able to find."

Jill stopped walking and wrapped her arms tightly over her chest. "Did they all get numbers too, then?"

Ian shook his head and moved closer. "Not that we know of. This guy is unpredictable. He's not playing by conventional rules. The only thing we've found that remained constant was his method and the time of death."

Jill swallowed hard. Perhaps, she didn't need all the information after all. "I don't want to know." Her eyes filled with tears and she stepped closer to the heat of him.

Ian's gaze dropped to her quivering lips. Control was just moments away from being lost and he could feel it as plainly as he could feel the heat of her breasts rammed against his chest. He tensed and narrowed his gaze on her eyes that were filled with fear and now damp with tears.

"I'm terrified," she gasped and a tear dropped from

each eye. "I can't sleep. I'm barely eating. I won't even let my boyfriend make love to me. It's like I'm already dead."

Ian's breath caught in his throat even at the mere mention of her making love to anyone. He wiped a tear from her eye with his knuckle and she wept harder and reached out to pull him closer.

Ian's reaction was quick. He tensed and moved back to evade her arms.

She wept harder. Outraged by the sting of rejection. "You're such an asshole. Don't you have any emotions at all? I just told you that I was scared out of my mind," she screamed and sank down into the sand at his feet. Sobbing hard and urgently trying to catch her breath.

Ian shook his head with a grimace and dropped down onto his knees in front of her. "What do you want from me?" he asked as breathlessly and as emotionally winded as he felt.

"A hug would be nice." She swiped vigorously at her tears. "I'd even settle for a warm smile and a pat on the shoulder — anything; any tiny indication that you have feelings. You do have feelings right?" Jill reached out and pinched him hard in the arm.

He cringed and grabbed her trembling hand.

"You felt that right? You are fucking human, aren't you?" she gasped. She'd never seen a man scowl so much in her life. He was the brooding type all right; he just stared at her and shook his head slowly as he digested her harsh words.

She ripped her hand out of his grasp and in turn grabbed his. Bringing his hand up to her chest, she placed it solidly over her breast and held it there with bated breath. "Do you feel that? Does that do anything for you? Because this is what you do to me." Her breathing was strained and out of control.

The beat of her heart pounded furiously beneath the rough hand that he now held there by his own volition. "God damn it," he growled and curled his fingers around the soft flesh of her breast, kneading it with a great sense of urgency. A little rougher than she would have liked, but she was trying to make a point, and, by god, it felt good to have his hand on her body. "What do want me to say? Do you want to know that you're all I think about? You're all I know. Right now... you are my life and I have a fucking job to do." He groaned and moved his hand up to wrap around the back of her neck. The tingle of his hand on her naked skin sent her heart into palpitations. Both of his hands were now holding her tightly: One around the back of her neck, the other gripping the ball of her shoulder tightly.

She thought for sure that he was going to bring her face closer, so close that their lips would tangle together in a heated battle of desire, but he was pressing her away, as if he were afraid of what might happen if he got too close.

His hands remained where they were, still holding her tightly at arm's length. His forearms flexed and hard. "I can't protect you if I...."

Jill licked her bottom lip. "What? If you feel something for me? Is that it?" Her voice was soft with need. "I'm not asking for your soul or even your heart. I'm asking for a little compassion. A little comfort. I trust you, Ian. I'm putting my life in your hands and I feel safe with you. Why can't you just open up to me and let me in. Why?" she cried harder when he released her from his grasp.

"Don't you have a boyfriend to comfort you?" His tone reeked of disdain.

Jill glared and stood up to put space between them. She dusted the sand off her shorts and glared at him as he stood up. "What is it with you two? He said you used to be his best friend."

"What else did he say?"

"He said you were a maniac and I shouldn't believe a word that you tell me."

"Oh, that's rich." Ian rolled his eyes and grabbed

her hand. "Let's go."

"Your bedside manner needs a little work," Jill dug her feet into the sand and tugged him back. "Let's try that again."

He was now standing so close again that her perky nipples lightly brushed the taut muscles of his chest.

"Why would Elias say something like that to me? And why did you hit him?" Her breasts pressed harder against his because it felt that exquisite and she was feeling bold.

"Aren't you going to be late for work?" He glared.

Jill looked down at her gold watch and grumbled.

After a ten-minute drive to the station and an argument that lasted the entire way, Jill finally got the infuriating agent to agree to let her drive her own car home from the station. She hated not having her car at home and had insisted until she got her way.

Which was fine with him because Jill's scent and the feeling of having touched her breast was wreaking havoc on his organs; one in particular. How could he not be affected by her little play for attention on the shore? God, how he had wanted to take her in his arms and lay her down beneath him. Every day it was becoming more and more of a struggle to keep his hands to himself, and day after day, it was becoming more and more difficult to talk himself out of falling in love with her. It's the last thing he wanted to do, but the more he got to know her, the more he wanted to know about her. He wanted to learn all sorts of things.

Before he pulled from the lot at the station, he called Will's cell phone and got the results of the blood work.

"Positively sure?" Ian felt the tension mount behind his eye sockets. His mind was once again on the task at hand.

"Absolutely. The blood from the parking structure matched Jill-seven in Whitefish. Which means that he's even more cunning and diabolical than we originally thought. Morrow wants this guy bad. He doesn't want two years to go by again and have this sicko strike out of nowhere again. He thinks its time to up the stakes and set a trap."

"She won't go for it." Ian said adamantly. He felt a certain amount of responsibility for Jill and it wasn't as much as her not going for it, as it was *himself* not going for it. It sounded too risky.

"She doesn't have to. The team in New Haven is looking into female agents who fit her description and they're working on a plan as we speak. The bureau wants this wrapped up before the guy strikes again, or word gets out to the media and some distant relative decides to sue us for wrongful death or some shit like that. I guess the old man is catching a lot of flack over Jill-fours death. Hell, the dumb-ass bureaucrats were the ones who pulled the manpower two years ago, weren't they?"

Ian remembered that all too clearly. The Jill Walkers of the region had been notified, some were helped to relocate for a short while, but Jill-four hadn't wanted to leave her home, or her new job and agreed to be put under surveillance. The FBI had someone on her tail for six months, seven days a week and nothing ever happened so the manpower was pulled and, by god, Ian hadn't been happy about leaving the nice lady. He'd actually become close friends with the woman during his six-month assignment just north of Hartford. She was almost like the big sister that he never had and he even helped her ten-year-old kid learn to hit a fastball.

And over two years later, just a couple of months ago, she was killed and Ian hadn't even had the balls to show up for her funeral. He knew he couldn't look that woman's kid in the eye after letting them both down. God, his chest ached just thinking about her; Jill Annabelle Walker, mother of Jacob Walker, survived by her two sisters Alyssa and Cyndy.

Ian slammed his hands into the steering wheel and swiped the tears from his eyes. "Fuck," he mumbled under his breath and returned to the present. He never wanted to feel that kind of pain ever again for as long as he lived.

Will was rambling on about his kids and his wife and how much he missed them and he was looking forward to this being over and done with.

Ian shook the remaining tears from his fingertips and cleared his throat. "I'll talk to you later, I need to call Pete and see what the hell he's planning."

"I'll be here, and, god, I love my job. Heck, that woman can cook! Have you tasted her minestrone soup? *Whooee*, her boyfriend's a lucky man."

Ian's scowl returned as he disconnected and dialed.

"Morrow," Agent Pete Morrow said from the office in New Haven, Connecticut. "Glad to hear from you. Did you get the results you were looking for?"

"It's not what I wanted to hear, but yeah, I got them. What's this I hear about a sting? Are you serious?" Ian asked.

"We need to make a bold move before he gets bored, or moves on. No one can get a handle on this guy and we don't have a clue as to how he ticks, so it's our best shot."

"I don't want her involved... not at all. In fact, I'd like to ask permission to kidnap her and take her to Brazil with me. We can raise chickens and make thatched skirts for the tourists." Ian chuckled slightly to relieve his pain. "What do you think?"

Pete Morrow got serious with his number one agent. "I think you need to stop blaming yourself. It's not your fault and there's not a damn thing that you could have done differently."

"I could have quit my job and moved into her fucking basement." Ian's tone soured. "I let that little boy down. I let her down and I won't let it happen again. Not to her... *not to this one.*"

"Are you in over your head, Hamlin? Be honest with me, Ian. I need you on this and if your head's in the clouds, you have to let me know."

"I'm fine, sir. My head is just where it should be."

"Glad to hear it. I'll call when we find a good body double for Miss Walker."

Chapter Nine

Jill finally finished up in makeup, but had dropped a smudge of foundation on the arm of her purple suit coat so she headed down the hall to her private dressing room and pulled the door closed behind her. The room was small, but it was functional. There was a small sofa, a desk and mirrors hung on almost every wall. Her outfit for the night was just about perfect, so she knew it would be tough to replace the jacket she had just ruined. Every night, she found that dressing for the evening news was her least favorite part of the nightly routine. She'd recite the weather in her sweatpants if they'd let her.

The closet was just to the right along the mirrored wall and since she usually did her own shopping, she never paid much attention to the extra outfits that had been hanging there. Tonight, she needed one, so she thumbed through them carefully, trying to find the right jacket to match her lilac colored rayon skirt.

The first one she brought out wasn't the right texture and made her hips look wide, so she returned it and grabbed another. She slid it on and when her hand emerged from the sleeve, she noticed the red smudge and brought it closer to her face. At first she thought she must have somehow cut her finger without knowing it, but then she looked down and noticed more drops before screaming bloody murder. Spots of white sparkles danced in front of her eyes before everything faded to black.

* * *

Ian didn't know he had the ability to drive like Jeff Gordon, but he did. He also didn't know what a heart attack felt like, but he was sure he was having one.

Taking the stairwell, because the elevator just wasn't running fast enough for his liking, he jumped three steps at a time until he reached the fourth floor of the Fowler building where Channel 12 broadcasts originated daily.

The door flew open and, so relieved to see him, Jill once again burst into tears and shivered slightly under the jacket that Reed Langley, her producer, had placed around her shoulders.

"Are you okay?" Ian clutched his chest and spoke breathlessly while looking around the room at the officers who had cordoned off her dressing room.

Jill just nodded and moaned quietly.

He did his best to show his humanity and lightly patted her on the top of the head. It's not exactly what she had in mind, but it made her head feel that much better.

He was off to investigate like the cop that he was. Jill sort of liked that about him, but wished he were more like Elias in the hug-giving department. She watched him enter her dressing room and then shuddered as she recalled the slick feeling of the blood on her fingers.

Ian raked his hand through his hair and tried to calm himself before he felt he urge to toss a chair through a window. That would most certainly make him feel better, but he had just been through that with the hotel in Memphis and he needed to save his money rather than continue to replace windows in his wake. He knew he needed to get a handle on his anger one of these days, but today was not the right day. Perhaps after he put a bullet in the killer's head, he'll feel the need to seek counseling for his anger problem.

On the floor in front of him were three different women's blazers that had been laid out on the floor and each one of them had been painted on the back with thick red blood in the shape of the number nine.

"It's fairly fresh," one investigator from the Vancouver police told Ian. The man held a fancy Nikon camera in his hands. "My guess is that it happened in the last hour or two because... well, it was still pretty wet and hadn't had time to dry before he hung them back up."

"Jesus," Ian groaned. "That means that he has access and he was here..." He gazed out the window and into space. "He was here... with her."

The Vancouver Police Department's officers were all growing impatient with the FBI's secrecy about this case. All eyes were on Ian Hamlin as he tried to make sense of it all.

"They must have a list of all personnel who are authorized on this floor, right?" He looked around at the expressions of the officers. "Find me that list. I want to know the name of every person who was here tonight and I want it yesterday."

Detective Jake Whitney offered his services and then took Ian aside. "This is starting to piss me off. Are you ready to tell me what's going on?"

"I'm not at liberty to say." Ian scowled.

"She's pretty shaken. I offered to take her home, but she refused. Said she wasn't leaving until you got here."

"She trusts me," Ian said flatly.

Detective Whitney rocked back on his heels and let out a whoop of stifled laughter.

"If that's what you want to call it. Go right ahead."

Ian glared and left the room without a reply.

* * *

Ian carried Jill into the house once he pulled her car into the garage and closed the door tightly behind them. He'd promised her that she'd have her car, so he left his SUV at the police station and drove her home in her Honda.

He moved passed Will, who was up waiting on the couch, and dropped Jill into the middle of her bed, and then abruptly turned to leave. The intimacy of the moment wasn't doing his aching heart one bit of good.

She caught his wrist with her delicate fingers. "Don't go," she wept quietly. "Please, Ian. Please stay with me."

"I can't protect you like this. Agent Harrison will be out on the couch." He wiggled out of her grasp and patted her hand lightly. "Do you want me to call Anita?"

"No," Jill said adamantly. "She doesn't need to know anything about this."

"I'd call Elias for you, but I'd rather slit my wrists." He barked and left without another word.

Jill cried quietly and felt more alone than she ever had in her life. It was only Thursday night, so she still had another day of work before she could get away for the weekend, and run away is what she intended on doing.

Elias had suggested spending the weekend at his penthouse in Seattle and, since he'd recently kicked Sara to the curb, he was ready to let Jill see where he spent the majority of his time.

Jill was looking forward to it more than ever because, again, Ian had shown that he's just not capable of throwing her a bone of any kind and that was starting to make her heart ache. At least when she was with Elias, her heart didn't ache on a daily basis. Perhaps it was because she didn't feel the same intense, excruciatingly passionate waves of emotion that she felt for Ian. But she still felt something for Elias and he was comforting.

Her tears dampened her pillow slightly and made a salty pool for her cheek to rest in as she closed her eyes and prayed for a peaceful night's sleep.

* * *

Two hours later, after a phone call and a couple cups of bad coffee, Ian watched a car pull in behind him. He got out, went to the driver's side window, and peered in.

"Thanks for coming," he said to agents Hardy and Reynolds of the Portland office. They were usually the day guys, but Jill's pleas for comfort had made his heart hurt since he'd slammed her door and marched out to the van.

He let himself in through the back door, after calling Will and telling him to open it up for him. Will sank back down on the couch to finish the chore of cleaning his gun. "What's up?" Will's curiosity was piqued by his partner's strange plea to be let into the house.

"How's she doing? Did she eat anything?" Ian's concern added to Will's curiosity even more.

"She hasn't come out of her room. I gave her a bottle of sleeping pills last night to take the edge off and I think she used them tonight. She's out like a light." Will smirked. "Sorry, I ate all the soup. You want a sandwich?"

Ian shook his head and headed toward Jill's room.

"I knew it." Will frowned at his partner. "Your head ain't right, man." Will's head shook from side to side. "This isn't personal, Hamlin. It's business and you have to get it together. What is it with this one?"

Ian dropped his chin to his chest and sighed before moving over and sinking down on the chair just across from Will's sofa bed. He was beyond overwrought. "When I was seventeen I saw her for the first time." He looked toward her closed bedroom door. "From my window. She was undressing in the house of my best friend next door. I'd never seen anything like it. I never got to meet her ... my so-called best friend wouldn't let me to go into his house. A week later, she up and moved out. I saw her about six months later on the beach and it was like fate slapping me in the face. I finally had my shot at meeting the most beautiful girl I had ever seen and I blew it. I stood there, just feet in front of her and froze. I didn't know what to say and she was so damn pretty I just walked away." Ian looked over at Will's agape expression and actually smiled. A wide smile that brightened his eyes and made his left cheek pucker slightly. "I've thought about her ever since and then I woke up in Memphis and I saw her face on TV. At first, I didn't fully recognize who she was. I just remembered her name was Jill and then it all snowballed from there."

"So, how'd you know it was her?" Will's eyes were glassy. Intrigued by his partner's confession.

"I went home to see my mom and I was just looking out the window and it came to me. It was like I was seventeen again and it just hit me. I still can't believe that after all this time, I'm here... in her living room." Ian looked around the house with a sappy expression that Will recognized right away.

"Dude!" Will exhaled and leaned back against the back of the sofa. "Are you in love with her?"

"Dude," Ian balked. "I don't even know her," he said, but he did know her and he knew he could never have her.

Will's head shook in astonishment. "Wow."

"That's not all of it." Ian smirked. "Her boyfriend... you know, the big blonde guy..."

"Yeah," Will said on the edge of his seat.

"He was that so-called best friend." Ian confessed and watched the color run from his partner's face.

"No!"

"Shhhh," Ian said and stood to do what he came in the house to do.

Her head was sunk down in her pillow, a puddle of drool pooled at the corner of her mouth, and the bottle of sleeping pills on her nightstand said a lot about the condition she was in when Ian sank down beside her in her bed. She'd fallen asleep in her skirt and a rayon tanktop that snuggled her breasts perfectly. It seemed every piece of clothing she wore was made just for her.

She hadn't even flinched when Ian sank down beside her, or even changed her breathing pattern. She was out for the count, so Ian felt comfortable snuggling in behind her and holding her close. For the first night in god knows how long, he actually slept soundly and at ease, knowing that nothing would happen to her. How could something happen? His arms were wrapped tightly around her waist and there was no space between his front side and her adorable backside. Ian made sure of that before he closed his eyes for the night.

* * *

Jill woke up alone in bed, but the scent of Ian lingered in her bedroom. At first she thought she was dreaming. In fact, she was positive because her dreams had been filled with nothing but Ian. Ian saving her life, Ian making her pancakes, even Ian raking the autumn leaves from the front yard. She shivered and hoped that she'd be alive to see autumn and its amazing colors. She inhaled deeply a couple of times and liked the scent that her nose was taking in. It was nothing short of heavenly.

"Hello," she grabbed the phone on the second ring. "It's fine. I'm awake." She sat up straight. "I'm good. How are you?" Jill's mind hadn't caught up with the realization that Elias's mother was calling.

"Elias just informed me that you'll be in Seattle this weekend and I was due for a visit. I was sort of hoping we could get together for lunch one day." Donna Webber said.

"I'd like that, Donna." Jill brushed the hair from her eyes. "I'm really sorry about that phone call. I hope I didn't startle you."

"It's fine, dear. Elias told me everything. I'll see you this weekend then."

"I'm looking forward to it." Jill said and then disconnected with a smile. She remembered certain things about Donna Swenson. Or rather Donna Webber. Mostly that the woman had kind eyes and was very involved in her charity work and doted on Dick Swenson every minute that she could. Jill remembered them as a very affectionate couple. Dick had been a widower for five years when he married Donna and it was as if she were his first young love, the way they held hands and kissed in the kitchen. It just made it that much more painful when news of Dick and Tanya's death rocked the household. Jill wished she could have been stronger and had been able to at least console Donna in the way that she wanted to. But it just wasn't possible. Tanya had meant so much to Jill, that spending just that one night in the house without the little girl was painful beyond words. So Jill packed up and left the next morning without as much as a goodbye to Elias or to Donna. Boy, she had regretted that day for so long. Now, fate was stepping in to help her heal old wounds and make amends with Dick's widow.

* * *

After spending the night tightly curled up with the unknowing Jill, Ian felt strangely uncomfortable about seeing her the next day. He kept his distance and took the day shift at the house, while Reynolds and Hardy followed her to the supermarket, her dentist appointment to have her teeth whitened and then straight to the television station. He hadn't heard a peep from her all day until his phone rang at six-thirty just as the primetime nightly news ended.

"Hamlin," he replied in his cop-tone.

"Hi," Jill said meekly. "I've decided to head to Seattle right after the late report tonight and I'd much rather drive up with you than drive alone."

"What? Elias doesn't have the common sense to come and get you."

"Hey, lay off. It's obviously you two don't get along and I'm sick of hearing about this bitter rivalry you have going." Jill snapped. Elias had already given her an earful this morning when he called to change their plans for the weekend. She was more inclined to believe what Elias was spewing because he was the only one doing any talking.

"What? I've barely said a goddamn thing about the guy. Hell, you know nothing about it."

"I know you bashed up his BMW after graduation." Jill retorted and waited for a response. "That's what I thought," she said when she heard the heaving breathing. For the life of her, she couldn't figure out why Ian was always so angry. He was just one big mystery; a mystery that she looked forward to solving in every way.

Ian's eyes popped open with rage and a twinge of humiliation. He hadn't been proud of that fact, but he couldn't take his actions back. Besides, Elias deserved it.

"So, you want me to drive you to Seattle at one in the morning?"

"*Please?*"

"Jill," Ian got over his pity party real quick and got serious. "Do you trust Elias?"

The silence at this point took Ian by complete surprise. He'd expected to get lectured, or yelled at, but she said nothing. "Jill," he said carefully.

"What?" she snapped viciously. "He's a good man and I like the way he hugs."

"You didn't answer my question."

"I don't like it when people hold out on me." She meant to direct that towards him, but it also pertained to her sometimes-puzzling boyfriend. "Elias wasn't honest with me about something, but he's a good man."

"I still would rather have you here in town where I can keep an eye on you."

"I can't stay here," Jill began. "It's fine during the week because I have work to look forward to, but I can't for the life of me sit in my living room and stare at my four walls. I'll go insane."

"Fine," Ian groaned. "I'll pick you up at one."

He disconnected and his phone immediately chirped again. "Hamlin."

"Hey, I'm at the airport. My wife's in the hospital with appendicitis." Will said breathlessly.

"Ah man, I'm sorry." Ian felt for his partner. "When will you be back?"

"Morrow said I'm done. They've got a body double and, for now, you're the man. He wants you to, and I quote, 'move into her basement'," Will chuckled lightly. "I swear, that's exactly what Pete said. Is this some sort of personal joke?"

If it was a joke, it wasn't fucking funny. "Ha, ha," Ian growled.

"Be cool, man, and I'll call you to let you know how her surgery goes."

Well, if that didn't just make his day that much more difficult. Jill was headed to his archenemy's for the weekend and his partner had just left him to play nursemaid to his ill wife and Mr. Mom to his four kiddos. "That's just great," Ian moaned and headed to the hotel for what could possibly be the last good night's sleep he'd have for god knows how long.

* * *

Traffic at one a.m. was a breeze. Such a breeze that Ian got comfortable behind the wheel of his rented SUV and hit the cruise control as they took off down the freeway headed north. Jill was nestled in by his side. Lionel Richie was softly playing on the stereo and, if life were good, Jill

180

would be resting her head on his shoulder, with her hand gently grazing his lap and he wouldn't be headed to Seattle to drop her off at the hands of Elias Fucking Webber.

Jill noticed the scowl just as Ian pulled onto the freeway. She knew this wasn't easy on him, having her out of eyesight for the entire weekend, but she needed to get some distance and put some space between her quivering loins and the man that induced them to do so. Looking over at him, she gave him a small smile. "I really appreciate this."

"It's fine. I'm usually up watching the house at this hour anyway. I might as well be doing something constructive... like driving you to see the love of your life."

Jill's jaw dropped, then she closed it tightly and pursed her lips. It wasn't really any of Agent Hamlin's business whether or not Elias was the love of her life. "That's very civil of you." Jill stared at the side of his face. Even in the dark she could see the frown lines that curled around his eyes. Even when she first saw him as young man, she had noticed that uneven scowl looked more at ease on his rugged face than a smile. "Can I ask you a question?" Jill wanted to pass the time. That and she felt darn curious about what Elias had said on the phone.

Ian glanced at her, looked down at her hands that were gripping her denim shorts in a tight knuckle grasp. He figured it had to do with the serious nature of what had brought them together, so he nodded.

Jill took a deep breath and remembered that Elias had warned her not to believe anything that the man had to say. "Why did you do it?"

Ian shot her a quick glance and reigned in his temper. He hadn't wanted to lash out at Jill, but he'd been waiting to beat the shit out of Elias Webber since the day of their high school graduation. "He didn't tell you?" Ian said, not at all surprised that the scumbag would offer the truth. Not when it would make *god's gift to women* seem like a world-class asshole.

181

"He mentioned something." Jill stared out the window and then continued when Ian refused to speak again. "He said that you were always jealous of the things he got and you just snapped one day because you were always so angry about everything. He said it wasn't his fault that his dad was rich and gave him everything he ever wanted. You just couldn't handle it anymore so you bashed in his car. He said you totaled it."

Ian's jaw tightened. "I did total it."

"So -- is that why?" Jill pushed it again. "Because you were jealous?"

"Is that what you think happened?" Ian asked her with a smirk.

"I don't know what happened. That's why I'm asking you. Do you ever break out of that cop-mode and talk like a normal human being?"

Ian blew out an exasperated breath, but remained silent.

After a few minutes, Jill spoke again. "Did you know that I used to live with him when I was younger?"

Ian's hands tightened on the steering wheel. Obviously, she would have known from talking to her boyfriend that he lived in the house next door. "Did he say I knew?"

"Oh, for Christ sake! Did you or did you not know that I once lived at Elias's house when he was seventeen. You're not on trial here, I'm just making conversation."

"Yes. All right. I remember you." Ian shouted and remained staring out the window so she wouldn't see the look of longing and adoration in his eyes.

Jill watched the side of his face with astonishment. "How come you never said anything? What is it with you two?"

Ian sat quietly until he comprehended what she had said. "You mean he never told you that he knew you back then?"

"No." Jill bellowed. "He didn't tell me, just like you

didn't tell me." Her arms crossed tightly in front of her chest.

"So - *what?*" Ian said a bit flustered as he tried to piece the information together. "He just happened to bump into you on the street one day and now you're going out with him?"

"It was a bar," Jill offered. "He bumped into me at the bar where Anita works. But he never mentioned that he knew me. I found out when I went to Sequim and I saw a picture of him and his mother."

"Donna," Ian said.

"Yes, a picture of him and Donna and then it just came to me, as if I had blocked it all out or something."

"So, what was his explanation about not telling you?"

"He said he thought the memory of Tanya would make me sad."

"Oh," Ian said flatly. He swallowed hard and clenched his jaw, getting ready for his declaration of guilt. "I saw you on TV," he confessed finally and turned down Lionel Richie to have a serious heart to heart with Jill-nine. "How well do you know him? I mean...I don't want sexually graphic details. I want to know what you know about his life and how long you've been dating." *This is going to be one long drive to Seattle*, Ian thought.

Jill relaxed and sank back in her seat. "I ran into him shortly after I was on the air and we've been together ever since. I know he has a house in Sequim and a penthouse in Seattle. He's an international banker who loves expensive cars, and I know that his ex is a bit unstable."

"Oh," Ian's jaw clenched again. "How so?"

"I wrote it all down on that sheet for you. Didn't you read it?"

He slammed his palm against his forehead. He'd bugged her and bugged her about doing it and then he had handed it straight to Will and told him to run with it.

Damn! My follow-through sucks. "I gave it to Will."

"Oh, well... if you had read it you would have read about the time I got the threatening phone calls and then the reason I returned early from the beach is because she called me and told me to get out of her bed and leave her fiancé alone. I think she was the one who keyed my car."

Ian just about drove off the side of the road. "Jesus!" He straightened out and steadied his breath.

Jill clutched the dash and sent him a glare. "Do you think there might be something to that?"

"Sara's always been a bit emotionally unstable, but I can't see her doing anything illegal."

Jill's head just about spun around in a complete circle. "How did you know her name was Sara? Elias said he hasn't spoken to you since the day you trashed his car back in high school." Her eyes narrowed fiercely.

Ian knew his mistake as soon as he opened his big mouth. He really didn't want to lie to her, so he kept his mouth shut and concentrated on the dark road in front of him.

"Jesus," Jill muttered under her breath. "You two are like two peas in a frigging pod. I can't get a goddamned straight answer to save my life. What? Did you happen to hear me talk about the psycho bitch while you were eavesdropping on my life?" Jill huffed. "I don't appreciate that by the way. In fact I hate it. I don't have any privacy and I can't even open my blinds anymore because you are always there. Watching me through binoculars." Tears welled in her eyes.

Ian didn't care that he'd most likely get a ticket or ram the guardrail; he pulled across all three lanes on the freeway and screeched to a halt alongside the dark road. He turned on her and leaned closer. "You don't like it, huh? Well you sure as hell didn't hold back in Sequim. You knew I was out there in the lawn."

"Oh... you are so arrogant."

"*Me?* I'm not the one who peeled off my clothes

and then opened the door to give the world a peak at my perfect nakedness. That was you. I think you liked that I was watching you."

"You're a freak!" Jill shouted. "I took off my clothes because I was sopping wet and I opened the door because I happen to love thunder and lightning. It excites me."

"I could see that." He looked down at her nipples and actually grinned at her. Her breath caught in her throat. She was so attracted to him that it hurt and when he smiled, the attraction doubled. "What about the window then?" Ian's voice grew husky. "You can't explain standing naked in front of that window, now can you."

"Bite me." She snarled and let out a playful giggle. The silence became insufferable but soon laughter broke out and hearing Ian Hamlin laugh was like music to her ears. In fact, it actually brought tears to her eyes.

"God, you scared the shit out of me that day." She started laughing too about the fact that Ian had seen her naked. "When that bolt lit up the sky and I saw you run by me, I just about lost bladder control." She laughed harder, reached out, and touched his thigh. The denim of his jeans was rough against her fingers, but he was warm and solid and she just wanted to touch him.

Ian stilled from the firm heat of her hand, and then cleared his throat. "I really am sorry. I had no idea that you were going to run into the house, strip down naked and then open the door. I couldn't believe my luck." He chuckled and gave her hand a squeeze. He felt comfortable with Jill; probably more comfortable with her than anyone he'd ever met. Suddenly, it was as if he wanted her to see his soft side. The awkward laughter stopped and they gazed at each other for what seemed like an eternity. His hand was hot on hers and it felt nice. *Nice and safe.* "See, I'm not that bad am I?" Ian brought her hand up to his lips and gave it a soft lingering kiss before releasing it from his clutch.

Jill buried her face in her hands. "Oh god, you heard everything I said that night? I didn't mean it. I was just angry." She felt true remorse for the night she went on and on about his lack of humanity, sitting there in her living room airing her frustrations to his partner of all people.

"It's okay. I know I'm a piece of work. My father tells me that all the time."

Jill smiled, fondly remembering the few times that she'd visited with Lily and Mitch Hamlin back when she lived with Donna and Dick Swenson. "How are your mom and dad?" Jill asked when she got her breathing back under control. Feeling his lips against her skin had sent a jolt of prickles straight to her happy place. *Just imagine what the man could do if he actually kissed my lips.* Jill quivered at the thought.

"You met my parents?" Ian groaned, in recollection that again, he was the only one who hadn't spoken to Jill all those years ago. "I can't believe you met my parents, and yet I was forbidden to set foot anywhere near you."

"By who?" Jill scoffed.

"Oh, he failed to mention that part too?" Ian's face tightened. Elias had said on more than one occasion that Ian wasn't invited in to meet the pretty nanny. Ian thought it was odd at the time, but *not-so-fondly* remembered other times in their friendship that they'd been crazy about the same girl. Besides, Elias had pretty much been living with Ian since his mother remarried anyway because he was so angry that his father's wishes of coming back had been denied time and time again by his mom. "Your boyfriend said and I quote, 'she's off limits.'"

"Nut-uh." Jill gasped. "Why would he say that?"

Ian just shrugged in lieu of an explanation and was mildly happy that they had almost reached their destination. That meant that he was once again saved from having to rehash his painful past. He slowed as he took the

off-ramp into downtown Seattle and then took Spencer
Avenue right to the front of Elias Webber's building.
"Well. It's been interesting."

Jill looked up the front of the tall building and
shivered. She would have much rather driven all the way
back home with Ian and tried to keep their conversation
going, but he got out and slammed his door and the easy
exchange released by that moment of levity came to a
crashing halt.

"Don't go anywhere alone. Don't stand too close to
the windows. Don't go to the bathroom alone. Don't..."

"Jesus, Ian. Relax." Jill smiled and grabbed her bag.
"I'll tell him you said hi." She grinned and entered the
building with an extra spring in her step.

Chapter Ten

Elias wasn't home when Jill made it up to the top
floor with the doorman, who kindly unlocked the door for
her and carried up her small travel bag. The penthouse was
grossly excessive in every way. Right down to the lights that
were motion activated. She took her time getting to know

her surroundings and, much to her pleasure, there wasn't a single sign of a woman's presence anywhere to be found. The place was white and lacked any décor that she found interesting. It definitely could use a woman's touch, a splash of color here and there and of course some window coverings.

She smiled when she opened the cabinet and found her favorite lotions, bath beads and a couple of vanilla scented candles. They were all unused and unopened and the man got points for doing his homework and paying attention to details. The way she was feeling after her drive up with the ever-so-sexy Ian Hamlin had tingling already. *Elias may even get lucky, that is if he hurries home and gets here before the sleepiness sets in.*

She changed into her silky pajamas and helped herself to a glass of wine before slipping under the covers of Elias's massive king-size bed. The sheets weren't satin as she had expected, but they were the softest cotton that her thighs had ever felt. It was like gliding on silk.

Jill let her heavy eyelids close and, once again, entered her dreams where Ian was waiting for her. She tried to ignore the no-faced man who would pop into her thoughts when she was awake, but it was harder to do when she closed her eyes. At times, all she could think about was some stranger catching her off guard. Usually she kept her wild imagination at bay, but at night, her fear sometimes took over. Her dreams took her to places she didn't want to go, so she tried hard to keep Ian in her mind. She was doing a pretty good job this particular night, so when she felt the warm slide of a hand up her naked thigh, she rolled over, yet kept her eyes tightly closed to appreciate the erotic fantasy transpiring in her mind. "Hey," she moaned with a hint of sensuality.

"Hey, yourself." He kept his hand tight around the contour of her hip, and then slid it under the fabric of her lace panties.

* * *

Jill woke up with a smile and felt invigorated after a good night's sleep and a lot of lovemaking. However, her smile did fade slightly when she rolled over and looked at Elias. Her dreams and fantasies had seemed so real that she expected to wake up this morning with Ian, not Elias. "Morning," she grumbled and sat up, pulling the covers demurely to her naked breasts.

"You were a tomcat last night. I'm guessing it was the wine." He bobbed his eyebrows and glanced over at the half empty bottle of merlot.

Jill blushed slightly and looked over at the clock that read eleven a.m. "Aren't we supposed to be meeting your mom in an hour?" Jill looked him directly in the eye and felt an overwhelming sense of guilt for making love to the man while thinking about another. *Elias didn't deserve this.* He deserved her love and her undivided attention. He was a good man. Not a perfect man, like she had previously thought, but a good man just the same.

"I'll be quick." Elias pulled her into his arms and she felt the stab of his morning erection against her hip. He nuzzled under her neck and then released her when she fidgeted around beneath him.

"Do you want me to make coffee?" She couldn't offer Elias her love so she compromised and offered fresh Columbian coffee instead.

"No. Why don't you make a bath and I'll make the coffee." He stood up and walked around the bed. His erection was quite impressive, along with the rest of his body, but Jill focused on his handsome face. "I'll be in to join you in a minute." He grazed her lips lightly and gave her a quick smack on the bottom.

Jill smelled the magnificent aroma of expensive gourmet coffee as Elias pushed open the bathroom door holding a cup of coffee in each hand and a tiny black box between his teeth. Jill's heart leapt into her throat. She wasn't ready for this. Even if she was ready for marriage, kids, and a house in the suburbs, she wasn't ready to give her life completely to Elias. Not yet. The idea had potential but it was too soon. *What about Ian? What about fate?* She swallowed hard and took a cup of coffee from him with trembling hands as he sank down under the bubbles.

He drew her closer and nudged his erection into the space between her legs. Jill shifted uncomfortably and waited with clenched teeth, but he didn't enter her just yet. Instead, he opened the little black box in front of her face.

Jill's eyes welled with tears. Not because she was moved by the large princess cut diamond that shimmered brightly and not because she was so happy that he was proposing. The tears were from pain. The pain of finding a wonderful man who gives great hugs. A man who was sensitive and kind and yet she just couldn't bring herself to love him. The ache stung deep.

"I know it's probably too soon, and I know you have lots of things going on in that pretty little head of yours, but I have it all worked out. You can come live with me here and you'll never have to work another day in your life. You can shop and get manicures and travel with me on business trips.... I love you, Jill and I want you to be my wife. Will you marry me?"

Why, God? Why? Jill gasped and sent him a small smile.

He slipped the ring on her finger and the fit was perfect. "I don't want you to say anything just yet. Please, Jill, just think about it."

Not work? Is the man insane? He doesn't know me at all. How could he not know how much I love what I do? That I've worked my whole life to get where I'm at and he wants me to give it all up and go shopping every day. I hate shopping. Jill shook her head at the thought and then did the unthinkable and let Elias have his way with her once again, while she thought about Ian's sexy scowl.

* * *

Elliot's Chowder House was where they met Elias's mother for lunch. Warm hugs were exchanged and then

Elias's phone rang and he took off for a quiet table while Jill and Donna talked of old times, good times, and sad times.

"So, you two just bumped into each other after all these years?" Donna sipped her chardonnay and sat back to let the sun warm her face. The temperature had already reached the day's projected high and it was barely noon.

"Yep. In Portland and then here in Seattle." Jill realized how odd that was and sat up a bit straighter, looking over at Elias on the phone and pondering the odds of that happening. "Small world I guess." She sipped some wine and fixed her gaze on Donna.

Donna looked out at the Sound with a sparkle of tears in her eyes from remembering the loss of her husband and stepdaughter. She looked fondly at Elias on the phone and then back to Jill.

Jill smiled warmly and sipped more wine before looking out over the water and realizing that, for the first time in many days, she felt okay about being outside and exposed to strangers. It was a nice feeling, but she also realized that she missed Ian.

She cleared her throat. "Do you ever talk to Lily Hamlin? If I remember you two were pretty close friends."

"Sure, Lily and I still talk. We see each other a couple times a year." Donna scowled over at Elias still yapping on the phone. "It's just a damned shame that those boys don't grow up and get past their differences. They were inseparable from the day they were born. Did everything together..." She sighed heavily. "Elias was always so jealous of Ian. Sometimes he'd watch Ian and his father outside playing football. It broke my heart. He was such an angry kid."

"Who? Ian?" Jill could see that. Even a blind person could see the rage in that man's eyes.

"Well, him too," Donna chuckled. "But I was talking about Elias. He was so hurt when his father left that something inside him just snapped. He screamed and yelled at me when I married Dick. He said I was ruining his life because he thought Donald was coming back some day. He just kept yelling that his daddy was coming back and I had done the unthinkable and married another man. I'd never seen anything like it. The pain behind his eyes was sort of unnerving because he'd always been such a quiet boy."

"He's a wonderful man." Jill soothed. "He's never been anything but sweet and gentle with me. I can't imagine him in a huff, much less screaming." Then Jill thought back to when he had discovered her and the pile of photos on his bed in Sequim. He most certainly had rage behind his eyes that night. And then there was the night that Ian had punched him in the face. He got a bit grabby that night. "Hmm. I don't remember him much, but he did seem sort of quiet to me when I lived with you." Jill looked over at Elias again. "I'm really sorry about leaving the way I did. I wanted to tell you how sorry I was for your loss, but it was just too painful." Jill had finally made her apology after all these years.

"It's fine, sweetie," Donna said sadly. "I know how much Tanya meant to you, and I know she sure loved you. She liked calling you Mom, didn't she?"

"Yeah." Jill smiled in recollection of Tanya's bright smile and curly red hair. "She was so sweet."

"It's a shame that they never found out who did it." Donna's eyes welled with tears once again. The loss back then was unbearable, but she had managed over the years to find happiness again. It's always hard to lose a spouse, but she honestly hadn't thought too much about Dick in the past couple of years. She had a new man in her life and she didn't like dwelling on the painful past. *Life is just too short*, in Donna's opinion.

Jill's head began to spin. "Did what?" Jill stammered, sitting up straighter in her chair. Muscles clenched. She could only speculate as to what Donna was talking about.

"Oh, dear," Donna muttered. "You left before they found out what caused the accident. I'm sorry, honey. It wasn't an accident. Someone had cut Dick's brake line."

Jill felt like someone had punched her in the stomach. The air from her lungs left with an exaggerated whoosh. All color ran from her face and that's when Elias came back and pressed a kiss against the side of her head. "What did I miss? Did you show Mom the ring?"

Donna smiled and wiped the tears from her eyes. "You're getting married?"

Elias nodded, but Jill shook her head with a painful frown. "I don't know yet."

"She will. I'm sure of it," he winked and Jill felt even sicker, if that was possible. "What is it, babe?"

"I'm not feeling too good. Can you take me home?"

* * *

Jill's head hit the pillow and she wanted to curl up in a ball and cry. Cry for Tanya and cry because all day all she could think about was some sick fuck wanting to kill her. Elias's warm hugs weren't enough to keep her feeling safe anymore. He crawled in beside her and gave her a kiss, once again nudging her with his eager erection.

She rolled away from him and sat up, still going over what Donna had told her about Elias and Ian no longer being friends and why Ian had punched him. She wanted answers and since Ian wasn't offering to fill in the gaps, she'd just have to work on Elias some more. "Was that the only reason that Ian trashed your car?"

"Jesus," he growled and dropped his head into his pillow. "Can we not talk about Ian right now. It's history."

"I just don't get it. If it were my car that got trashed, I'd want to hit the guy, not the other way around. Why weren't you the one throwing punches? Is there something more to the story?"

"I already told you," he sat up abruptly and

narrowed his eyes. For only the third time since she'd known the man, he looked angry. "He's been filling your head with his lies, am I right?"

Jill shrugged. She knew she could probably bluff her way through this interrogation. Play man against man, so to speak.

"I told you, he's just jealous and he'll stop at nothing to get between us. Please don't listen to his lies. He's just jealous and he's out for revenge."

Jill's eyes narrowed. "Revenge for what?"

Elias let out his breath. "It wasn't my fault. She came on to me. She said she wanted something better than he had to offer. I swear it wasn't my fault."

Ah ha. Jill chuckled lightly. "He trashed your car because of a girl." She had a hard time believing that one. That would mean that Ian Hamlin actually was capable of those kinds of warm fuzzy feelings. *Perhaps he is human after all.*

Elias pulled her into his arms. *That was a close call. She bought it and twisted it into what she believed happened and that was that. No further explanation required.* "Please don't let him come between us. I love you Jill and I want you..." He pressed her down onto the bed under him and nuzzled her ear. "And I always get what I want."

Jill succumbed once again to Elias and his wishes, but her mind remained on Ian. *If a man could be that passionate about a girl in high school, just imagine how much passion he might possess as a man.* She quivered under Elias and once again kept her eyes closed tightly.

* * *

Elias woke from his catnap around four p.m. Jill was nowhere to be seen. He lifted his weary head and shouted out to her. "Sweetie," he called and then picked up the phone that began ringing by his side. "Dad," he groaned. "I told you I'll call you tomorrow."

Jill emerged from the kitchen draped in his long

oxford shirt and nothing else. She carried a glass of water in one hand and a bowl of red grapes in the other. He gave her a wink and kissed the tip of her upturned nose. "Dad, I've got company. I can do this tomorrow."

Donald Webber wasn't a man that you say no to. Even when you are his son and CEO of the man's company. "I'm headed to New York and I want this wrapped up today," Donald demanded. "You should have called the broker this morning, first thing. I want this property and I'm going to get it." After all Donald Webber was the original poster child for getting what you want. Ever since Elias was old enough to speak, Donald had instilled in the young man that he could have anything his heart desired as long as he had the balls to do what it takes to make it happen. *Anything is possible; you just have to want it bad enough.* Elias had literally lived by his father's words every day of his life. If he wants it, he gets it. Just like his father had always said.

"Fine, I'll be there in ten minutes," Elias growled and disconnected before reaching for his Dockers. "I'm sorry honey, I have to go into the office for a bit. My old man gets what he wants after all."

"I thought you were a banker," Jill said with suspicious eyes. "Banks aren't open on Saturday. What's the dang deal?"

Elias blushed slightly and realized his mistake and the little fib he had told the day he met her. "Please don't be angry. It's not that big of a deal, but I have a little confession to make. I'm not a banker."

Jill's body tensed, but she remained calm and kept her heart rate below one-forty. "And you couldn't tell me this because... you're a secret agent and you were protecting me from Russian spies." She said with disdain, clearly appalled that once again he had lied.

"That's a good one — but no," Elias sank down beside her on the bed. "I'm sorry. I'm the CEO of Webber Software and that was my father, founder and pain in my ass. I never meant to lie to you."

Webber Software was about as big as Microsoft. And Jill knew all about the company. Their products were everywhere. Hell, the computer she used at work was loaded with their software and world-renowned technology.

"Why didn't you just tell me that?"

"I was taking a different approach. I've been burned a couple of times by gold-diggers and I wanted to know that you liked me for me, not for my position. I just had to make sure," he said with feeling.

"Then you should have told me you were a grade school teacher for the blind and deaf." Jill said sternly.

"That wouldn't really explain the Porsche and the house in Sequim, now would it?" He cocked a brow.

Jill let out an exasperated groan. "I guess not." She was pretty irritated, but only slightly. Just irritated enough to pull on her clothes and hand Elias his shirt back.

He took it with sad eyes and dropped jaw.

"I'm not going anywhere," Jill said. "Relax. I'm not a bit happy that you lied, but it makes sense and, besides, there's a serial killer who wants to take a whack at me, so I'm really in no hurry to rush home." She gave him a quick kiss and he enveloped her in his arms once again.

"Please move in here with me. The security is the best in the city and we'll be happy. I'll hire you a private Jean Claude Van Damme and you'll be safe here with me. Please?" he pouted.

"I can't, Elias. I love my job, I love my house and I love my life."

He grumbled and was out the door without another word.

* * *

Ian finally had a good night's sleep under his belt by Sunday morning and that made him less irritable about the fact that Jill still wasn't home. He rolled over in bed and looked out her bedroom window. He knew it probably was inappropriate and a bit immoral to have spent the night sleeping in her bed, but he couldn't help it. He missed her and her scent was driving him mad.

Anita had moved the rest of her things over to her fiancé's house, so her room had been cleared of all her belongings and her bed. Anita was thrilled to hear that Ian was moving in and that she didn't have to worry about Jill's stalker any more. Ian hadn't realized that Anita was still in the dark about the serial killer scenario, but he kept his cool and tried to keep their conversation light in nature. Just like Jill –had always done, he was coddling the pregnant Anita. As for the reason Ian chose to sleep in Jill's bed – well ... he hated the couch. The couch was too squishy and uncomfortable to sleep on, and Jill's scent was like a foghorn calling him home.

He nuzzled his nose into her pillow once again before kicking the covers off and stretching. Judging by the stiff erection he had going on this morning, he'd been thinking about her all night. Probably imagining her in bed with him. In her bed. Surrounded by her stuff. Stuff that was so intrinsically Jill that it made his heart flutter in his chest.

He'd enjoyed their drive up to Seattle so much that their conversation had played over and over in his mind all weekend. He had really started getting to know her on that three-hour drive. He knew that she was an exhibitionist at heart. He knew that she loved her job more than anything and had worked hard to get to where she was. He knew that her scent was intoxicating and that she made the cutest damn chipmunk sound when she was embarrassed and he knew what her laughter sounded like. Genuine laughter that filled his ears and warmed his heart. He knew that he hated that he could never have her more than he hated imagining her making love to Elias Fucking Webber and furthermore, Ian knew that he missed her.

The fact that he was moving into her house

probably should have been mentioned on the drive to Seattle, but he had been distracted by her incessant questions and, of course, her natural beauty. So he failed to mention that when she got back from Seattle, she would begin sharing every minute of every day with him. He could only hope that she likes the idea, because Agent Teri Wyatt, undercover body double, would soon be in Vancouver and the surveillance van had been pulled from the neighborhood so that, once everything was in place, the killer would hopefully, build up a false sense of security and make a move. For the next week or two it was just going to be Ian and Jill. Together, alone in that house where he was supposed to remain and stay out of sight, as if he were a ghost sent there to watch over her. It was the FBI's best shot at finally nabbing the guy. Ian, for one, was all for it.

* * *

Jill couldn't help the intense feeling of panic, loss and disappointment when Elias pulled his Porsche into her driveway and neither the FBI van nor Ian's Ford Explorer were parked on the street, or even around the corner from her house. It sort of made her uneasy as she grabbed for the door handle with a shaking hand.

"You sure you don't want to drive straight back to Seattle with me right now?" Elias said sternly, gripping her wrist tightly. The sun had just started its descent behind the horizon and he hated leaving her, especially since her life was in danger and he had to head to Chicago to close a major deal. "You say the word and I'll take you away from here. How's the Four Season's in Chicago sound? Or a two-week sailing trip around the San Juan's?" He smiled. At least he tried.

"No, I have to work, but I appreciate the offer." She leaned over the console and gave him a quick kiss. "Walk me in?"

"Of course," he turned off the ignition and grabbed her bag from the backseat. Jill had to laugh when she looked at his hair, which had been seriously ruffled from the windy ride back to Vancouver with the top down. "What?" he grinned and patted the top of her hair. "Yours isn't much better, sweetie pie."

Jill grappled with the front door and finally got it opened. When what she saw finally registered in her brain, her heart flip-flopped in her chest. "Jesus, what the hell are you doing here?" She had to sound mildly distressed by the fact that Ian was on her couch; otherwise, Elias might have gone for the man's jugular.

Only it was Ian who wanted to go for someone's jugular. He did his best to keep his cool, but Jill could see the blind fury in his eyes. "Well, hello to you too." He nodded at Elias. "He's leaving," Ian said sternly.

Elias shut the door calmly and stepped in front of Jill. "The lady asked you a question. What are you doing in her house? I assume you weren't invited."

"None of your fucking business." Ian stood up and aggressively moved toward Elias. Jill jumped in between them because she liked her furniture and the knick-knacks she had collected her whole life and having them broken in a childish brawl was not an option. Not today.

"Chill out." She barked and looked at both of them. "Where's Will?"

"His wife had surgery. I'm your new roommate for the next two weeks. Elias has to leave and stay away from you until this is over. Got it?" He sounded way to happy about the fact that Elias had to leave Jill alone. At least for the time being anyway.

"No way. She's not staying here with you. And *you* have no right to tell *me* what to do." Elias's tone was flat and if Jill hadn't known better, she would have wondered if the man had a pulse. He was so damn calm all the time. It was almost eerie.

"Give me one good reason, Webber," Ian glowered. "One good reason to arrest you and throw away the key."

"Ha. I dare you to try." Elias scoffed, which made Ian even more outraged.

Ian moved closer, pinning Jill tightly between himself and Elias.

Jill somewhat enjoyed having Ian that up close and personal. In fact it was sort of erotic being the filling in a hunk-sandwich. She quickly snapped out of it. Ian's heart was beating in time with her own. Now that was erotic.

"Look," Jill took control. "Elias is leaving and if he has to stay away until this is over, so be it." She looked over her shoulder at Elias and gave him a weak smile. "And as for you," she tapped hard on Ian's chest with her index finger. Her pulse raced faster as she did so because his deep blue eyes were now focused solely on her mouth. Breathing became more difficult as he stepped away and reigned in his frustrations, but she continued, "You will not bark orders at me in my own house. Now let's try this again."

A low grumble erupted from his lips and he motioned to the couch. "Please sit." He flashed a phenomenally fake smile at Elias and grabbed her elbow to help her along faster. "From this point out, we are strictly concentrating on making Jill seem vulnerable. I will be living in the house with no one's knowledge. I will not come and go. I will be here twenty-four hours a day until we get set up. Jill will be closely followed to the station. We have two men working security there and she'll be perfectly safe," Ian drew in a breath, and then narrowed his eyes on the man who had made his life miserable. "And to keep up this illusion you are not to be hanging around. We have one shot at this and if you don't keep your distance, I'll finally get to fulfill my fantasy of cuffing you, or better yet, bashing your head in when you try to resist."

Jill swallowed hard. *This went way beyond childhood envy. Why the hell was Ian so damn angry?* She grabbed Elias's arm when the big man made a move to stand up. "It's fine, Elias. He has a point and I'd like to just get this over with. I'll be fine."

Elias gave her a swift, hard kiss on the lips that not only stunned Jill, but also made her feel very uncomfortable. The kiss hadn't felt loving, it had felt *possessive.* He wrapped a proprietary arm around her shoulder and scowled hard at Agent Hamlin. "I don't like the fact that you're using her to catch a maniac. Figure something else out because this isn't happening."

"Oh, it's happening all right." Ian barked and once again, Jill stood up to get between the infantile men. "You aren't going to be in harm's way, I promise you...." He gazed deeply into her eyes, taking her breath away in the process. "You trust me, don't you, Jill?"

Jill nodded vigorously and wanted so badly to wrap her arms around him, or vice versa. Instead, she tugged Elias toward the door.

Ian plopped back down on the couch and gave Elias a sneaky little wave and smirked as the big man hesitantly walked to the door. "Don't worry, Webber. I'll take excellent care of her."

Jill said goodbye to Elias on the porch and got another hug before reentering her house and slamming the door. She marched aggressively toward Ian and raised her hands to her hips, ready to demand an explanation and not willing to take just any answer this time.

Ian looked completed relaxed on her couch, eating her homemade cookies and reaching for the remote control. The man looked like he belonged there. Jill shook the fantasy from her mind and moved in front of the television before he could click it on.

"What'd I do?" Anger was still present behind his eyes. "The guy wasn't going to cooperate."

"He was doing just fine under the circumstances. He's worried about me and he has a right to be. What is wrong with you? I want the truth this time."

Ian scowled. Nothing new there, but it was where

his eyes were directed that bothered her the most. *Damn it.* Jill shoved her left hand into her pocket as Ian stood up and got within inches of her face. "Congratulations," he muttered with a pained expression. "Elias Webber always gets what he wants, doesn't he?" He attempted to step by her, but she grabbed for his hand and caught his wrist.

Ian stilled. He could feel himself losing control and it was about to spill over no matter what he did. The anger grew inside him. The hurt and pain and after all these years. It still felt like yesterday that his wife packed her bags and told him she was leaving.

Jill flinched hard and closed her eyes when he groaned and raised his hand. A moment later she heard glass shattering and noted that the remote control was no longer in Ian's hand, it was most likely in the side yard. Fear skittered threw her veins alongside a bit of anger. She moved away from him and waited for his eyes to refocus on her face.

His breathing returned to normal and he felt a little bit better, that is until he looked into Jill's eyes and saw her fear. "I'll fix that," he groaned and had to get as far away from her as he could, so he marched up the stairs, berating himself the entire way up.

The light rap on the upstairs office door jolted him out of his pity party and the smell of minestrone soup wafted around him, causing him to sniff a couple of times. It smelled heavenly. "I'm not hungry."

"Bullshit," Jill growled. "You're drooling. Come down at eat like a civilized person. I'll make some coffee."

"Fine," he grumbled and watched her hips sashay out of the room. How she managed to get him into such states of erotic fog and pure aggressive need was a mystery to him. He knew he wanted her and now he knew for sure that he could never have her. It was as clear as the ring on her finger.

When he got downstairs, he noticed the table had been set for two. It made his heart ache that much more.

Ian had always been dealt a lousy hand, but seeing Jill making him dinner in her kitchen was just plain cruel. It wasn't until he got caught watching her hips sway that he noticed the ring had been removed from her finger. A painful spasm took him by surprise. *Was this a sign that things weren't what they seemed, or did she just not want to get her new bauble dirty while cooking?*

Jill still wouldn't and couldn't look him in the eye. She'd turned around just in time to see the yearning in his eyes as he watched her move around the kitchen, but damn she was still irritated by his apparent bout of jealousy. She'd wanted an explanation and all she got was a hole in her window.

Ian moved around her cautiously, jockeying for a position in the small kitchen to see if he could help, but the truth was, he was just trying to be closer to her. Every so often, her hand would graze over his thigh or the back of his arm as she reached for the coffee mugs. The silence was unbearable, as was his growing need to touch her.

Finally, when he couldn't take it any longer, he watched her set the coffee cups down on the table and then grabbed both her hands to make her stop and listen. He rubbed slowly along the soft palms of her hands and then rested his fingers on the erratic pulses of her wrists.

Jill hesitantly moved closer to the man and waited for him to speak first.

"I didn't mean to scare you earlier. I'm sorry."

She cleared her throat with an excruciatingly slow swallow before speaking in a soft, seductive voice. "Why can't you just open up to me? We might as well get to know each other if we are stuck here... together."

"I have a job to do and that job doesn't entail being your friend. I'm here for one reason and one reason only."

Jill's heart sank. "Then why did I see pain in your eyes when you saw the ring? Why did that matter so much to you that you broke my window? Where the hell did that come from?" Her tone became erratic and filled with emotion. The man had already destroyed both her doors and one window. She didn't want to take any chances, so she tried to keep the impatience from her voice.

Ian took a deep breath and let it out slowly. Unconsciously, he had moved so close that their bodies had aligned vertically and sparks of electric heat roared between them. The heat was almost agonizing, but he remained pressed up against her as he breathed her in. "God, you are so beautiful." He heard himself say as if he had no control over his mouth and what came out of it.

Jill blinked heavily and leaned closer to breathe him in. He felt so wonderful against her that nothing mattered more than finally feeling his warm, full lips against hers.

A deep guttural moan resounded low in his throat, and as his mouth covered hers, the moan escaped and he deepened the kiss, held her hips tightly in place with his rough fingers and slid his tongue into the hot depths of her sweet, sweet mouth.

Jill's eyes filled with tears. The deep feelings that he inspired with his lips sent a shiver of wanton desire up her loins and straight to *neverland*. Never in her life had she felt that kind of passion from one damn kiss. She tried wiggling her hips to bring him even closer and heighten the pulsing feeling that needed to be extinguished, but the stranglehold he had on her was keeping her right where he needed her to be. Right where his strong erection needed to be to feel the warmth of her; the heat of her.

Jill's hands grasped the hard muscles of his arms, then she wrapped her arms around him and pulled him closer to her breasts, to her heart. Right where she wanted him to be.

Another deep moan escaped his lips and the table was cleared with one swipe of his hand. Silverware clicked on the floor, along with the sound of ceramic breaking. Jill's teeth clanked against his as he lifted her up and laid her down beneath him on the cold hard oak table.

Writhing above her, he couldn't keep his hands off her breasts. Those sweet firm breasts that he'd fantasized about caressing so many times. *This was really happening,* Jill thought. Ian is the man she was supposed to be with, she knew that now, more than ever. Fate had been kind to her, and in just the knick of time. Passion flared between them, sending her into a fog of pure satisfaction. The incredible pull she felt from his hand on her erect nipple had her moaning and arching her hips to seek him out. She'd never felt passion like this before. This was once-in-a-lifetime passion and she never wanted it to end.

The teakettle on the stove whistled loudly, taking Ian's mind and his hand off Jill's flesh. He looked down at her swollen lips and heaving chest and reality slapped him in the face.

Jill's eyes looked desperate. "No," she moaned as he eased off her and extended his hand. She didn't take it. Instead, she pursed her lips and wiped the tears from her eyes. "That's what I thought." She groaned and ran into the bedroom, slamming the door loudly in her wake.

Ian dropped to the floor in the kitchen and buried his face in his hands. He had just made the biggest bonehead mistake ever. For one thing, the house was still bugged and, for another, he'd just let Jill know how he honestly felt.

* * *

Monday morning, Jill woke up with swollen eyes from crying most of the night. Of course, after the dining room table debacle she wasn't about to leave the confines of her bedroom, even if she had been starving and thirsty and wanting an explanation. One that she knew she most certainly would never get. Ian had let his guard down last night. She understood the implications of what had happened and it mattered not to her why he felt so compelled to hold back his feelings, it just mattered that he had them.

She saw last night as a victory of sorts. A bittersweet

victory, but at least she knew now that he felt just as strongly as she did and that meant that Elias's ring would remain in that little black box... indefinitely.

She heard the shower running when she finally emerged from her bedroom. Shuffling into the kitchen, she noticed the dishes were all cleaned off the floor, coffee had already been made and the window had been patched up with a piece of cardboard. *It would do for now.* The window was small, so it's not like the killer could crawl through it. Jill shivered under her bathrobe and poured herself a cup of coffee.

Just as she turned around, she saw Ian, standing in her living room wrapped in a towel and nothing more. The water droplets were still running down his chest, his damp hair was disheveled and his eyes looked weary. Most likely, because Ian hadn't slept a wink last night after losing control and finally attacking the woman like he'd longed to do since the first day he ever saw her.

He looked surprised to see her standing there in her robe, but just nodded in acknowledgement and grabbed his toiletry bag before returning to the steaming bathroom.

Jill returned to her room and waited patiently until she heard the bathroom door creak open. She met him at the door, opened her mouth to talk and then Ian grabbed her by the wrist and dragged her into Anita's old bedroom.

She glared hard and didn't appreciate his caveman character. "What the hell is wrong with you?"

Ian shut the door and shuffled his bare feet. He was dry now, but the towel was still wrapped precariously around his hips. "The house is still bugged and I like my job very much, so can we please not talk about last night."

Jill looked around at the empty walls. She missed Anita terribly. *Where's a girl's best friend when you need her?* Jill sighed. "My room's bugged too?"

"No..." A salacious grin tugged at his lips. "But your room has a bed."

Jill giggled nervously and stepped toward him with fire in her eyes. He backed up, so she stepped forward again causing him to back up and hit the wall. "Are you afraid of me, Agent Hamlin?"

If he hadn't been almost naked and pressed up against the wall by a beautiful woman, he might have said no, but he nodded slowly and she backed off. "Do you want to talk about it?"

He shook his head with his vintage scowl. "Are you really going to marry him?" Ian's voice squeaked and for the first time since she had met Ian Hamlin, he actually looked afraid —very afraid.

"Honestly, I don't know." Jill stared into his deep, blue eyes. Of course what she wanted to say was something along the lines of, "*Of course not, you idiot. I've loved you forever, now take me to bed and make me scream,*" but of course, she couldn't say that, so she continued in a rational manner. "I've sort of been waiting around for someone and I thought I could be really happy with Elias, but then..." She swallowed hard. *One kiss does not a future make.* She reminded herself over and over again. "How old are you?" she asked out of nowhere.

Ian's eyes flickered, wondering where that came from. "I'm thirty, why?"

Jill chuckled slightly with a great sense of relief, but it still didn't prove that this would work out. What if Ian was just a common slam-hound and her hormones were causing dissension in her relationship with a perfectly good man? *Okay, so Elias isn't perfect. He lies. He's bad in bed, he grinds his teeth and spends way too much time on his hair, but he's still a good man.* Jill shook her head to end the debate that was going on in her brain. "Have you ever been completely head over heels in love with anyone?"

Ian's face tightened with rage and embarrassment, because he was sure that his cheeks just blushed slightly. "Sure, who the hell hasn't?" he groaned and Jill stepped close once again.

Sucking the playfulness right out of the room, she got serious and pursed her lips. "Is that why you trashed his car? Because of a girl?" Jill asked.

"I thought we closed the door on this conversation."

"You may have, but I still have a lot of questions. Like why you hit him? And why he's the only one talking. Don't you want to defend yourself, or make a rebuttal plea? Anything?"

"Look," Ian frowned and crossed his arms in front of his chest. *He had an amazing chest; hairless and perfectly sculpted, it was a shame to cover it up. Men like Ian Hamlin shouldn't ever cover up their bodies.* In fact, Jill thought it might be fun if Ian just wore that towel and nothing more for the next two weeks. That would make her life more fun and it would certainly improve the décor of her home. "I don't know what kind of bullshit the guy's been spewing about me and I could really give a fuck."

"Yeah, but don't you care?"

"About what?"

"I don't know," Jill shrugged, "He's the only one talking. He makes you out to sound like some jealous punk still out for revenge. He's even convinced that you're out to come between us."

"All I care about is keeping you safe and catching this psycho before he strikes again. Elias Webber is old news. It's over, I've moved on and frankly I could care less what you think about me. You're a big girl and you can choose what you want to believe. I don't have to explain myself." Anger grew in his tone. "Now, can I please get dressed?"

Jill blinked a couple of times. Ian Hamlin was a pretty honorable guy in her eyes. She smiled and stepped back. "For what it's worth, I don't think you're over it. If you were over it, that little vein in your neck wouldn't protrude every time I bring up his name. If you were over it, you wouldn't look pissed off all the time. But, hey, that's just my opinion." Jill said smugly and then walked out of the room and into the bathroom.

Chapter Eleven

Jill called the glass repairman to come fix the gaping hole in her window before leaving for work. *Of course Ian is going to have to pay for it. So far, the man has rung up quite a tab. He has a lot of making up to do.*

She hated the idea that Ian wasn't taking her to the station, but she trusted him and she wanted this to be over just as badly as the FBI did.

She did her best to remain panic free as she drove into the parking structure and turned off the ignition. Ian had given her a can of pepper spray as a precaution and she gripped it tightly in her hand. Much to her surprise and pleasure, Reed and Tom Riley were waiting for her outside the elevator. She guessed that Ian had updated the staff about the threat and therefore everyone was watching her back. She sure appreciated that and her fear subsided slightly as she entered the elevator on the arm of her producer and her mousy little assistant, Tom.

* * *

Ian had never thought of himself as a handy guy,

but there wasn't much else to do while Jill was at work, so he grabbed tools out of her garage and fixed everything and anything that he could find that was broken. He owed her at least that much.

He took a nap on her bed, folded her clothes that he'd pulled from the dryer and around one a.m. went on a search for something to whip up for dinner. He had a lot to make up for. With no real cooking experience, he opted for leftover Chinese food and had just warmed it up when he heard the roar of the garage door.

He set the plates on the table, opened the bottle of wine, and had just sat down when Jill finally made it inside the house. "How was your day, dear?" he joked and, for the most part, Jill appreciated the levity. Her hands were still trembling from her ride home; he noticed that right away and stood up to offer some sort of comfort, remembering she had asked for that in the past.

"Are you okay?" He patted her hand, but didn't dare do something like wrap his arms around her and hold her tight. God, how he wanted to do that. "You're shaking. What happened?"

"I'm fine. It was just sort of scary being alone at night... without you." She looked at him with those big brown doe eyes. She looked so sad. It broke his heart.

"Here, I made dinner. Do you want some wine?" He tried easing her over to sit down but she remained firmly planted and a tear rolled down her cheek. "What is it? What do you want?"

Jill remained quiet because the walls were listening and she didn't want to jeopardize his job. She knew his job meant the world to him just like he knew the same about her. She extended her arms in a loving manner.

Ian looked at her with a troubled stare, but then relinquished his fear and hesitation and took her into his arms. She felt so exquisite. *Like we were meant to be this close all the time.*

Her tears finally spilled relentlessly as she held him

close and this is all that she wanted. She wanted to know that his hugs were just as good or even better than Elias's, and they were better. His arms were much stronger around her shoulders and she could feel his heart beating rapidly in his chest as she melted into his grasp and let him rock her gently until the tears receded and she could breathe easy again.

Ian inhaled the scent of her hair and hadn't done something this intimate since before his wife had left. He hadn't been with a woman in so long and yet, just holding Jill in his arms in a platonic embrace seemed like heaven to the man. Of course, he could fool himself into believing that was enough for him, but clearly he wanted more. He eased her away and looked her in the eye. "You okay now?"

Jill smiled as brightly as she could under the circumstances. "Thanks, Ian."

He winked and poured her a glass of wine.

Dessert consisted of two chocolate chip cookies each, a cup of tea for Jill, and black coffee for Ian. They watched a late-late movie together, but on separate ends of the couch. Ian didn't trust himself and neither did Jill. Jill felt like a teenager again, sitting on her parent's couch watching television with a boy. It was a fun feeling and, even more importantly, it kept her mind off any impending doom.

The phone rang at a little after three and Jill snatched it up.

"Hi," she said sheepishly and then went to her room to talk in private. "I'm fine." She explained to Elias. "We're watching a movie."

"Did he say anything to you? 'cause you shouldn't believe a word he says. You can't trust him, Jill."

"I don't want to talk about this anymore. Okay." Her tone meant business.

"So, have you had enough time to think about my proposal?"

"Honestly Elias, I haven't really, I'm sorry. It's not a good time for me...you know what I mean." She didn't want to have this conversation over the phone. Dumping a man over the phone is not something she would ever do, and besides the future was not etched in stone. Anything could happen.

"I understand." Elias blew out his breath with a hiss. "What's he doing now?"

"Jesus Christ, Elias, grow up. This isn't high school and Ian's not trying to steal your girlfriend." She slammed down the phone and stuck her tongue out at the picture of Elias on her mirror. "Men," she growled and made her way back out to the couch. Ian's eyes were closed and his breathing was already heavy.

She curled in beside him and took the opportunity to hold him close. Laying her head on his chest, she eased the blanket up around them and closed her eyes, as she was lulled to sleep by the rising and falling of his chest.

* * *

By the end of Thursday's broadcast, Jill was so excited about going home that she practically ran to her car. She ran to her car a lot these days because she was usually panicked and freaked out about dying, but tonight she was excited to head home and see Ian. They hadn't finished their game of Scrabble from the night before and that's all that she had thought about all day. *Sitting across from Ian at the table. Or sitting next to him on the couch.* Not a minute had gone by when she hadn't thought of him. They'd spent the last four days together and if she wasn't sure that she loved him before, she was positive now.

Everything seemed to have come together. She didn't ever bring up Elias, and even took down the picture of him on her mirror. That kept things peaceful and she found that the best way to get through to Ian was through his stomach. The old adage was right and Jill loved to cook and bake. Ian had probably gained five pounds since he moved in, but he seemed more relaxed and at ease lately.

She had even got him to crack a smile a couple of times, by god. She loved the sound of his laughter.

Mostly he laughed at her when she tried to make up words that didn't exist, or he'd laugh about the way she insisted on keeping the towels perfectly aligned in the bathroom or the fact that she liked ketchup on her eggs.

Of course, she in turn laughed at him for polishing his silverware before he ate. It was a nervous habit he had, but it made him look like a pretentious snob, which wasn't him at all. She also laughed when he showered because he liked to sing and sing he did. Usually it was either Ted Nugent, or Sting, but this morning it was The Backstreet Boys. Her stomach ached after that little concerto. Everything Ian did seemed to make her smile and she loved that her house looked perfect every night when she returned home. Having a bored FBI agent living with her was better than having Martha Stewart as a roommate, and he was so much more fun to look at.

Jill pulled into the driveway just as Ian was finishing up his phone conversation with the men in the van that was now parked three blocks away. "Are you sure?" Ian pulled Jill by the arm as she entered the house. He held her protectively close. "Okay, if you think so." Ian's scowl had returned, as had his cop face, and his protective instinct that sent a quiver down her spine. His hand was gripped tightly around her wrist. She wasn't going anywhere, not any time soon. "Fine. No, we can't take that chance. Don't move on it, let's just see what happens." Ian disconnected and let out an exasperated breath.

"What is it?" Jill fumbled with her words. "What happened?"

"You were followed home." Ian said sternly and flipped off the kitchen light.

Terrified is a pretty good word to describe how Jill felt. She shuddered and tried to find solace in his arms. He backed off, but kept a tight grip on her wrist.

"Jesus, Ian." Jill said shakily.

"I can't think when you're that close to me."

"Fine," Jill shrugged from his grasp and ran for her room.

Ian caught up to her before she had a chance to flip on the light. He pinned her against the wall in her room. "Don't turn on the light, and listen to me, goddamn it." He groaned and she wiggled and suddenly burst into tears. "Shhhh," Ian said quietly. "I know you're scared, but you have to listen to me."

At least she got to be close to him again. She looked at him in the darkened room. The light from the hallway flickered in his eyes as he blinked and looked at her tears. "We can't take a chance and scare this guy off, so please just do what I say."

"What?" Jill sniffled. "What do you need me to do?"

"Go to the front door and open it..."

Jill's knees buckled under her. He caught her in his arms and shushed her again.

"Just open the door, call out to the cat a couple of times, but stay on the porch. Just look at the grass and don't look around at the street. Just call the cat and then come back in."

Jill took a deep breath. "Anita took the cat. I don't have a cat anymore."

"Yeah, but he probably doesn't know that and we want to see what he does when he sees you. There are four men outside and I'm right here. Don't be afraid." He pressed a kiss into her hair and sent her a very weak smile. "Can you do this? Do you trust me, Jill?"

Jill nodded and quickly pulled her robe over her clothes to make the illusion real. She walked to the front door and paused before flipping the deadbolt into the unlocked position. She looked back over her shoulder at Ian who already had his gun drawn and was back to being Mr. Cop. With trembling fingers, she twisted the door handle and did her best at remaining calm. She opened the door, remembered everything she had learned in drama class and played her part well.

"Whiskers!" She yelled out and walked the length of the porch. "Whiskers. Here kitty kitty." She held on tightly to the porch swing for support as she called out again. Besides feeling like a complete moron for calling out to an imaginary cat, she was still trembling inside and her voice was high and squeaky as she called out one more time and then retreated into the safety of her home.

Ian stared at her and then grabbed his cell phone when it vibrated on his hip. "Hamlin."

"He's definitely interested," Agent Hardy said. "He's two houses down and from the looks of it, he's...oh god -- you know -- doing himself in the front seat."

Ian cringed and sent Jill a sympathetic glance. "Did you run the plates?"

"We're waiting for the results right now." Silence ensued while the other agent waited for his computer to catch up. "Yep, got it. Car belongs to a Marvin Akers. Vancouver address. Should we move in?"

"No," Ian almost shouted. "We can't take a chance at screwing this up and I'm not bringing him in on a petty Peeping Tom charge. We need more. The car might be stolen." Ian continued. "Don't lose him. Tail him when he leaves and then let me know if he ends up at the right address."

"We'll stay on him."

Ian disconnected and went to Jill. "You did good."

"Now what?" she stuttered.

"Now we wait," Ian pulled her into his arms but kept his gun at his side. He pulled her into her room and shut the door for privacy. "You sleeping with me on the couch again, or do you feel comfortable in your room?"

"You knew?" Jill stared bright eyed at the great pretender. "You knew I snuck out to sleep with you?"

"I'm not dead. Of course I knew."

Jill smiled warmly. "Will you stay with me?

Please."

"Do you have to do that?" Ian growled.

"What?" she said demurely.

"Bat your pretty little eyelashes at me," he said with a smirk.

"Did it work?" Jill grinned and climbed into bed.

He followed, but stayed on the outside of the covers, completely out of arm's reach.

* * *

After the previous night's scare, Agent Hamlin, Agent Reynolds, and Agent Hardy had a powwow early the next morning about what had transpired and how it couldn't be allowed to happen again.

"I want out. I can't take it any more and if last night happens again, then Agent Wyatt needs to already be in the house. If she's going to pretend to be Jill, then she should be living here with Jill and I should be out there trying harder to find this fucker. What did he do after he left?"

"We lost him in an apartment building just south of town. The car was reported stolen this morning right around six a.m. when Marvin Akers went to leave for work. We impounded the car and hope to get prints back soon."

"Excellent. Call Teri Wyatt and we'll sneak her in tonight in the backseat of Jill's car." Ian said. Then he watched Jill emerge from the bathroom wrapped in a towel. It's not that he wanted to leave her, it's that he knew he couldn't protect her like this. Not like this, not with the way he felt about her.

Jill stopped in the hallway and watched him finish his conversation. She'd heard every word and was not at all happy that Ian was leaving, but what could she do? Drop down on her knees and beg him to stay? Drop her towel and beg him to make love to her, or drop her chin to her chest and cry? She didn't do any of that, she just sent him a weak smile and went into her bedroom and shut the door.

A minute or two went by before she heard the

phone ring. It took her a couple of seconds to snap out of her state of sorrow before she answered. "Hello. I'm fine."

"When can I see you again?" Elias wondered. He'd been waiting a week to see her and had hated every day that they had been apart.

"I don't know." Jill said solemnly, and then heard the knock on her door. She opened it and motioned Ian inside. He closed the door and walked toward her. "I have to go," Jill said with a gulp. Ian's gaze was burning a hole right through her and into her soul. She loved Ian more than she could have possibly imagined and it became more and more painful every day. Jill listened to Elias say he loved her and then she hung up and stepped back, bumping her butt against the edge of the bed. Ian's eyes still hot on hers, she licked her lips and made sure her towel was still secured around her breasts. Her damp hair tickled her naked shoulders and she shivered in anticipation.

"I'm sending in my replacement. She'll be here tonight but I'll keep in touch." Ian sounded like a cop through and through, yet he was looking at her like a man should look at a woman. Like he had to have her.

"What if I don't want you to go?" she said sadly. "Why are you doing this?"

"Because last night should never have happened. Agent Wyatt should have been here. It should have been her out on the porch and I'm not taking any more chances with you." He moved toward her and raised his hand up to stroke her cheek lightly. "I can't let anything happen to you. Not now. Not ever."

Jill's eyes closed at the sheer pleasure that his caress induced. She leaned into his hand and pressed a kiss into the palm of his hand.

Ian's heart fluttered as he embraced her tightly. "This is our last day together. How about another game of Scrabble? Winner takes all."

Jill shook her head. She could think of a hundred

things she'd rather do with Ian and each idea involved being naked with the man. She reached her hand up to release the towel, but he caught her wrist and creased his brow.

"I can't protect you if I get too involved." Ian stepped back and stared at her beautiful face. "Don't you get that by now? You distract me, Jill." And he walked from the room.

*   *   *

Jill waited patiently after the late night news for Agent Teri Wyatt to secretly get into the back of her car. She really hated the idea of going home to a house without Ian in it. It almost felt like a break-up, and after her lame attempt at seducing him this afternoon, she felt like a hussy incarnate. Boy, she had blown it big time. She'd called him twice to apologize for her behavior, but all she had gotten was his voice mail.

"All set, Miss." Agent Hardy helped Jill into her car. "This will all be over soon. I promise." He winked and watched her drive off with another agent on her tail.

"Hi, I'm Teri." Agent Teri Wyatt said from the floor of the backseat. "You keep a really clean car. I'm impressed," she joked with the fretful Jill.

"Nice to meet you," Jill said, but she wanted Ian back. "So, what's the plan?"

"Tomorrow morning you are going to follow an ordinary Saturday routine ... do some stretches on the front porch, then you're going to slowly jog around the neighborhood, then take off for the lake. Don't worry. There'll be agents nearby until you get to the lake, where Agent Hamlin will pick you up and I will continue on with your usual route. We'll see if we pick up a tail and go from there. This guy seems to be totally unpredictable, so we'll do this a couple of times this weekend and then we'll try something different on Monday."

"Sounds okay," Jill said with a great deal of bravado. "Have you been with the FBI long?"

"Ten years or so." Teri said. "How long have you been a weathergirl?"

"Meteorologist," Jill said sternly. "Not very long. This is my first on-air job."

"That makes sense." Teri said. "Hamlin told me that you were pretty adamant about going to your job every day. You must really love it."

"Do you love your job?"

"More than life itself," Teri said with pride.

"How well do you know Ian?"

"I've met him twice. Pretty sexy guy, too bad he's such a moody prick. Is he always that angry, or is it just me?"

Jill laughed as she pulled into the garage. "It's not you." She chuckled lightly and then thought hard about it. "It might be women though. Is he married, divorced, widowed?"

"I heard divorced." Teri said as the garage closed tightly and she crawled off the floor. "So, roomie. What should we do tonight? Popcorn and chick flicks or male-bash?"

"Male-bashing sounds good to me. Mind if I have a martini?" Jill smirked.

"Knock yourself out." Teri grinned and checked out the house thoroughly before letting Jill out of the garage. When it was deemed safe and Teri's gun was re-holstered, Jill made a martini and got down to business.

* * *

Ian listened to his sweet Jill's voice before signing off and heading to his desolate hotel room for the night. He was counting the minutes before he got to see her again and was looking forward to their rendezvous at the lake tomorrow morning. He had volunteered to watch after her while they tried to bait the bad-guy with a fake Jill. It was the only way he would agree to such a risky plan and, besides, he wanted to see her again.

He slept an entire eight hours and woke up with a

start as the alarm chimed by his head. He showered, shaved and put on a pair of denim shorts, a black t-shirt and topped it off with a dark blue New York Yankees baseball cap and a pair of dark sunglasses before heading to Vancouver Lake for his date with Jill-nine. His gun was tucked under the waistband of his shorts and, with watchful eyes, he eyeballed the crowd on the shore and waited behind the cover of the large downed trees on the other side of the lake where he was supposed to meet Jill.

When she arrived, she was damp with perspiration due to the sweltering heat and her brisk jog. She took a deep breath in and stretched out the stitch in her side. It had been a week or two since she'd had regular exercise and she was feeling it this morning.

"It looks like thunderclouds." Ian joked and placed his hat on her head and handed her a sweatshirt to put on to keep her disguised. She slid sunglasses over her eyes and sank down in the sand. "You're not going to do something crazy like run around naked in the sand are you?"

"Very funny." Jill scoffed and playfully tugged on his hand before entwining her fingers with his. "I hated being without you last night."

"This is how it has to be." Ian said as he lay back in the sand and continued holding her hand. It was nice, comfortable, and unsettling all at once.

"Can you turn off your cop-persona for ten minutes and just be a man please?"

"Fine," Ian groaned. "I missed the hell out of you too. It took me two hours to finally fall asleep and when I did, all I thought about was how good your bed smells."

"That's more like it." Jill smiled and leaned back to lie down beside him. She shuffled her position and leaned up on her elbow to look him in the eye. "Do you believe in fate or love at first sight?"

He swallowed hard and diverted his gaze to the ominous looking clouds overhead. "No and no."

"Why not?"

"Because it's all bullshit."

"You sound like a man scorned." Jill said and then made a bold move and laid her head down on his chest to feel his heart beating wildly in his chest.

Ian's eyes rolled back in his head as he squirmed under the weight of her head. Attempting to keep control of his ever-growing feelings for her had him clenching his jaw. He laced his fingers into the back of her hair and massaged her scalp with intense need.

"I believe that fate brought you back to me," Jill confessed breathlessly. "I told Anita about how I saw you at the police station and she convinced me that you weren't real, that you were a figment of my imagination because I'd been waiting for you for the past twelve years and then I met Elias. I thought my mind was playing tricks on me and trying to keep me from being happy with another man. That's why I was so dazed when you were in my house that first night. Because I felt you, and you were real." Tears welled in her eyes as she lifted her head and looked him in the eye. "Do you remember me from the beach that day too?" She leaned closer to his face. Her lips looked warm and inviting.

He couldn't believe what he was hearing. She remembered him and his luck was definitely changing for the better. Ian kissed her then. Softly at first, but then it was if he couldn't get enough of her and he rolled until she was pinned tightly beneath him. With a nervous quiver and a growing need for her, he gazed into her eyes. "How could I forget you? You were the most beautiful girl I had ever seen." He kissed her again and brushed his lips against hers as he spoke. "You looked like an angel that day on the beach. I remember you were wearing a red bikini and you had a kid on each hand. Two boys, I think it was and I...." He bent and took her again with great need and felt the warm, slick slide of her tongue against his, taking his breath away. Their kiss intensified with desire and an intimacy that rocked his soul. He broke from the kiss, kept his gaze locked on her and raked a thumb hungrily across her jaw line. "I think I've loved you ever since."

Jill closed her eyes to hide her tears of joy; she kissed him back and held him tightly to her with trembling hands. "Why didn't you say anything, that day on the beach? I smiled and you just blinked and walked away. God, Ian, I've thought about you every day since then and I think I've loved you since the moment that I looked into your eyes."

"Oh god, Jill," Ian groaned and rested his forehead firmly against hers. "I didn't know what to say. My mom had said that you were so devastated after you learned about Tanya's death that you couldn't even stay in the house. I didn't know what to say. I recognized you right away, but it just didn't feel right to bring up where I knew you from, but I wanted to. I really wanted to tell you how sorry I was that Tanya and Dick had been killed." He kissed her again and then wiped the tears from her eyes. "You really think it's fate?" He chuckled lightly.

"I don't know, Ian, but I do know that I love you. I've always loved you."

He blinked slowly a couple of times, realizing the cold hard truth of the matter. He groaned and rolled over to dismount from the precarious position that he had taken between her legs. Clothed or not, it was wrong to even want to be inside her. "But you're still Elias's girl. I can't do this, Jill."

"I'm not going to marry him. Hell, I don't even love him. I've never loved him. I love you. It's you I want. It's always been you." Jill said a bit flustered.

Ian smiled warmly at her and entwined his fingers in hers once again. "If I didn't know that I want you forever I'd throw you down in the sand and fuck you so hard your eye sockets would hurt," he said with a grimace. *That would be a perfect way to get back at Elias fucking Webber,* but it wasn't his style. Ian had always thought of himself as a noble man, even if sometimes he lost his temper. "But I do know that I want to be with you and even if I hate the guy, I couldn't do that. I'm sorry."

Jill smiled. *What a wonderful man. Who would have ever thought that Ian The Scowler Hamlin would be so regal and chivalrous? Wow,* that made her thighs quiver even more.

* * *

When Jill wasn't at her house, Elias had pulled around the corner and, out of the corner of his eye, he had seen the dark head of hair go bobbing down the lane toward the lake and he knew Jill loved the lake. She had mentioned once or twice that she loved jogging the back country trails that led to the shore, so he put his sunglasses back down across the bridge of his nose and followed the streets to the parking lot on the west side of Vancouver Lake. He couldn't believe that Ian had the audacity to let Jill go running alone in the woods, but then again, he wouldn't put anything past that guy.

Elias watched for ten minutes before getting out and walking along the shore in hopes of finding her. And he hoped to get a few minutes alone with her, for it had been one long week without anyone to make love to. He finally caught sight of a man who looked a lot like Ian, but with the hat and sunglasses on, he just couldn't tell for sure.

Elias followed this man along the beach and waited until the man ducked out of sight behind a couple of downed logs before running over to get a better look. The man waited in a secluded area, pacing in the sand as if impatiently awaiting someone. A half a minute later, a woman met up with the man and he recognized her right away. It most certainly was Jill and once the man took off his hat, Elias knew for certain it was Ian. The sight of them sitting in the sand hand-in-hand was difficult for Elias to comprehend, much less swallow. His breathing grew jagged as if someone had a vice grip on his chest.

Elias watched with clenched fists as Ian lay down in the sand, then Jill laid her head on Ian's chest, and a fire roared in his belly. He hadn't remembered a time in his life - well, with the exception of when his mother brought home Dick Swenson and that little brat Tanya — when he felt that much anger. Sure, he'd gotten mad once or twice. Sometimes ... well mostly when he was a teenager and his father had left. Now the blood in his veins had reached its boiling point and his eyes glazed over from the sight: the god-awful sight of Ian Hamlin embracing his Jill. *Oh, god, now Ian is kissing her -- my Jill.* Elias had to walk away before he completely snapped and did something truly irreversible.

* * *

Jill and Ian remained on the beach talking and laughing together until he got the call that Agent Wyatt was headed back toward them. Jill returned the sweatshirt to Ian and then smiled brightly at the man she loved.

"When will I see you again?"

"When I catch this guy. So be careful. And stay close to Hardy this afternoon." He shook his head, not at all happy that Jill had demanded that she keep her appearance at the children's hospital fundraiser this afternoon at Esther Short Park. He knew how much her job and her charitable obligations meant to her, so he didn't push. He just frowned and waited for her to resume her run and head back to her house to get ready for the fundraiser barbecue.

Chapter Twelve

The fundraiser was a smashing success. It was Jill's first public appearance as Vancouver's newest news celebrity, and for the most part, she felt okay about being out in public. She knew three agents and Ian would most likely be watching and, since their love-fest at the lake, Jill couldn't wipe the smile off her face.

Anita made her way through the crowd with Ryan on one hand and a bag of baby stuff in the other — the farmer's market was coincidentally being held in the same park as the Children's Hospital annual summer blast fundraiser. "Oh, golly," Anita hugged her friend tightly and burst into tears. "Sorry. I'm all over the place these days. I just miss you so fucking much." Anita snorted with laughter and gave Jill a big kiss. "Man, it's packed. Vancouver must love you." She chuckled and rubbed her barely bulging belly. It was protruding just enough to make it obvious that she was pregnant and not just getting fat.

Ryan smiled gleefully from the other side of her. "I think she bought out a couple of vendors over there." He motioned to the farmer's market. "Homemade baby food, a couple of knitted thingy-ma-jigs, and *like* enough socks to keep junior's toes nice and comfy."

Ryan's beaming attitude about being a daddy just made Jill's smile that much wider.

"Well, did you tell Elias to kiss off yet?" Anita sat down and took a long pull off her water bottle.

"No," Jill grinned. "But I did tell Ian how I feel."

"NO!" Anita shouted a little louder than she intended. "So, what happened?"

"Not much, except that he feels the same and I'm so flipping happy I can't stand it." Jill giggled wildly and looked over the crowd to see if her man was watching.

"So, is the sex hot?"

"I don't know." Jill laughed. "We just kissed a couple of times, but I tell you, the chemistry is pretty damn strong. I can't even look at him without getting weak in the knees."

"That's a wonderful sign." Anita grinned and gave Ryan's tummy a pat. She looked lovingly into his eyes and smiled. "We've decided on an October wedding. Nothing fancy, just family and friends at my folks' house. I don't think I really have to even ask, it's sort of a given, but will you be my maid of honor?"

Jill's eyes filled with tears. *Hopefully, if I'm alive in September.* She wanted so badly to confide in her friend about the hell she'd been going through. But it wasn't an option.

"Of course I will. I'd be honored." Jill gushed and felt a pang of panic envelop her thoughts.

Anita smiled and said her goodbyes. Congratulating her on catching a hunky piece of ass like Ian Hamlin. She also apologized again for pushing Jill into a relationship with Elias and not being more supportive about Ian from the beginning. "How old is he?" Anita asked right before letting go of Jill's hand.

"Thirty," Jill laughed and waved goodbye.

* * *

Before the crowd dispersed and the sun started its descent in the sky, Jill made her way through the crowd escorted by her producer, Reed Langley. "I'm really glad you were able to make it. I'm sure your fans have appreciated the opportunity to meet you. I should have your picture plastered on a bus as soon as this mess is over." He winked and made sure that she was safely in her car before walking away. Out of the corner of her eye, Jill saw the back of Tom's head, but she was too late to honk or try to wave. She shrugged and put her car into drive.

Jill smiled to herself just because she was just that damn happy, and pulled out of the lot, followed closely by two undercover police officers and the Hardy boys again. She turned right on Second Avenue and headed down the hill toward her neighborhood in Wallingford Heights. At first she thought that her foot had just slipped off the brake pedal somehow, but when she tried it again and the pedal went straight to the floor, she knew she was in trouble. All she could do was brace herself and pray that she wouldn't hurt anyone. Scenarios raced through her mind as she picked up speed. The hill wasn't that steep, it was just long and went on and on, making it impossible for her to stop — until she hit the Pepsi truck parked at the bottom.

* * *

Ian wasn't the first one on the scene, but he was the angriest. Cussing-out is an understatement as to what he did to the agents who were supposed to be protecting her this afternoon. He berated them, screamed, yelled, and almost slammed his fist through Agent Hardy's window before they had a chance to explain that it was just a car accident and it wasn't their fault. Ian apologized as he finally approached the ambulance where Jill was lying on the gurney waiting to be taken to the hospital.

Her eyes fluttered opened when she smelled his musky male scent, or maybe when she sensed his fierce scowl. Somehow, she knew that he would blame her for insisting on going to the fundraiser in the first place.

"Jesus fucking Christ, Jill, are you trying to cause my premature death?" He meant it to be playful but this wasn't the first time since he'd met the pretty woman that she'd almost given him a heart attack. "Are you okay? What hurts?"

"Just my neck and head. The airbag helped, but they think I might have a concussion from the side impact.

I'm okay. Really I am."

Ian jumped up into the ambulance and pulled the door closed on one side before bending over and kissing her gently. "I'll meet you at the hospital. Are you sure you're okay?"

"I'm fine," Jill lied and held back the tears to keep up the illusion that she wasn't terrified out of her mind. Her accident just made the theory that someone wanted her dead all that more real for her and it was terrifying.

"I love you," he whispered in her ear and then hopped back out.

* * *

Jill was taken first into the St. Joseph's Hospital emergency room to be looked over, then to a semi-private wing to be looked at by a doctor. When she was finally escorted upstairs to her own private room, the aches and pains became much more noticeable. She'd been checked out thoroughly, her head sent through the cat-scan, her legs and arms x-rayed and she came away from that accident pretty damn lucky. Her car that she loved so much was, of course, totaled and sitting in the police station impound yard waiting for its autopsy.

Ian peeked his head into Jill's room after all the uniformed officers asked their questions and took her information. Their eyes met in a star-crossed lover's gaze, before the doctor popped in followed by a nurse who measured her vital signs, and then finally they were alone. The sky outside was already black, with millions of stars twinkling high above her window as she gazed out and got a handle on her fear.

"What happened?" Ian climbed in beside her, planting a soft kiss on her forehead. "The cops said you couldn't stop."

"Can I ask you something?" Jill looked into his deep blue eyes without blinking. She'd thought about the possibility for hours, actually ever since she realized that her brakes had failed. It was almost too impossible to fathom, but then again, how much did she really know about Elias. Could he have done something so cruel, so horrific that it made her shudder to think about?

"Sure," Ian said with concern.

"Was Elias weird when he was a kid?"

"I don't know where this is coming from... What do you mean by weird?"

Jill sucked back a tear. "I don't know. He seems so calm all the time, but his mother said that when she married Dick, he got so angry. You don't think..." Jill stopped herself before going any further. She had a psychopathic serial killer on her ass; the accident could have nothing to do with Elias. "Never mind. I think I just need to sleep."

"You go ahead and sleep. I'll be right here all night." Ian pressed a kiss into her dark hair and tried to once again reign in his fear, his anger, and the gnawing feeling in his gut that Jill might just be onto something.

When her eyes finally stopped fluttering, he slipped away to make a phone call to the Vancouver police.

"I want every inch of that car swept for fingerprints, DNA, blood, foreign lint... everything. This may be just the break we need." Ian said to Detective Whitney. Either that or he had more to worry about than he originally thought. Ian preferred to concentrate on his first theory.

* * *

The following morning, Anita and Ryan were Jill's first visitors, followed by Detective Whitney of the Vancouver Police Department and then Reed Langley with a giant bouquet of roses from the office staff at the station. They had all finally left her alone and Ian was nowhere to be seen, which made her uneasy. The grinding, churning feeling in her gut led her to sit up straight and take matters into her own hands.

There was something that she needed to know;

something that she had to find out for herself. So she pulled her clothes out of the plastic hospital bag and got dressed. Despite the pounding in her head, she was eager to escape the watchful eye of the FBI for a little investigating of her own. She grabbed her purse and personal effects out of the plastic bag under her hospital bed and left Ian a note saying that he could reach her on her cell phone if he needed her but there was something that she had to do.

The uniformed officer just outside her door was busy flirting with a pretty young nurse, so Jill took the opportunity and fled quickly to the elevator. She called a cab, waited patiently near the west entrance to the hospital and within minutes she was en route to the train station with a final destination of Seattle.

When she was finally safe on the Amtrak train headed north, she closed her eyes and listened to the sounds of the train leaving the station. For a fleeting moment, she panicked that she had just left behind her only protection – the men who were keeping her safe, but her quest to discover the truth about Elias overrode her fear. It was a liberating feeling for Jill to leave the city limits and soon all she could think about was finding out the truth once and for all.

* * *

The penthouse was reasonably secure, but all Jill had to do was bat her eyelashes at the doorman she had met previously and tell him a tall tale about why she was there.

Gus smiled and gave her an escorted ride up to the seventeenth floor of Windsor Towers and right into the penthouse of Elias Webber.

"Thanks, Gus. I'll just be a minute. I promise," Jill waved. When he was out of sight, she began her search. The first thing she did was flip through the filing cabinet in his den and pulled open the drawers of his desk. Although she didn't know what she was looking for, it was fun playing detective. Even if it meant that she had flown the coop, against medical advice, and had to run to the bathroom to vomit every couple of minutes, it would be well worth it if she found what she was looking for. She vowed to God that if she lived through this, she'd never run from a hospital AMA ever again.

After finding a piece of bread in the kitchen to munch on, she pulled open the drawer to the left of where the knives were kept and found a manila folder.

Strange place to keep a file. Jill stuffed a bite of bread in her mouth and then choked it up when she began reading about her own life. Pictures of her and Anita. Pictures of just Anita behind the bar at Ross's Bar and Grill. Photos of herself entering the studio. She would have thrown up if anything were left in her stomach. She read the date of the report on her life and felt more violated than she ever had. The date was ten days after she had been on the air for the first time.

Something in her gut told her that Elias and their chance meeting wasn't all that much of a chance after all.

Her cell phone chirped in her purse and of course she knew who it had to be.

"Hi," she said with a quivering lower lip, then had to hold the phone away from her ear because Ian was screaming and cussing up a storm. "Can I just explain?" she shouted and waited for the string of obscenities to desist.

"There's not a damn thing you can say to make this better. Jesus, you are trying to kill me, aren't you?" Ian shouted.

"I needed to do this. I needed to find something out for myself."

"Where the hell are you?"

"Seattle," she said and the held the phone away from her ear again.

"Damn it, Jill. You better not be where I think you are. Jesus!" He groaned and was quite certain that Jill wasn't taking the threat on her life seriously enough. "For fuck's sake, what the hell is wrong with you?"

"Me? What the hell is wrong with you? I need to do this."

"Jill," Ian took a deep breath. "They found a couple of long blonde hairs snagged in the undercarriage of your car. Please tell me that you aren't anywhere near Elias Webber."

"I'm not. I promise." Jill lied and gulped loudly, shaking the image of Elias actually trying to kill her. She felt somewhat better that she knew Elias had to go to Chicago again and he was nowhere near his penthouse. "I'll be back on the six o'clock train."

"You took the damn train?" Ian's eyes just about popped from their sockets. "I'll pick you up. Don't get off the damn train until you see the whites of my eyes. Got it?"

"You know, I really hate it when you bark orders at me."

"I promise to never bark at you again, once I know you're safe."

"That's a start, I guess." Jill nibbled on her lip and thought about what Ian had said about hair. "I'll see you soon. I love you."

She made her way to the bathroom and found a brush in the second drawer down. Carefully she pulled a couple of hairs from the brush, carried them back to the kitchen and stuffed them into a plastic baggie. Her favorite show as a kid was Quincy. That man could solve any crime with a hair follicle or a piece of lint. It was amazing.

Once she got what she came for and headed for the door with the file tucked under her arm, her cell phone chirped again. Her breath caught in her throat when she saw that it was Elias calling from his cell phone. "Hello," she swallowed hard and kept the anger and disappointment from surfacing.

"What are you doing in my penthouse?"

"Where are you?" Jill stammered and looked

around with wide eyes and a painful knot in her stomach.

"Gus called me. What do you want, Jill?" He sounded strange. Guarded and almost disturbed by her presence. Something was amiss. Jill could feel it in her bones.

"Are you in town?" Jill said. "I came to see you."

"Bullshit!" he shouted. "I thought I knew you. I thought we had something special. Why would you throw that all away for a man who'll just throw you out like yesterday's garbage? He's using you, Jill. He's poisoned you against me and he's just using you to get back at me. I told you not to trust him. I warned you, Jill." Elias shouted. "All I wanted was you."

Jill's fury rose once again. "Me? *You* don't know *me*? That's a hoot. I don't know *you* at all. Everything you have told me has been a lie. Everything. I can't marry you, Elias. I don't even know you..."

"I love you," Elias shouted. "*That's* not a lie. Why am I not good enough for you? Why would you listen to his lies? None of it is true. You have to believe me."

Jill hung her head low and then strengthened her resolve to finally learn the truth. "Did you do it, Elias? Did you kill Dick and Tanya?" Jill's voice hit a high note as her voice squealed out of control.

She heard nothing but silence on the other end. Then she heard a sniffle. "Is that what he told you?" Elias asked quietly.

"Jesus, Elias. Ian hasn't told me anything. He won't even bring himself to say your name half the time. This has nothing to do with Ian. You haven't been honest with me from day one and now I can't even trust that you wouldn't hurt me." She bit her lip and walked to the elevator after slamming the door to his penthouse. "It's over, Elias. I'll send you the ring. I'm sorry... it's over."

"I love you..." she heard him yell out just as she disconnected and hugged herself tightly to stop the shaking.
* * *

Four hours later at ten minutes after six, Jill watched through the glass as Ian approached her train. It wasn't until she saw the whites of his eyes that she stepped off the platform, although it was pretty hard to see any white in his eyes due to the fierce scowl, the bloodshot veins and the shadow of the trees that was cast on his ruggedly handsome face.

"Don't start with me, okay? My head is killing me." Jill said with a pained expression.

Ian yanked her wrist and made her keep up with his quick steps toward his SUV. As soon as she was safely buckled inside, he roared out of the parking lot, drove half a mile up the road, then pulled off Marine Drive into a grassy field just west of the Portland Airport.

Jill grabbed the dashboard with white knuckles, then released it once they came to a screeching halt. "Thanks, that really made my head feel so much better. Have you ever considered anger management classes?" Jill returned his fierce scowl and then was hauled over the center console and into the man's lap.

He kissed her hard and long, letting her know just how bad he had felt about her taking stupid chances and evading the protection that he'd worked so hard to procure for her. Passionate wasn't a strong enough word to describe a man like Ian Hamlin. There wasn't a word in Jill's vocabulary that could be used to describe the feelings he inspired in her. She tried a number of times, but all she could come up with was, *unadulterated passion.* The pain in her head seemed to dissipate once she concentrated on how good his kisses felt. How good his body felt, hard and lean under her fingertips.

The kiss softened and became less demanding. He finally peeled his panicked lips off her and sighed hard against her quivering mouth. "Anger management never worked for me," he grumbled before taking her face in his hands. "Did you at least find what you were looking for?"

"Yes," Jill moaned and maneuvered until she was

straddling his legs and had him nestled in right where she wanted him to be. She kissed him again, and then trailed kisses down his neck until she felt a change in him and his throat seemed to tighten under her lips.

He looked into her eyes and shook his head in remembrance of why exactly he couldn't be with her in that way. "Why do you do this to me?"

"Because I've never wanted anything so much in my entire life. I'm not going to marry him."

Ian watched her eyes and quickly talked himself out of taking her right here in the front seat of his rental car. *She deserves more*, plus he hated making love in cop mode. It always seemed more like a fast-fuck, because his mind was always on the job and he tended to not take his time. He wanted to take his time -- especially with Jill. Most especially because he hadn't done it in two years. Hell, he wanted her so bad he could taste it. He shook his head and a muscled worked in his jaw.

"Why the hell did you have to go run off to Seattle for? Why did you insist on taking such a fucking stupid chance? Huh, answer me?"

"Screw you," Jill shouted and retreated from his lap. "I know I shouldn't have run off, but I had to. I had to know for myself, damn it!"

Ian didn't like that one bit, nor did he like that he was rock hard and as turned on as he was. It was excruciating. He stared out the window minute for a heartbeat or two and then called for a taxicab with his cell phone.

Jill didn't know what was more upsetting, the fact that he was just being his normal abrasive self, or that she was as aroused as she was. Damn, the man set a fire to her loins that she just couldn't extinguish. She should be mad at hell at the way he was treating her, but she knew him. He was better than this and the man had feelings. Granted he was a raving lunatic most of the time, but he still had feelings just the same. *Damn him.* Jill fumbled with her seatbelt once the cab driver appeared behind them.

Ian got out, said a few words to the driver, handed him twenty dollars and then helped Jill out of the SUV. "Go straight home. Agent Wyatt is waiting. And stay put..." he realized at that moment what a huge prick he had been. "Please."

"Fate sucks." Jill slammed the door of the cab and looked out to see him saunter away. That just put her in a state. She'd never felt the urge to smack anyone up side the head before in her life, but right now that's the first thing she wanted to do to him... of course, more pleasurable things would follow. "Driver, please follow that SUV." Jill said smugly and sat back while the taxi took her over the bridge into Vancouver and stopped at the Hamilton Towers Hotel just off Main Street a couple of blocks from the television station. "Thanks." Jill got out and watched the cab drive off.

* * *

Ian's head had just plopped down on his pillow when he heard the soft rapping sound on his hotel room door. He groaned a couple of times, rolled up onto his feet and swung the door open, expecting the chambermaid, but was surprised and mildly amused to see Jill.

His agape expression caused her to flush slightly.

"Can I come in?"

He stepped back and let her by. He had to admit that he was happy to see her. Even though she had blatantly disobeyed him, he was thrilled beyond words that they were alone.

She inspected the room and, just as she had expected, it was dark, dreary and looked as if an undercover cop had been living in it for two weeks.

"We have some unfinished business," Jill said sternly and moved toward him. "Can you please turn it off?" She fumbled with the buttons on his denim shorts. His t-shirt had been removed before she got there and he was barefoot, which was fine by her. It just meant that there

236

was less work to do.

"Turn what off?" he groaned as her knuckles lightly caressed his rock-hard dick.

"The scowl. The cop face... Just turn it all off. I want to make love to Ian right now, and I'd rather have Agent Hamlin out of the picture."

He chuckled lightly and grabbed her by her wrists. He brought her hands up to his lips and kissed her palms gently. One at a time, slowly tantalizing her with his soft lips and wet tongue. "I'm afraid that's not possible. If you want me," Ian looked into her eyes and softly slid the tip of his tongue up her wrist, kissing it softly as he moved up her arm, "you have to take all of me. The good, the bad, the ugly and the cop. It's all I know, baby."

"I told him that I couldn't marry him," Jill said with a whimper and that was all she needed to say.

Elation, relief and perhaps a bit of *hallelujah* lit up his face. When he kissed her, she saw nothing but sparks, fireworks and her chemistry lessons. A bright smile lit up her face as he lifted her into his arms and placed her on the bed below him. She giggled slightly because she couldn't get enough of him and he made her feel like a silly little virgin.

He raked his rough fingers down her arms and locked gazes with her. She needed him as badly as he needed her. Within minutes, her skirt was flung to the floor along with her white blouse, her bra and those pretty little black panties that he'd only seen hanging from the shower rod. Jill was now naked and whimpering beneath him, and Ian felt a surge of power as she finished unzipping his fly. She watched his sultry gaze as she slid his shorts down the contour of his lean hips. Euphoria lit up her eyes when he was finally just as naked as she was. She'd never seen anything like it and, for the first time in her life, she wanted to sit up and give it a nice long lick as if it were her favorite flavor of ice cream in a waffle cone. She snickered slightly and blushed when he finally responded to her yearning for him.

This was a special occasion indeed and for Ian it was like nothing he'd ever felt before. It was like coming home. When he finally eased deep inside her with an exerted thrust, he felt the world lift from his shoulders, and she felt so damn good clutched around his dick that he moaned and groaned and rubbed his face into the hollow of her neck like a puppy that needed love. Ian needed this. More than he had ever imagined.

* * *

After the third round of making love, Ian grunted hard and rolled over, taking his weight off the woman of his dreams. "God, I love you," he groaned and eased himself up onto his elbow to look into her dark sensuous eyes. "Fate does not suck." He grinned and played with her perky nipple with his roughened fingers.

"I was mad. And horny." She giggled and splayed her hand across his chest, right where she could feel his heartbeat the strongest. Jill had to agree with him now because she had just experienced four of the most intense orgasms of her life. She never knew that making love could be so much fun, but she was happy that she hadn't ever had it this good before, because it just made being with Ian all the more special. Ian was the man she was meant for. They fit together perfectly, as if they were only made to be with each other. "I love you too, and I trust you," Jill said earnestly.

"Where did that come from?" he asked.

A tear rolled down her cheek. He leaned over and kissed it away.

Jill sat up and reached for her purse. She pulled the manila file folder out and handed it to him. "I just think trust is important."

Ian sat up and thumbed through the file. That quickly broke the mood and sent him once again into cop mode. "This is some serious shit, Jill. What are you thinking?"

"You're the cop, you tell me." Jill raked a hand through her hair before pulling it up and securing it with a rubber band. She popped open the bottle of Advil and tossed a couple into her mouth.

"I want you to draw your own conclusions about Elias Webber. What are you thinking?" Ian insisted.

"I think that our running into each other was no coincidence. I think that he had me followed to see where I hung out, where I shopped — but I don't know why." Jill cleared her throat. "I think that he could have possibly been the one who was responsible for Dick and Tanya's death and I think it might have been him who cut my brake line." She let another tear roll down her cheek.

"Who said your brake line was cut?"

"Wasn't it?" Jill said with wide eyes

Ian nodded. "How did you know?"

"Donna told me how Dick and Tanya were killed and then, when my brakes failed, I just put two and two together. She said that Elias hated Dick and hated that she married him and he wanted his parents back together so badly. I think it's possible that he made it happen. He's always told me that he gets what he wants." Jill explained.

Ian pulled her closer. "I'm sorry."

"For what?"

"For everything," he said. "I know it must be hard to think this about someone that you thought you knew. Someone that you once thought about marrying. I haven't made it easy on you and I'm sorry." He kissed her warmly.

"You've been doing just fine. It's me who hasn't made things easy on you."

"I could have hugged you more."

"True," Jill smiled.

"I hate to be the bearer of bad news but we still have a little matter of a serial killer on your ass. Don't forget about that."

"How can I?" Jill sputtered. "I have you to remind me every second of every damned day."

"Let's not think about it right now." He pulled her onto his chest and gave her a sensual wink. "I think it's your turn to be on top."

She smiled and held on for the ride of her life.

The sky had darkened and their clothes were on once again before Jill was ready to hand Ian the baggie full of hair. She hadn't wanted a ten minute interrogation about where she got it from, so she handed it to him just as he got her into the back of a taxicab.

"What's this?" He lifted the bag up to the light.

"Just see if it matches what you found under my car, please?"

He nodded and said nothing more.

* * *

Chapter Thirteen

The weather had been reported on both the five and six-thirty news and Jill had just sat down to take off her hoards of makeup and get ready to have some dinner.

Ian popped his head into the makeup room. "Can I have a moment with Miss Walker please?"

The makeup technician gave Jill a worried look and then left them alone.

"What's up? You look like a man on a mission." Jill tried to keep the mood light, but hated that he looked like a cop.

"Where did you get the hair?"

"Did it match?" Jill hoped with all her might that it didn't. Her stomach clenched as she saw a muscle twitch in his neck.

He nodded. "Where did you get it?"

"It matched..." She almost wept, but nausea rolled in her stomach instead. Never in her wildest dreams could she have imagined that a man like Elias, who was so convincing with his love, would stoop so low as to attempt to take her life, most likely in a bout of jealous rage. Her body was wracked with embarrassment as well as horror. How could she have let a man like that anywhere near her? "Oh god, I didn't want to believe it. I'm such a fool. How could he do that to me?"

"It matched, but it wasn't male." Ian narrowed his eyes on his woman. "Where... did... you... get... it?" he asked again, very slowly this time.

"Elias's house. I found it on a brush in the bathroom drawer," Jill explained as she digested the truth. "Oh god... that means it was..."

Ian had already punched some numbers on his cell phone and interrupted her thought process.

"I need an APB put out on one Sara Marie Hamlin, age twenty eight... Last known address 1345 West Spencer Avenue, Windsor Towers, penthouse three, Seattle, Washington...."

Jill listened to him rattle off Sara's stats like he knew them by heart. The man even knew the color of her eyes and date of birth.

Ian clutched her shoulder as she tried to liberate herself from his grasp. He held on strongly and sent her a long look of warning. He finally finished his conversation and gave her hand a squeeze before she ripped it out of his clutch.

"Sara Hamlin?" Jill gasped. "Is she related to you?"

"She's my ex-wife." Ian said, frowning.

Jill literally slapped her palm against her forehead.

241

Duh. It all made sense, but then it didn't. "Why didn't you tell me? I think that's something you should have mentioned, especially since I once told you that she threatened my life. Jesus, Ian, you're as bad as he is."

"Think about that for one minute, Jill, and you'll see that I'm nothing like him."

Jill stormed away from him and sank down on the sofa in the corner. She stewed about it for a minute or two. "Nope, I don't get why you didn't tell me that. In fact, it kind of pisses me off."

"Okay," Ian exhaled loudly, making his way toward her. "If I had told you that two years ago, at my ten-year high school reunion, I had run into Elias and three weeks later my wife had come home and said she wanted to be more than a cop's wife... she didn't love me anymore... she loved Elias — would you have believed me when I told you that I loved you, or would you have believed that I was out for revenge?" He cocked a dark eyebrow at her.

Damn, the man does have a point.

"But." Jill tried to say, but Ian was too quick and had already pressed his lips firmly against hers. "I guess that makes sense." She cocked her brow, and then returned his kiss. "Oh god. I'm so sorry."

"It's okay. She was too beautiful for me anyway. People always told me I was a fool for marrying her. She was just a groupie and liked telling people that she was married to an FBI agent. What can I say; I was a fool in love," Ian grinned and kissed her again. "It worked out okay though."

"Why do you say that?"

"I got you and now that bitch is going to jail." He actually chuckled, then got solemn after he thought about the seriousness of the situation. "I doubt that she tried to kill you. She isn't that bright. She probably just thought she'd scare you."

"Well, it scared me all right." Jill hugged him tighter and, in her peripheral vision, noticed the door creak open.

Elias was standing in the doorway, looking as if he'd just lost his best friend... or the love of his life... or both. "They said I'd find you in here. I thought you'd be alone though."

"Elias," Jill stood up and looked from one to the other. *Sometimes fate does work in mysterious ways. Perhaps it's time to see the bigger picture.* "Maybe you two should finally sit down and hash this out."

"There's nothing to talk about," Elias said through clenched teeth. "I took Sara and now he's come after you. He's using you. Why can't you see that?"

"No," Ian cocked a dark brow at his former friend. "I trashed your car. You took Sara. It's over. You got your revenge, now let's just drop it. By the way, do you know where she is?" Ian actually sounded civil toward the man.

"No, I haven't seen her in weeks." Elias said. "Why?"

"She attempted to kill Jill, or scare her. Either way, she's in big trouble." Ian said sternly.

"She tried to kill you?" Elias went to Jill's side, and wrapped an arm around her shoulder. "Oh god, it's all my fault. I treated her like garbage and threw her out on her ass. God, I'm such a fucking jerk."

"You can say that again," Ian said with a smirk and then got serious and decided that enough was enough. He'd been miserable for two years and it was time to move on, forgive and try to get past the pain. He adjusted his leather jacket, fidgeting with the zipper. "Why'd you do it anyway? My God, she was my *wife.*"

Elias sank down in the makeup chair and fiddled with his thumbs. Both Ian and Jill could see the pain and perhaps remorse in his eyes. He bit into his quivering lip and sighed. "God, dude, I'm such fuck up. Ever since we were kids, I wanted to be you. You had the best mom in the world and, my god, your dad was awesome. Do you know how lucky you were? I wanted to have a dad like yours. Someone who came to games and taught me how to fish." Elias's eyes filled with the threat of tears. Finally, after all these years, he too was ready to relinquish the pain he'd held inside for so long. "Man, I envied you so much that it just started eating away at me. It was like this gnawing in my gut and, by the time we graduated and Cindy Lewis was head over heels in love with you, I just snapped. I told her that she deserved someone better, she deserved a guy who could buy her jewelry and then I did — I bought her a diamond pendant and she fucked me right there in my car after the ceremony and I felt so ashamed."

Jill reached out to him and patted his hand. It was only then she understood fully what had happened between them. It seemed it was just an ongoing case of revenge

He looked at her and sighed, at last knowing full well what love felt like. Before Jill, he'd never felt a sense of loss when it came to women. He'd used them for his own selfish reasons but had never felt a deep love for anyone. Now that he knew how it felt to feel love-loss, he could empathize with Ian.

Ian stood up, rammed his hands into the pockets of his Levis and shook his head. It was hard to shake the image of Elias *doing it* with his high-school sweetheart, but more importantly, it was hard for Ian to believe how Elias envied him. "You were jealous? Of me? I was so jealous of you I couldn't see straight. When you got that car right before our junior year, I remember fantasizing about bashing the hell out it because I was so damn jealous because all I got for my seventeenth birthday was a skateboard and a new pair of Nikes. And, damn man, *you're* the one who had all the girls. You used to talk smack about it all the time in the locker room." Ian's heart sank. All this time, if they just had been honest with each other, the pain they inflicted on each other could have been avoided. It all seemed so petty now. Especially since fate had stepped in and it seemed that Ian had found the woman that he was meant to be with. Elias actually had done him a huge favor by taking Sara away. "Dude, why didn't we ever talk about this shit?"

Elias shook his head. "I lied. God I lied to you and to everyone. Truth is, the first time I got laid was right before our junior year and it wasn't anything to brag about. I was so damned tongue-tied when it came to girls that I didn't even stand a chance." He stood up and kicked at the floor with his black shiny shoes. "Hell, it took me three whole days to say hi to Jill when she moved in." He looked over at Jill who had tears streaming down her cheeks, yet was smiling brightly. "Do you even remember me?" Elias wanted to know.

"I remember that you were really quiet. You liked your movies and you were a real asshole to that sweet little girl. She was afraid of you. Did you know that?" The memory and her suspicions made Jill angry and she stepped forward to get in his face. Her eyes lit up, ablaze with anger and fury at how awfully Elias had treated Tanya. In her heart, she knew that Elias couldn't have been the one responsible for the deaths of the child and her father, but she was angry just the same. "She was just a baby. A sweet little girl who wouldn't hurt a fly. Why?" She screamed and planted an open-faced slap right on his left cheek. "Why did you have to kill her?"

The pain from the slap stung deep, but not as deep as having Jill think he was a murderer. "I didn't do it." Elias wept. "I swear to god, Jill. I didn't do it and, yeah, I was mean to her. I hated that my father left and he wanted to come back and my mom kept saying no and then she married Dick and that ruined everything. My god, Jill. You know me better than that? Don't you?"

Elias pleaded with his eyes and his father's words ran through his mind, over and over again. *You can have whatever you want, son, as long as you have the balls to make it happen.* His stomach clenched in a knot. The color ran from his face. *It can't be true.* How could his father have done something so horrific? Then again, he wouldn't put it past the man; he was as cruel and conniving as they came. Perhaps it was time to have a little chat with Dad about Dick and Tanya Swenson. "My parents reconciled right after the funeral. My dad moved back in... oh god," he groaned. "It was the happiest day of my life. Son-of-a-bitch!" He stood up abruptly and Ian and Jill exchanged wondering gazes.

Elias didn't want to end up like his father, he hated his father. This entire debacle was just one big slap in the face; a huge reminder of the genes he carried. Elias wanted to be better than his father. "I owe you an apology, Ian. I envied that you had a wife. She was beautiful and I wanted to hurt you... I'm truly sorry." He extended his hand to Ian.

Ian took it immediately and sent him a crooked smile.

"I'm sorry about your car."

It was good for Ian to let go of the anger after all this time. He didn't feel the need to pummel the man anymore, or to scowl for that matter. It truly was water under the bridge and it all worked out for the best in the end. Perhaps someday, they'd even have a good laugh about it all. *Nah, probably not,* Ian thought. But he did think that, given time, they might be able to manage being friends again.

"And you," Elias turned to Jill. "I saw you on the news and at first, yeah, I just wanted to see if I could get you after all these years. Can you ever forgive me and find it in your heart to give me another chance? I truly fell in love with you."

Jill looked at his sad and confused face, took his hand and gave it a light squeeze. "I do forgive you. I know you're a very confused man with shaky morals, so I'll cut you some slack," Jill's voice quivered slightly. "But to be completely honest... you never stood a chance." She looked over at Ian with intense love apparent in her eyes.

"I've loved Ian since I saw him at Compo Beach back when I was twenty years old. I waited a long time to see him again and he's been in my mind all along. That wasn't fair to you and for that I apologize, but I intend to go on loving Ian for as long as he'll have me."

Elias looked distraught and heartbroken. "I don't deserve you anyway." He hesitantly smiled and gave her a warm hug. "I need to go have a little heart to heart with good old dad." He almost looked happy that he finally knew just how evil his old man truly was.

"You want some help?" Ian stood up and offered his law enforcement services.

"Thanks, but this has been a long time coming. I'd rather talk to Donald myself... but thanks, Ian."

"Hey," Ian stopped him before he left the room. "If you happen to see Sara will you give me a call?"

"Of course," Elias said and started to leave. He stopped short of the door and turned to face Ian again. "Do you think you'll ever be able to forgive me, Hammy?"

Ian chuckled at hearing Elias call him that after all these years. His childhood nickname again reminded him of his once-strong friendship with Elias Webber. "Let's just say that anything is possible."

Elias gave Jill another quick smile and swiftly stepped outside.

"Wow." Ian dropped his ass down on the couch and buried his hands in his face. He grumbled a couple of times, and Jill wanted to hold him. "Just go," he said without letting her see his tears. Tears that he'd waited years to let out. Yet, he was a big tough cop with a bad attitude, how could he break down in front of a woman?

"I'm not going anywhere, Ian Hamlin. Remember, I have to accept you for you, the good, the bad, the ugly and — the sad." She grinned and pulled him into her arms once he relinquished control and bawled like a baby. Her shoulder had never been softer, or wetter for that matter.

Jill consoled the tearful Ian and listened as

he let it all out. After years of keeping his rage, envy and hatred inside, he needed this just about as badly as Jill needed him. She kissed his salty lips and looked up at the time. "I have to go get ready. Are you staying the rest of the night with me?"

Ian shook his head. "I have to go see Detective Whitney and talk to him about Sara and let him know Elias had nothing to do with the accident. I was a bit premature on that one and besides, Hardy and Reynolds are still downstairs and Meier is in the booth. You'll be fine. I'll call you tonight on your cell phone."

"I meant what I said," Jill smiled and leaned in for another sweet, intense kiss. "I love you."

"Not nearly as much as I love you." Ian held her tightly and inhaled deeply. This entire ordeal was still far from over and, until he captured this ruthless killer, he knew Jill was still in grave danger.

* * *

Jill's late night forecast informed the residents of the Pacific Northwest that rain was imminent with tomorrow's thunderstorm activity, but by Thursday temperatures would be back up into the nineties and the blue skies and scorching temperatures would remain throughout the weekend. She beamed at the camera and really truly loved what she did. There hadn't been a day since she started that she loathed coming to work, even days when all she could think about was getting hacked up, or days when she didn't want to leave Ian. Her job was fun. It was the best thing that had ever happened to her. As she wiped the makeup off her brow at midnight, she realized that's probably how Ian feels about his job.

Her stomach clenched as she took a deep breath. Ian lived in Connecticut. She knew this when she fell in love with him. If she indeed wanted to love him for the rest of her life, she'd probably have to pack up and relocate. *It isn't that bad,* Jill thought as she changed into her jeans and pink tanktop After all, she'd spent lots of time back east

248

and she liked Connecticut. It could be worse; he could be a special agent in Duluth, Minnesota, or Cleveland, Ohio. Connecticut would be okay. But she'd miss Anita and her baby. Jill got solemn for a moment and thought about having her own babies. Maybe she wouldn't work again. Maybe she'd just have babies and stay home every day to raise them while her husband ran around the country stalking mass murderers.

On that note, Jill abruptly stopped thinking about the future. She stepped into her sandals and entered the elevator without waiting for Agent Meier. Her mind reeled with all she'd been thinking about. Sure, it was sort of exciting to think about being with a man who makes a living cleaning up the rotten apples in the world, but damn she liked her life. She pressed the button to go down and when the elevator jolted and then didn't respond, she hit the button again. Nothing. She tried the open door button and when it didn't work, she panicked and started pounding on the doors and screaming at the top of her lungs.

After a minute or two, when her voice was lost and her hands were red and nearly bruised from her anxiety attack, she saw a couple of hairy hands through the crack in the door. The hands pushed the door open enough for her to see a face.

One of the custodial crew working on the top floor smiled at her. "Need some help puurrty lady?"

"Oh, yes. Thanks." Jill took his extended hand and was helped out of the elevator by the strange man. "I never knew I was claustrophobic." Jill shuddered and looked at the grinning man in dark overalls. He looked goofy; big ears, thick glasses, just standing there with his hands in his pockets, sporting a broad, mischievous grin.

"You're so puurrty," he said stepping toward her.

Jill's muscles froze in terror, but she did manage to let out yet another blood-curdling scream.

* * *

Ian got the call from Agent Hardy just as he was leaving the Vancouver Police Station so it didn't take him long to make his way to the television station where Jill had disappeared from the elevator.

"Maintenance crew said it stopped on the fifth floor, but she never made it downstairs." Hardy explained to Ian and then waited to get screamed at again.

Ian was trying to keep his cool. He knew she had to be somewhere in the building because the entrances were all tightly locked this time of night, except for the elevator that led to the parking garage and that elevator hadn't made it to the parking garage. It was still stuck between floors four and five. "Why wasn't Meier on that damn elevator with her?"

Hardy shrugged. "Said he waited outside her dressing room, grabbed some coffee and then when he got back, she was gone."

"Fuck." Ian shouted and pulled his gun from his holster that was snugly wrapped around his body at kidney level. "I assume you've checked the entire fifth floor then."

"And the fourth. The stairwells are clean, but like I said. She could have been taken to any of the floors in the service elevator. I'm sure she's still in the building."

Ian heard the sirens of the Vancouver Police and knew that the cavalry was here. "She's got to be here somewhere." Ian said and took off on his own to find Jill.
* * *

Jill looked around at her surroundings once she was finally dropped to the floor by her captor. The fluorescent lights overhead flickered on and she knew she was in trouble. *Who would think to look for me in the men's room?* The only sound she could hear was the monotonous trickle of a leaking urinal. "What do you want?" she asked between sobs. Her hands were tied tightly behind her back and as she sat in the corner of the men's bathroom, she thought this was the end.

"You're so puurrty," he said again and just looked

at her. His matted hair was neatly combed over the large bald spot on his bulbous head. His glasses were so thick that his eyes seemed to bulge out at her when he tilted his head to the side and grinned at her. "I'm not gonna hurt you. I just want to hold you."

Jill screamed one more time; as loud as she could, channeling the primal fear inside her. The custodian came closer and pressed his gloved hand over her mouth and unzipped his dark blue coveralls. Jill closed her eyes and sucked in a breath, turning her head to the side to escape the horror.

"You're just so puurrty," he mumbled into her hair and then she opened her eyes and saw the glimmer of a long silver blade in one of his hands.

Closing her eyes again, she stilled and let out a whimper as she heard the scissors open and close. Open and close and then open and close again. The pressure of him holding her head still was causing vomit to rise in her throat and all she could do was sit still and pray.

When he finally let go of her head, he was holding a wad of her long locks in his hand and as he freed himself from his pants and laid his erection in the bed of hair on his hand, Jill felt the room spin, but she managed one more blood curdling scream before the tiny dots danced in front of her eyes and the room went black.

      * * *

Ian thought he heard a scream. It might have been his imagination, but the scream sounded close, and it sounded hollow. *Like from a closet,* he looked up. *Or a bathroom.* He checked the women's room and called Agent Hardy on his phone to relay his position.

The women's was clear, so he kicked open the men's bathroom that was just down the hall.

The custodian didn't stand a chance. He was holding his penis in one hand and long scissors in his other. Standing over an unconscious Jill, the custodian gawked at the man holding a gun and dropped the scissors.

They clanged to the ground, bouncing around near Jill's face.

Ian took one shot without even yelling the words "freeze," or "drop it" or even the all important, "FBI, you're under arrest."

The custodian dropped to the cold tile floor beside Jill.

Jill's eyes fluttered open, but she was safe. Safe in Ian's arms as he rocked her and told her it was over. "You're safe now. You're okay, honey," he cooed into her now much shorter hair before she looked into his eyes and then puked in his lap.

Ian cleaned himself off as the ambulance took away the suspect. Ian had made a clean shot to the upper right chest, but made sure it wasn't fatal. He sure felt like killing the motherfucker, but it wasn't his nature to kill a man in cold blood. Sure, he fantasized about it a number of times, but he was a federal agent not Rambo.

Jill was helped to the studio by Ian as she waited with a couple of other agents; one of them was Teri Wyatt, her now-former roommate. "Well, it was nice knowing you, Jill. I hope someday you think back on this and laugh," Teri joked to keep the situation light. "You were very brave and we're all very proud of you."

"Thanks," Jill said and sipped from her juice bottle. "Thanks for everything."

"Don't mention it." Teri waved and was out the door on her way to her next exciting assignment.

Jill eased back into her seat and watched the room fill with more people. Police officers sipping coffee, federal agents wiping their brows in relief that they'd caught a very dangerous criminal. Jill sighed. It almost seemed anticlimactic. After all her fear and the times she had thought that this sicko was going to get her and then it was over just like that. Not that she was in any way complaining.

Boy, she was happy that she had survived unscathed. Well, with the exception of her hair. She ran her fingers through it and cringed. She was going to need a trip to the salon tomorrow and perhaps a manicure because her nails had been either broken in her car accident, or broken when she had tried to claw her way out of the elevator. She looked down at her hands and noticed the horrible shape of her nails and then noticed that they were no longer trembling.

She smiled. It was a nice feeling. A nice feeling indeed.

* * *

Ian took Jill home to his tiny hotel room because he wanted to make loud, head-banging love to her and didn't feel like letting his colleagues and fellow agents know about his affair with the pretty lady. After all, what he had done was a fairly looked-down-upon thing. *Falling in love with my assignment.* That was on the top of the big FBI taboo list. That and blowing your cover were two really good reasons to get your ass tightly snuggled into a sling.

He preferred keeping his ass wiggling free.

As did Jill. She hadn't known that adrenaline was such an aphrodisiac or that Ian had the stamina of a mustang. Her body ached after a couple rounds with the love of her life.

They finally got some well-deserved sleep, but were both awakened by the phone.

"Hamlin," Ian growled. "Thanks," he grinned over at Jill's warm eyes. Even in the morning with sex hair and sleep lines, she was the most beautiful woman in the world to him. "I'll be there sometime this afternoon. Tell her not to say anything until her lawyer gets there." And he hung up, wrapped his arm around the back of Jill's head and grimaced. "Have you looked at your hair?"

"No," Jill laughed. "I had enough trauma for one night. Was that about Sara?"

"Yep, they found her last night. She's in jail in

Seattle and Elias has hired her a good attorney. I guess the guy can feel remorse." He leaned over to kiss Jill and silently thanked Elias for taking Sara away so he was free to love Jill, the way fate intended him to. "I think I might go have a word with her before she talks herself into a noose. I think it's high time that I forgive and forget."

"I'm proud of you." She smiled and snuggled closer to his naked body. "God, it feels good to breathe easy again." Jill felt her shoulders relax and then closed her eyes. "When do you think they might get all those damn bugs out of my house?"

"Probably this afternoon. You'll be a free woman again soon." Ian laid his head back down on her naked breasts and lightly flicked her nipple with the tip of his tongue. "Fate's pretty twisted isn't it."

Jill moaned sensually and wiggled her hips. "I thought you didn't believe in fate."

Ian rolled over, relinquishing the pleasure of his tongue on her breast. He eased his body down between her legs and inhaled sharply as he bent to kiss her lips. An entire minute went by before he finally plunged himself inside her and then stilled as he filled her up completely.

He brushed the hair from her eyes. "A lot of women had to die for me to find you. I'd like to think that fate doesn't exist, but how else do you explain how I found you again."

Jill moaned and wiggled her hips, needing to accept even more of him. Getting enough of Ian was something she just couldn't do. "Let's just chalk it up to love at first sight and random coincidence."

"I guess we could do that." He smiled and began rocking into her because he couldn't stand it any longer. The pleasure was agonizing, and he needed to move and make her squeal. "Whatever you want to call it. I'm glad I found you and I thank God that I turned on the TV when I did."

Jill laughed and then gasped when he hit a good

spot. "Thank God for TV." She groaned as he clasped his hot mouth down over her lips and rocked her into oblivion.

* * *

Ian spent a good part of the morning in the office of FBI headquarters in downtown Portland. He'd heard the news that the suspect had survived from surgery but still hadn't made it out of the recovery room. Agents Hardy and Reynolds were talking in the corner and Ian looked around the room and got used to the idea that this just might be his new home.

He'd thought about it all night long as he lay there and watched Jill sleep. Her eyes fluttered slightly as she had dreamed, but for the first time since he'd met her, she looked peaceful. *It probably has to do with my magnificent lovemaking ability.* Or so he liked to think. However, all last night, all he could concentrate on was how they were going to make this work. He could easily give up his position in New Haven, but he'd never in a million years ask Jill to give up being the first weathergirl in the history of Vancouver, Washington.

His cell phone chirped on his hip. "Hamlin," he said much friendlier than usual.

"Hey," Agent Pete Morrow said sternly from the New Haven office. "We've been doing a little research here and we found something that might be of interest to you."

"Go ahead," Ian sank down at a desk, a desk that could possibly be his sometime soon.

"Remember how the victims' families said that nothing strange had happened before the other Jill's deaths? Jill-six's father mentioned that nothing out of the ordinary had happened surrounding the time of her death and pretty much everyone else said the same?"

"Sure," Ian seemed fairly relaxed. After all, it was over. They got their man; they were just waiting until he got out of recovery so they could start the process. "What about it?"

He heard Pete Morrow exhale slowly. "We missed something pretty substantial. The team before you really botched the first couple of murders."

"How so?" Ian sipped his coffee and narrowed his eyes. He hadn't been involved with the first two murders. He'd come along just as the third one had been discovered and they realized they had a serial on the loose.

"Apparently, Jill-seven received a letter in the mail, about seven months ago. All the card had on it was a big, red 7."

"No," Ian dropped his coffee on the desk. He grabbed it up quickly, but not before it leaked out onto a pile of files. "I should have put a bullet in his brain."

"I have calls into Jill-eight's mother and husband. We're going to see if she received anything six months prior to her death. This could be the piece we were missing. I'm sorry we missed it."

"Fuck," Ian groaned. "If we would have known!"

"There's no way we could have. I mean, who in their right mind would think anything of that card six months after the fact. Unless they knew what to look for, it's just impossible. I just thought you should know. Nice job yesterday. I'll see you back here as soon as it gets wrapped up."

"Uh huh," Ian disconnected. "Six months?" he shook his head and wondered why the killer didn't wait six months to strike at Jill. Why after all this time and all their hard work would they find a viable MO on this guy, after he'd suddenly thrown caution to the wind and hit her early? He shook his head to make sense of it all and then got back on the phone.

"What did you find?" he asked Agent Meier, who had been leading the investigation at the suspect's house.

"Perp's name is Charles Akers. His brother is Marvin, the guy whose car he stole. Lives alone in an old apartment building on Second Avenue near the TV station. The landlord said he's lived there for four years. I've got a bad feeling about this." Meier said with a frown. "He doesn't have a car. Rides his bike to work every day. His pay is minimal and I'm just not connecting the dots here."

Ian sucked in his breath and he too had doubts about whether or not it was really over. Perhaps this Charles guy wasn't the killer. It all started to make sense, as Ian thought about Jill -- alone in her house. "What did they find at the television studio, anything yet?"

"The team is still investigating. What are you thinking?"

"Shit," Ian growled. "I need to call Harrison." He hung up on Meier and dialed Will Harrison's home number in New Haven.

"Hey," Will said with surprise. "I heard you got the fucker. Congrats."

"Maybe," Ian growled. "Listen, remember that timeline of events I gave you, the one I hounded Jill about. You know her phone calls, the flowers, all that?"

"Yeah, I remember."

"Where is it?"

"Ah," Will scratched his head and snapped his fingers. "On my desk," Will moved around his kids, tripping over toys, stuffed animals and wooden blocks on his way to the den. "Want me to fax it over?"

"Yeah," Ian said. "How's Trina?"

"Perfectly fine. Thanks for asking. You coming back soon?"

"Soon," Ian lied. *I'm not going anywhere, not for a long, long time.*

* * *

Jill sank back into the bubbles of her bath and lit a couple of candles on the ledge near her feet. She turned on the stereo, and changed the station to the light rock station that she loved to listen to during her bath time. Her hair barely made it back into a ponytail now that it had been reshaped into a trendy new hairstyle, thanks to her encounter with the freak. She shivered as she submerged under the hot water. The thought of the sight of him and what he had done with her hair made her stomach turn, but it could have been so much worse. Getting her hair cut off was the least horrible thing that could have happened to her at the hands of a serial killer. By god, she felt happy to be alive today.

Music swam in her ears as she laid her head back to appreciate being alive and in love.

* * *

Ian waited patiently for the fax machine to spit out the document he'd been waiting for. Once it had fully emerged from the machine, he took it over to his desk and got out his own calendar of events. The one that chronologically graphed the deaths of Jills four, five, six, seven, and eight.

Jill's phone calls weren't jibing with his serial killer timeline. The first call to her home came at the time that the killer would have been in Connecticut. The second one, when he actually talked to her, would have been around the same time that he was in Memphis. And the flowers? Boy, things just didn't add up.

He punched in Jill's phone number and got no answer. He tried it three more times, each time causing his heart to thump harder and faster. His pulse slightly rocketed.

He dialed Pete Morrow in New Haven. "Hey, I think now is the time that we should reach the other Jill Walkers in the area and see if they have received any strange mail. It might be our best shot." He hurried through the maze of cubicles still on the phone, walking faster with every tick of the clock.

"But it's over." Pete said.

"Maybe not." Ian told him what Meier had found out and then told him about the timelines not matching up.

"Do you see where I'm going with this?"

"Where's Jill-nine right now?"

"I'm already on my way," Ian said from the elevator. He hit the street just as he disconnected with his superior back east. He'd just gotten into his SUV when his phone chirped again. "Hamlin," he said quickly.

"Hey, it's Hardy." Agent Hardy said from the TV studio. "We found his locker. Pictures of Jill everywhere. Even some videotape that he stole from the production room. They also found semen residue in Marvin Aker's car that matched his DNA. He was the man that night in front of her house. Looks like he's had his eye on her for a while. Even has a couple women's hairbrushes, a skirt and a handkerchief with her initials on it. He's our guy all right."

Ian's head threatened to explode. "He may be her stalker, but I'm almost positive he's not the killer." Ian growled. *Fucking traffic.* He couldn't make it out of the downtown area fast enough for his liking. "I'm on my way to her house now. Call Meier and tell him to call Morrow in Connecticut. I don't think this is over. Not by a long shot." Ian disconnected and drove like a bat out of hell.

* * *

Jill didn't answer when he knocked loudly on her door. He tried it one more time, and screamed out her name a couple of times. Then he took a step back and kicked in the door with his foot, the black shiny gun held tight in his hand as adrenaline spiked in his blood. The doorjamb splintered under the weight of his kick and he moved swiftly throughout the house, screaming her name.

Her foot had just left the bathtub when she heard the screaming. She quickly pulled the towel off the rack and turned down the radio just as Ian slammed open the bathroom door and caught her completely by surprise. Dripping with bubbles and hot water, Jill's body tensed at the sight of Ian standing there with gun drawn, looking more panicked than she'd ever seen him before.

"Jesus, Jill! Didn't you hear me calling you?"

Jill stuttered and was pulled into his arms before she could explain that the music was too loud and she had been refreshing the hot water.

His hot trembling mouth covered hers as he lifted her naked body against the door that he had just kicked shut. Fumbling feverishly with his jeans, it was if his body had been taken over with rapture and getting inside Jill couldn't happen fast enough for his liking. He held her up against the door, as his kiss deepened. Her head banged lightly on the door as he deepened the kiss and invaded her mouth with his probing tongue. Breathing became tattered as he whispered that he loved her over and over again.

Jill kept her naked legs wrapped tightly against his hips as he finally freed himself and shoved hard into her. The painful sting of tears streamed down his cheeks as he wept and thrust hard and harder into her, taking her body in a loving yet possessive way. He'd never felt the kind of passion for a woman that overrode his mind and messed with his head, -- that is until now. Primal fear of losing Jill seemed to cause Ian to appreciate every beat of her heart.

Finally, tensing in her arms, he trembled and came hard; his knees buckled causing them both to fall to the tile floor.

He caught her in his arms and kissed her feverishly as she gazed into his eyes. Those eyes that she'd dreamt about for so many years. Those eyes were now filled with so much love for her that it brought tears to her own eyes. The intensity of his stare compared only with the intensity of his lovemaking and his kisses.

Ian sucked in a deep, meaningful breath and pressed his forehead against hers when he spoke. "I'm never letting you out of my sight for the rest of my life. Never again." He kissed her lightly and grabbed the towel off the floor to wrap around her naked shoulders.

Jill's heart still hadn't stopped pounding in her

chest from their frenzied lovemaking, but she gave him a weak smile and looked down at his gun lying on the floor of her bathroom. "What happened?"

"It's not over, baby. I'm so sorry, but it's not over," he groaned and lifted her off his lap so he could stand up. She wrapped the towel against her breasts and tried to take a deep breath. It didn't happen. Her lungs seized up and she began hyperventilating.

Ian lifted her into his arms and moved her into her room, and laid her down on her bed.

"Baby, breathe. Breathe, Jill."

Jill watched his worried eyes and finally took a deep breath as she grabbed his hand and held it tightly. She couldn't believe this was happening. After everything she'd been through, it wasn't over. She couldn't take it anymore. Bursting into tears, she wept hard in Ian's arms as he consoled her like she'd wanted him to all those times before. To her surprise and liking, he had very wonderful, warm shoulders to cry on.

Jill stayed as close to Ian as she could until he finally insisted that she get dressed and accompany him to finish up some work he had to do. She pulled on a pair of khaki shorts, a tanktop, and a pair of Keds.

When she finally emerged from her bedroom, she gawked at the broken front door. *The man has done it again.* She smirked and sent him a critical gaze.

"I'll fix that," he shrugged and pulled her into his arms for a mind-bending kiss coupled with magic hands and fingers that made her completely forget about the damned door.

* * *

For the first time since Jill had taken the position of meteorologist at Channel 12 in Vancouver, she wasn't the one reading tonight's forecast. Instead she followed Ian to the FBI building in downtown Portland and curled up on the couch in the office of Agent Hardy while Ian finished up his paperwork and made some phone calls.

"How about some coffee?" Agent Hardy said to Jill.

She shook her head and Ian walked in and handed her a cup of hot tea. She smiled warmly, thankful that the man knew her so well.

Agent Hardy looked at the couple and snickered.

"What?" Ian barked.

Hardy rocked back on his heels and let out a snort. "Nothing," he grinned. "Your secret is safe with me."

Ian scowled at the man, then got back to business. "What happened when he woke up?"

"Confessed to the phone calls and said he never intended to hurt her. Just an obsessed fan and, since he worked at the studio, he had access to her personal records. As soon as he's released from the hospital, he'll be taken over to the courthouse and booked. What did you find out from your office?"

Ian looked over at Jill, then back to Hardy. "I haven't heard yet. I need to make a call... in private."

"Sure," Hardy said, making himself scarce while Ian left Jill alone and went into another office, where Ian called the Connecticut office.

"So, any news?"

Pete Morrow kicked his feet onto his desk. "Two of the three Jill Walkers in and around Portland received postcards with numbers on them. One was a ten and the other was..."

"Eleven," Ian groaned. "I get it. Now what?"

"Unfortunately, I need you back here. We can't keep surveillance on any of them for six months. It's just not possible.

"Bullshit," Ian's blood boiled. "They can't do that to me again. He's here. He's so close I can feel it."

"So, what are you saying?" Morrow smirked. "Are you going to quit and move into her basement?"

"If I have to."

"You don't have to." Pete smiled into the phone.

"Quit that is. I'll submit your transfer order as soon as you say the word."

Ian couldn't help the smile that spread across his whiskered face. "Thanks for understanding."

"Well, I figure it's my only option and I'd rather have you working in Portland than lose you altogether. Who knows, maybe you'll find your way back someday when this is all over."

Ian smiled. He highly doubted it, but he smiled just the same.

"I suspect she's worth it"

Ian chuckled lightly about his partner, who couldn't keep his mouth shut to save his life. "What did Will tell you?" Ian shook his head with a smirk.

"Just that she's something special." Pete said.

"So, is that all?"

"No, I'm still waiting to hear from the hospital where the first Jill Walker worked. They're getting in touch with the nurse who found her. For now, we're still concentrating on the idea that all the women might have gotten a number around the six months prior to their deaths. Right now, it's our best bet and since the killer probably knew number one, we're starting there."

"How long do I have before surveillance gets pulled off Jill-nine?"

"It's already been pulled. The team will debug her place this afternoon. Unfortunately you're on your own, so sit tight and watch your back. Remember, we're probably looking at a timeline of six months here, so chances are she's safe for the time being."

"Easy for you to say," Ian said in recollection of everything that had happened to his poor Jill in the past couple of weeks. *Sara, a stalker, and a serial killer? It's a wonder the woman isn't catatonic or hooked on Valium. Shit.* Ian suddenly remembered he was supposed to visit his ex-wife in the slammer that afternoon. He quickly left the inner office and entered the office where Jill was fast asleep on the couch. He lightly nudged her cheek with his hand. She woke and smiled weakly when he explained that he was taking her to stay with Anita and Ryan.

* * *

On the way home from Seattle, Ian actually began to feel sorry for Sara, but of course was still angry as hell that'd she pull such a stunt just to make a point. He recalled how she broke down in sobs, confessing her undying love for Elias. She had even apologized to Ian for breaking his heart and Ian surprised himself by actually telling her that all was forgiven. "Just water under the bridge," he had said to her and then did one better. "You can't help who you love." And boy didn't he know it. Nothing short of death would keep him from loving Jill.

Elias had been there too, standing beside Sara and her high-powered attorney in the interview room. The two men had taken a couple of minutes to share a conversation over a couple cups of mediocre coffee. Ian shook his head and stared out the window of his SUV, remembering Elias's somber mood and genuine remorse for his past actions. *Perhaps forgiveness is the right thing to do.* He pulled Elias's business card from his t-shirt pocket and smiled, knowing full well that he'd see him again someday.

He continued down the freeway, headed south, still pondering how Sara had been stupid enough to do such a thing. Sara never was much of a thinker and she'd actually thought that she could scare Jill into leaving Elias alone, so Ian felt obliged to speak in Sara's behalf and get the charges reduced from attempted murder to reckless endangerment. She'd still be serving some hefty time, but at a minimum security jail instead of the state penitentiary in Walla Walla.

An hour later, his phone rang as he pulled into Anita and Ryan's driveway where he was picking up Jill. "Hamlin,"

"Good news." Pete Morrow said. "Well, if you want to call it good news. We got a call back from the nurse who found Jill one and she remembered something that might be of importance."

Ian got excited for a minute and cut his engine. "So, you're killing me here. What is it?"

"Apparently, when she found Jill Walker's body, there was a long stripe of blood down the mirror. At first she didn't think anything of it, because she had just found the body of her friend, but she remembered telling the first officers on the scene, local cops who didn't even bother to take a photo of the streak. But it could have been the number one. Don't you think?"

"Wow. That's something I guess. Did the woman say anything else?"

"No, that was it, but I think we should take another look at the first victim and start again from there. I don't suppose you can convince Jill-nine to take a week off and accompany you here for vacation. Hell, New Haven has lots to offer a girl."

"I'll see what I can do." Ian laughed. *New Haven has nothing to offer a girl, but Darien, Connecticut, might be a different story.*

Chapter Fourteen

Labor day weekend, Jill and Ian took a five-hour plane ride across the United States and ended up in New Haven, Connecticut. Jill hadn't been back to Connecticut in the ten years since she'd graduated from college and finally quit giving up her summers off to work for spoiled rich people and play with their kids.

The couple weeks prior to their trip back east, Ian

had seemed a little more relaxed, but still insisted on driving her to work daily. He still hadn't mentioned the fact that the FBI had backed off completely and he had requested his transfer to the Portland bureau just so that he could keep an eye on her daily. He had an office in Portland, but was still hesitant to tell her that he'd taken permanent measures to be with her all the time. For one, he didn't want her to panic and, secondly, he hadn't even made his full intentions known. He was saving that for a special occasion.

Will Harrison greeted them at the airport and drove them back to Ian's small house to drop Jill off so they could meet up with Pete Morrow and look into the newly re-opened investigation on the first victim. They pulled up to his house and, much to his dismay, the lawn was brown, his shrubs had wilted and looking at the pile of newspapers made him realize he forgot to halt his subscription months ago.

"I'll be fine," Jill said as Ian opened his front door and dropped their luggage inside. He was hesitant about leaving her alone, but knew she'd be bored to tears at his office.

Jill looked around, took a couple of whiffs and grinned over at Ian. "This place needs a woman's touch."

He kissed her hard on the mouth and grabbed a handful of her breast. "Then touch everything!"

She giggled and straightened out just as Will joined the party.

"Lock the door, don't talk to strangers, and there's a couple of loaded guns in his underwear drawer." Will said with a straight face, and winked at Ian. "We'll be back in three hours, tops."

"Go then," Jill shuffled them out the door, with a smile for Will and a warm kiss for Ian. "Hurry back. I love you."

"Ahhh," Will crooned from the front steps, giving his partner hell for being a love-struck dope. "That's so sweeeet!"

    * * *

When they finally arrived back at headquarters in downtown New Haven, Jennifer Mullen was waiting patiently in the conference room, ready to once again go over the details of her friend's death. After four years of trying to forget that horrifying day, her mind tried to focus on every little detail about her fellow nurse's death that night at the mental hospital.

"Agent Hamlin," Ian extended his hand. "We really appreciate your help, Miss Mullen. We'll try to make this as quick and painless as possible." He cleared his throat and got right to the point. "Can you tell us anything about the patient whose room Jill was found in? Had you witnessed any violent behavior from him in the past?"

"No, the man was hospitalized for severe depression and was under suicide watch, but he'd been cleared of any wrongdoing. We went over this four years ago with the New Haven police. He didn't do this." Jennifer said adamantly.

"How about other patients? Did any of the other patients have bad feelings for nurse Walker? Did she ever mention anything to you about any threats? Any weird conversations? Anything at this point would help."

       "Like I said, it was four years ago. I don't remember a whole lot. We had several patients on our floor. A couple of chronic manic depressives, some sexually confused individuals and Jane."

"Jane?"

"Jane Walker." Jennifer said as agents Harrison and Hamlin exchanged glances.

"Jane Walker?" Agent Morrow flipped through the pages of his file and couldn't find her name on the original police report from four years ago. "Who was Jane Walker?"

"Oh, Jane was a strange bird. I'd known her for years. Her parents had recently committed her for a three-month stint because she'd been recently diagnosed with chronic depression."

"Jane Walker." Ian flipped his notepad and showed his findings to Will Harrison. "We met her parents, a couple of months ago. The conjoined twins, right?"

Will nodded.

Jennifer nodded vigorously. "Yep, that's her."

"So, this Jane Walker? Was she violent?"

"No. No," Jennifer shook her head. "She was such a sad woman. She'd been in a number of times for depression, and that last time the doctors determined they had been wrong about her condition. Just about the time that Jill was killed, Jane had been diagnosed with schizophrenia."

"Really?" Ian glanced at Will with a cocked brow and a rumbling in his gut. "The hospital should still have a file on this girl then right?"

"Sure, we keep copies of the records, but about a week after the murder, her parents moved her to a hospital in Hartford. One that specializes in her condition."

"Thank you, Miss Mullen. You've been a great help."

"My pleasure," Jennifer extended her hand and then was escorted out by Agent Harrison.

Ian and Pete stared at their feet and tried to make sense of it all. "We should speak to her parents. How did the police miss this?" Ian said. "What a coincidence. Her sister's name was Jill Walker. She died thirteen years ago."

"Well, what are you waiting for? I'll take the hospital records; you stop by her parents place. "Damn it, I'd hate to learn we'd dropped the ball on this one." Pete said.

"We?" Ian chided. "Hey, I was in Seattle four years ago."

"Yeah, yeah. You're the best...blah blah blah. How the hell am I going to survive without you?" Pete said.

Ian shrugged with a grin and was out the door.

* * *

The drive to the Walker's place was quick because traffic was light and Will and Ian were going on and on, bouncing theories off each other as they wound through the suburban neighborhood. Ian remembered his way through the streets from his previous visit with the Walkers.

"Let me handle this," Will said. "I'll do the talking because you're too involved."

Ian grumbled as a response.

Mrs. Walker was in her front yard watering roses and Gordon Walker was in the garage sanding a dresser. Both the parents of Jane Walker immediately stopped what they were doing and met each other in the driveway before the agents approached.

"Mr. and Mrs. Walker?" Ian shielded his eyes from the bright sun. "Agents Hamlin and Harrison. We met a while back."

Gordon nodded without expression.

"We'd like to ask you a few questions about Jane? If that's okay?"

Ruth and Gordon embraced tightly as Ruth broke into long drawn out sobs in front of the Federal agents.

"Come on in." Gordon held his wife tightly and led the agents in through the front door.

Ian noticed the photo on the mantle of the girls still joined at the hip. He looked around behind the parents and on the wall was a photo of Jane's high school graduation, her college graduation, and her diploma from UCONN.

"Good school," Ian nodded toward the degree on the wall. "That's my alma mater."

"Really?" Gordon sat down and entwined his fingers with his wife's more delicate ones. "What can we do for you?"

"We need to talk to you about Jane's stay at

Riverview Hospital. About four years ago, while she was there, a nurse named Jill Walker was murdered and somehow our initial investigation didn't include any information from your daughter. Do you know where she might be? We'd like to talk to her about that night." Ian said, trying to keep his pulse at a safe level.

Gordon swallowed hard. "We haven't seen Jane for about seven months now."

"Did you know about the murder of the nurse?"

"Yes," Gordon said with an exaggerated swallow.

"Did Jane ever mention anything about the murder? Could she possibly have seen something or have any information to contribute?" Ian asked and then when he noticed the change in Gordon's eyes, he continued. "Can you tell us anything about Jane's condition?"

Gordon looked at his wife, but remained silent. He fidgeted with his hands and couldn't look Agent Hamlin in the eye.

Ian's eyes narrowed, but he knew now was not the time to lose his temper and start screaming at these people, who were obviously holding something back. He'd already drawn a conclusion on his way to their home that something was amiss. Jane either knew something of importance, or perhaps she'd seen something and that's why her parents had taken her away from the hospital. Either way, Ian intended on getting answers. "Look," Ian sat down across from the couple. "We're trying to help. There's a lot riding on this. In fact a woman's life is at stake and the faster we can get through this, the faster we can go about saving her life and the lives of many other women out there. Perhaps you could give us some insight into where she might be."

Ruth sobbed hard and wrenched her hand out of Gordon's ironclad grasp. She stood up and stared into Ian's eyes. "Oh god. What have we done? What's happened? Did it happen again?"

270

Ian had a deep suspicion that they were on the right track. Finally, after all this time, he was getting somewhere. "Yes, ma'am. It has. What can you tell us? Please. This is a matter of life and death and we can stop it if you just tell me now what I need to know."

Ruth sat back down and buried her face in her hands.

Her husband held her tightly around the shoulders. "Jane and Jill were, like we said before, conjoined twins. They spent seventeen years by each other's sides and then Jill wanted to take the chance at separating. Jane didn't want to at first. She feared that Jill wouldn't survive because Jill was weaker and her liver was failing. I think to some extent Jill knew she was dying and just wanted to give her sister a normal life. She'd always been the more level-headed and brave-hearted one." Gordon's eyes filled with tears, as he held tighter to his wife's hand. "Jill didn't survive the surgery and Jane blamed herself." The room was quiet except for Ruth's moans of disapproval. "She became severely depressed shortly after and even once tried committing suicide about eight years ago."

Ruth sobbed harder and looked into her husband's eyes. "Don't!" She sniffled loudly.

Will handed her the box of tissues off the coffee table beside him. She gave him a weak smile. "Thanks."

Ian nodded to Gordon and continued listening to the amazing story.

"After many tears and days of not knowing if she'd try to kill herself again, we had her spend some time at Riverview whenever her depression became too much for us to handle. She started becoming paranoid and was always in fear that someone was after her." He looked sympathetic to his wife's pain, but continued on. "Her symptoms worsened and she even told us that she'd seen Jill a couple of times. We of course feared the worst and decided to seek more intensive therapy for her."

Ian understood that this must be incredibly hard on

them after all this time, but he was still in one-hundred-percent cop-mode at that point. "Go on."

Gordon cleared his throat and began again after taking a short break to get a handle on his emotions. "A couple of weeks before the nurse was murdered, she'd been diagnosed with paranoid schizophrenia. Paranoia overwhelmed her and soon she was convinced that her sister wasn't really dead."

"What?" Ian said, cutting Gordon off and trying to piece together the incoming information. "Why would she think that?"

Gordon swallowed hard. "It was the disease. She thought Jill was alive and was coming back for revenge."

Both Ian and Will glanced at each other. Ian felt the tiny hairs on the back of his neck stand at attention and something beyond his normal gut instinct had him tightening his jaw.

"The doctors said that her behavior and paranoia were completely normal for someone with her condition, but we feared that there was more to it because of her idea that it was her own fault that Jill had died. She was convinced that it was her fault and nothing we said helped. We were still pondering the idea of medication when we heard about the death of the nurse."

Ian felt the air rush from his lungs in realization that they may have found their killer. *A woman no less.* "Did you speak to her doctor about your concerns? Was she put under suicide watch or did they perhaps think she was a physical threat to anyone at that time?"

Gordon's head shook slowly. "We couldn't tell the doctors. They would have restrained her, or worse...committed her in the maximum security wing." He sucked back a tear. "Two days after the murder, we visited with Jane and she had told us that Jill ... meaning her dead sister ... had come for her organs. She was convinced that Jill had come to harvest her organs and that's why she killed the nurse..."

Pain and anguish forced Gordon to stop and suck back his tears. "The nurse was probably only trying to sedate her during one of her neurotic attacks." Gordon's face paled.

"She told you this?" Will spoke before Ian could. "Why didn't you come forward? She would have been better off if you'd gone to the police right away. She would have had a chance."

Ruth was eerily white and motionless, still mortified that her husband had betrayed their only living child.

Ian cleared his throat and shook his head with a scowl. "Unbelievable."

Gordon fumbled with his words, trying to make Ian understand. "We had her transferred out of the hospital before the investigation was over. We tried, honest to God; we tried to do the right thing. We were going to have her committed...to get some real help, so she wouldn't hurt anyone else. Honest, we were just looking out for her."

"Then what happened?" Will asked, cutting Ian off. From the looks of it, he knew his friend and partner was about to blow.

"She escaped from the Mountain View Hospital in Hartford the first week. She was gone for about six months until she came back home. At that time, we discussed going to the police. But she's our baby... you have to understand. She's all we have..." he moaned and stifled his tears. A man resigned to finally telling the truth, Gordon continued, despite his wife's long look of warning. He knew it was time. It had to stop. "She used to rock herself to sleep and moan about Jill coming for her. I was still working full time and when it got to be too much for Ruth to handle on her own we sought a more aggressive approach. We had her committed for two years and when she came home, the medication seemed to have worked. She was fine. She said the voices stopped and she was herself again. She got a job at a CPA firm here in town and lived with us while she saved for her own place."

Ian still wasn't convinced that they'd done the right thing by lying. These people had inadvertently gotten many women killed. They had aided a murdered in his opinion and he had no room in his heart to feel sorry for them. He stood and began pacing to reign in his emotions.

Will send Ian a stern look, warning him to keep his mouth shut and his ears open as Gordon continued.

"But then she just up and disappeared one day. Every so often, she would call us and ask for money, or a refill for her prescription and we'd transfer some money into her account, or send her a Western Union wire. I had to find her medication in a small village in Mexico. And sometimes on the Internet. Sometimes I could get enough to last her three or four months, sometimes six but then we just stopped hearing from her all together."

Ian still wanted to arrest them and Will wanted to give them both a big hug. He had kids and a couple of daughters of his own. He'd probably have done the exact same thing.

The agents exchanged looks and inhaled sharply, at the same time. "When was the last time you heard from her and where was she?"

"About seven months ago, she called from a hotel in Stratford. We wired her some money."

"How much?" Ian snapped. The pieces were quickly falling into place. "How much and where did you send it?"

"Uhh." Gordon looked at Ruth. "Four thousand dollars. To a Western Union office. I can't remember which one exactly."

"And that's it?" Ian asked. "You sent her money, then what?"

"She hasn't called or written since." Gordon's eyes filled with tears and trepidation once again. "It happened again, didn't it? Another woman was killed?"

Ian and Will exchanged glances and both nodded. Ian pulled his little black notebook out of his pocket and flipped the pages. "Can you give us a recent photo of Jane and perhaps a physical description?"

"You can't arrest her! It's not her. She's kind and gentle and it's just the voices in her head. It's a disease! You can't blame her." Ruth wept hard against her husband's shoulder.

"She's about five-foot-nine, two hundred pounds. Her hair was shoulder-length last time we saw her..." Gordon handed them a framed photo of Jane from the previous Christmas. Besides the fact that she was a mass murderer, she just looked like a normal woman from suburbia.

"God have mercy, we had no idea she'd do it again. I'm so sorry, we didn't know." Gordon looked up at Ian. "I've got some of her old records in the den." He stood up and Ian and Will followed.

Ruth couldn't face the fact that Gordon was helping the officers, so she retreated from the room while Gordon showed the agents to his den and dug out as much information as he could. Jane's bank records, recent Visa statements, her most recent medication prescription numbers, names of her former psychiatrists... anything that would be of help. Perhaps it was the guilt that he'd been holding onto for all these years, or perhaps he just understood that his daughter was that sick and out there hurting others.

After securing the records under his arm, Will gave Gordon a sincere smile. "We can't thank you enough." He shook Gordon's hand. "We'll be in touch."

Ian was the first one back into the car. He slammed his door shut and shook his head with contempt. "I feel like we should at least bring them in. What they did was so fucking wrong..."

Will lit up a cigarette. "When you become a parent, you'll see things a lot differently, pal. I don't particularly feel like throwing them both in the slammer. Frankly that won't make me feel a damn bit better about all this." A cloud of smoke seeped from his lips. "Let's let the lawyers decide what to do with them."

Ian growled and headed back to headquarters.

* * *

Two days later, after the FBI had issued a new member on the ten most wanted list. Ian pulled into the driveway of his parent's house in Darien, Connecticut. After having several more conversations with Gordon Walker over the past few days, he knew that someday, somehow Jane would slip up or contact her parents again. The FBI now had Gordon's complete cooperation. They had phone taps in place. Her Visa was being tracked, her photo was displayed everywhere and he had confidence that they'd find her eventually. He just hoped that he could keep Jill safe until that happened. He did breathe easier about at least knowing whom he was now looking for.

His smile returned, more relaxed than the last time he'd been home. With Jill by his side, he felt like the luckiest man alive. "You okay?" He asked her as he cut the engine and saw her glancing across the front yard at the house that she had once lived in.

"Fine," Jill said and gave his hand a squeeze before opening her door and sliding out from the passenger seat. "It looks a lot different than I remember." She was still staring at the house next door.

"They completely renovated a couple of years ago. New landscaping in front and everything. Come on." He tugged on her hand and grabbed their overnight bag from the back.

Lily Hamlin was on the porch wearing a purple apron over her beige trousers and a pair of pink slippers. "Well, aren't you a sight for sore eyes." She hugged her one and only son and pulled back to get a good look at him. "Forgiveness looks good on you. You're actually smiling." She grinned and pinched his cheek.

"Yeah, yeah." He groaned and pulled Jill into the

spotlight. "You remember Jill Wallokowski, don't you?"

"How could I forget a name like Wallokowski?" She grinned and gave Ian a quick mischievous wink. "How are you, Jill? Besides the obvious — I heard all about what's been happening with you from Donna Webber. The woman is mad as hell that Elias couldn't keep his hooks in you. Now I finally have something to gloat about after all these years." She gave Jill a warm hug and then looked again at Ian's broad smile. "Damn, Ian, you look like a happy man."

"You have no idea, Mom," he grinned and walked into the house. "Hey, Dad. You remember Jill don't you?"

"Of course. You're all I've been hearing about lately. Jill this and Jill that and Ian this and Ian that. My wife needs a hobby."

"Bite your tongue," Lily grouched and untied her apron. "How long are you in town for?"

"Just overnight. We're meeting Elias in Boston tomorrow." Ian said with a relaxed smile. It was still hard for him to believe that after all this time he was so willing and eager to forgive a man that he once hated. Boy, it was nice for him to breathe free again. *Who knew forgiveness felt this wonderful?* "He's got some big hot-shot yacht up at the Cape that's he's dying to show off. Same old Elias." Ian grinned and planted a big kiss on Jill.

Jill looked around at the house and it was everything that she had expected. It felt like home. The couches were newer and overstuffed. Pastel colors painted the walls and even the throw pillows sang of happiness. A lot of love was present in this house and watching Ian's parents bicker in the kitchen and then embrace lovingly almost brought her to tears. She saw Ian sneak off into the living room, but she remained where she was and watched Lily finish baking pie. Then she heard Ian's shouts.

She followed the sound of his groans and then was pulled onto his lap as he stared at the television. Ian nuzzled into her neck and whispered a few sweet nothings in her ear. Even though Ian had mentioned that she still had a cloud of doom hanging over her head, she felt good about her life. Not knowing what was going to happen next was kind of a rush. Ian wasn't like any man she'd ever dated before. He never spoke of his plans, of whether he'd be asking her to move to New Haven. She'd already decided that she'd follow him to the ends of the earth. He just had to say the word. She loved him that much.

"Who do you like?" Ian motioned to the television set as the two teams took the field after the commercial.

"I don't like football," Jill crinkled her nose.

"What?" Ian's eyes popped open wide. "How can you not like football?" He tickled her hard until she squealed and writhed around in his lap. "I don't think I can marry a woman who doesn't like football."

Jill's eyes popped open and filled with imminent tears of joy. "Marry?"

"Yeah. What did you think I meant when I said I was never going to let you out of my sight for the rest of my life?"

"I...I thought you were just saying that. I mean...I..."

Ian kissed her gently on the mouth and tangled his hands into her dark hair. "You were the first girl I ever saw completely naked and if it's all right with you, I'd like you to be the last." He grinned against her lips and then kissed her again.

Jill scoffed and leaned back to look him in the eye. "Yeah right, you liar."

Ian's jaw dropped. "Liar?" He bucked his hips to get her to get off his lap. Tugging her toward the stairs, he pulled her up the tall flight of stairs and into his childhood bedroom. His baseball trophies and ribbons of every color still sat atop his old dresser. The bed had been upgraded to a queen-size guest bed, but it would always be his room. "See." A salacious grin tugged at the corners of his mouth. "Look out there and tell me what you see."

Jill smiled smugly and moved past him. His hand

rested lightly on the small of her back as she leaned over the windowsill and saw her old bedroom just beyond the side lawn. "You little pervert," Jill growled playfully and then was pulled backwards onto the bed. "You watched me through your window?" She grinned and then her eyebrows bobbed teasingly.

"That turns you on doesn't it?" Ian chuckled lightly and rubbed her back as she blushed slightly about her embarrassing fetish. "So...will you marry me?"

"Well, jeez...let me think about that." She kissed him tenderly and smiled against his lips. "Yes. I will marry you."

Ian never looked happier.

Epilogue

Four and a half months later.

"It's a boy," Ryan McNamara gushed proudly into the phone when he called Jill and told her the happy news. Jill had been biting her nails, waiting by the phone after learning that her best friend had gone to the hospital early that morning. It was ten thirty on Sunday night when Ryan finally called to say the baby had arrived.

"Eight pounds, four ounces and he's doing just fine. Anita's exhausted, but she wants you to come up if you can."

"Are you kidding?" Jill beamed and wiped the tears of joy from her eyes. "I'll be there soon." She disconnected, threw on some sweatpants and called Ian's cell phone. "The baby's here. I'm headed up to the hospital right now. I just wanted to let you know I won't be home when you get here, but there's dinner in the fridge and..."

"Whoa..." Ian scolded her. "Wait just a minute. I haven't finished here and I thought we talked about this."

Jill rolled her eyes completely back into her skull. It had been five months since anything spooky had happened. No strange nines appeared anywhere around her and ever since Ian had moved into her place full time and started a couple new cases in the area, she felt safer than ever. "I'll be fine. It's one little trip to the hospital. What could happen?" She held out her left hand and admired her elegant diamond engagement ring.

"Famous last words," Ian growled, not at all happy that after all this time Jill would even think about leaving the house alone at night. "What's the rule?"

Jill groaned loudly and dramatically. "Blah blah blah. She's my best friend and I'm the godmother. Hell, you're the godfather. Drop what you're doing and come with me."

"You know I can't do that." Ian grinned from behind his binoculars. He'd been staking out a very important person and couldn't just leave his post to run off and play *god-daddy*. He watched Jill walk through the living room and into the kitchen to grab her purse. He chuckled lightly to himself. He knew that if she were to ever find out that he and his team were once again following her every move, she'd probably toss his ass out into the doghouse. Needless to say, he kept his mouth shut and shook his head in resignation. "What time will you be home?"

"I don't know. I'll stay as long as Anita needs me to. I'll call you when I'm about to leave." Jill grinned and despite her bravado, she still worried daily that she was in danger. She tried to keep it in the back of her mind, but because Ian was as overprotective as they came, sometimes it was hard to think of anything else. "I love you."

"I love you too. Call me the minute you leave the

hospital."

"Yes sir." Jill chuckled, disconnected, and headed to the hospital.

Every so often she felt a tingle of fear ripple up her spine and could swear that someone was watching her, but she ignored it tonight and took the freeway up toward Salmon Creek where the hospital was. She'd been so excited for this day to come. It was almost as if she really did get to share Anita's baby, just like they had joked about so many times in the past.

Anita had finished school, but was taking at least two years off before attempting to become the next Jacques Cousteau. Anita learned shortly after her and Ryan's wedding that the young man was fairly well-to-do thanks to his daddy's company that he owned stock in. He was just a firefighter because it's what he'd always wanted to do and he loved it. They had married in a small ceremony in her parent's backyard in southeast Portland. The same house that she had grown up in. Jill was her maid of honor, of course, and even six months pregnant, Anita had been a beautiful, glowing bride.

Jill smiled to herself as she pulled into the hospital parking lot. She was planning a wedding very similar to Anita's. Small outdoor ceremony with just friends and family and most of the FBI team of investigators that she'd gotten to know over the past summer. She couldn't be happier about the fact that in just three short months she would become Mrs. Ian Hamlin. Of course, she would still be called Jill Walker on the news, but Wallokowski was finally going to be thrown out the window. Something she's wanted to do her whole life.

She got out, tucked the presents she had bought for Anita under her arm and took off through the double doors at the side entrance of St. Christopher's Memorial Hospital.

When she finally found Anita's room, her best friend's eyes were closed, the room was dark, but she could hear the creaking of a rocker. Jill tiptoed into the room and saw Ryan rocking his newborn son as his wife took a well-deserved nap.

"Hi, Aunt Jill," Ryan cooed. He suddenly looked like a man to Jill. Far cry from just ten months ago when Anita would complain that he said "like" too much and wanted to chase pussy.

Jill's eyes welled with tears. "He's beautiful. Did you finally agree on a name?" She touched the baby's tiny red cheek. It was so soft she just wanted to eat him up.

"It's Dean." Ryan whispered. "Dean Christopher."

"He's so tiny." Jill gushed and turned to see Anita's smiling yet tearful face. "He's so beautiful, sweetie. I'm so proud of you. You got your family." Jill wiped the tears from her eyes and nodded toward Ryan. "There's your boyfriend." She chuckled lightly and wrapped her arms around Anita's weary shoulders.

"Where's Ian?"

"Stakeout." Jill smiled. "So, was it as horrible as everyone says?" Jill grinned and sat down next to her friend on the bed.

"It's even more beautiful than I could have ever imagined. You just wait. It's the most amazing miracle. And it didn't even hurt." Anita grumbled ironically, with a wince.

Ryan tried to hide his amusement, but he remembered her screams. How could he forget all the colorful words she called him during labor? He just kept rocking his son and smiled at his wife and her best friend who was now curled up beside her.

"Two years." Jill sighed, staring starry-eyed at the tiny baby in Ryan's arms.

"Two years, huh?" Anita chuckled. "I'll give you five more months and then you'll be begging that man to impregnate you."

"You think so, huh?" Jill beamed at her friend. "You might be right. Damn, I hate it when you're right."

Jill visited for about an hour and had just stepped off the elevator when she finally stopped grinning and pulled her cell phone out to call Ian. "I'm coming home." She was so happy to hear his voice. "He's beautiful. His name is Dean Christopher and he's just so perfect." Jill gushed and tried to keep her emotions in check. Her eyes were still teary when she walked out the double doors.

"You sure you want to wait?" Ian joked. It was her idea to wait a couple years before having kids. He agreed for the most part, but he wouldn't mind starting right away. *At least trying will be fun.*

"I don't know." Jill said haughtily. "You shouldn't ask me that right now. I'm too emotional."

"Fine," Ian joked. "We'll talk about it tomorrow. But can we at least practice tonight?"

Jill laughed and dropped her phone to the ground when she felt the painful sting in her lower back.

Ian never knew he could move so fast. One minute he was joking with his fiancé about making love and the next, he was jumping from the surveillance van with his gun drawn. He had watched Jill walk out the side doors of the hospital and had himself in a position to see the route to her car from almost every angle, but because the parking lot was practically full, he hadn't been able to see the entire picture.

Jill was already lying on the cold, hard asphalt when he moved into position on the other side of her car. He aimed his gun at the suspect who was leaning over Jill's unconscious body. He'd always thought that if given the chance he'd just shoot to kill, but instead he simply found himself saying, "It's over, Jane."

Jill survived her brush with Jane Walker reasonably unscathed. She had a couple of small burn marks on her lower back from Jane's tazer gun, broke a couple of nails when she fell, but other than that, she looked good.

"You've been tailing me this entire time? Why didn't you just tell me?" Jill said once she could properly see again. Sirens and flashing lights were surrounding her. Detective Whitney was there, as were the agents that she once referred to as the Hardy Boys and Agent Meier, whom she recognized from several months ago.

"I didn't want you to worry." Ian pressed a kiss against her lips. "You've been busy planning our wedding. I didn't want to burden you." He joked to keep the mood light. Elated would be an understatement as to how he felt about finally wrapping up the Jill Murders once and for all. Now he could concentrate fully on his other investigations and spend more quality time actually *with* Jill instead of watching her from afar.

"Do you know why she did it? I want to know everything." She was finally ready to hear the gory details now that she was out of danger.

"It's a long story. How much time do you have?" Ian cocked a brow and helped her into her car.

"For you?" Jill attempted a small smile. "I have the rest of my life. Can we go home and make a baby now?" She finally let the tears stream out. It had been a very long, hard, and painfully frightening year. She was more than ready for some eternal bliss.

The corners of Ian's mouth bowed into a smile. "We can sure try."